**Praise for *New York Times* bestselling author
Linda Lael Miller**

"Linda Lael Miller creates vibrant characters and stories I defy you to forget."
—#1 *New York Times* bestselling author
Debbie Macomber

"[Linda Lael] Miller's name is synonymous with the finest in western romance."
—*RT Book Reviews*

"[Linda Lael] Miller tugs at the heartstrings as few authors can."
—*Publishers Weekly*

**Praise for *New York Times* bestselling author
B.J. Daniels**

"[B.J.] Daniels keeps getting better with every visit to Whitehorse and the charged atmosphere and layered details of two separate storylines will keep you compulsively reading until the climactic and exciting ending."
—*RT Book Reviews* on *Lassoed* (4½ stars)

"B.J. Daniels will absolutely move to the top of your list of must-read authors."
—*Fresh Fiction* on *Mercy*

The daughter of a town marshal, **Linda Lael Miller** is the author of more than one hundred historical and contemporary novels. Now living in Spokane, Washington, the "First Lady of the West" hit a career high when all three of her 2011 Creed Cowboy books debuted at #1 on the *New York Times* bestseller list. In 2007, the Romance Writers of America presented her with their Lifetime Achievement Award. She personally funds her Linda Lael Miller Scholarships for Women. Visit her at www.lindalaelmiller.com.

New York Times and *USA TODAY* bestselling author **B.J. Daniels** lives in Montana with her husband, Parker, and three springer spaniels. When not writing, she quilts, boats and plays tennis. Contact her at www.bjdaniels.com or on Facebook under B.J. Daniels, or follow @bjdanielsauthor on Twitter.

New York Times Bestselling Author

LINDA LAEL MILLER

HERE AND THEN

HARLEQUIN® BESTSELLING AUTHOR COLLECTION

ISBN-13: 978-1-335-01639-3

Here and Then

Copyright © 2017 by Harlequin Books S.A.

The publisher acknowledges the copyright holders of the individual works as follows:

Here and Then
Copyright © 1992 by Linda Lael Miller

Lassoed
Copyright © 2011 by Barbara Heinlein

Recycling programs for this product may not exist in your area.

Printed in U.S.A.

HARLEQUIN®
™ www.Harlequin.com

CONTENTS

HERE AND THEN

Linda Lael Miller

For Jane and Dick Edwards,
the kind of friends I always hoped I'd have.

Chapter 1

Aunt Verity's antique necklace lay in an innocent, glimmering coil of gold on the floor of the upstairs hallway. An hour before, when Rue Claridge had been carrying her suitcases upstairs, it had not been there.

Frowning, Rue got down on one knee and reached for the necklace, her troubled gaze rising to the mysterious, sealed door in the outside wall. Beyond it was nothing but empty space. The part of the house it had once led to had been burned away a century before and never rebuilt.

Aunt Verity had hinted at spooky doings in the house over the years, tales concerning both the door and the necklace. Rue had enjoyed the yarns, but being practical in nature, she had promptly put them out of her mind.

Rue's missing cousin, Elisabeth, had mentioned the necklace and the doorway in those strange letters she'd written in an effort to outline what was happening to her. She'd said a person wearing the necklace could travel through time.

In fact, Elisabeth—gentle, sensible Elisabeth—had claimed she'd clasped the chain around her neck and soon found herself in the 1890s, surrounded by living, breathing people who should have been dead a hundred years.

A chill wove a gossamer casing around Rue's spine as she recalled snatches of Elisabeth's desperate letters.

You're the one person in the world who might, just might, believe me. Those wonderful, spooky stories Aunt Verity told us on rainy nights were true. There is another world on the other side of that door in the upstairs hallway, one every bit as solid and real as the one you and I know, and I've reached it. I've been there, Rue, and I've met the man meant to share my life. His name is Jonathan Fortner, and I love him more than my next heartbeat, my next breath.

A pounding headache thumped behind Rue's right temple, and she let out a long sigh as she rose to her feet, her fingers pressing the necklace deep into her palm. With her other hand, she pushed a lock of sandy, shoulder-length hair back from her face and stared at the sealed door.

Years ago there had been rooms on the other side, but then, late in the last century, there had been a tragic fire. The damage had been repaired, but the original structure was changed forever. The door had been sealed, and now the doorknob was as old and stiff as a rusted padlock.

"Bethie," Rue whispered, touching her forehead against the cool, wooden panel of the door, "where are you?"

There was no answer. The old country house yawned around her, empty except for the ponderous nineteenth-century furniture Aunt Verity had left as a part of her estate and a miniature universe of dust particles that seemed to pervade every room, every corner and crevice.

At thirty, Rue was an accomplished photojournalist. She'd dodged bullets and bombs in Belfast, photographed and later written about the massacre in Tiananmen Square, covered the invasion of Panama, nearly been taken captive in Baghdad. And while all of those experiences had shaken her and some had left her physically ill for days afterward, none had frightened her so profoundly as Elisabeth's disappearance.

The police and Elisabeth's father believed Elisabeth had simply fled the area after her divorce, that she was lying on a beach somewhere, sipping exotic tropical drinks and letting the sun bake away her grief. But because she knew her cousin, because of the letters and phone messages that had been waiting when she returned from an assignment in Moscow, Rue took a much darker view of the situation.

Elisabeth was wandering somewhere, if she was alive at all, perhaps not even remembering who she was. Rue wouldn't allow herself to dwell on all the *other* possibilities, because they didn't bear thinking about.

Downstairs in the big kitchen, she brewed a cup of instant coffee in Elisabeth's microwave and sat down at the big, oak table in the breakfast nook to go over the tattered collection of facts one more time. Before her were her cousin's letters, thoughtfully written, with no indications of undue stress in the familiar, flowing hand.

With a sigh, Rue pushed away her coffee and rested her chin in one palm. Elisabeth had come to the house the two cousins had inherited to get a new perspective on her life. She'd planned to make her home outside the little Washington town of Pine River and teach at the local elementary school in the fall. The two old ladies across the road, Cecily and Roberta Buzbee, had seen Elisabeth on several occasions. It had been Miss Cecily who had called an ambulance after finding Elisabeth unconscious in the upstairs hallway. Rue's cousin had been rushed to the hospital, where she'd stayed a relatively short time, and soon after that, she'd vanished.

Twilight was falling over the orchard behind the house, the leaves thinning on the gray-brown branches because it was late October. Rue watched as a single star winked into view in the purple sky. *Oh, Bethie,* she thought, as a collage of pictures formed in her mind... an image of a fourteen-year-old Elisabeth predominated—Bethie, looking down at Rue from the door of the hayloft in the rickety old barn. "Don't worry," the woman-child had called cheerfully on that long-ago day when Rue had first arrived, bewildered and angry, to take sanctuary under Aunt Verity's wing. "This is a good place and you'll be happy here." Rue saw herself and Bethie fishing and wading in the creek near the old covered bridge and reading dog-eared library books in the highest branches of the maple tree that shaded the back door. And listening to Verity's wonderful stories in front of the parlor fire, chins resting on their up-drawn knees, arms wrapped around agile young legs clad in blue jeans.

The jangle of the telephone brought Rue out of her reflections, and she muttered to herself as she made her way across the room to pick up the extension on the wall next to the sink. "Hello," she snapped, resentful because she'd felt closer to Elisabeth for those few moments and the caller had scattered her memories like a flock of colorful birds.

"Hello, Claridge," a wry male voice replied. "Didn't they cover telephone technique where you went to school?"

Rue ignored the question and shoved the splayed fingers of one hand through her hair, pulling her scalp tight over her forehead.

"Hi, Wilson," she said, Jeff's boyish face forming on the screen of her mind. She'd been dating the guy for three years, on and off, but her heart never gave that funny little thump she'd read about when she saw his face or heard his voice. She wondered if that meant anything significant.

"Find out anything about your cousin yet?"

Rue leaned against the counter, feeling unaccountably weary. "No," she said. "I talked to the police first thing, and they agree with Uncle Marcus that she's probably hiding out somewhere, licking her wounds."

"You don't think so?"

Unconsciously, Rue shook her head. "No way. Bethie would never just vanish without telling anyone where she was going…she's the most considerate person I know." Her gaze strayed to the letters spread out on the kitchen table, unnervingly calm accounts of journeys to another point in time. Rue shook her head again, denying that such a thing could be possible.

"I could fly out and help you," Jeff offered, and Rue's practical heart softened a little.

"That won't be necessary," she said, twisting one finger in the phone cord and frowning. Finding Elisabeth was going to take all her concentration and strength of will, she told herself. The truth was, she didn't want Jeff getting in the way.

Her friend sighed, somewhat dramatically. "So be it, Claridge. If you decide I have any earthly use, give me a call, will you?"

Rue laughed. "What?" she countered. "No violin music?" In the next instant, she remembered that Elisabeth was missing, and the smile faded from her face. "Thanks for offering, Jeff," she said seriously. "I'll call if there's anything you can do to help."

After that, there didn't seem to be much to say, and that was another element of the relationship Rue found troubling. It would have been a tremendous relief to tell someone she was worried and scared, to say Elisabeth was more like a sister to her than a cousin, maybe even to cry on a sympathetic shoulder. But Rue couldn't let down her guard that far, not with Jeff. She often got the feeling that he was just waiting for her to show weakness or to fall on her face.

The call ended, and Rue, wearing jeans and a sweatshirt, put on a jacket and went out to the shed for an armload of the aged applewood that had been cut and stacked several years before. Because Rue and Elisabeth had so rarely visited the house they'd inherited, the supply had hardly been diminished.

As she came through the back door, the necklace

caught her eye, seeming to twinkle and wink from its place on the kitchen table. Rue's brow crimped thoughtfully as she made her way into the parlor and set the fragrant wood down on the hearth.

After moving aside the screen, she laid twigs in the grate over a small log of compressed sawdust and wax. When the blaze had kindled properly, she added pieces of seasoned wood. Soon, a lovely, cheerful fire was crackling away behind the screen.

Rue adjusted the damper and rose, dusting her hands off on the legs of her jeans. She was tired and distraught, and suddenly she couldn't keep her fears at bay any longer. She'd been a reporter for nine eventful years, and she knew only too well the terrible things that could have happened to Elisabeth.

She went back to the kitchen and, without knowing exactly why, reached for the necklace and put it on, even before taking off her jacket. Then, feeling chilled, she returned to the parlor to stand close to the fire.

Rue was fighting back tears of frustration and fear, her forehead touching the mantelpiece, when she heard the distant tinkling of piano keys. She was alone in the house, and she was certain no radio or TV was playing....

Her green eyes widened when she looked into the ornately framed mirror above the fireplace, and her throat tightened: The room reflected there was furnished differently, and was lit with the soft glow of lantern light. Rue caught a glimpse of a plain woman in long skirts running a cloth over the keys of a piano before the vision faded and the room was ordinary again.

Turning slowly, Rue rubbed her eyes with a thumb and forefinger. She couldn't help thinking of Elisabeth's letters describing a world like the one she'd just seen, for a fraction of a second, in the parlor mirror.

"You need a vacation," Rue said, glancing back over her shoulder at her image in the glass. "You're hallucinating."

Nonetheless, she made herself another cup of instant coffee, gathered up the letters and went to sit cross-legged on the hooked rug in front of the fireplace. Once again, she read and analyzed every word, looking for some clue, anything that would tell her where to begin the search for her cousin.

Thing was, Rue thought, Bethie sounded eminently sane in those letters, despite the fact that she talked about stepping over a threshold into another time in history. Her descriptions of the era were remarkably authentic; she probably would have had to have done days or weeks of research to know the things she did. But the words seemed fluent and easy, as though they'd flowed from her pen.

Finally, no closer to finding Elisabeth than she had been before, Rue set the sheets of writing paper aside, banked the fire and climbed the front stairway to the second floor. She would sleep in the main bedroom—many of Elisabeth's things were still there—and maybe by some subconscious, instinctive process, she would get a glimmer of guidance concerning her cousin's whereabouts.

As it was, she didn't have the first idea where to start.

She showered, brushed her teeth, put on a nightshirt and went to bed. Although she had taken the necklace off when she undressed, she put it back on again before climbing beneath the covers.

The sheets were cold, and Rue burrowed down deep,

shivering. If it hadn't been for the circumstances, she would have been glad to be back in this old house, where all the memories were good ones. Like Ribbon Creek, the Montana ranch she'd inherited from her mother's parents, Aunt Verity's house was a place to hole up when there was an important story to write or a decision to work out. She'd always loved the sweet, shivery sensation that the old Victorian monstrosity was haunted by amicable ghosts.

As her body began to warm the crisp, icy sheets, Rue hoped those benevolent apparitions were hanging around now, willing to lend a hand. "Please," she whispered, "show me how to find Elisabeth. She's my cousin and the closest thing I ever had to a sister and my very best friend, all rolled into one—and I think she's in terrible trouble."

After that, Rue tossed and turned for a while, then fell into a restless sleep marred by frightening dreams. One of them was so horrible that it sent her hurtling toward the surface of consciousness, and when she broke through into the morning light, she was breathing in gasping sobs and there were tears on her face.

And she could clearly hear a woman's voice singing, "Shall We Gather at the River?"

Her heart thundering against her chest, Rue flung back the covers and bounded out of bed, following the sound into the hallway, where she looked wildly in one direction, then the other. The voice seemed to be rising through the floorboards and yet, at the same time, it came from beyond the sealed door of the outside wall.

Rue put her hands against the wooden panel, remembering Elisabeth's letters. There was a room on the other side, Bethie had written, a solid place with floors and walls and a private stairway leading into the kitchen.

"Who's there?" Rue called, and the singing immediately stopped, replaced by a sort of stunned stillness. She ran along the hallway, peering into each of the three bedrooms, then hurried down the back stairs and searched the kitchen, the utility room, the dining room, the bathroom and both parlors. There was no one else in the house, and none of the locks on the windows or doors had been disturbed.

Frustrated, Rue stormed over to the piano on which she and Elisabeth had played endless renditions of "Heart and Soul," threw up the cover and hammered out the first few bars of "Shall We Gather at the River?" in challenge.

"Come on!" she shouted over the thundering chords. "Show yourself, damn it! Who are you? *What* are you?"

The answer was the slamming of a door far in the distance.

Rue left the piano and bounded back up the stairs, because the sound had come from that direction. Reaching the sealed door, she grabbed the knob and rattled the panel hard on its hinges, and surprise rushed through her like an electrical shock when it gave way.

Muttering an exclamation, Rue peered through the opening at the charred ruins of a fire. A trembling began in the cores of her knees as she looked at blackened timbers that shouldn't have been there.

It was a moment before she could gather her wits enough to step back from the door, leaving it agape, and dash wildly down the front stairs. She went hurtling out through the front door and plunged around to the side, only to see the screened sun porch just where it had always been, with no sign of the burned section.

Barely able to breathe, Rue circled the house once, then raced back inside and up the stairs. The door was still open, and beyond it lay another time or another dimension.

"Elisabeth!" Rue shouted, gripping the sooty door-jamb and staring down through the ruins.

A little girl in a pinafore and old-fashioned, pinchy black shoes appeared in the overgrown grass, shading her eyes with a small, grubby hand as she looked up at Rue. "You a witch like her?" the child called, her tone cordial and unruffled.

Rue's heartbeat was so loud that it was thrumming in her ears. She stepped back, then forward, then back again. She stumbled blindly into her room and pulled on jeans, a T-shirt, socks and sneakers, not taking the time to brush her sleep-tangled hair, and she was climbing deftly down through the ruins before she had a moment to consider the consequences.

The child, who had been so brave at a distance, was now backing away, stumbling in her effort to escape, her freckles standing out on her pale face, her eyes enormous.

Great, Rue thought, half-hysterically, *now I'm scaring small children.*

"Please don't run away," she managed to choke out. "I'm not going to hurt you."

The girl appeared to be weighing Rue's words, and it seemed that some of the fear had left her face. In the next instant, however, a woman came running around the corner of the house, shrieking and flapping her apron at Rue as though to shoo her away like a chicken.

"Don't you dare touch that child!" she screeched, and Rue recognized her as the drab soul she'd glimpsed in the parlor mirror the night before, wiping the piano keys.

Rue had withstood much more daunting efforts at intimidation during her travels as a reporter. She held her ground, her hands resting on her hips, her mind cataloging material so rapidly that she was barely aware of the process. The realization that Elisabeth had been *right* about the necklace and the door in the upstairs hallway and that she was near to finding her, was as exhilarating as a skydive.

"Where did you come from?" the plain woman demanded, thrusting the child slightly behind her.

Rue didn't even consider trying to explain. In the first place, no one would believe her, and in the second, she didn't understand what was going on herself. "Back there," she said, cocking a thumb toward the open doorway above. That was when she noticed that her hands and the knees of her jeans were covered with soot from the climb down through the timbers. "I'm looking for my Cousin Elisabeth."

"She ain't around," was the grudging, somewhat huffy reply. The woman glanced down at the little girl and gave her a tentative shove toward the road. "You run along now, Vera. I saw Farley riding toward your place just a little while ago. If you meet up with him, tell him he ought to come on over here and have a talk with this lady."

Vera assessed Rue with uncommonly shrewd eyes— she couldn't have been older than eight or nine—then scampered away through the deep grass.

Rue took a step closer to the woman, even though she

was beginning to feel like running back to her own safe world, the one she understood. "Do you know Elisabeth McCartney?" she pressed.

The drudge twisted her calico apron between strong, work-reddened fingers, and her eyes strayed over Rue's clothes and wildly tousled hair with unconcealed and fearful disapproval. "I never heard of nobody by that name," she said.

Rue didn't believe that for a moment, but she was conscious of a strange and sudden urgency, an instinct that warned her to tread lightly, at least for the time being. "You haven't seen the last of me," she said, and then she climbed back up through the charred beams to the doorway, hoping her own world would be waiting for her on the other side. "I'll be back."

Her exit was drained of all drama when she wriggled over the threshold and found herself on a hard wooden floor decorated with a hideous Persian runner. The hallway in the modern-day house was carpeted.

"Oh, no," she groaned, just lying there for a moment, trying to think what to do. The curtain in time that had permitted her to pass between one century and the other had closed, and she had no way of knowing when—or if—it would ever open again.

It was just possible that she was trapped in this rerun of *Gunsmoke*—permanently.

"Damn," she groaned, getting to her feet and running her hands down the sooty denim of her jeans. When she'd managed to stop shaking, Rue approached one of the series of photographs lining the wall and looked up into the dour face of an old man with a bushy white beard and a look of fanatical righteousness about him. "I sure hope *you're* not hanging around here somewhere," she muttered.

Next, she cautiously opened the door of the room she'd slept in the night before—only it wasn't the same. All the furniture was obviously antique, yet it looked new. Rue backed out and proceeded along the hallway, her sense of fascinated uneasiness growing with every passing moment.

"Through the looking glass," she murmured to herself. "Any minute now, I should meet a talking rabbit with a pocket watch and a waistcoat."

"Or a United States marshal," said a deep male voice.

Rue whirled, light-headed with surprise, and watched in disbelief as a tall, broad-shouldered cowboy with a badge pinned to his vest mounted the last of the front stairs to stand in the hall. His rumpled brown hair was a touch too long, his turquoise eyes were narrowed with suspicion, and he was badly in need of a shave.

This guy was straight out of the late movie, but his personal magnetism was strictly high-tech.

"What's your name?" he asked in that gravelly voice of his.

Rue couldn't help thinking what a hit this guy would be in the average singles' bar. Not only was he good-looking, in a rough, tough sort of way, he had macho down to an art form. "Rue Claridge," she said, just a little too heartily, extending one hand in friendly greeting.

The marshal glanced at her hand, but failed to offer his own. "You make a habit of prowling around in other people's houses?" he asked. His marvelous eyes widened as he took in her jeans, T-shirt and sneakers.

"I'm looking for my cousin Elisabeth." Rue's smile was a rigid curve, and she clung to it like someone dangling over the edge of a steep cliff. "I have reason to believe she might be in...these here parts."

The lawman set his rifle carefully against the wall, and Rue gulped. His expression was dubious. "Who are you?" he demanded again, folding his powerful arms. Afternoon sunlight streamed in through the open door to nowhere, and Rue could smell charred wood.

"I told you, my name is Rue Claridge, and I'm looking for my cousin, Elisabeth McCartney." Rue held up one hand to indicate a height comparable to her own. "She's a very pretty blonde, with big, bluish green eyes and a gentle manner."

The marshal's eyebrows drew together. "Lizzie?"

Rue shrugged. She'd never known Elisabeth to call herself Lizzie, but then, she hadn't visited another century, either. "She wrote me that she was in love with a man named Jonathan Fortner."

At this, the peace officer smiled, and his craggy face was transformed. Rue felt a modicum of comfort for the first time since she'd stepped over the threshold. "They're gone to San Francisco, Jon and Lizzie are," he said. "Got married a few months back, right after her trial was over."

Rue took a step closer to the marshal, one eyebrow raised, the peculiarities and implications of her situation temporarily forgotten. "Trial?"

"It's a long story." The splendid eyes swept over her clothes again and narrowed once more. "Where the devil did you get those duds?"

Rue drew in a deep breath and expelled it, making tendrils of her hair float for a few moments. "I come from another—place. What's your name, anyhow?"

"Farley Haynes," the cowboy answered.

Privately, Rue thought it was the dumbest handle she'd ever heard, but she was in no position to rile the man. "Well, Mr. Haynes," she said brightly, "I am sorry that you had to come all the way out here for nothing. The thing is, I know Elisabeth—Lizzie—would want me to stay right here in this house."

Haynes plunked his battered old hat back onto his head and regarded Rue from under the brim. "She never mentioned a cousin," he said. "Maybe you'd better come to town with me and answer a few more questions."

Rue's first impulse was to dig in her heels, but she was an inveterate journalist, and despite the fact that her head was still spinning from the shock of sudden transport from one time to another, she was fiercely curious about this place.

"What year is this, anyway?" she asked, not realizing how odd the question sounded until it was already out of her mouth.

The lawman's right hand cupped her elbow lightly as he ushered Rue down the front stairs. In his left, he carried the rifle with unnerving expertise. "It's 1892," he answered, giving her a sidelong look, probably wondering if he should slap the cuffs on her wrists. "The month is October."

"I suppose you're wondering why I didn't know that." Rue chatted on as the marshal escorted her out through the front door. There was a big sorrel gelding waiting beyond the whitewashed gate. "The fact is, I've—I've had a fever."

"You look healthy enough to me," Haynes responded, and just the timbre of his voice set some chord to vibrating deep inside Rue. He opened the gate and nodded for her to go through it ahead of him.

She took comfort from the presence of the horse; she'd always loved the animals, and some of the happiest times of her life had been spent in the saddle at Ribbon Creek. "Hello, big fella," she said, patting the gelding's sweaty neck.

In the next instant, Rue was grabbed around the waist and hoisted up into the saddle. Before she could react in any way, Marshal Haynes had thrust his rifle into the leather scabbard, stuck one booted foot in the stirrup and swung up behind her.

Rue felt seismic repercussions move up her spine in response.

"Am I under arrest?" she asked. He reached around her to grasp the reins, and again Rue was disturbed by the powerful contraction within her. Cowboy fantasies were one thing, she reminded herself, but this was a trip into the Twilight Zone, and she had an awful feeling her ticket was stamped "one-way." She'd never been on an assignment where it was more important to keep her wits about her.

"That depends," the marshal said, the words rumbling against her nape, "on whether or not you can explain how you came to be wearing Mrs. Fortner's necklace."

Leather creaked as Rue turned to look up into that rugged face, her mind racing in search of an explanation. "My—our aunt gave us each a necklace like this," she lied, her fingers straying to the filigree pendant. The piece was definitely an original, with a history. "Elis— Lizzie's probably wearing hers."

Farley looked skeptical to say the least, but he let the topic drop for the moment. "I don't mind telling you," he said, "that the Presbyterians are going to be riled up some when they get a gander at those clothes of yours. It isn't proper for a lady to wear trousers."

Rue might have been amused by his remarks if it hadn't been for the panic that was rising inside her. Nothing in her fairly wide experience had prepared her for being thrust unceremoniously into 1892, after all. "I don't have anything else to wear," she said in an uncharacteristically small voice, and then she sank her teeth into her lower lip, gripped the pommel of Marshal Haynes's saddle in both hands and held on for dear life, even though she was an experienced rider.

After a bumpy, dusty trip over the unpaved country road that led to town—its counterpart in Rue's time was paved—they reached Pine River. The place had gone into rewind while she wasn't looking. There were saloons with swinging doors, and a big saw in the lumber mill beside the river screamed and flung sawdust into the air. People walked along board sidewalks and rode in buggies and wagons. Rue couldn't help gaping at them.

Marshal Haynes lifted her down from the horse before she had a chance to tell him she didn't need his help, and he gave her an almost imperceptible push toward the sidewalk. Bronze script on the window of the nearest building proclaimed, Pine River Jailhouse. Farley Haynes, Marshal.

Bravely, Rue resigned herself to the possibility of a stretch behind bars. Much as she wanted to see the twentieth century again, she'd changed her mind about leaving 1892 right away—she meant to stick around until Elisabeth came back. Despite those glowing letters, Rue wanted to know her cousin was all right before she put this parallel universe—or whatever it was—behind her.

"Do you believe in ghosts, Farley?" she asked companionably, once they were inside and the marshal had opened a little gate in the railing that separated his desk and cabinet and wood stove from the single jail cell.

"No, ma'am," he answered with a sigh, hanging his disreputable hat on a hook by the door and laying his rifle down on the cluttered surface of the desk. Once again, his gaze passed over her clothes, troubled and quick. "But I do believe there are some strange things going on in this world that wouldn't be too easy to explain."

Rue tucked her hands into the hip pockets of her jeans and looked at the wanted posters on the wall behind Farley's desk. They should have been yellow and cracked with age, but instead they were new and only slightly crumpled. A collection of archaic rifles filled a gun cabinet, their nickel barrels and wooden stocks gleaming with a high shine that belied their age.

"You won't get an argument from me," Rue finally replied.

Chapter 2

Rue took in the crude jail cell, the potbellied stove with a coffeepot and a kettle crowding the top, the black, iron key ring hanging on a peg behind the desk. Her gaze swung to the marshal's face, and she gestured toward the barred room at the back of the building.

"If I'm under arrest, Marshal," she said matter-of-factly, "I'd like to know exactly what I'm being charged with."

The peace officer sighed, hanging his ancient canvas coat from a tarnished brass rack. "Well, miss, we could start with trespassing." He gestured toward a chair pushed back against the short railing that surrounded the immediate office area. "Sit down and tell me who you are and what you were doing snooping around Dr. Fortner's house that way."

Rue was feeling a little weak, a rare occurrence for

her. She pulled the chair closer to the desk and sat, pushing her tousled hair back from her face. "I told you. My name is Rue Claridge," she replied patiently. "Dr. Fortner's wife is my cousin, and I was looking for her. That's all."

The turquoise gaze, sharp with intelligence, rested on the gold pendant at the base of Rue's throat, causing the pulse beneath to make a strange, sudden leap. "I believe you said Mrs. Fortner has a necklace just like that one."

Rue swallowed. She was very good at sidestepping issues she didn't want to discuss, but when it came to telling an outright lie, she hadn't even attained amateur status. "Y-yes," she managed to say. Her earlier shock at finding herself in another century was thawing now, becoming low-grade panic. Was it possible that she'd stumbled into Elisabeth's nervous breakdown, or was she having a separate one, all her own?

The marshal's jawline tightened under a shadow of beard. His strong, sun-browned fingers were interlaced over his middle as he leaned back in his creaky desk chair. "How do you account for those clothes you're wearing?"

She took a deep, quivering breath. "Where I come from, lots of women dress like this."

Marshal Haynes arched one eyebrow. "And where is that?" There was an indulgent tone in his voice that made Rue want to knuckle his head.

Rue thought fast. "Montana. I have a ranch over there."

Farley scratched the back of his neck with an idleness Rue perceived as entirely false. Although his lackadaisical manner belied the fact, she sensed a certain lethal energy about him, an immense physical and emotional power barely restrained. Before she could stop it, Rue's mind had made the jump to wondering what it would be like to be held and caressed by this man.

Just the idea gave her a feeling of horrified delight.

"Doesn't your husband mind having his wife go around dressed like a common cowhand?" he asked evenly.

Color flooded Rue's face, but she held her temper carefully in check. Marshal Haynes's attitude toward women was unacceptable, but he was a man of his time and all attempts to convert him to modern thinking would surely be wasted.

"I don't have a husband." She thought she saw a flicker of reaction in the incredible eyes.

"Your daddy, then?"

Rue drew a deep breath and let it out slowly. "I'm not close to my family," she said sweetly. For all practical intents and purposes, the statement was true. Rue's parents had been divorced years before, going their separate ways. Her mother was probably holed up in some fancy spa somewhere, getting ready for the ski season, and her father's last postcard had been sent from Monaco. "I'm on my own. Except for Elisabeth, of course."

The marshal studied her for a long moment, looking pensive now, and then leaned forward in his chair. "Yes. Elisabeth Fortner."

"Right," Rue agreed, her head spinning. Nothing in her eventful past had prepared her for this particular situation. Somehow, she'd missed Time Travel 101 in college, and the Nostalgia Channel mostly covered the 1940s.

She sighed to herself. If she'd been sent back to the big-band era, maybe she would have known how to act.

"I'm going to let you go for now," Haynes announced thoughtfully. "But if you get into any trouble, ma'am, you'll have me to contend with."

A number of wisecracks came to the forefront of Rue's mind, but she valiantly held them back. "I'll just… go now," she said awkwardly, before racing out of the jailhouse onto the street.

The screech of the mill saw hurt her ears, and she hurried in the opposite direction. It would take a good forty-five minutes to walk back to the house in the country, and by the looks of the sky, the sun would be setting soon.

As she was passing the Hang-Dog Saloon, a shrill cry from above made Rue stop and look up.

Two prostitutes were leaning up against a weathered railing, their seedy-looking satin dresses glowing in the late-afternoon sun. "Where'd you get them pants?" the one in blue inquired, just before spitting tobacco into the street.

The redhead beside her, who was wearing a truly ugly pea green gown, giggled as though her friend had said something incredibly clever.

"You know, Red," Rue replied, shading her eyes with one hand as she looked up, and choosing to ignore both the question and the tobacco juice, "you really ought to have your colors done. That shade of green is definitely unbecoming."

The prostitutes looked at each other, then turned and flounced away from the railing, disappearing into the noisy saloon.

The conversation had not been a total loss, Rue decided, looking down at her jeans, sneakers and T-shirt. There was no telling how long she'd have to stay in this backward century, and her modern clothes would be a real hindrance.

She turned and spotted a store across the street, displaying gingham dresses, bridles and wooden buckets behind its fly-speckled front window. "'And bring your Visa card,'" she muttered to herself, "'because they *don't* take American Express.'"

Rue carefully made her way over, avoiding road apples, mud puddles and two passing wagons.

On the wooden sidewalk in front of the mercantile, she stood squinting, trying to see through the dirty glass. The red-and-white gingham dress on display in the window looked more suited to Dorothy of *The Wizard of Oz* fame, with its silly collar and big, flouncy bow at the back. The garment's only saving grace was that it looked as though it would probably fit.

Talking to herself was a habit Rue had acquired because she'd spent so much time alone researching and polishing her stories. "Maybe I can get a pair of ruby slippers, too," she murmured, walking resolutely toward the store's entrance. "Then I could just click my heels together and voilà, Toto, we're back in Kansas."

A pleasant-looking woman with gray hair and soft blue eyes beamed at Rue as she entered. The smile faded to an expression of chagrined consternation, however, as the old lady took in Rue's jeans and T-shirt.

"May I help you?" the lady asked, sounding as though she doubted very much that anybody could.

Rue was dizzied by the sheer reality of the place, the woman, the circumstances in which she found herself. A fly bounced helplessly against a window, buzzing in bewilderment the whole time, and Rue felt empathy for it. "That checked dress in the window," she began, her voice coming out hoarse. "How much is it?"

The fragile blue gaze swept over Rue once again, worriedly. "Why, it's fifty cents, child."

For a moment, Rue was delighted. Fifty cents. No problem.

Then she realized she hadn't brought any money with her. Even if she had, all the bills and currency would have looked suspiciously different from what was being circulated in the 1890s, and she would undoubtedly have found herself back in Farley Haynes's custody, post haste.

Rue smiled her most winning smile, the one that had gotten her into so many press conferences and out of so many tight spots. "Just put it on my account, please," she said. Rue possessed considerable bravado, but the strain of the day was beginning to tell.

The store mistress raised delicate eyebrows and cleared her throat. "Do I know you?"

Another glance at the dress—it only added insult to injury that the thing was so relentlessly ugly—gave Rue the impetus to answer, "No. My name is Rue... *Miss* Rue Claridge, and I'm Elisabeth Fortner's cousin. Perhaps you could put the dress on her husband's account?"

The woman sniffed. Clearly, in mentioning the good doctor, Rue had touched a nerve. "Jonathan Fortner ought to have his head examined, marrying a strange woman the way he did. There were odd doings in that house!"

Normally Rue would have been defensive, since she tended to get touchy where Elisabeth was concerned, but she couldn't help thinking how peculiar her cousin must have seemed to these people. Bethie was a quiet sort, but her ideas and attitudes were strictly modern, and she must surely have rubbed more than one person the wrong way.

Rue focused on the block of cheese sitting on the counter, watching as two flies explored the hard, yellow rind. "What kind of odd doings?" she asked, too much the reporter to let such an opportunity pass.

The storekeeper seemed to forget that Rue was a suspicious type, new in town and wearing clothes more suited, as Farley had said, to a cowhand. Leaning forward, she whispered confidentially, "That woman would simply appear and disappear at will. Not a few of us think she's a witch and that justice would have been better served if she'd been hanged after that trial of hers!"

For a moment, the fundamentals of winning friends and influencing people slipped Rue's mind. "Don't be silly—there're no such things as witches." She lowered her voice and, having dispatched with superstition, hurried on to her main concern. "Elisabeth was put on trial and might have been hanged? For what?"

The other woman was in a state of offense, probably because one of her pet theories had just been ridiculed. "For a time, it looked as though she'd murdered not only Dr. Fortner, but his young daughter, Trista, as well, by setting that blaze." She paused, clearly befuddled. "Then they came back. Just magically reappeared out of the ruins of that burned house."

Rue was nodding to herself. She didn't know the rules of this time-travel game, but it didn't take a MENSA membership to figure out how Bethie's husband and the little girl had probably escaped the fire. No doubt they'd fled over the threshold into the next century, then had trouble returning. Or perhaps time didn't pass at the same rate here as it did there....

It seemed to Rue that Aunt Verity had claimed the necklace's magic was unpredictable, waning and waxing under mysterious rules of its own. Elisabeth had mentioned nothing like that in her letters, however.

Rue brought herself back to the matter at hand—buying the dress. "Dr. Fortner must be a man of responsibility, coming back from the great beyond like that. It would naturally follow that his credit would be good."

The storekeeper went pale, then pursed her lips and sighed, "I'm sorry. Dr. Fortner is, indeed, a trusted and valued customer, but I cannot add merchandise to his account without his permission. Besides, there's no telling when he and that bride of his will return from California."

The woman was nondescript and diminutive, and yet Rue knew she'd be wasting her time to argue. She'd met third-world leaders with more flexible outlooks on life. "Okay," she said with a sigh. She'd just have to check the house and see if Elisabeth had left any clothes or money behind. Provided she couldn't get back into her own time, that is.

Rue offered a polite goodbye, only too aware that she might be stuck on this side of 1900 indefinitely.

Although she power walked most of the way home— this drew stares from the drivers of passing buggies and wagons—it was quite dark when Rue arrived. She let herself in through the kitchen door, relieved to find that the housekeeper had left for the day.

After stumbling around in the darkness for a while, Rue found matches and lit the kerosene lamp in the middle of the table.

The weak light flickered over a fire-damaged kitchen, made livable by someone's hard work. There was an old-fashioned icebox, a pump handle at the sink and a big cookstove with shiny chrome trim.

Bethie actually wanted to stay in this place, Rue reflected, marveling. Her cousin would develop biceps just getting enough water to make the morning coffee, and she'd probably have to chop and carry wood, too. Then there would be the washing and the ironing and the cooking. And childbirth at its most natural, with nothing for the pain except maybe a bullet to bite on.

All this for the mysterious Dr. Jonathan Fortner.

"No man is worth it, Bethie," Rue protested to the empty room, but Farley Haynes did swagger to mind, and his image was so vivid, she could almost catch the scent of his skin and hair.

Desperately hungry all of a sudden, she ransacked the icebox, helping herself to milk so creamy it had golden streaks on top, and half a cold, boiled potato. When she'd eaten, she took the lamp and headed upstairs, leaving the other rooms to explore later.

She'd had quite enough adventure for one day.

In the second floor hallway, Rue looked at the blackened door and knew without even touching the knob that she would find nothing but more ruins on the other side. Maybe she'd be able to get back to her own century, but it wasn't going to happen that night.

Reaching the master bedroom, Rue approached the tall armoire first. It soon became apparent that Bethie hadn't left much behind, certainly nothing Rue could wear, and if there was a cache of money, it wasn't hidden in that room.

Finally, exhausted, Rue washed as best she could, stripped off her clothes and crawled into the big bed.

Farley didn't make a habit of turning up in ladies' bedrooms of a morning, though he'd awakened in more than a few. There was just something about this particular woman that drew him with a force nearly as strong as his will, and it wasn't just that she wore trousers and claimed to be Lizzie Fortner's kin.

Her honey-colored hair, shorter than most women wore but still reaching to her shoulders, tumbled across the white pillow, catching the early sunlight, and her skin, visible to her armpits, where the sheet stopped, was a creamy golden peach. Her dark eyelashes lay on her cheeks like the wings of some small bird, and her breathing, even and untroubled, twisted Farley's senses up tight as the spring of a cheap watch.

He swallowed hard. Rue Claridge might be telling the truth, he thought, at least about being related to Mrs. Fortner. God knew, she was strange enough, with her trousers and her funny way of talking.

"Miss Claridge?" he said after clearing his throat. He wanted to wriggle her toe, but decided everything south of where the sheet stopped was out of his jurisdiction. "Rue!"

She sat bolt upright in bed and, to Farley's guarded relief and vast disappointment, held the top sheet firmly against her bosom.

Farley Haynes was standing at the foot of the bed, his hands resting on his hips, his handsome head cocked to one side.

Rue sat up hastily, insulted and alarmed and strangely

aroused all at once, and wrenched the sheets from her collarbone to her chin.

"I sure hope you're making yourself at home and all," Farley said, and the expression in his eyes was wry in spite of his folksy drawl. He wasn't fooling Rue; this guy was about as slow moving and countrified as a New York politician.

Although the marshal hadn't touched her, Rue had the oddest sensation of impact, as though she'd been hauled against his chest, with just the sheet between them. "What are you doing here?" she demanded furiously when she found her voice at last. She felt the ornate headboard press against her bare back and bottom.

He arched one eyebrow and folded his arms. "I could ask the same question of you, little lady."

Enough was enough. Nobody was going to call Rue Claridge "honey," "sweetie" or "little lady" and get away with it, no matter *what* century they came from.

"Don't call me 'little' anything!" Rue snapped. "I'm a grown woman and a self-supporting professional, and I won't be patronized!"

This time, both the intruder's eyebrows rose, then knit together into a frown. "You sure are a temperamental filly," Farley allowed. "And mouthy as hell, too."

"Get out of here!" Rue shouted.

Idly, Farley drew up a rocking chair and sat. Then he rubbed his stubbly chin, his eyes narrowed thoughtfully. "You said you were a professional before. Question is, a professional what?"

Rue was still clutching the covers to her throat, and she was breathing hard, as though she'd just finished a marathon. If she hadn't been afraid to let go of the bedclothes with even one hand, she would have snatched up the small crockery pitcher on the nightstand and hurled it at his head.

"You would never understand," she answered haughtily. "Now it's my turn to ask a question, Marshal. What the *hell* are you doing in my bedroom?"

"This isn't your bedroom," the lawman pointed out quietly. "It's Jon Fortner's. And I'm here because Miss Ellen came to town and reported a prowler on the premises."

Rue gave an outraged sigh. The housekeeper had apparently entered the room, seen an unwelcome guest sleeping there and marched herself into Pine River to demand legal action. "Hellfire and spit," Rue snapped. "Why didn't she drag Judge Wapner out here, too?"

Farley's frown deepened to bewilderment. "There's no judge by that name around these parts," he said. "And I wish you'd stop talking like that. If the Presbyterians hear you, they'll be right put out about it."

Catching herself just before she would have exploded into frustrated hysterics, Rue sucked in a deep breath and held it until a measure of calm came over her. "All right," she said finally, in a reasonable tone. "I will try not to stir up the Presbyterians. I promise. The point is, now you've investigated and you've seen that I'm not a trespasser, but a member of the family. I have a right to be here, Marshal, but, frankly, you don't. Now if you would please leave."

Farley sat forward in his chair, turning the brim of his battered, sweat-stained hat in nimble brown fingers. "Until I get word back from San Francisco that it's all right for you to stay here, ma'am, I'm afraid you'll have to put up at one of the boardinghouses in town."

Rue would have agreed to practically anything just

to get him to leave the room. The painful truth was, Marshal Farley Haynes made places deep inside her thrum and pulse in response to some hidden dynamic of his personality. That was terrifying because she'd never felt anything like it before.

"Whatever you say," she replied with a lift of her chin. Innocuous as they were, the words came out sounding defiant. "Just leave this room, please. Immediately."

She thought she saw a twinkle in Farley's gem-bright eyes. He stood up with an exaggerated effort and, to Rue's horror, walked to the head of the bed and stood looking down at her.

"No husband and no daddy," he reflected sagely. "Little wonder your manners are so sorry." With that, he cupped one hand under her chin, then bent over and kissed her, just as straightforwardly as if he were shaking her hand.

To Rue's further mortification, instead of pushing him away, as her acutely trained left brain told her to do, she rose higher on her knees and thrust herself into the kiss. It was soft and warm at first, then Farley touched the seam of her mouth with his tongue and she opened to him, like a night orchid worshiping the moon. He took utter and complete command before suddenly stepping back.

"I expect you to be settled somewhere else by nightfall," he said gruffly. To his credit, he didn't avert his eyes, but he didn't look any happier about what he'd just done than Rue was.

"Get out," she breathed.

Farley settled his hat on his head, touched the brim in a mockingly cordial way and strolled from the room.

Rue sent her pillow flying after him, because he was so insufferable. Because he'd had the unmitigated gall not only to come into her bedroom, but to kiss her. Because her insides were still colliding like carnival rides gone berserk.

Later, ignoring Ellen, who was watchful and patently disapproving, Rue fetched a ladder from the barn and set it against the burned side of the house. At least, she thought, looking down at her jeans and T-shirt, she was dressed for climbing.

She still wanted to find Elisabeth and make sure her cousin was all right, but there were things she'd need to sustain herself in this primitive era. She intended to return to the late twentieth century, buy some suitable clothes from a costume place or a theater troupe, and pick up some old currency at a coin shop. Then she'd return, purchase a ticket on a train or boat headed south and see for herself that Bethie was happy and well.

It was an excellent plan, all in all, except that when Rue reached the top of the ladder and opened the charred door, nothing happened. She knew by the runner on the hallway floor and the pictures on the wall that she was still in 1892, even though she was wearing the necklace and wishing as hard as she could.

Obviously, one couldn't go back and forth between the two centuries on a whim.

Rue climbed down the ladder in disgust, finally, and stood in the deep grass, dusting her soot-blackened hands off on the legs of her jeans. "Damn it, Bethie," she muttered, "you'd better have a good reason for putting me through this!"

In the meantime, whether Elisabeth had a viable excuse for being in the wrong century or not, Rue had to make the best of her circumstances. She needed to find a way to fit in—and fast—before the locals decided *she* was a witch.

Ellen had draped a rug over the clothesline and was busily beating it with something that resembled a snowshoe. Occasionally she glanced warily in Rue's direction, as though expecting to be turned into a crow at any moment.

Rue wedged her hands into the hip pockets of her jeans and mentally ruled out all possibility of searching Elisabeth's house for money while the housekeeper was around. There was only one way to get the funds she needed, and if she didn't get busy, she might find herself spending the night in somebody's barn.

Or the Pine River jailhouse.

The idea of being behind bars went against her grain. Rue had once done a brief stint in a minimum-security women's prison for refusing to reveal a source to a grand jury, but this would obviously be different.

Rue headed for the road, walking backward so she could look at the house and "remember" how it *would* look in another hundred years. A part of her still expected to wake up on the couch in Aunt Verity's front parlor and discover this whole experience had been nothing more than a dream.

Reaching Pine River, Rue headed straight for the Hang-Dog Saloon, though she did have the discretion to make her way around to the alley and go in the back door.

In a smoky little room in the rear of the building, Rue found exactly what she'd hoped for, exactly what a thousand TV Westerns had conditioned her to expect.

Four drunk men were seated around a rickety table, playing poker.

At the sight of a woman entering this inner sanctum, especially one wearing pants, the cardplayers stared. A man sporting a dusty stovepipe hat went so far as to let the unlit stogie fall from between his teeth, and the fat one with garters on his sleeves folded his cards and threw them in.

"What the hell...?"

After swallowing hard, Rue peeled off her digital watch and tossed it into the center of the table. "I'd like to play, if you fellas don't mind," she said, sounding much bolder than she felt.

The man in the stovepipe hat had apparently recovered from the shock of seeing the wrong woman in the wrong place; he picked up the wristwatch and studied it with a solemn frown. "Never seen nothin' like this here," he told his colleagues.

Being one of those people who believe that great forces come to the aid of the bold, Rue drew up a chair and sat down between a long-haired gunfighter type in a canvas duster and the hefty guy with the garters.

"Deal me in," she said brightly.

"Where'd you get this thing?" asked the one in the high hat.

"Kmart," Rue answered, reaching for the battered deck lying in the middle of the table. She thought of bumper stickers she'd seen in her own time and couldn't help grinning. "My other watch is a Rolex," she added.

Stovepipe looked at her in consternation and opened his mouth to protest, but when Rue shuffled the cards deftly from one hand to the other without dropping a single one, he pressed his lips together.

The gunfighter whistled. "Son of a— Tarnation, ma'am. Where'd you learn to do that?"

Rue was warming to the game, as well as the conversation. "On board Air Force One, about three years ago. A Secret Serviceman taught me."

Stovepipe and Garters looked at each other in pure bewilderment.

"I say the lady plays," said the gunslinger.

Nobody argued, perhaps because Quickdraw was wearing a mean-looking forty-five low on his hip.

Rue dealt with a skill born of years of practice— her grandfather had taught her to play five-card draw back in Montana when she was six years old, and she'd been winning matchsticks, watches, ballpoint pens and pocket change ever since.

Rue had taken several pots, made up mostly of coins, though she had raked in a couple of oversize nineteenth-century dollar bills, in this game when the prostitute in the pea green dress came rustling in.

The woman's painted mouth fell open when she saw Rue sitting at the table, actually playing poker with the men, and her kohl-lined eyes widened. She set a fresh bottle of whiskey down on the table with an irate thump.

"Be quiet, Sissy," Quickdraw said, talking around the matchstick he was holding between his teeth. "This here is serious poker."

Sissy's eyes looked, as Aunt Verity would have said, like two burn holes in a blanket, and Rue felt a stab of pity for her. God knew, nineteenth-century life was hard enough for respectable women. It would be even rougher for ladies of the evening.

Quickdraw picked up Rue's watch, which was lying next to her stack of winnings, and held it up for Sissy's inspection. "You bring me good luck, little sugar girl, and I'll give you this for a trinket."

"I think I may throw up," Rue murmured under her breath.

"What'd you say?" Stovepipe demanded, sounding a little testy. Losing at poker clearly didn't sit well with him.

Rue offered the same smile she would have used to cajole the president of the United States into answering a tough question at a press conference, and replied, "I said I'm sure glad I showed up."

Sissy tossed the watch back to the table, glared at Rue for a moment, then turned and sashayed out of the room.

Rue was secretly relieved and turned all her concentration on the matter at hand. She had enough winnings to buy that horrible gingham dress and rent herself a room at the boardinghouse; now all she needed to do was ease out of the game without making her companions angry.

She yawned expansively.

Garters gave her a quelling look, clearly not ready to give up on the evening, and the game went on. And on.

It was starting to get embarrassing the way Rue kept winning, when all of a sudden the inner door to the saloon crashed open. There, filling the doorway like some fugitive from a Louis L'Amour novel, was Farley Haynes.

Finding Rue with five cards in her hand and a stack of coins in front of her, he swore. Sissy peered around his broad shoulder and smiled, just to let Rue know she'd been the one to bring about her impending downfall.

"Game's over," Farley said in that gruff voice, and

none of the players took exception to the announcement. In fact, except for Rue, they all scattered, muttering various excuses and hasty pleasantries as they rushed out.

Rue stood and began stuffing her winnings into the pockets of her jeans. "Don't get your mustache in a wringer, Marshal," she said. "I've got what I came for and now I'm leaving."

Farley shook his head in quiet, angry wonderment and gestured toward the door with one hand. "Come along with me, Miss Claridge. You're under arrest."

Chapter 3

Farley Haynes set his jaw, took Miss Rue Claridge by the elbow and hauled her toward the door. He prided himself on being a patient man, slow to wrath, as the Good Book said, but this woman tried his forbearance beyond all reasonable measure. Furthermore, he just flat didn't like the sick-calf feeling he got whenever he looked at her.

"Now, just a minute, Marshal," Miss Claridge snapped, trying to pull free of his grasp. "You haven't read me my rights!"

Farley tightened his grip, but he was careful not to bruise that soft flesh of hers. He didn't hold with man-handling a lady—not even one who barely measured up to the term when it came to comportment. To his way of thinking, Rue Claridge added up just fine as far as appearances went.

"What rights?" he demanded as they reached the shadowy alley behind the saloon. He had the damnedest, most unmarshal-like urge to drag Rue against his chest and kiss her, right then and there, and that scared the molasses out of him. The thought of kissing somebody in pants had never so much as crossed Farley's mind before, and he hoped to God it never would again.

"Forget it," she said, and her disdainful tone nettled Farley sorely. "It's pretty clear that around this town, I don't *have* any rights. I hope you're enjoying this, because it won't be long until you find yourself dealing with the likes of Susan B. Anthony!"

"Who?" Farley hadn't been this vexed since the year he was twelve, when Becky Hinehammer had called him a coward for refusing to walk the ridgepole on the schoolhouse roof. His pride had driven him to prove her wrong, and he'd gotten a broken collarbone for his trouble, along with a memorable blistering from his pa, once he'd healed up properly, for doing such a damnfool thing in the first place.

He propelled Miss Claridge out of the alley and onto the main street of town. Pine River was relatively quiet that night.

They reached the jailhouse, and Farley pushed the front door open, then escorted his captive straight back to the jail's only cell.

Once his saucy prisoner was secured, Farley hung his hat on a peg next to the door and put away his rifle. It didn't occur to him to unstrap his gun belt; that was something he did only when it was time to stretch out for the night. Even then, he liked to have his .45 within easy reach.

He found a spare enamel mug, wiped it out with an

old dish towel snatched from a nail behind the potbellied stove, and poured coffee. Then he carried the steaming brew to the cell and handed it through the bars to Miss Claridge. "What kind of name is Rue?" he asked, honestly puzzled.

This woman was full of mysteries, and he found himself wanting to solve them one by one.

His guest blew on the coffee, took a cautious sip and made a face. At least she was womanly enough to mind her manners. Farley had half expected her to slurp up the brew like an old mule skinner and maybe spit a mouthful into the corner. Instead, she came right back with, "What kind of name is Farley?"

If she wasn't going to give a direct answer, neither was he. "You're a snippy little piece, aren't you?"

Rue smiled, revealing a good, solid set of very white teeth. Folk wisdom said a woman lost a tooth for every child she bore, but Farley figured this gal would probably still have a mouthful even if she gave birth to a dozen babies.

"And *you're* lucky I know you're calling me 'a piece' in the old-fashioned sense of the word," she said pleasantly. "Because if you meant it the way men mean it where—when—I come from, I'd throw this wretched stuff you call coffee all over you."

Farley didn't back away; he wouldn't let himself be intimidated by a smudged little spitfire in britches. "I reckon I've figured out why your folks gave you that silly name," he said. "They knew someday some poor man would rue the day you were ever born."

A flush climbed Rue's cheeks, and Farley reflected that her skin was as fine as her teeth. She was downright pretty, if a little less voluptuous than he'd have preferred—or would be, if anybody ever took the time to clean her up.

Considering that task made one side of Farley's mouth twitch in a fleeting grin.

He saw her blush again, then lift the mug to her mouth with both hands and take a healthy swig.

"God, I can't believe I'm actually drinking this sludge!" she spat out just a moment later. "What did you do, boil down a vat of axle grease?"

Farley turned away to hide another grin, sighing as he pretended to straighten the papers on his desk. "The Presbyterians are surely going to have their hands full getting *you* back on the straight and narrow," he allowed.

Rue stared at Farley's broad, muscular back and swallowed. She was exhausted and confused and, since she hadn't had anything to eat in almost a century, hungry. She kept expecting to wake up, even though she knew this situation was all too real.

She sat on the edge of the cell's one cot, which boasted a thin, bare mattress and a gray woolen blanket that looked as though it could have belonged to the poorest private in General Lee's rebel army.

"Did you ever get around to having your supper?" Farley's voice was gruff, but there was something oddly comforting about the deep, resonating timbre of it.

Rue didn't look at him; there were tears in her eyes, and she was too proud to let them show. "No," she answered.

Farley's tone remained gentle, and Rue knew he had moved closer. "It's late, but I'll see if I can't raise Bessie over at the Hang-Dog and get her to fix you something."

Rue was still too stricken to speak; she just nodded.

Only when the marshal had left the jailhouse on his errand of mercy did Rue allow herself a loud sniffle. She stood and gripped the bars in both hands.

Maybe because she was tired, she actually hoped, for a few fleeting moments, that the key would be hanging from a peg within stretching distance on her cell, like in a TV Western.

In this case, fact was not stranger than fiction—there was no key in sight.

She began to pace, muttering to herself. If she ever got out of this, she'd write a book about it, tell the world. Appear on *Donahue* and *Oprah*.

Rue stopped, the nail of her index finger caught between her teeth. Who would ever believe her, besides Elisabeth?

She sat on the edge of the cot again and drew deep breaths until she felt a little less like screaming in frustration and panic.

Half an hour had passed, by the old clock facing Farley's messy desk, when the marshal returned carrying a basket covered with a blue-and-white checkered napkin.

Rue's stomach rumbled audibly and, to cover her embarrassment at that, she said defiantly, "You were foolish to leave me unattended, Marshal. I might very well have escaped."

He chuckled, extracted the coveted key from the pocket of his rough spun trousers and unlocked the cell door. "Is that so, Miss Spitfire? Then why didn't you?"

She narrowed her eyes. "Don't be so damn cocky," she warned. "For all you know, I might be part of a gang. Why, twenty or thirty outlaws might ride in here and dynamite this place."

Farley set the basket down and moseyed out of the cell, as unconcerned as if his prisoner were an addle-pated old lady. Rue was vaguely insulted that the law-man didn't consider her more dangerous.

"Shut up and eat your supper," he said, not unkindly.

Rue plopped down on the edge of the cot again. Farley had set the basket on the only other piece of furniture in the cell, a rickety old stool, and she pulled that close.

There was cold roast venison in the basket, along with a couple of hard flour-and-water biscuits and an apple.

Rue ate greedily, but the whole time she watched Farley out of the corner of one eye. He was doing paperwork at the desk, by the light of a flickering kerosene lamp.

"Aren't you ever going home?" she inquired when she'd consumed every scrap of the food.

Farley didn't look up. "I've got a little place out back," he said. "You'd better get some sleep, Miss Claridge. Likely as not, you'll have the ladies of the town to deal with come morning. They'll want to take you on as a personal mission."

Rue let her forehead rest against an icy bar and sighed. "Great."

When Farley finally raised his eyes and saw that Rue was still standing there staring at him, he put down his pencil. "Am I keeping you awake?"

"It's just..." Rue paused, swallowed, started again. "Well, I'd like to wash up, that's all. And maybe brush my teeth." *In my own bathroom, thank you. In my own wonderful, crazy, modern world.*

Farley stretched, then brought a large kettle from a

cabinet near the stove. "I guess you'll just have to rinse and spit, since the town of Pine River doesn't provide toothbrushes, but I can heat up some wash water for you."

He disappeared through a rear door, returning minutes later with the kettle, which he set on the stove top.

Rue bit her lower lip. It was bad enough that the marshal expected her to bathe in that oversize bird cage he called a cell. How clean could a girl get with two quarts of water?

"This is a clear violation of the Geneva Convention," she said.

Farley looked at her over one sturdy shoulder, shook his head in obvious consternation and went back to his desk. "If you hadn't told me you and Lizzie Fortner were kinfolk, I'd have guessed it anyway. Both of you talk like you're from somewhere a long ways from here."

Rue sagged against the cell door and closed her eyes for a moment. "So far away you couldn't begin to comprehend it, cowboy," she muttered.

Farley's deep voice contained a note of distracted humor. "Since I didn't quite make out what you just said, I'm going to assume it was something kindly," he told her without looking up from those fascinating papers of his.

"Don't you have something waiting for you at home—a dog or a goldfish or something?" Rue asked. She didn't know which she was more desperate for—a little privacy or the simple comfort of ordinary conversation.

The marshal sighed and laid down his nibbed pen. His wooden chair creaked under his weight as he leaned back. "I live alone," he said, sounding beleaguered and a little smug in the bargain.

"Oh." Rue felt a flash of bittersweet relief at this announcement, though she would have given up her trust fund rather than admit the fact. Earlier, she'd experienced a dizzying sense of impact, even though Farley wasn't touching her, and now she was painfully aware of the lean hardness of his frame and the easy masculine grace with which he moved.

It was damn ironic that being around Jeff Wilson had never had this effect on her. Maybe if it had, she would have a couple of kids and a real home by now, in addition to the career she loved.

"You must be pretty ambitious," she blurted out. The sound of heat surging through the water in the kettle filled the quiet room. "Do you often work late?"

Farley put down his pen again and scratched the nape of his neck before emitting an exasperated sigh. "I don't plan on spending my life as a lawman," he replied with a measured politeness that clearly told Rue he wished she'd shut up and let him get on with whatever he was doing. "I've been saving for a ranch ever since I got out of the army. I mean to raise cattle and horses."

At last, Rue thought. Common ground.

"I have a ranch," she announced. "Over in Montana."

"So you said," Farley replied. It was plain enough that, to him, Rue's claim was just another wild story. He got up and crossed the room to test the water he'd been heating. "Guess this is ready," he said.

Rue narrowed her eyes as he came toward the cell, carrying the kettle by its black iron handle, fingers protected from the steam by the same rumpled dish towel he'd used to wipe out the mug earlier.

"I'm not planning to strip down and lather up in front of you, Marshal," she warned, standing back as he unlocked the cell door and came in.

He laughed, and the sound was unexpectedly rich. "That would be quite a show," he said.

Rue wasn't sure she appreciated his amusement. She just glared at him.

Farley set the kettle down in the cell, then went out and locked the door again. He handed Rue a rough towel and a cloth through the bars, then ambled over to collect his hat and canvas duster.

"Good night, Miss Claridge." With that, he blew out the kerosene lantern on his desk, plunging the room into darkness except for the thin beams of moonlight coming in through the few windows.

It was remarkable how lonely and scared Rue felt once he'd closed and locked the front door of the jailhouse. Up until then, she'd have sworn she wanted him to go.

She waited until she was reasonably sure she wouldn't be interrupted before hastily stripping. Shivering there in that cramped little cell, Rue washed in the now-tepid water Farley had brought, then put her clothes back on. After wrapping herself in the Civil War blanket, she lay down on the cot and closed her eyes.

Although Rue fully expected the worst bout of insomnia ever, she fell asleep with all the hesitation of a rock dropping to the bottom of a deep pond. She awakened to a faceful of bright sunlight and the delicious smell and cheerful sizzle of bacon frying.

At first, Rue thought she was home at Ribbon Creek, with her granddaddy cooking breakfast in the ranch house kitchen. Then it all come back to her.

It was 1892 and she was in jail, and even if she managed to get back to her own time, no one was ever, *ever* going to believe her accounts of what had happened to her.

She would definitely write a novel. A movie would inevitably follow. Priscilla Presley could play Rue, and they could probably get Tom Selleck for Farley's role, or maybe Lee Horsely....

Rue rose from the bed and immediately shifted from one foot to the other and back again.

"'Morning," Farley said with a companionable smile. He was standing beside the stove, turning the thick strips of pork in a cast-iron skillet.

"I have to go to the bathroom," Rue told him impatiently. "And don't you dare offer me a chamber pot!"

The marshal's white teeth flashed beneath his manly mustache. Expertly, he took the skillet off the heat, setting it on a trivet atop a nearby bookshelf, then ambled over to face Rue through the bars.

"Don't try anything," he warned, gesturing for Rue to precede him into freedom.

She stepped over the grubby threshold, concentrating on appreciating the sweet luxury of liberty, however brief it might be.

The marshal ushered her outside and around the back of the small building. Behind it was a small, unpainted cabin, and beyond that was an outhouse.

Rue wrinkled her nose at the smell, but she was in no position to be discriminating.

She went inside and, peering through the little moon some facetious soul had carved in the door, saw Farley standing guard a few feet away, arms folded.

When they were back in the jailhouse, he gave her

soap and a basin of water to wash in before setting the bacon on to finish cooking. Rue felt a little better after that, though she longed for a shower, a shampoo and clean clothes.

"I suppose you'll be releasing me this morning," she said after Farley had brought her a metal plate containing three perfectly fried slices of bacon, a dry biscuit and an egg so huge, it could have been laid by Big Bird's mother. "After all, if playing poker were a crime, you'd have to arrest Stovepipe and Garters and Quickdraw."

Farley, who was perched on the edge of his desk, consuming his breakfast, laughed. Then he chewed a bite of bacon with such thoroughness that Rue grew impatient.

Finally, he responded. "I reckon you're referring to Harry and Micah and Jim-Roy, and you're partly right. It isn't against the law for *them* to play poker, but Pine River has an ordinance about women entering into unseemly behavior." Farley paused, watching unperturbed as Rue's face turned neon pink with fury. "You not only entered in, Miss Claridge—you set up housekeeping and planted corn."

"That's the most ridiculous thing I've ever heard!" Rue thought about flinging her plate through the bars like a Frisbee and beaning Farley Haynes, but she hadn't finished her breakfast and she was wildly hungry. "It's downright discriminatory!"

Farley went to the stove and speared himself another slab of bacon from the skillet. "Nevertheless," he went on, "I can't ask the good citizens of this town to support you forever."

"If you'd just wire Elisabeth in San Francisco—"

"Nobody's heard from Jon and Lizzie," Farley interrupted. "They were in such a hurry to get started on their honeymoon, they didn't bother to tell anybody where they were going to stay once they got to California. They weren't planning to return until Jon's hand has healed and he's ready to start doctoring again."

Rue finished her breakfast with regret. Although loaded with fat and cholesterol, the food had tasted great. "People have mentioned a little girl. Did they take her with them?"

Farley nodded. "Yes, ma'am. Looks like we'll just have to wait until Jon decides to write a letter to somebody around here. When he left, he wasn't thinking of much of anything besides Lizzie."

After handing her empty plate through the bars, Rue folded her arms and sighed. "They're really in love, huh?"

The marshal's blue eyes sparkled. "You might say that. Being within twelve feet of those two is like being locked up in a room full of lightning."

Rue took comfort in the idea that this whole nightmare might not have been for nothing. If Bethie was really happy and truly in love with the country doctor she'd married, well, that at least gave the situation some meaning.

"I understand there was a fire and that nobody really knows how Dr. Fortner and his little girl escaped."

Farley stacked his plate and Rue's neatly on the trivet and poured the bacon grease from the frying pan into a crockery jar. "That's right. Of course, what's important is, they're alive. There are a lot of goings-on in this world that don't lend themselves to reasoning out."

"Amen," agreed Rue, thinking of her own experiences.

After fetching a bucket of water from outside, Farley put another kettle on to heat.

"You are going to give back my poker winnings, aren't you?" Rue asked nervously. She needed that money to buy some acceptable clothes and pay for a room. Provided she could find someone willing to rent her one, that is.

Farley took a mean-looking razor from his desk drawer, along with a shaving mug and a brush. "It'd serve you right if I didn't," he said calmly, studying his reflection in a cracked mirror affixed to the wall near the stove. "But I'll turn the money over to you as soon as I decide to let you go."

Rue's temper simmered at his blithely officious attitude, but she held her tongue. It was a technique she usually remembered after a conflagration, not before.

She watched, oddly fascinated, when Farley poured water from the kettle into a basin and splashed his face. Then, after moistening his shaving brush, he turned the bristles in the mug and lathered his beard.

Presently, he began using the straight razor with what seemed to Rue to be extraordinary skill.

The whole process was decidedly masculine, and it had a very curious—and disturbing—effect on Rue. Every graceful motion of his hands, every turn of his head, was like a caress; it was as though Farley were removing her clothes and taking the time to explore each new part of her as he bared it. And that odd feeling that she'd just collided with a solid object was back, too; she gripped the bars tightly to hold herself up.

When Farley gave her a sidelong look and grinned, she felt as though the bones in her pelvis had turned to warm wax.

Rue had spent a lot of time on a ranch, and she'd traveled and met people, read hundreds of books, watched all sorts of movies, so she had a pretty fundamental understanding of what was happening in her body. What she *didn't* comprehend was exactly what it would be like to make love, because that was something she hadn't gotten around to doing quite yet. It wasn't that she was scared or even especially noble—she just hadn't found the right man.

Farley finished shaving, humming a little tune all the while, rinsed his face and dried it with the towel draped around his neck.

The jailhouse door opened, and Rue noticed that Farley's hand flashed with instinctive speed and grace to the handle of the six-gun riding low on his hip.

His fingers relaxed when a big woman dressed in black bombazine entered. Her eyes narrowed in her beefy face when she caught sight of the prisoner. Two other ladies in equally somber dress wedged themselves in behind her.

"Something tells me the Presbyterians have arrived," Rue murmured.

"Worse," Farley whispered. "These ladies head up the Pine River Society for the Protection of Widows and Orphans, and they're really mean."

The trio stared at Rue, their mouths dropping open as they took in her jeans, sneakers and T-shirt.

"Poor misguided soul," one visitor said, raising bent fingers to her mouth in consternation and pity.

"Trousers!" breathed another.

The heavy woman whirled on Farley, and Rue noticed that a muscle twitched under his right eye.

"This is an outrage!" the lady thundered, as though

he were somehow to blame for Rue's existence. "Where on earth did she get those dreadful clothes?"

"I can speak for myself," Rue said firmly, and the other two women gasped, evidently at her audacity. "This is called a T-shirt," Rue went on, indicating the garment in question, "and these are jeans. I know none of you are used to seeing a woman dressed the way I am, but the fact is, these clothes are really quite practical, when you think about it."

"Well, I never!" avowed the leader of the pack.

Rue's mouth twitched. "Never what?" she inquired sweetly.

Farley rolled his eyes, but offered no comment. It was plain that, although he wasn't really intimidated by these women, he wasn't anxious to cross them, either.

"Are you a saloon woman?" demanded the leader of the moral invasion. The moment the words were out of her mouth, she drew her lips into a tight line and retreated a step, no doubt concerned that sin might prove contagious.

Rue smiled. "No, Miss— What was your name, please?"

"My name is *Mrs.* Gifford," that good lady snapped.

Holding one hand out through the bars, Rue smiled again, winningly. "I'm very glad to meet you, Mrs. Gifford. My name is Rue Claridge, and I'm definitely not a 'saloon woman.'" She dropped her voice to a confidential whisper. "Just between you and me, I think I'm probably overqualified for that kind of work."

Mrs. Gifford turned away and gathered her bombazine-clad troops into a huddle. While the conference went on, Rue stood biting her lower lip and wondering whether or not Farley would turn her over to these people. She thought she'd rather take her chances with a lynch mob, if given the choice.

Farley scratched the back of his neck and sighed. Judging from his body language, Rue was pretty sure he wanted to let her go and get on with the daily business of being a living, breathing antique.

Finally, Mrs. Gifford approached the cell again. "There will be no more prancing up and down the street in trousers and no more poker playing," she decreed firmly.

Under any other circumstances, Rue would have defended her right to dress and gamble as she liked, but she wasn't about to risk getting herself into still more trouble. For all she knew, *Mr.* Gifford was a judge with the power to lock her away in some grim prison.

"No more poker playing," Rue conceded in a purposely meek voice. "As for the—trousers, I promise I won't wear them any farther than the general store. I mean to go straight over there and buy a dress as soon as the marshal here lets me out of the pokey."

The delegation put their heads together for another consultation. After several minutes, Mrs. Gifford announced, "Rowena will walk down to the mercantile and purchase the dress," she said, indicating one of the other women.

"Great," Rue responded, shifting her gaze to the marshal. "Will you give Rowena fifty cents from my winnings so I can get out of here?" If the Society tried to make her go with them, she'd make a break for it.

Rowena, who was painfully thin, her mousy brown hair pulled back tightly enough to tilt her eyes, swallowed visibly and backed up when Farley held out the money.

"Poker winnings," she said in horror. "My hands will never touch filthy lucre!"

Now it was Rue who rolled her eyes.

"*I'll* get the dress," Farley bit out furiously, grabbing his hat from its peg and putting on his long canvas duster. A moment later, the door slammed behind him.

The church women stared at Rue, as though expecting her to turn into a raven and fly out through the barred window.

Thank God I didn't land in seventeenth-century Salem, Rue thought wryly. *I'd surely be in the stocks by now, or dangling at the end of a rope.*

Basically a gregarious type, Rue couldn't resist another attempt at conversation, even though she knew the effort was probably futile. "So," she said, smiling the way she did when she wanted to put an interviewee at ease, "what do you do with yourselves every day, besides cooking and cleaning and tracking down sinners?"

Chapter 4

When Farley returned from his mission to the general store, looking tight jawed and grim, he opened the cell door and handed a wrapped bundle to Rue.

Rue's fiery, defiant gaze swept over Mrs. Gifford and her cronies, as well as the marshal, as she accepted the package. "If you people think I'm going to change clothes with the four of you standing there gawking at me, you're mistaken," she said crisply.

Farley seemed only too happy to leave, although the Society hesitated a few moments before trooping out after him.

If she hadn't been so frazzled, Rue would have laughed out loud at the sheer ugliness of that red-and-white gingham dress. As it happened, she just buttoned herself into the thing, tied the sash at the back and tried with all her might to hold on to her sense of humor.

When the others returned, Farley slid his turquoise gaze over Rue in an assessing fashion, and she thought she saw the corner of his mouth twitch. The ladies, however, were plainly not amused.

"Just let me out of here before I go crazy!" Rue muttered.

Farley unlocked the cell again and stepped back, holding the door wide. In that moment, an odd thought struck Rue: she would miss being in close contact with the marshal.

Their hands brushed as he extended the rest of her poker winnings, and Rue felt as though she'd just thrust a hairpin into a light socket.

"I'll try to stay out of trouble," she said. All of a sudden, her throat felt tight, and she had to force the words past her vocal cords.

Farley grinned, showing those movie-cowboy teeth of his. "You do that," he replied.

Rue swallowed and went around him, shaken. She'd been in an earthquake once, in South America, and the inner sensation had been much like what she was feeling now. It was weird, but then, so was everything else that had happened to her after she crossed that threshold and left the familiar world on the other side.

The Society allowed her to leave the jailhouse without interference, but the looks the women gave her were as cool and disapproving as before. It was plain they expected Rue to go forth in sin.

Once she was outside, under a pastel blue sky laced with white clouds, Rue felt a little stronger and more confident. The air was fresh and bracing, though tinged with the scent of manure from the road. Rue's naturally buoyant spirits rose.

She set out for the house in the country, determined to take another crack at returning to her own time. Not by any stretch of the imagination had she given up on finding Elisabeth and hearing her cousin tell her face-to-face that she was truly happy, but Rue needed time to regroup.

She figured a couple of slices of pepperoni pizza with black olives and extra cheese, followed by a long, hot bath, wouldn't hurt her thinking processes, either.

Soon Rue had left the screeching of the mill saw and the tinny music and raucous laughter of the saloons behind. Every step made her more painfully conscious of the growing distance between her and Farley, and that puzzled her. The lawman definitely wasn't her type, and besides…talk about a generation gap!

When Rue finally reached Aunt Verity's house, she stood at the white picket fence for a few moments, gazing up at the structure.

Even with its fire-scarred side, the place looked innocent, just sitting there in the bright October sunshine. No one would have guessed, by casual observation, that this unassuming Victorian house was enchanted or bewitched or whatever it was.

Rue drew a deep breath, let it out in a rush and opened the gate. With her other hand, she touched the necklace at her throat and fervently wished to be home.

The gate creaked as she closed it behind her. Rue proceeded boldly up the front walk and knocked at the door.

When the crabby housekeeper didn't answer, Rue simply turned the knob and stepped inside. *Remarkable,* she thought, shaking her head. Bethie and her new husband were off in California and the maid had probably left for the day, and yet the place was unlocked.

"Hello?" Rue inquired with a pleasantry that was at least partially feigned. She didn't like Ellen and would prefer not to encounter her.

There was no answer, no sound except for the loud ticking of a clock somewhere nearby.

Rue raised her voice a little. "Hello! Anybody here?"

Again, no answer.

Rue hoisted the skirts of her horrible gingham dress so she wouldn't break her neck and bounded up the front stairway. In the upper hall, she stood facing the burned door for a moment, then pushed it open and climbed awkwardly out onto a charred beam, praying it would hold her weight.

The antique necklace seemed to burn where it rested against her skin. Clutching the blackened doorjamb in both hands and closing her eyes, Rue whispered, "Let me go home. *Please,* let me go home."

A moment later, she summoned all her courage and thrust herself over the threshold and into the house.

When she felt modern carpeting beneath her fingers, jubilation rushed through Rue's spirit, though there was a thin brushstroke of sorrow, too. She might never see her cousin Elisabeth again.

Or Farley.

Rue scrambled to her feet and gave a shout of delight because she was back in the land of indoor plumbing, fast food and credit cards. Looking down at the red-and-white dress, with its long skirts and puffy sleeves, she realized the gown was tangible proof that she actually had been to 1892. No one else would be convinced, but

Rue didn't care about that; it was enough that *she* knew she wasn't losing her mind.

After phoning the one restaurant in Pine River that not only sold but delivered pizza, Rue stripped off the dress, took a luxurious bath and put on khaki slacks and a white sweater. She was blow-drying her hair when the doorbell rang.

Snatching some money off the top of her bureau, Rue hurried downstairs to answer.

The pizza delivery person, a young man with an outstandingly good complexion, was standing on the porch, looking uneasy. Rue smiled, wondering what stories he'd heard about the house.

"Thanks," she said, holding out a bill.

The boy surrendered the pizza, but looked at the money in confusion. "What country is this from?" he asked.

Rue could smell the delicious aromas rising through the box, and she was impatient to be alone with her food. "This one," she replied a little abruptly.

Then Rue's eyes fell on the bill and she realized she'd tried to pay for the pizza with some of her 1892 poker winnings. The mistake had been a natural one; just the other day, she'd left some money on her dresser. Apparently, she'd automatically done the same with these bills.

"I'm a collector," she said, snatching back the bill. "Just a second and I'll get you something a little more… current."

With that, Rue reluctantly left the pizza on the hall table and hurried upstairs. When she returned, she paid the delivery boy with modern currency and a smile.

The young man thanked her and hurried back down the walk and through the front gate to his economy car. He kept glancing back over one shoulder, as though he expected to find that the house had moved a foot closer to the road while he wasn't looking.

Rue smiled and closed the door.

In the kitchen, she consumed two slices of pizza and put the rest into the refrigerator for later—or earlier. In this house, time had a way of getting turned around.

On one level, Rue felt grindingly tired, as though she could crawl into bed and sleep for two weeks without so much as a quiver of her eyelids. On another, however, she was restless and frustrated.

As a newswoman, Rue especially hated not knowing the whole story. She wanted to find her cousin, and she wanted to uncover the secret of this house. If there was one thing Rue was sure of, it was that the human race lived in a cause-and-effect universe and there was some concrete, measurable reason for the phenomenon she and Elisabeth had experienced.

She found her purse and the keys to her Land Rover and smiled to herself as she carefully locked the front door. Maybe the dead bolt would keep out burglars and vandals, but here all the action tended to be on the *inside*.

Rue drove into town, past the library and the courthouse and the supermarket, marveling. It had only been that morning—and yet, it had *not* been—that the marshal's office and the general store and the Hang-Dog Saloon had stood in their places. The road, rutted and dusty and dappled with manure in Farley's time was now paved and relatively clean.

Only when she reached the churchyard did Rue realize she'd intended to come there all along. She parked by a neatly painted wooden fence and walked past the old-fashioned clapboard church to the cemetery beyond.

The place was a historical monument—there were

people buried here who had been born back East in the late seventeen hundreds.

Rue paused briefly by Aunt Verity's headstone, crouching to pull a few weeds, then went on to the oldest section. Almost immediately, she found the Fortner plot, a collection of graves surrounded by a low, iron fence.

She opened the little gate, which creaked on rusty hinges, and stepped inside.

Jonathan Fortner's grave was in the center and beside his stone was another one, marked Elisabeth Fortner. Rue felt tears sting her eyes; maybe Bethie was still alive in that other dimension, but she was long dead in this one. So were her husband and all her children.

After she'd recovered from the shock of standing beside Bethie's grave, Rue studied the other stones. Sons, daughters, sons-in-law and daughters-in-law, even grandchildren, most of whom had lived to adulthood, were buried there. Obviously, Jonathan and Elisabeth's union had been a very fruitful one, and that consoled Rue a little. More than anything else, her cousin had wanted a lot of children.

When Rue turned, she was startled to see a handsome young man crouched by the metal gate, oiling the creaky hinges. He smiled, and something about the expression was jarringly familiar.

"Friend of the family?" he asked pleasantly. Rue had him pegged for the kind of kid who had played the lead in all the high school drama productions and taken the prettiest girl in his class to the prom.

Rue allowed herself a slight smile. "You might say that. And you?"

"Jonathan and Elisabeth Fortner were my great-

great-grandparents," he said, rising to his feet. He looked nothing like Bethie, this tall young man with his dark hair and eyes, and yet his words struck a note of truth deep inside Rue.

For a moment, she was completely speechless. It seemed that every time she managed to come to terms with one element of this time-travel business, another aspect presented itself.

Rue summoned up a smile and offered her hand. "I guess you could say Bethie—Elisabeth—was my great-great-cousin. My name is Rue Claridge."

"Michael Blake," he replied, clasping her fingers firmly.

Rue searched her memory, but she couldn't recall Aunt Verity ever mentioning this branch of the family. "Do you live in Pine River, Michael?"

He shook his head and, once again, Rue felt a charge of recognition. "Seattle—I go to the university. I just like to come out here once in a while and—well—I don't know exactly how to explain it. It's like there's this unseen connection and I'm one of the links. I guess this is my way of telling them—and myself—that I haven't broken the chain."

Rue only nodded; she was thinking of the overwhelming significance a simple decision or random happenstance could have. If Bethie hadn't stumbled into that other dimension or whatever it was, then Michael would probably never have existed. In fact, just a few months before, when Elisabeth had not yet stepped over the threshold to meet and fall in love with her country doctor, there had surely been no Michael Blake. That would explain why Aunt Verity had never talked about him or his family.

On the other hand, Michael had grown to youthful manhood; he had a life, a history. He was as solid and real as anyone she'd ever met.

Rue's head was spinning.

"Are you all right?" Michael asked, firmly taking her elbow and helping her to a nearby bench. "You look pale."

Rue sat down gratefully and rubbed her right temple with a shaking hand. "I'm fine," she said hastily. "Honestly."

"I could get you some water...."

"No," Rue protested. "I'm okay. Really."

Michael brought a small black notebook from his jacket pocket, along with a stub of a pencil. "My grandmother would really like to meet you, since you're a shirttail relation and everything. She lives with my mom and dad in Seattle. Why don't you give her a call sometime?"

Rue grinned at the ease with which he invited a total stranger into the inner circle of the family, but then that was the sort of thing kids did. "Thanks, Michael."

He wedged one hand into the pocket of his jacket, holding the can of spray lubricant in the other. "Well, I guess I'd better be getting back to the city. Nice meeting you."

"Nice meeting you," Rue said hoarsely, looking away. *Did you think about what it means to change history, Bethie?* she thought. *I know I never did.*

Michael had long-since driven away in a small blue sports car when Rue finally rose from the bench and went to stand beside her cousin's grave once again.

"Maybe I should just leave it all alone," she murmured as a shower of gold, crimson and chocolate-colored leaves floated down onto the little plot from the surrounding maple trees. "Maybe it would be better to walk away and pretend I believe the official explanation for your disappearance, Bethie. But I just can't do it. Even though I know I could stir up ripples that might be felt all the way into this century, I have to hear you say, in person, that you want to stay there. I have to look into your eyes and know that you understand your decision."

And I have to see Farley Haynes again.

The stray, ragtag thought trailed in after the others, and Rue immediately evicted it from her mind. For all practical intents and purposes, Farley was just a figment of her imagination, she reminded herself, little more than a character she'd seen in a movie or read about in a book.

The idea left a keen, biting sense of loneliness in its wake, but Rue was determined to accept the fact and get on with her life.

Of course, before she could do that, she had to see Bethie just once more.

Instead of going home, Rue drove into Seattle.

She visited a coin shop first, where she purchased an expensive selection of bills and coins issued between 1880 and 1892. After that, Rue visited a dusty little secondhand store tucked away in an alley behind a delicatessen, and bought herself a graceful ivory gown with tatting on the cuffs and collar, and a waist-length capelet to match. A little searching unearthed a pair of brown, high-button shoes and a parasol.

Rue coughed as the shop's proprietress shook out the ancient garment and prepared to wrap it. "Is this a theatrical costume, or was it a part of a real wardrobe?"

The other woman smiled wistfully. "I suspect this gown came from a camphor trunk in someone's attic, since it's in relatively good condition. If you'll look closely at the handwork, you'll see it's made to last."

"Is it washable?"

"I wouldn't try that. The fabric is terribly old; water or dry-cleaning solution might dissolve the fibers."

Rue nodded, feeling fond of that romantic old relic of a dress already, and hoping she could make it hold together long enough to get back to 1892, have a couple of practical calico dresses made and find Elisabeth. Between her poker winnings and the old currency she'd purchased at the coin shop, Rue figured she'd have enough money to catch a boat or a train to San Francisco, where Elisabeth and Jonathan were supposed to have gone.

As Rue was driving back to Pine River, a light rain began to fall. She found a classical station on the car radio—Rue's musical tastes covered the full range, but on that particular night, Mozart had the greatest appeal.

It truly startled her to realize, just as she reached the outskirts of Pine River, that there were tears on her face.

Rue rarely cried, not because she was in any way above it, but because she'd long ago learned that weeping solved nothing. In fact, it usually just complicated matters.

Nevertheless, her cheeks seemed as wet as the windshield, and her feelings were an odd, explosive tangle. Methodically, she began to separate them.

Meeting Michael Blake had given her a shattering sense of the gossamer threads that link the past with the present and the future. If for some reason Elisabeth changed her mind about staying in 1892 and following through with the new destiny she'd created for herself by making that choice, Michael and a lot of other people would simply be obliterated.

To make matters worse, the problem wouldn't stop with Michael's generation. Whole branches of the family tree that might have lived and loved, laughed and cried, would never come into being at all.

Rue's hands began to tremble so badly that she had to pull over to the side of the road and sit with her forehead resting against the steering wheel.

Finally, after several minutes, she was able to drive on, but she was still crying, and there were more feelings to be faced and dealt with.

Next came the most prickly fact of all, the one Rue could no longer deny: she was lonely. From an emotional standpoint, she sometimes felt as though everyone on the planet had stepped into a parallel dimension. She could see them and hear their voices, but they seemed somehow inaccessible, forever out of reach.

Only her grandfather, Aunt Verity and Elisabeth had been able to reach through the invisible barrier to touch her, and now they were all gone.

Rue sniffled. There was one positive aspect to this experience she and Elisabeth shared, however: it opened the door to all sorts of possibilities. Maybe the philosophers and poets were right and she *would* see her loved ones again someday. Maybe Aunt Verity and Gramps were carrying on happy lives in some other time and place, just as Elisabeth seemed to be.

It was all too mystical for a pragmatic mind like Rue's.

Darkness had fallen by the time she reached home but, as always, the atmosphere of the house was friendly.

After carefully hanging up the dress she'd purchased and setting the high-button shoes side by side on the floor of the armoire, Rue went downstairs and made supper: a grilled cheese sandwich and a cup of micro-wave soup.

She was too tired and overwrought to think clearly or make further plans. After a warm bath, Rue crawled into bed, read two chapters of a political biography and promptly drifted off to sleep.

In the early hours of the morning, Rue dreamed she was back in Baghdad, at the start of the Gulf War, hid-ing out in the basement of a hotel with several other news people and trying not to flinch every time a bomb exploded. She forcibly woke herself from the nightmare, but the loud noises continued.

Rue's fingers immediately rushed to the necklace at her throat. Once again, the pendant felt warm, al-most hot, to the touch. And the predawn air reverber-ated with gunshots.

Muttering, Rue tossed back the covers and stumbled through the hallway to the sealed door. Sure enough, it opened when she turned the knob, and now she could hear drunken male laughter and the nervous whinny-ing of horses on the road, though the thick darkness prevented her from seeing anything.

There was more shooting, and Rue cringed. Obvi-ously, a few of the boys where whooping it up, as they used to say on TV, and that made her furious. Some-one could be shot!

She gripped the sooty sides of the doorframe and yelled, "Hey, you guys! Knock it off before you hurt somebody!"

Surprisingly, an immediate silence fell. Rue listened

for a moment, smiled and closed the door. True, she had unfinished business in 1892, but she wasn't going to attend to it in her nightgown.

There was no point in trying to go back to sleep, thanks to the James Gang. Rue set up her portable computer at the kitchen table and brewed a cup of herbal tea in the microwave. Then she sat down, her toes hooked behind the rung of her chair, and began tapping out an account of the things that had happened to her. Like Bethie with her letters, Rue felt a fundamental need to record her experiences with an orderly succession of words.

Rue had been writing steadily for over half an hour, and the first thin light was flowing in through the window above the sink, when suddenly the keyboard vanished from beneath her fingertips.

Rue looked up, stunned to see that the room had changed completely. Dr. Fortner's cast-iron cookstove stood near the back door. There was no tile, only rough wood flooring, and the wooden icebox had returned, along with the bulky pump handle and the clunky metal sink.

Just as quickly, the modern kitchen appeared. The computer keyboard materialized in front of Rue, and the sleek appliances stood in their customary places.

Rue swallowed hard, remembering the time she'd been standing in the front parlor, looking into the mirror above the mantel. The room had altered that day, too, and she'd even caught a glimpse of a woman dusting a piano.

These experiences gave new credence to Aunt Verity's hazy theory that the necklace had a mind of its own.

She sat back in her chair, pressing her palms to her cheeks, half expecting to find she had a raging fever. Instead, her face felt cool.

After a few moments spent gathering her composure, Rue got out Elisabeth's letters and read them again, carefully, word by word. Not once did Bethie mention seeing a room change; she'd gone back and forth between the present and the past all right, but only by way of the threshold upstairs.

Clearly, the common denominator was the necklace.

Rue rubbed the antique pendant thoughtfully between her thumb and forefinger. She, unlike her cousin, had twice caught glimpses of that other world while just going about her business. Did that mean the invisible passageway between the two eras was changing, expanding? If that were the case, it might also shrink just as unpredictably, or disappear entirely.

Forever.

Rue sighed and shoved splayed fingers through her hair, then began pounding at the keys of her computer again, rushing to record everything. She had always believed that reality was a solid, measurable thing, but there was something going on in and around the house that superceded all the normal rules.

There were no more incidents that day, and Rue spent the time resting and making preparations to return to old-time Pine River. She carefully aired and pressed the fragile dress she'd bought, watched a few soap operas and made herself a tuna sandwich for lunch.

Then on a foray into the dusty attic, she found one of Aunt Verity's many caches of unique jewelry and helped herself to a brooch and set of tarnished, sterling combs.

Later, in her bedroom, she put on the dress and sat at

the vanity table, putting her hair up and learning to use the combs strategically. When she'd mastered the technique, Rue sat looking at her reflection for a long time, liking the wistful, romantic image she made.

The faintly musty scent of the fabric was a subtle reminder, however, that she and the garment belonged to two distinctly different times.

Carefully, Rue unpinned her hair, took off the dress and got back into her jeans and sweatshirt. She felt a strong draw to 1892, but she wasn't quite ready to go back. She needed to gather all her internal forces and make this trip count.

Just to make certain there wouldn't be any unscheduled visits to the Outer Limits, Rue unclasped the necklace and carefully placed it inside an alabaster box on the vanity. She wondered briefly if the pendant was capable of slipping back and forth between then and now all on its own.

That concept caused Rue a case of keen, if momentary, panic. She reached for the necklace, drew back her hand, reached again. Finally, she turned purposefully and walked away, determined not to be held hostage by a chunk of antique gold on a chain.

The pull of the necklace was strong, though, and Rue had to leave the house to keep away from it.

She decided to call on the Buzbee sisters, the two spinsters who lived on the other side of the road, and find out if they could shed any light on the situation.

Roberta Buzbee, a plain and angular woman, greeted Rue at the door. She seemed pleased to have company and, after explaining that her sister was "indisposed," invited Rue in for tea.

They sat in the front parlor before a blazing applewood fire. It was a cozy room, except for the shrunken head prominently displayed on top of the piano. Rue didn't ask how the sisters had come to acquire the memento because she was pretty sure Miss Roberta would tell her. In detail.

"Have there been any developments in the search for your cousin Elisabeth?" Miss Roberta asked. The sisters had been among the first people Rue had spoken with when she'd arrived in Pine River and begun to look for Bethie, and she knew they'd never bought the official theories.

Rue shrugged and avoided the older woman's gaze for a moment, wishing she dared admit the truth. The situation was simply too delicate. "I'm going to find her," she said, and all the considerable certainty she possessed was contained in those words. "No matter what it takes, no matter what I have to do, I'm going to see Bethie and make sure she's okay."

Miss Roberta nodded primly and took a graceful sip of her tea.

Rue cleared her throat softly and began again. "Miss Roberta, have other people disappeared from that house? Temporarily or permanently?"

The other woman looked distinctly uncomfortable. "Not just that. People have *appeared*, too," she confided. "Folks in old-timey clothes, mostly."

This was new to Rue; she scooted to the edge of her chair. "Like who?" she asked, wide-eyed.

"Well, there was a woman—never liked her. Verity took her under her wing, though, and she finally left town. Once in a while, Sister and I catch sight of a buggy that comes along and turns in at your driveway.

And there's another woman who can be seen hanging out clothes on a fine spring morning."

Ellen, Rue thought. Lizzie's housekeeper. "Ghosts?" Rue asked, to keep the spinster talking.

Miss Roberta clucked her tongue. "Oh, my, no. There aren't any such things—just places where the curtain between our time and theirs has worn a little thin, that's all. Time's all of a piece, Sister and I believe, like a big tapestry. Would you like some lemon cookies? I just baked them this morning."

Rue loved homemade sweets, no matter how agitated her state of mind might be, and she eagerly agreed.

While her hostess was in the kitchen, though, Rue was restless. She picked up a small book that was lying on the coffee table—the title, *My Life in Old Pine River,* suggested the subject was local history. She began thumbing through page after page of old pictures in the center of the book.

Rue's heart twisted when she came across a photograph of Elisabeth standing with the townsfolk in front of a new-looking covered bridge, a slight and mysterious smile curving her lips.

Chapter 5

Seeing an impossibly old photograph of Elisabeth left Rue shaken. Even though she knew from personal experience that time travel was possible, the mysteries of it all still boggled her mind.

"Is something wrong, dear?" Miss Roberta asked as she appeared in the doorway with the promised cookies. "You look as though you wouldn't trust your knees to hold you up."

Rue sighed and rubbed her temple. "This picture…"

Miss Roberta put the platter of cookies down on the coffee table and bent to look at the book in Rue's lap.

Even as she acted, Rue knew discretion would have been a better course than valor, but she was tired of being the only one who knew. She needed the understanding and support of another human being.

She tapped the page lightly with an index finger,

and when she spoke, her voice was thready and hoarse. "This woman, standing here by the bridge...this is Elisabeth."

The spinster perched gracefully on the arm of the sofa, took the volume from Rue and raised it for a closer view. "My land, that does *look* like Elisabeth. I've been through this book a thousand times.... This little girl sitting on the big rock by the stream grew up to be our mother...but I swear I've never noticed this woman. Well, well, well. What do you make of that?"

"What, indeed?" Rue murmured, longing to take an aspirin.

Miss Roberta was pensive. "Maybe she was an ancestor of yours. That would account for the resemblance. What I can't understand is how something so obvious could have escaped my attention."

Rue accepted the book when it was offered and scrutinized the picture again. The woman standing in that crowd was definitely Elisabeth herself, not just someone who resembled her, and the handsome, dark-haired man at her side was probably Jonathan Fortner.

Rue smiled, though she could just as easily have cried, so fragile were her emotions. Elisabeth and Jonathan looked right together.

"Next thing you know," Miss Roberta said irritably, "we'll be appearing on *Unsolved Mysteries,* the whole lot of us. We'll have our pictures on the front of those dreadful newspapers they sell at the supermarket, and all because of that troublesome old house of Verity's."

Lowering her head for a moment to hide her smile, Rue nodded. She suspected the neighbor woman secretly hoped an explosion of notoriety would thrust the boundaries of Pine River outward, thus bringing some excitement to an otherwise humdrum town.

Rue ate a cookie and finished her tea, but only to be polite. Now that she'd seen the photograph of Elisabeth, she was more anxious than ever to make contact with her cousin. Bethie looked happy in that old picture, but that didn't mean she wasn't in over her head in some way. After all, during her marriage to Ian McCartney, Elisabeth had put a brave face on things, but she'd also been miserable for the duration.

Dr. Fortner looked like a hard-headed, autocratic type, though there was no denying he was a formidable hunk, and the male sex had virtually ruled the world in the nineteenth century. Maybe the good doctor was dominating Elisabeth in some way, forcing her to stay when she really wanted to come back to her own time.

Just the idea made Rue's blood simmer. Nobody, but *nobody* was allowed to mistreat Elisabeth.

When she could leave without seeming hasty, Rue thanked Miss Roberta for the cookies and tea, and set out for the other side of the road. By that time, it was already getting dark, and a crisp autumn wind was stirring the flame-colored trees.

Reaching the house, Rue built a fire and then carefully assembled all the items she'd purchased for her journey back to 1892—the dress, the brown high-button shoes, the musty, fragile old money, the silver combs.

Since she hadn't bought stockings, Rue made a concession and wore panty hose. She put on a bra, too, because there were certain comforts she just wasn't willing to sacrifice, even for the sake of authenticity. Besides, nobody in 1892 was going to get a look at her underwear, anyway.

Once she'd donned the dress—she had to suck in her stomach and fasten the buttons in front, then turn the gown around again and put her hands through the armholes—Rue did up her hair. Then, reluctantly, wishing she could wear her sneakers as she had before, she slipped her feet into the pinchy-toed shoes.

She folded the money she'd bought in the coin shop, along with the funds she'd won in the poker game, and tucked the bundle securely into her bodice. The hated red-and-white gingham dress was carefully folded into a neon pink designer sports bag, along with a toothbrush and toothpaste, a paperback book, a bottle of aspirin and some snack-size candy bars.

Once she was seated at the kitchen table, the bag perched on her lap, Rue put on the necklace and waited. A sense of urgent excitement buzzed in her stomach, and she was certain something was about to happen.

Rue sat waiting for so long that she finally unzipped the bag and brought out the novel. She was halfway through chapter two when suddenly the necklace started to vibrate subtly and the light changed, dimming until she could barely see.

The first thing Rue was aware of after that was an incredibly bad smell. The second was the moon shape cut out of the crude wooden door in front of her.

Realizing she'd landed in somebody's outhouse, Rue bolted to her feet, sending the book and the sports bag tumbling to the floor. *"Yuk,"* she grumbled, snatching up her belongings again and then turning the loosely nailed piece of wood that served as a primitive lock and bolting out into the sunlight.

An elderly cowboy touched his hat and smiled at her, and the gaps between his teeth made Rue think of a string of Christmas-tree lights with some of the bulbs burned out. "No hurry, ma'am," he said. "I can wait."

Rue's face throbbed with the heat of embarrassment. It was disconcerting enough to be flung back and forth between two different centuries. Landing helter-skelter in somebody's privy was adding insult to injury.

She hurried past a line of laundry flapping in the breeze, not recognizing the house in front of her or the ones on either side, possessed by an entirely new fear. Maybe she wasn't in 1892, or even in Pine River, for that matter.

Rue's hand tightened on the handle of her bag. Reaching a side gate in the white picket fence, she opened it and stepped out onto a wooden sidewalk. She glanced wildly up and down the street, looking for anything familiar.

She swayed slightly, so great was her relief when she saw Farley come out of a saloon and amble toward her, holding his rifle casually in one hand. With his free hand, he pushed his hat back a notch, and the sigh he gave was one of exasperation.

"You're back," he said.

Rue wrinkled her nose. "How long was I gone?"

Farley's marvelous turquoise eyes narrowed as he studied her. "How long were you…what the sam hill are you talking about?"

"An hour?" Rue shrugged and smiled charmingly, pleased that she was confusing Marshal Haynes. He deserved it for being so arrogant. "Two hours? A week?"

"I haven't seen you in about four days." He frowned, and his expression was pensive now. "I figured you'd gone back to your folks or something."

Rue wanted to ask if he'd missed her, but she couldn't

quite bring herself to take the risk. "I've been…around," she said, holding out the skirts of the gown she'd bought especially for this trip. "Like my dress?"

Farley wasn't looking at her outfit, however. He was staring at the blindlingly pink bag she was carrying. "That's the damnedest colored satchel I've ever seen," he muttered, reaching out to touch the material. "Where did you get that?"

"Nordstrom," Rue answered with a slight grin. "It's a store in Seattle." Obviously, she couldn't go into much more detail. As it was, if Farley went looking for the place in the Seattle *he* knew, he'd never find it.

"Where are you staying?" he asked suspiciously.

Much as Rue enjoyed Farley's company, she had no desire to do another stretch in his jail. She looked around, biting her lip, and fortunately caught sight of a sign swinging from the lowest branch of an elm tree in a yard down the street. "There," she said. "At Mrs. Fielding's Rooming House."

Farley sighed again. "That's interesting," he commented at some length, "because Geneva Fielding only takes in gentleman boarders, as a rule."

Rue bit her lower lip. "Okay, so I lied," she blurted out in a furious whisper. "If I'd told you the truth, you wouldn't have believed me. I don't *have* a place to stay, since you won't let me set foot inside Elisabeth's house, but you don't need to worry. I'm not going to loiter or anything. I plan to buy a ticket on the next stagecoach out of town."

The marshal raised one eyebrow. "That so? There won't be one leaving for nearly a week."

"Damn!" Rue ground out. If it weren't for the inconvenience this news was bound to cause her, she would

have laughed at the expression of shock on Farley's face.
She set the bag on the sidewalk and placed her hands on
her hips. "Now I suppose you're going to say it's illegal
for a lady to swear and I'm under arrest!"

One corner of Farley's mouth twitched almost im-
perceptibly. "It's true enough that a lady can't cuss on
the street and still be within the law. Thing is, I'm not
sure whether that ordinance could cover *you* or not."

Rue opened her mouth, closed it again. As a child,
she'd been a tomboy, and as an adult, she'd thought more
in terms of being a woman than a lady. It hurt that Farley wasn't sure how to classify her.

He allowed her a smile so brief it might have been
nothing more than a mirage, then took her elbow in his
free hand. "Miss Ella Sinclair takes in roomers now and
again. Do you still have that poker money you won the
other night?"

It was a moment before Rue could speak, since a series of small shocks was still jolting through her system
from the place where Farley was touching her. "Ah...
er...yes, I have a little money." She swallowed hard,
awed at the cataclysmic shifts taking place in the deepest, most private passages of her spirit. Farley began to
walk purposefully onward, and Rue hurried to keep up.
"I've got to be careful, though, because I don't know
how much I'll need for train fare to San Francisco."

"It'll cost you about seventy-five cents to go from
here to Seattle by stage. As for the train ticket, that'll
be considerably more."

Mentally, Rue was counting the currency tucked into
her bodice, but she kept having to start over because of
the distracting sensations Farley's grip on her elbow was
causing. She figured she probably had enough money

for the trip, provided she skimped on meals and didn't run into any emergencies.

"Is there a place around here where a woman can get a job?" she asked. Farley stopped in front of a narrow blue house with a white weather vane on the roof.

His look was one of wry annoyance as he cocked his thumb back toward the main part of town. "Sure. They're always looking for dancing girls at the Hang-Dog Saloon."

"Very funny," Rue whispered, stepping away from him. "I'll have you know that I'm a trained journalist, with a college education...."

Farley grinned. He plainly knew full well that what he was going to say would infuriate Rue, and so did she...long moments before he actually spoke. "I guess that's where your kinfolks went wrong. Sending you to college, I mean. That's probably how you got all those muddleheaded ideas you're always spouting."

After telling herself silently that it would be immature to stomp on the man's instep, Rue managed to reply in a relatively moderate tone of voice. "It would serve you right if I told you *exactly* where I got all my 'crazy ideas,' Mr. Haynes. However, since you'd almost certainly be too boneheaded to absorb the information, I won't bother." She opened the gate latch. "Goodbye."

Farley was right beside Rue as she strode up the flagstone walk. "You'll need me to vouch for you," he said, his eyes laughing at her even though his sensual mouth was somber. "Even that might not be enough, given the reputation you've made for yourself in this town by wearing pants, playing poker and getting yourself thrown into jail."

Before Rue could answer, the front door of the house

swung open and a woman appeared. She was tall, with blue eyes and thin, blond hair, and she wore a paisley shawl pulled tightly around her shoulders. Her smile was tremulous and hopeful—and it was entirely for Farley.

A laughable stab of jealousy knifed through Rue, but she didn't feel at all amused.

Farley touched his hat brim in a courtly way. "Miss Ella, this is…er…a friend of mine. Miss Rue Claridge." Rue didn't miss the fact that he'd remembered her last name, though she had no idea what conclusions to draw from the discovery. "She needs a place to stay, just until the stage pulls out on Tuesday."

Miss Ella folded her arms and assessed Rue with disapproving eyes, and her nostrils flared slightly in rebellion. "I'm sorry, Farley." Her voice was irritatingly shrill. "I don't have a single room left."

"Then I guess she'll just have to stay at my place," Farley said, resigned. With that, he took hold of Rue's elbow again and propelled her back toward the gate.

Miss Ella took only a few moments to weigh the implications of that. The hard leather heels of her shoes clicked purposefully against the floorboards of the porch as she hurried after Farley and Rue. "Wait!" she warbled. "There is Mama's old sewing room.… It's just a matter of moving out a few trunks and the like."

Rue smiled to herself, though in some ways she'd found the idea of being Farley's houseguest appealing.

Farley winked at her, causing Rue's heart to go into arrest for at least five beats, before turning to look back at Miss Ella. "That's very kind of you," he said cordially.

For the first time, it occurred to Rue that Farley

Haynes was a well-spoken man, for a small-town, nine-teenth-century marshal. Silly questions boiled up in her heart and rose into her mind like vapor, and Rue was grateful that he'd be going on about his business soon. Hopefully before she made a complete fool of herself.

Sure enough, he escorted the ladies only as far as the porch, then tugged at his hat brim, muttered a polite farewell and left.

Rue felt as though she'd been abandoned on a distant planet.

The look in Miss Ella's eyes was not a friendly one as the woman opened the front door and swept into the thin, blue house.

Rue followed, lugging her pink bag. By that time, sleeping in somebody's barn sounded a shade more inviting than rooming with Miss Ella Sinclair.

"That'll be one dollar in advance," the spinster said, holding out one hand, palm up.

Pulling her money from her bodice embarrassed Rue, but she did it defiantly all the same, to let the landlady know she wasn't intimidated. "Here," she said, peeling off a bill.

"Thank you," Miss Ella replied crisply. "I'll just go and ready up that room I mentioned." With that, she swept off, leaving Rue standing awkwardly in the front parlor, still holding her bag.

The landlady returned in a surprisingly short time for someone who'd allegedly had to move trunks out of a sewing room. Of course, Rue knew there had never been a shortage of beds in this house in the first place; Miss Sinclair was smitten with Farley, and she didn't want him taking in a female boarder.

Rue's quarters turned out to be a closet-size room

wedged underneath the stairway. There was very little light and even less air. Someone had made a disastrous attempt at decoration, papering the place with hideous red cabbage roses against a pea green background. It looked as though a child had stood on the threshold and pitched overripe tomatoes at the walls.

"Dinner is at seven," Miss Ella announced. "Please be prompt, because Papa is always ravenous when he returns from a day at the bank."

Rue nodded and set her bag on the foot of the narrow cot she'd be sleeping on every night until the stagecoach came through and she could be off to Seattle. It hardly looked more comfortable than the bed in Pine River's solitary jail cell.

"Thank you." Rue rushed on without thinking, and the instant the question was out of her mouth, she regretted it. "Where's the bathroom?"

"There's a chamber pot underneath the bed," the landlady answered with a puzzled frown. "And as for bathing, well, each boarder is assigned one particular night when he can bathe in the kitchen. Yours will be..." She paused, tapping her mouth with one finger as she considered. "Thursday."

Rue sat down on the edge of the cot with a forlorn sigh. She didn't mind being in the wrong century, she didn't even mind boarding in a house where she wasn't wanted, but not being able to take a shower every day was practically unbearable.

Miss Ella waggled her fingers in farewell and went out, closing the squeaky door behind her.

Rue got out her paperback book, stretched out on the lumpy cot and sighed. She'd stayed in worse places, though most of them had been in third-world countries.

Somewhere between chapters four and five, Rue dozed off. When she awakened, she had a headache and cramps in all her muscles, and she was clutching her sports bag like some pitiful orphan abandoned at Ellis Island.

Since crying wasn't a workable method of operation, she got up, poured tepid water from a chipped pitcher into a mismatched bowl and splashed her face. After that, she opened the window a crack and took a few deep breaths.

Soon Rue was feeling better. She ferreted out the supply of candy bars tucked away in her bag and ate a single piece, then decided to brave Miss Sinclair's parlor. She would borrow a cloak, if she could, and go out for a walk before dinner.

The landlady was nowhere to be found, as it happened, but a young woman who introduced herself as Miss Alice McCall volunteered a long woolen cape. Gratefully, Rue wrapped herself against the evening chill and went out.

There were no streetlights in this incarnation of Pine River, and certainly no neon signs. The blue-gray color of television screens didn't flicker beyond the windows, but oil lanterns sent out a wavering glow.

A crushing wave of loneliness washed over Rue, a bruising awareness that the lights behind those thick panes of glass didn't shine for her.

She was a stranger here.

In the center of town, the golden glimmer of lamps spiced with bawdy piano tunes spilled out of the saloon windows into the streets. Rue was drawn not by the drinking and the ugliness, but by the light and music.

The sudden flare of a match startled her, and she

jumped. Farley was leaning against the outer wall of the feed and grain, his trusty rifle beside him, smoking a thin brown cigar.

"Looking for a poker game?" he inquired dryly.

Rue tossed her head to let him know just how much contempt she had for his question, then gestured toward the cigar. "Those things will kill you," she said. She didn't really expect to turn Farley from his wicked ways; she just wanted to make conversation for a few minutes.

He chuckled and shook his head. "You have an opinion on just about everything, it seems to me."

Rue sighed. It wasn't the first time someone had called her opinionated, and it probably wouldn't be the last. "There are worse things," she said, drawing her borrowed cloak more tightly around her. She hoped she would catch up with Elisabeth before too long, because she didn't have the clothes for cold weather.

"I can't deny that," Farley confessed good-naturedly. He started walking along the board sidewalk, and Rue just naturally strolled along beside him.

"Miss Sinclair is—what did you people call it?— oh, yes. She's sweet on you, Marshal. She's set her cap for you."

Now it was Farley who sighed. "Umm," he said.

"Typical male answer," Rue replied briskly. "Who are you, Farley? Where did you go to school?"

His boots made a rhythmic and somehow comforting sound on the wooden walk as he moved along, keeping a thoughtful silence. Finally, he countered, "Why do you want to know?"

"I'm just curious," Rue said. They'd reached the end of the main street, and Farley crossed the road and started back the other way, the ever-present rifle in his hand. "You're educated, and that isn't all that common in the old...in the West."

Farley laughed, and the sound was low and rich. The smell of his cigar was faint and somehow a comfort in the strangeness of that time and place. "My pa was a hard-scrabble farmer in Kansas," he said, "and my ma never got beyond the fourth grade in school, but she loved books, and she taught me to read from the Bible and the *Farmer's Almanac*. Once in Texas, I herded cattle for a man who must have had two hundred books in his house, and he let me borrow as many as I could carry." Farley paused, smiling as he remembered. "I stayed on with that outfit for three years, even though the money wasn't for spit, and I read every damn one of those books."

Rue felt a swell of admiration, along with the usual jangling this man always caused in her nervous system. And she wished she could take him by the hand and show him the library her grandfather had built up on the ranch in Montana. "Awesome," she said.

"Awesome," Farley echoed. They were passing one of the saloons, and he glanced in over the swinging doors, apparently just making sure all was well with the warm-beer set. "I've never heard that word used that way."

Rue smiled. "Kids say 'awesome' in... Seattle." It was true enough. They just weren't saying it *yet*. "I'm impressed, Farley. That you've read so many books, I mean."

"If you ever want to borrow any," he said with an endearing combination of modesty and shyness Rue had never dreamed he was capable of, "just let me know. I've got some good ones."

They had reached the residential part of town, and Rue knew seven o'clock must be getting close. "Thanks," she said, lightly touching Farley's arm. "I might do that."

The instant her fingers made contact with the hard muscles of his forearm, Rue knew she'd made a mistake. The ground seemed to tremble beneath her feet, and she felt more than slightly dizzy.

When Farley leaned his rifle against a building and gripped the sides of her waist to steady her, the whole situation immediately got worse. He gave a strangled groan and bent his head to kiss her.

His tongue touched either side of her mouth, then the seam between her lips. She opened to him as she had never done for another man, and he took full advantage of her surrender.

Much to Rue's chagrin, it was Farley who finally broke away. He gripped her shoulders and held her at a distance, breathing hard and muttering an occasional curse word.

"I'll see you back to the Sinclair place," he said after a long time.

Rue was shaken and achy, wanting the marshal of Pine River as she had never in her life wanted a man before. "Farley, what's wrong?" she asked miserably.

He took her elbow and started hustling her along the walk. "Nothing. You're leaving for Seattle on Tuesday and I'm staying here to start a ranch. Let's remember that."

For the first time, Rue fully understood how Elisabeth could care enough about a man to give up every comfort and convenience of the twentieth-century.

Her own attraction to Farley Haynes had just reached a frightening pitch.

She swallowed. "I guess you'll marry someone like Miss Sinclair, once you're ready to settle down. A man out here needs a wife."

Farley didn't look at her. "I guess so," he said, and his voice sounded gruff. They'd reached the Sinclair's front gate, and he reached down to unfasten the latch. "In the future, Miss Claridge," he said tightly, "it might be a good idea if you didn't go out walking after dark. It's not safe or proper, and the good people of the town don't set much store by it."

Rue was riding an internal roller coaster, had been ever since Farley had kissed her, and she'd exhausted her supply of sensible remarks. "Good night," she said, turning and rushing toward the house.

The Sinclairs and their boarders were just sitting down to supper, and Rue joined them only because she was famished. This was one night when she would definitely have preferred room service.

"What do you do, Miss Claridge?" the head of the household asked pleasantly. He was a tall, heavy man with slate gray hair and a rather bulbous red nose. "For a living, I mean?"

His daughter smiled slyly and lowered her eyes, obviously certain that the new boarder was about to make a fool of herself.

"I'm an heiress," Rue said. The statement was true; it was just that her money was in another dimension, stamped with dates that would be nothing but science fiction to these people. "My family has a ranch in Montana."

"What brings you to Pine River, Miss Claridge?"

asked the young woman who had loaned Rue her cloak earlier.

"I came to see my cousin, Elisabeth Fortner."

Mr. Sinclair put down his fork, frowning, but his daughter did not look at all surprised. Of course, Rue would have been the subject of much female conjecture in the dull little town.

"Jonathan's wife?" Mr. Sinclair inquired, frowning heavily. "The woman we tried for murder?"

"Yes," Rue answered. "The woman you tried...and acquitted."

Pointing out Elisabeth's innocence of any crime didn't seem to lighten the mood at the table. It was as though being accused had been enough to taint not only Bethie, but all who came before and all who could come after.

Once again, Rue wondered how happy her cousin could expect to be in this town. Probably the memory of Elisabeth McCartney Fortner's murder trial would live on long after Bethie herself was gone, and time would undoubtedly alter the verdict.

"More chicken and dumplings, Miss Claridge?" cooed Miss Sinclair with particular malice.

Rue's stomach had suddenly closed itself off, refusing to accept so much as one more forkful of food. "No, thank you," she said. Then she excused herself from the table, carried her dishes into the kitchen and took refuge in her room under the stairway.

After making a reluctant trip to the privy behind the house—Rue refused to use the chamber pot under any circumstances—she washed and brushed her teeth, then climbed into bed. There was one lamp burning on the bedside stand, but the oil was so low that reading was out of the question.

Rue turned down the wick until the room was in darkness, then lay back on her pillow, thinking about Farley and the way she'd felt when he kissed her. She raised one hand to her chest, amazed at the way her heart was pounding against her breastbone, and that was when she made the frightful discovery.

The necklace was gone.

Chapter 6

Rue bounded out of bed, lit the lamp and tore through her sheets and blankets in a panic. There was no sign of the necklace.

Only too aware that she would be trapped in this backward century if she didn't find the antique pendant, she sank to her knees and went over every inch of the floor.

Rue was rifling through her sports bag when the last of the lamp oil gave out and the tiny room went dark. For a long moment, she just knelt there on the splintery wood, breathing hard and fighting a compulsion to scream hysterically.

Finally, reason prevailed. She couldn't retrace her steps through town until morning. Flashlights hadn't been invented yet and, besides, if Farley caught her out prowling the sidewalks at that hour, he'd probably toss her back in jail just on general principle.

Lying very still, Rue forced herself to concentrate on her breathing until she was calmer. Soon her heartbeat had slowed to its regular rate and the urge to rush wildly around Pine River upending things in search of the missing necklace had abated slightly. For all her self-control, Rue didn't manage to sleep that night.

Finally the sun peeked over the blue-green, timber-carpeted hills, and Rue bolted out of her room like a rubber-tipped dart shot from a popgun. She'd long since washed, dressed and brushed her teeth.

She went over every step she'd taken the day before, hoping to find the necklace wedged between one of the boards in the sidewalk or lying beside the Sinclairs' gate or on the path to the privy. After a full morning of searching, however, Rue still had no necklace, and she was pretty forlorn.

In a last-ditch effort, she made her way to Farley's office. The front door was propped open with a rusty coffee can filled with ordinary speckled rocks.

"Hello?" Rue called, peering around the frame.

Farley was just hanging his hat on its customary peg, and a large, rumpled-looking man was snoring away on the cot in the cell.

When Farley smiled in recognition, Rue felt as if two of the floorboards had suddenly switched places beneath her feet. "Good day, Miss Claridge," the marshal said.

He acted as though he hadn't kissed her the night before, and Rue decided to go along with the pretense.

She stepped into the room reluctantly, torn between approaching the marshal and bolting down the sidewalk in utter terror. Rue hadn't felt this awkward around a guy since junior high. "I wonder if you would mind

checking your lost-and-found department for my necklace," she said, sounding as prim as Miss Ella Sinclair
or one of the Society.

Farley's dark eyebrows knit together for a moment,
then he went to the stove and reached for the handle of
the coffeepot. "We've never seen the need for a lost-
and-found department here in Pine River," he said
with a good-natured patience that nonetheless rankled.
"Folks pretty much know what belongs to them and
what doesn't."

Rue sagged a little. "Then no one has reported finding a gold necklace?"

Farley studied her sympathetically and shook his
head. "Coffee?"

Rue had never been a frail woman, but these were
stressful circumstances, and she knew a dose of Farley's
high-octane brew would probably turn her stomach inside out. "No, thanks," she said distractedly. "Did you
know it's been proven that caffeine aggravates P.M.S.?"

"What aggravates what?"

"Never mind." Rue turned to go, muttering. "I've
got to find that necklace...."

There was nowhere else to look, however, so Rue returned to the Sinclair house. The place was empty and,
since she'd probably missed lunch, Rue headed for her
room. As she was opening the door, a distraught, feminine moan drifted down the stairway.

Holding the skirts of her secondhand dress, Rue
swept around the newel post and up the stairs. The sound
was coming from beneath the first door on the right.
She knocked lightly. "Hello? Are you all right in there?"

"Yes." The answer was a fitful groan.

Rue opened the door a crack and saw Alice McCall

lying on a narrow bed in her chemise. A crude hot-water bottle lay on the lower part of her stomach.

"Cramps?" Rue inquired.

"It's the curse," Alice replied, whispering the words as though confessing to some great sin.

Remembering the aspirin in her bag, Rue said, "I think I can help you. I'll be right back." She raced downstairs to her room to fetch the miracle drug she'd brought from her own century and then, after pausing in the kitchen to battle the pump for a glass of water, returned to Alice's room.

The poor girl was pale as death, and her wispy, reddish blond hair was limp with perspiration.

She looked at the pair of white tablets in Rue's palm and squinted. "Pills?"

"They're magic," Rue promised with a teasing lilt to her voice. Aspirin would probably work wonders for someone who had never taken it before. "Just swallow them and you'll see."

Alice hesitated only a moment. Then she took the tablets and washed them down, one by one, with delicate sips of water.

"Would you like me to fix you a cup of tea?" Rue asked.

"You're very kind, but, no," Alice responded, her face still pinched with pain. It would be a while before the aspirin worked.

Rue sat down at the foot of the bed, since there was no chair, and took in the small, tidy room at a glance. Although Alice's bedroom had a window and the wallpaper was actually tasteful, the place was as sparsely furnished as a monk's cell. Two dresses hung on pegs on the wall, one for everyday and one for Sundays and special occasions. Over the bureau, with its four shallow drawers, was a mirror made of watery greenish glass. A rickety washstand held the requisite pitcher and bowl.

Above the bed was a calendar, clearly marked 1892, with a maudlin picture of two scantily clad children huddling close in a blizzard. The month of October was on display, and the twenty-third was circled in a wreath of pencil lines.

"Is your birthday coming up?" Rue asked, knowing Alice had seen her glance at the calendar.

Alice smiled wanly. "No. That's the day of the Fall Dance at the schoolhouse."

Rue wondered if Alice, like Miss Ella Sinclair, was sweet on Marshal Haynes. The idea took a little of the sparkle off her charitable mood. "Are you hoping to dance with anybody special?"

Color was beginning to return to Alice's cheeks, though Rue couldn't be sure whether that was due to the aspirin or the prospect of spending time with that special someone. "Jeffrey Hollis," she confided. "He works at the mill."

"Are the two of you dating?"

Alice looked puzzled. "Dating?"

"Courting," Rue corrected herself.

Alice laughed softly. "*I* am definitely courting Jeffrey," she replied, "but I think somebody will have to tell him that he's supposed to be courting me in return." She lay back on the pillow, her lashes fluttering against her cheeks, and then, without further adieu, she floated off to sleep.

Rue covered her newfound friend with a plaid woolen blanket and sneaked out of the room. Back in her own quarters, she ate another candy bar, read two more chapters of her book, and closed her eyes to meditate on the problem of the lost necklace.

Mentally, she retraced every step she'd taken the day before, from the moment she'd found herself in a stranger's privy until she lay down in bed and realized the pendant was gone. And again the chilling thought came to her that that weird, spooky piece of jewelry might have taken to traveling through time all on its own.

Rue squeezed her eyes shut and dragged in a series of slow, deep breaths in an effort to keep her cool, all the while feeling like a one-woman riot.

If she got stuck in this place, she vowed silently, she would pay Elisabeth back by moving into her house like a poor relation. She would stay for fifty years and consciously work at getting more eccentric with every passing day.

Rue brought herself up short. She refused to worry about the future or about the missing necklace. It was time to stop thinking about problems and start looking for solutions.

The first order of business was to find Elisabeth. Once she'd done that, once she knew for a fact that her cousin really wanted to stay in the Victorian era, she could worry about getting home. Or about making a life for herself right there in old Pine River.

With Farley.

She imagined cooking for him, pressing his shirts, washing his back.

The images stirred hormones Rue hadn't even known she had, and a schoolgirl flush rolled from her toes to the roots of her hair in a single crimson wave.

Good grief! she thought, bolting upright on the cot.

Cooking? Ironing? Washing his back? *What's happening to me? I'm regressing at warp speed!*

Rue sighed and rose from the bed. Lying around in her room in the middle of the day was a waste of daylight. She would check on Alice, then go out and retrace her steps again. Maybe she would find the necklace, or maybe some earthshaking idea would come to her.

Miss McCall was still sleeping, and some of the color had returned to her cheeks, so Rue knew the aspirin was doing its work. She closed the door of Alice's room carefully and turned toward the front stairway.

Mr. Sinclair was standing there, barring her way, a worrisome smile on his face. He was a portly man, with gray hair, shrewd brown eyes, florid cheeks and a somewhat bulbous nose.

"Miss Claridge," he said, as though Rue might have forgotten her name and he was generous enough to enlighten her.

Rue retreated a step, feeling uneasy. She'd seen that look in a man's eyes many times during her travels, and she knew the banker had decided to make a pass. "Good afternoon," she said warily, with a little nod.

"Exploring the house?" He crooned the words, and somehow that was more unnerving than if he'd shouted them.

Rue raised her chin a notch, still keeping her distance. "Of course not," she said with cool politeness.

"Your room is on the first floor, I believe." Sinclair's eyes never linked with hers all the while he was speaking. Instead, his gaze drifted over her hair, her throat, her shoulders and then her breasts.

"I was looking in on Miss McCall," Rue said, folding her arms to hide at least one part of her anatomy from his perusal. "She's suffering from—feminine complaints."

In the next instant, the master of the house reached out with one beefy hand and took hold of Rue's jaw. While his grip was not painful, it was definitely an affront, and she immediately tried to twist free.

"Now, now," Sinclair murmured, as though soothing a fractious child, "don't run away. I wouldn't want to have to tell Farley I caught you going through my personal belongings and get you thrown back into jail."

Rue felt the blood drain from her face. This kind of bore was easy enough to deal with in her own time, but just then the year was 1892 and Sinclair was probably among the most influential men in town. "What do you want?" she asked, hoping she was wrong.

She wasn't.

He ran a sausage-size thumb over her mouth. "Just an hour of your time, Miss Claridge. That's all."

Rue thrust herself away from him. "I wouldn't give you a *moment,*" she ground out, "let alone an hour!"

Smiling genially, Sinclair hooked his thumbs in his vest pockets. "That's a pity. More jail time will surely ruin what little is left of your reputation."

Rue inched backward toward the stairway leading down to the kitchen. "I'll deny everything. And Farley will believe me, too!" She wasn't too sure about that last part, but she wanted to keep Sinclair distracted until she was out of lunging distance.

His bushy eyebrows rose in mocking amusement. "Silly child. What the marshal believes doesn't amount to a hill of beans. Not against the say-so of a man who controls everybody's finances."

Knowing she had reached the stairs, Rue whirled

and raced down them. She snatched her bag from the little room she had occupied so briefly and fled out the front door.

Now, for all practical intents and purposes, she was homeless. She couldn't go back to her own century because she'd lost the necklace, and since Farley would probably take Sinclair's word over hers, arrest was no doubt imminent.

Much as Rue enjoyed Farley's company, she wasn't about to be locked up again. One stretch in the hoosegow on trumped up charges was more than enough; she had no intention of serving another.

Even so, Rue was forced to admit to herself that she was drawn to Farley's quiet strength. She made her way through the deep grass behind the mercantile and the Hang-Dog Saloon, stopping now and then to crouch down when she heard voices. After nearly half an hour of evasion tactics, she reached the little barn behind the marshal's house and slipped inside.

Farley's horse, a big roan gelding, nickered companionably from its stall.

"At least somebody around here likes me," Rue said, looking around the small structure and deciding the loft would make the best hiding place.

After letting out a long sigh, she tossed her bag up and then climbed the rickety ladder—not an easy task in a long skirt.

The hay in the loft was sweet smelling, and afternoon sunlight flooded in through a gap in the roof. Rue sat cross-legged and automatically unzipped the side flap on her bag, since that was where she had hidden her money.

The currency, like Aunt Verity's necklace, had vanished.

Rue gave a little cry of frustration and fell backward into the hay. A few minutes later, she checked the main compartment of the bag, but nothing was missing. Evidently the thief—possibly even Sinclair himself—had stumbled upon the money first and been content with that.

Despite her fury, Rue had to smile, wondering what the robber would have made of her miniature candy bars and other modern inventions.

Following that, she took the advice her grandfather had given her long ago and quietly accepted the fact that she was in big trouble. As much as she would like things to be different, the reality was that her money was gone, one of Pine River's most prominent citizens planned to accuse her of stealing, and she'd lost the only means she'd had of returning to her own time. Only when she'd faced these problems squarely would solutions begin to present themselves.

At least, she *hoped* solutions would begin to present themselves. Nothing came to her right away.

The sun was setting and crickets were harmonizing in the quack grass outside the barn when she heard sounds below and rolled over to peer through a crack between the floorboards of the loft.

Farley was there. He filled a feedbag and slipped it over the gelding's head, then began currying the animal. The graceful play of the muscles in the marshal's back and shoulders did odd things to Rue's heartbeat, but she couldn't help watching him work.

The lawman caught her completely off guard when he suddenly whirled, drew his pistol and pointed it at the underside of the loft.

"All right, just come down from there," he ordered. "And keep your hands where I can see them."

Some days, Rue reflected dismally, it just didn't pay to get out of bed.

"Don't shoot, Marshal," she said. "It's only me, Rue Claridge, Pine River's Most Wanted."

When Rue peered over the top of the ladder, Farley was just sliding his pistol back into its holster. He'd hung his hat on a peg on the wall, and his attractively rumpled brown hair glimmered even in the fading light. "What the hell are you doing up there?" he demanded, setting his hands on his hips.

Rue sighed and swung her legs over the side of the loft, gripping the pink sports bag in one hand. "Holding, of course. When Mr. Sinclair put the moves on me, I told him to get lost, and he said he'd have you arrest me...."

Farley scratched his head, obviously impatient and puzzled.

Rue tossed her bag to the floor and then climbed resignedly down the ladder to face her fate. "Here." She held out her hands, wrists together. "Handcuff me."

The marshal looked sternly down his nose at Rue. "You've gone and gotten yourself thrown out of the only boardinghouse that would have you?"

Sudden color pulsed in Rue's cheeks. "Didn't you hear a word I've said? Sinclair wanted me to—to be intimate with him. I refused, of course, and he said he'd have me arrested for robbing his house."

Farley's turquoise eyes narrowed. "Let's see that satchel," he said brusquely.

Rue resented the invasion of privacy, but she also knew she had no real choice, so she handed over the bag.

The marshal turned it end over end, trying to find

the opening, and Rue finally reached out and pulled back the zipper herself.

Farley stared at the small mechanism as though it were a bug under a microscope. "What the—"

"It's called a zipper," Rue said with a sigh. "They won't be invented for another twenty-five or thirty years, so don't bother looking for them in your favorite store."

Now Farley studied Rue with the same thoroughness as he'd examined the zipper on her neon pink bag. "You don't talk like anybody I've ever known before, except for Mrs. Fortner, of course. Where did you come from?" he asked quietly.

Rue folded her arms. She might as well tell the truth, she decided, since nobody was going to believe her anyway. "The future. I came from the far end of the twentieth century." She snatched the bag from his hands, suddenly anxious to convince him, to have one person on the face of the earth know what was happening to her. "Here," she said, pulling the paperback spy novel out and thrusting it in Farley's face. "Look. Did you ever see a book like this before, with a soft cover? And read the copyright date."

Farley turned the book in his hands, clearly amazed by the bright red cover and the gold-foil lettering spelling out the title and the author's name.

"Nobody can come from the future," he insisted stubbornly, but Rue could see that the paperback puzzled him.

"I did," she said. After setting the bag down, she politely took the book, opened it to the copyright page and held it out again. "There. Read that."

Farley took in the printed words, then raised baffled eyes to Rue's face. "It's a trick," he said.

"How could it be?" Rue demanded, growing impatient even though she'd known she would never convince him. "Paperback books and zippers don't exist in 1892, Farley!"

"You could have gotten those things at some fancy science exhibition in St. Louis or Chicago or somewhere." Clearly, Farley meant to stand his intellectual ground, even though it was eroding under his feet. "All I know is, it's got to be some kind of hoax."

Rue rolled her eyes. Then she bent and pulled out one of her precious snack-size candy bars. "How about this?" she challenged, holding out the morsel. "Did I get this at an exhibition, too?"

Farley frowned, examining the wrapper.

"You have to tear off the paper," Rue prompted. "Then you eat what's inside."

Farley looked suspicious, but intrigued, also. He tore away the paper, letting it drift to the floor.

Rue picked the litter up and crumpled it on one hand, while Farley carried the candy bar over to the doorway and studied it in the last light. The look of consternation on his face was amusing, even under the circumstances.

"Go ahead, Farley," she urged. "Take a bite."

The marshal glanced at her again, then nibbled cautiously at one end of the chocolate bar. After a moment, he smiled. "I'll be damned," he muttered, then consumed the rest of the candy. "Got any more of those?"

"Yes," Rue answered, thrusting out her chin, "but I'm not going to let you wolf them down. Especially not when you're about to arrest me for something I didn't do."

"I'm not going to arrest you," Farley replied reasonably, looking at Rue with curious amusement. "We've only got one jail cell here in Pine River, as you know, and it's already occupied. I'll just have to give you my bed and bunk out here in the barn until you get on that stage next Tuesday."

Rue didn't protest, nor did she turn the conversation back to the reality of time travel. Farley was still telling himself he was the victim of some elaborate prank, no doubt, but at least she had the satisfaction of knowing she'd planted the seed of possibility in his mind. Maybe after some rumination, he'd begin to take the idea seriously.

It the meantime, they were clearly going to pretend nothing out of the ordinary was going on.

If someone had to sleep in the barn, Rue reasoned, better Farley than she. She lowered her eyes. "There's a problem with my leaving on the stage," she confessed. "Somebody snitched all my money."

Farley sighed. "With luck like yours, it's purely a wonder you ever managed to win at poker the other night," he said, gesturing toward the door. "Come on, Miss Rue. Let's go in and rustle up some supper. We'll figure out what to do with you later."

Rue picked up her bag, straightened her shoulders and preceded him through the doorway of the barn. An inky twilight was working its way down the timbered hills toward them, and there was a bite in the air.

The inside of Farley's log cabin was cozy and surprisingly neat. Books lined one whole wall, from roof to floor, and a stone fireplace faced the door. An attached lean-to housed a small kitchen area, and Rue suspected the tattered Indian blanket hanging from the ceiling hid Farley's bed.

She went to stand beside the fireplace, hoping the

warmth would dispel the sweet shivers that suddenly overtook her. She had a peculiar sense, all of a sudden, of being a piece on some great celestial board game, and she'd just been moved within easy reach of both victory and defeat.

"Hungry?" Farley asked, clattering metal against metal in the lean-to kitchen.

"Starved," Rue said, too tired, confused and frustrated for any more deep thought. She'd missed both breakfast and lunch, and the candy bars weren't taking up the slack.

Farley came out of the lean-to. "The stew'll be warmed up in a few minutes," he said. As he went around the cabin lighting kerosene lamps, he seemed uncharacteristically nervous.

Rue, on the other hand, felt totally safe. "So you're a cook as well as a reader," she said, wanting to hear him talk because she liked the sound of his voice, liked knowing he was there.

He grinned and shook his head. "No, ma'am," he replied. "My food is provided as a part of my wages, like this cabin. The ladies of the town take turns cooking for me."

The thought made Rue violently jealous, and that was when she realized the horrible truth. Somehow, she'd fallen in love with Farley Haynes.

Talk about Mr. Wrong.

"Oh," she said finally.

Farley shook his head and crouched to add wood to the fire. "Maybe you shouldn't stand so close," he said, and his voice was suddenly hoarse. "Ladies have been known to catch their skirts afire doing that."

Rue moved away to look at Farley's collection of

books, and her voice shook when she spoke. "Have you really read all these?"

"Most of them more than once," Farley replied. She heard him retreat into the lean-to, then he called to her to join him. "Stew's warm," he said.

After drawing a deep breath, raising her chin and pushing back her shoulders, Rue marched into the tiny kitchen.

Farley had set a place for her at the small, round table, and there was a lantern flickering on a shelf nearby. The atmosphere was cozy.

He ladled stew into two bowls, set a loaf of hard bread on a platter and sat down across from her.

Once she'd taken several bites of the stew, which was delicious, Rue was a little less shaky, both inwardly and outwardly. She smiled at Farley. "This is quite a place you've got here."

"Thank you," Farley replied, "but I'll be glad when I can take up ranching and let somebody else wear my badge."

A bittersweet sadness touched Rue's heart. "Have you got a place picked out?" she asked, breaking off a piece of bread.

Farley nodded. "There's a half section for sale north of town. I've almost got enough for the down payment, and the First Federal Bank is going to give me a mortgage."

"Mr. Sinclair's bank," Rue murmured, feeling less festive.

Farley was chewing, and he waited until he'd swallowed to answer. "That's right."

An autumn wind tested the glass in the windows, and Rue was doubly glad Farley had taken her in. "If there was any justice in this world, you'd go right over there and arrest that old lecher right this minute for sexual harassment."

A modest flush tinted Farley's weathered cheekbones. "He hasn't broken the law, Rue. And that means he can't be arrested."

"Why?" Rue demanded, only vaguely registering the fact that Farley had called her by her first name. "Because he's a man? Because he's a banker? I was innocent of any crime, and that didn't keep you from slapping *me* behind bars."

"I've never slapped a woman in my life," Farley snapped, looking outraged.

Rue sat back in her chair, her eyes brimming with tears she was too proud to shed. "It's hopeless," she said. "Absolutely hopeless. You and I speak different languages, Farley Haynes."

"I would have sworn we were both talking English," he responded, reaching calmly for his glass of water.

"I give up!" Rue cried, flinging out her hands.

Farley reached for her bowl and carried it to the stove. "What you need," he said, "is some more stew."

Rue watched him with a hunger she would have been too embarrassed even to write about in the privacy of her journal, and she swallowed hard. "Stew," she said. "Right."

Chapter 7

The stew was remarkably good, hot and savory and fresh, and Rue consumed the second helping without quibbling. She was fiercely hungry, and the food eased her low-grade headache and the shaky feeling that invariably overtook her when she failed to eat regular meals.

After supper, Farley heated water on the stove, and Rue insisted on washing the dishes. It was fun, sort of like playing house in an antique store.

The lean-to was a small place, though, and when Farley poured himself a cup of coffee and then lingered at the table, flipping thoughtfully through a stack of papers, Rue was more painfully conscious of his presence than ever. She tried not to think about him, but it was an impossibility. He seemed to fill the little room to its corners with his size, his uncompromising masculinity and the sheer strength of his personality.

In Rue's opinion, the effect on her nerves, her muscles and her most-secret parts was all out of proportion to the circumstances, strange as they were. She felt like a human volcano; lava was burning and bubbling in the farthest reaches of her body and her spirit. Simple things like drying the chipped crockery bowls they'd eaten from and setting them on the shelves took on the significance of epic poetry.

She was wrestling with the enormous enamel coffeepot, trying to pour herself a cupful, when she felt Farley looming behind her. He displaced her grip on the pot's handle and filled her cup.

He was only standing at her back, it was nothing more dramatic than that, yet Rue felt a devastating charge radiate from his body to hers. In the next moment, the invisible field, woven of lantern light, cosmic mystery, half-forgotten dreams and stardust enfolded her, and she sagged backward against Farley's steely stomach and chest.

Farley made no sound. He simply took the cup from Rue's hand, set it on the stove and closed his strong arms lightly around her waist. For all that she had never been in such trouble, even on her most memorable assignments as a journalist, Rue felt as though she'd stumbled upon some magical sanctuary where nothing and no one could ever hurt her.

In the meantime, the seismic tumult was building inside Rue, gaining force moment by moment. She knew the inevitable eruption would be more than physical; it would be an upheaval of the soul, as well. And she wanted it despite the danger.

Presently—whether a minute or an hour passed, Rue could not have said—Farley raised his hands slowly, gently, to weigh her breasts. When his thumbs moved over her nipples, making them harden and strain against the fabric of her dress, Rue groaned and tilted her head back against his shoulder.

He touched his lips to her temple, warming the delicate flesh there, and then he bent his head slightly to nibble the side of her neck. Rue would have throttled any other man for taking such liberties, but her need for Farley had sneaked up on her, and it was already so pervasive that she couldn't tell where the craving stopped and her own being began.

When he lifted her into his arms, Rue's logical left brain finally struggled to the surface and gurgled out a protest, but it was too late. The fanciful right side of her brain was hearing rapturous symphonies, and the notes drowned out all other sounds.

Farley carried her out of the kitchen—Rue was vaguely aware of the fire as they passed the hearth—then he took her behind the Indian blanket that served as a curtain. There was a look of grim resignation on his face as he laid her on the neatly made bed and stood gazing down at her for a long moment. It was as if he thought she'd cast a spell over him and he was trying to work out some way to break it.

She couldn't tell him that she was under an enchantment, too, that she had never done anything like this before. All she could do was lie there, all but the most primitive essence of her identity seared away by the heat of her desire, needing him. Waiting.

He took off her funny, old-fashioned shoes and tossed them aside, then began unbuttoning her dress. Only when she lay completely naked on his bed, totally vulnerable, did he speak.

"God help me," he said in a raw whisper, "I've wanted to see you like this since that day I found you wandering in Doc Fortner's house. I've wanted to touch you...."

Rue took his hand in hers, emboldened by the turquoise fire in his eyes and the frantic fever in her own spirit, and pressed his palm and fingers to her breast. "Touch me," she said softly, and the words were both a plea and an affirmation.

Farley complied for a long, torturously delicious interval, then while Rue waited in sweet agony, he withdrew. She watched, dazed, as he removed his clothes.

His body had the stealth and prowess of a stalking panther as he stretched out beside her on the rough, woolen blanket that served as a bedspread. Then he kissed her, first caressing her lips with his, then commanding her mouth to open for the entrance of his tongue.

The conquest was a triumphant one, far more potent than any ordinary kiss. Rue's body arched beside Farley on the bed, and he reached beneath her to cup her bottom in one hand and press her close against his thighs and the solid demand of his manhood.

She was afraid when she felt him, terrified of his size and power, and yet this knowledge did nothing to stem the furious tide of her passion.

Farley kissed Rue, again and again, all the while caressing and shaping her with his hands, until she was in a virtual delirium of need. Perspiration shimmered on every inch of her flesh, and tendrils of her hair clung wetly to her neck and temples.

At last, Farley positioned himself between her legs, then put his hands under her shoulder blades and raised her breasts for conquering. When he captured one eager nipple with his mouth, Rue cried out in despairing surrender, begging him to take her.

For all her travels, for all her reading and her sophistication, when Farley entered her, Rue was startled. There was pain, and it lingered, but it was also promptly overshadowed by a consuming, joyous rage made up of heavenly light and dragon's fire.

Rue pressed her hands to Farley's back, and the play of his muscles under her palms was as much a part of their lovemaking as the ferocious rhythm of joining and parting that was even then transforming them both.

For all the breathless promise of the past half hour or so, when Rue finally achieved satisfaction, she was all but swept away by the force of it. She strained beneath Farley in wild, glorious and totally involuntary spasms, her teeth clenched against the shouts of triumph rattling in the back of her throat. She was just settling back to the bed, breathless and disoriented, when Farley clasped her bottom hard in his hands, pressed her tightly against him and made a series of deep, abrupt thrusts. To Rue's surprise, she reached another climax when Farley had his; her release was a soft, languid implosion, like a blessing on the tempest that had preceded it.

When he'd finally spent the last of his energy, Farley collapsed beside Rue, his breathing hard and raspy. She pressed her face into the taut, moist flesh on his shoulder, at once hiding from her lover and seeking him out.

"I knew it would be like that," Farley muttered after they'd lain entwined for a long time, listening to the beating of each other's hearts, the crackle of the fire and the night sounds of the lively timber town beyond the cabin walls.

Rue's eyes filled with tears, but she wasn't mourning the time before, when she and Farley had been innocent of each other. No matter what happened, whether she lived the rest of her life with this man or without him, in this century or another, she'd given herself truly and totally to Farley Haynes, and she would never forget the splendor of it.

"I thought it was a lie," she finally confessed. "What people said about making love, I mean. I never knew— until now."

Farley sighed and raised his head to look through her eyes, as though they were clear as windowpanes, and straight into her soul. He kissed her forehead and then rested his scratchy chin where his lips had just touched. "I'm sorry," he said, his voice low and hoarse. "I offered you safe haven here, and then I took advantage."

Rue had just been transported to a whole other plane of womanhood, and the journey had had just as great an impact on her senses and emotions as being tossed from one time period to another. She was incapable, for the moment, of working out whether Farley's apology was appropriate or not. "It's not as though you threw me down on the bed and forced me," she pointed out, loving the feel of his back, supple skin over firm muscles. "I wanted you."

Farley drew back to search her eyes again, and the gesture made her feel more naked than she had earlier when he'd methodically relieved her of her clothes. "You are the most forward-thinking female I have ever encountered," he said somberly, but then a grin broke over his face. "I think I like that about you."

Rue swallowed, and her ability to think in rational terms was beginning to dissipate like fog in bright sunshine. Farley was joined to her, and he was getting hard again, and she didn't want him to leave her. "Stay inside me, Farley. Please."

Bracing himself by pressing his hands on the mattress on either side of her, Farley began to move slowly. "I'll find out the truth about you," he said, his words growing short and breathy as he increased his pace, "if it's the last thing I ever do."

Pressing her shoulders deep into the feather pillows and tilting her head back in magnificent surrender, Rue gasped out, "I'd love to tell you—I'd love to show you the place I came from...." And from that moment on, Rue was beyond speaking.

Farley dipped his head to lave one of her distended nipples with his tongue. His attentions were merciless and thorough, and soon Rue was pitching under him like a wild mare trying to shake off a rider.

Once that session had ended, Rue cuddled against Farley's side—his rib cage had about as much flexibility as the staves of a wooden barrel—and promptly drifted off to sleep. When she awakened, the Indian blanket that separated the bed from the rest of the cabin was framed in silvery moonlight and Farley's side of the mattress was empty.

Rue scrambled off the bed, found one of Farley's shirts hanging from a peg in the wall and shoved her arms through the sleeves. The clock on the plain, board mantel over the fireplace read 3:17 and despite the fact that she had no claim on the marshal's time, a sense of alarm crowded her throat.

Obviously, Farley had gone out for some reason—maybe there had been shouts or a frantic knock at the door or even shots fired, and she'd been too drunk on lovemaking to hear. In fact, she hadn't even noticed when Farley left.

Rue's imagination tripped into overdrive. She'd seen enough Clint Eastwood movies to know what awful things could happen to a lone lawman. The difference was that now she wouldn't be able to toss away her pop-corn box, fish her car keys out of her purse and go home to an apartment filled with modern conveniences. This was the real thing, and she just happened to be hope-lessly in love with the peace officer in question.

On some level, Rue had known from the moment she met Farley that something significant was going to hap-pen between them. But she hadn't expected the event to be on a par with the destruction of the dinosaurs or the formation of the Grand Canyon.

Rue groped her way into the lean-to kitchen, blinded by her emotions rather than a lack of light, and looked at herself in Farley's shaving mirror. Except that her hair was tangled and she was wearing a man's shirt, she seemed unchanged. Inside, however, Rue was wholly different; she'd been converted, not into someone else, but into a better, richer and more genuine version of herself.

Trembling, Rue poured a cup of coffee from the pot on the stove and sank into one of the two chairs at the table. Since it had been sitting on the heat for hours, the brew was black as coal oil and only slightly more palatable. Rue figured there was probably enough caf-feine in the stuff to keep her awake well into the next century—be it the twentieth or the twenty-first—but she took a second sip anyway.

Through the closed windows and thin walls of Far-ley's house, Rue could hear the sounds of laughter and bad piano music and an ongoing argument between a man and a woman. She was overwhelmingly relieved when the door opened and the marshal himself walked in.

He set his rifle in the corner, hung his hat and long canvas duster on their pegs and then began unfastening his gun belt. All the time, he watched Rue in the dim, icy glow of the moonlight.

Rue didn't want to express her relief at seeing him; she didn't have the right. "I hope I didn't keep you from your work," she said with as much dignity as a person wearing only a man's shirt and a glow of satisfaction can be expected to summon up.

Farley didn't answer. He simply came to the table, took Rue's hand and brought her to her feet. He took her back to the bedside, and she crawled under the covers, her heart turning to vapor and then gathering in her throat like a summer storm taking shape on the horizon.

She watched as Farley took off his clothes for the second time that night, more shaken than before by his magnificence and quiet grace.

He stretched out beside her under the blankets and with a few deft motions of one hand, relieved her of the long shirt she wore. Having done that, Farley curved one arm around Rue and arranged her close against his side, her head resting on his shoulder.

Farley did not make love to Rue; instead, he simply held her, sheltering her in his solidity and strength. For Rue, the experience was, in its own way, just as momentous as full surrender had been earlier. The simple intimacy met fundamental needs that had not only been unsatisfied before, but unrecognized.

Rue slept soundly that night and awakened with the

first light of dawn, when Farley gently displaced her
to get out of bed.

"What do I do now?" Rue asked softly. Sadly. "I can't
stay here. The whole town will know if I do."

"The whole town already knows," Farley answered,
pulling on a pair of dark trousers and disappearing
around the edge of the blanket curtain. "There aren't
many secrets in a place like Pine River."

Rue slipped under the covers with a groan of mortification, but she could still hear the clatter and clink of
stove lids, the working of a pump handle, the opening
and closing of a door.

Presently, the smell and sounds of sizzling bacon
filled the air, along with the aroma of fresh coffee.
Rue got up, struggled back into her clothes and peered
around the blanket.

She could see Farley in the lean-to, standing at the
stove. The sight of him, with his hair wetted down and
combed, a meat fork in one hand, filled her with a ten-
derness so keen that it was painful.

Rue approached hesitantly. For the first time in her
life, she didn't know what to say.

Farley turned a strip of bacon in the black skillet and
ran his turquoise eyes companionably over her length.
For an instant, Rue was beneath him again, in the throes
of complete physical and spiritual communion, and the
sensation left her disconcerted.

The marshal made short work of her poetic mood.
"If you're sore," he said, "I've got some balm out in
the barn."

Rue sighed. This was the same man who had evoked
such violently beautiful responses from her the night
before and had later held her snugly against his side,

making no demands. Now he was offering her the same medicine he would use on a cow or a horse.

"Thanks," she answered belatedly, "but I'll be fine."

Farley shrugged, took two plates down from a shelf and began dishing up breakfast.

"Interesting," she murmured thoughtfully, pulling back a chair.

He set a plate filled with fried food in front her. "What's interesting?"

"You," Rue reflected. "You're a nineteenth-century male, and here you are cooking for a woman. Even waiting table."

Farley arched an eyebrow. "It's that or risk letting you do the cooking," he replied.

Rue laughed, but her amusement faded as daylight strengthened the thin glow of the lanterns and reality settled in around her. It was morning now; the enchanted night was over and she was stranded in the wrong century, with the wrong man.

"Farley, what am I going to do?" she asked again. "My money is gone, I don't have anywhere to stay and it's beginning to look like my cousin and her husband are going to make their home in San Francisco and never contact anybody in Pine River again."

"Jon and Lizzie will come back when they're ready," Farley said with certainty. "And you can stay here with me."

"Oh, right," Rue snapped, irritated not with Farley for making the suggestion, but with herself for wanting to go on sharing his life and his bed for as long as possible. "The good women of Pine River will love that."

Farley grinned. "No, they won't."

"You're being pretty cocky right now," Rue pointed

out, annoyed, "but the truth is, you're afraid of those
women, Farley Haynes. They have the power to make
both our lives miserable, and you know it."

Farley's smile tightened to a look of grim obstinance,
and Rue wondered hopefully if the night before had
worked some ancient, fundamental magic in the deepest parts of his being, the way it had in hers.

"Those old hens will just have to do their scratch-
ing and pecking in somebody else's dooryard," he said.

"What the devil is that supposed to mean?" Rue
countered, reaching for another slice of crispy bacon.
The man made love with the expertise of a bard taking
up the pen, and he had some pretty modern attitudes,
but sometimes he talked in cowboy riddles.

Farley got up to refill his coffee mug and Rue's.
"Hell," he grumbled, "even the prissy Eastern lieuten-
ants and captains I knew in the army didn't boss a man
around the way those old biddies do."

Rue stifled a giggle, but said nothing.

Farley came back to the table, set their mugs down
and shook an index finger at her. "Mind you don't take
to carrying on the way they do, because I won't put up
with it."

Rue swallowed, unsure how to react. On the one
hand, it was an affront, Farley's presuming to issue
orders that way. On the other, though she would have
chewed one of Aunt Verity's antique crystal doorknobs
before admitting as much to him, she liked the gentle
forcefulness of his manner. Here, at last, was a person
as strong as she was.

"I don't see where my actions are any concern of
yours," she finally managed to say.

He sighed and shook his head, as though marveling that someone so simpleminded could have reached adulthood without being seriously injured in the process. "After last night," Farley told her, making an insulting effort at clarity as he spoke, "there's nothing we can do but get married."

Rue wouldn't have been more stunned if he'd thrown his food all over her. *"Married?"* she squeaked. In that instant, she realized that it was the dearest, most secret wish of her heart to marry Farley Haynes. At the same time, she knew she'd have to be demented even to entertain the idea.

Okay, so she loved Farley, she thought. He didn't feel the same way toward her; in mentioning marriage, he was probably just following the code of the West, or something like that. And there was still the matter of their coming from two different centuries, two different *worlds*. To love Farley, to stay in this time with him, would be to give up everything she knew and much of what she was.

Rue was a strong woman, and that was both her blessing and her curse. Not even for Farley and a lifetime of the tempestuous dances he'd taught her in the night just past could she give up her own identity. She was of another time; she was a journalist, a person with many more bridges to cross, both professionally and personally.

Of course, if she did marry the marshal, she would have a place to stay until she made contact with her cousin, found the necklace and returned to her own century. Farley would undoubtedly make thorough love to her practically every night, and the mere prospect of that brought all Rue's feminine forces to a state of hypersensitivity.

"I'll send somebody over to the next town for the justice of the peace," Farley said, as if the matter had been settled.

"Now just a minute," Rue protested, thumping the tabletop lightly with one fist. "I haven't said yes to your proposal, if you can call it that. It just so happens that I don't want to get married—I don't even plan to stay around here, once I've seen my cousin."

Farley looked untroubled by this announcement. "What if we made a baby last night?" he asked, figuratively pulling the rug out from under Rue's feet. "I don't think things are any different in Seattle or Boston or wherever it is you really come from. Life is damn near impossible for an unmarried woman with a child."

Rue laid both her hands to her stomach. Nature might very well be knitting a tiny being in the warm safety of her womb. She was filled with wanting and fear. "Oh, my God," she whispered.

Farley stood and carried his plate to the sink. Then he came back to the table, stood beside Rue's chair and bent to simultaneously taste her lips and rub her lower abdomen with one hand. "If there's no baby inside you now," he said huskily, "I'll put one there when I get back."

A hot shiver shook Rue; she was amazed anew at the depths of the passion this man could rouse in her with a few words and caresses. "When will that be?"

He nibbled at her lower lip before answering. "About noon, if nothing goes wrong," he said. Then he walked away to strap on his gun belt, reload his pistol and shrug into his duster. Farley put on his battered hat and reached for his rifle in a smooth, practiced motion. "Try to stay out of trouble until I can get you married," he urged, grinning slightly. Then he opened the door and left.

Rue was restless, and the choices confronting her seemed overwhelming. Go or stay. Love or pretend to be indifferent. Follow her heart or her head. Laugh or cry.

More to keep herself busy than because she was a devotee of neatness, Rue heated water on the cookstove, washed the dishes, wiped off the table and swept the floor. Following that, she made the bed. It was while she was doing that that she found the stash.

Her foot caught on a loose floorboard as she was plumping the pillows, and she crouched to press the plank back into place. The same curiosity that had made her such a good journalist made her a very bad house-guest; Rue couldn't resist peeking underneath.

A cigar box was tucked away in the small, dark place, and Rue lifted the lid to find a respectable collection of five-dollar gold pieces. This money, surely, was meant to be the down payment on Farley's ranch.

Kneeling now, Rue set the box on the side of the bed and studied one of the coins. Where she came from, the small, ornate bit of gold would be worth far more than five dollars, but here it was ordinary money.

Carefully, Rue closed the lid and set the box back in its place. If Farley had been anyone but who he was, she might have taken that money, used it to get to San Francisco, but she couldn't steal his dreams.

The best thing to do was look for the necklace.

The day was chilly, and Rue wished for a shawl as she walked along the sidewalks of Pine River, searching for the lost piece of jewelry that was her only link with the world she knew.

She searched all morning without any luck, and her

shoulders were sagging with discouragement when she started toward Farley's office. Hopefully, since he was willing to give her a baby, he might also offer lunch.

As she was passing Ella Sinclair's boardinghouse, Rue realized there was one place she hadn't looked—the outhouse she'd materialized in. Her heart started to pound. She wasn't sure which one it was, but she knew it was in this neighborhood.

Lifting her skirts, Rue dashed around the house she'd been passing, avoiding manure and mud in the yard as best she could, and hurtled herself into the outhouse she found there, but to no avail—the necklace wasn't there. She began to run through backyards, entering and searching each outhouse she came to. So intent was she on finding the lost necklace that she was barely aware of the rumbles of consternation, shock and amusement around her.

When she spotted her pendant caught between two boards—thank the Lord—she let out a shriek of delighted triumph and snatched it up.

In practically the same instant, a strong arm curved around her from behind, and Rue was yanked backward against an impervious chest. She knew by the quivering in her spirit and the straightforward method of operation that she'd been apprehended by Farley Haynes. Again.

"I was only getting my necklace," she told him, wriggling to get free. "I lost it in the back of this wagon the other day, when I hitched a ride into town."

With his free arm, Farley swept off his hat and wiped his forehead with his sleeve. "That's just fine," he drawled, obviously furious. "Now I suggest you start apologizing to these people you've been disturbing."

Rue wanted to laugh and to cry, she was so relieved

at finding the necklace. She dropped it into her skirt pocket. "Anything you say, Marshal," she responded sweetly. "Are we still getting married?"

The question stirred a buzz in the crowd that had gathered, and Rue was amused. Farley had just assumed she was up to no good, plundering the good citizens' outhouses for heaven only knew what scurrilous purpose, and she wouldn't have put it past him to arrest her. Therefore, in her opinion, a little embarrassment served him right, because after the previous night's activities, he should have trusted her more.

"Yes," he said as grimly as a judge pronouncing a death sentence.

Rue smiled all the while as she offered her apology to the crowd, every once in a while reaching into her pocket to make sure the necklace was there, She could not yet return to her own time because she hadn't found Elisabeth, but the door was no longer closed to her, and that was the important thing.

Chapter 8

Some thoughtful citizen had brought fried chicken, biscuits and gravy for Farley's lunch, and he shared the feast with the solitary prisoner and Rue. The marshal's eyes were narrowed, however, as he regarded her across the surface of his messy desk.

"I thought I told you to stay out of trouble," he said.

Rue's cheeks pulsed a little as she thought of the episode. "I was only looking for my necklace, Farley," she answered reasonably. She took a bite from a crispy fried chicken leg and chewed thoroughly before going on. "If you had any idea how important that pendant really is, you wouldn't make such a big deal about a little disturbance."

Farley's frown deepened. He took another piece of chicken from the lunch basket, which was lined with a blue-and-white cotton napkin. "I know ladies like their trinkets," he allowed. "My mother had a brooch made of marcasite and jet that she wouldn't have parted with to save her own scalp. But I have a feeling this necklace of yours is important for some other reason."

He was remarkably astute, Rue thought, but she wasn't about to explain the necklace's peculiar power—mainly because she didn't begin to understand it herself.

She reached into her pocket and touched the twisted chain, and that was when she felt the strange warning vibration. By instinct, she realized that the pendant was up to its old tricks again; she was about to be sent helter-skelter into some other part of history, and not necessarily the one she belonged in, either.

No, she thought desperately, *not now. Not without saying goodbye....*

The room seemed to waver and shift, like a reflection in old bottle glass. Glimpses of the orchard behind Aunt Verity's house were superimposed over the stove, the bars in the cell door, Farley himself. Rue wrenched her hand from her pocket and the visions faded instantly, along with the sense of an impending spiritual earthquake.

She gripped the edge of Farley's desk with both hands, swaying slightly with mingled sickness and relief.

Farley immediately jumped up to bring her a dipperful of cold well water from the bucket near the stove.

"Are you sick?" he demanded. "Do you want me to go and get the doc?"

Rue smiled thinly and squeezed her eyes shut for a moment, still trying to regain her equilibrium. "Yes. Find Dr. Jonathan Fortner, please," she joked. "And his wife Elisabeth, while you're at it."

Farley crouched beside her chair, looking up into her face with troubled eyes, eyes of such a beautiful Arizona turquoise that it hurt Rue's heart to return their gaze. "What just happened here?" he demanded quietly.

I almost left you, Rue answered in stricken silence.

"Rue," Farley insisted, setting the empty dipper on the desk and holding both her hands in his. "Are you suffering from some sickness of the head? Is that your big secret? Did you run away from one of those mental hospitals?"

Rue laughed, a little hysterically, but with genuine amusement. She could answer only one of his questions with an unequivocal no. The other two he would have to take on trust. She shook her head. "I didn't escape from an asylum, Farley," she said softly.

She could see by his face that he believed her, maybe only because he wanted to, and that was the biggest relief she'd had since finding the necklace in the outhouse.

"I sent for the justice of the peace," he said. "He'll be here in a few hours."

Rue had never, in all her life, had to deal with such a degree of temptation. She wanted so much to marry Farley, to have the right to share his joys and sorrows, his table and his bed, but to vow eternal fidelity when she fully intended to return to her own time as soon as possible would be unthinkable. She would simply disappear, and Farley would be left to wonder, to the end of his days, what had become of her.

"We can't," she said.

"We will," he replied, rising and walking away to hang the dipper on its nail near the bucket.

Nothing was resolved when, fifteen minutes later, Rue left the jailhouse. Since she had nowhere in particular to go, she set out for the house in the country where all this had begun. She meant to find a tree in the orchard, climb up as high as she could and sit there and think, her back to the rough trunk, the way she'd done as a child, in a time far in the future.

She was surprised to find a fancy carriage in the yard next to the farmhouse. There was lots of bustle and activity; a little girl ran full tilt, first in one direction, then another, her small arms outspread in a child's joy at simply existing. A handsome, dark-haired man was taking bags and satchels from the vehicle's boot....

It was only then that the belated realization struck Rue.

Elisabeth was back from San Francisco.

A tearful joy filled her. She struggled with the latch on the front gate, grew impatient and vaulted over the low fence, catching her skirts on the pickets. "Bethie!" she cried in breathless, exultant frustration; even though she had not yet caught sight of her cousin, she knew she was there somewhere.

Sure enough, Elisabeth came bursting through the doorway of one of the outbuildings at the sound of Rue's voice. She heedlessly dropped the crock she was carrying to the ground, and her blond hair tumbled around her shoulders as she ran.

"Rue!" she shrieked, laughing and sobbing the name. "Rue!"

Rue was dimly aware of the man and the little girl looking on in confusion, but she could only think of Elisabeth in those moments. Elisabeth, her best friend, her only real family.

"Bethie," Rue said, and then the two women were

embracing and weeping, as women have always done, and probably will do, when meaningful separations end.

Finally, Bethie gripped Rue's upper arms in hands that had been strengthened by life in simpler but more physically demanding times, her blue-green eyes shimmering with tears, her face bright with joy.

"What are you doing here?" she wanted to know.

Rue laughed even as she wiped her cheek with one palm. "I sort of stumbled onto the place, the way I suspect you did," she confessed. "Once I got here, I was determined to find you, to make sure you were all right."

"I'm more than all right," Elisabeth answered, touching her stomach. "I never thought it was possible to be so happy, Rue. I'm going to have a baby."

The man and the child gravitated toward the two cousins while Rue was absorbing this news. She felt a pang of jealousy, which surprised her, and she even went so far as to hope she was pregnant herself—which was ridiculous, because that could only complicate matters.

"This is my husband Jonathan," Elisabeth said, and her skin took on the lustrous glow of a fine pearl as she introduced him. The child, who was as lovely as her father was handsome, huddled against Bethie's side and smiled shyly up at Rue. "And this is Miss Trista Fortner," Elisabeth added, as proudly as if she'd somehow produced the little girl herself, just that very moment. "Jonathan, Trista, I'd like you to meet my cousin Rue."

Elisabeth's husband was movie-star gorgeous, in a smooth, urbane way. Farley was just as good-looking, but he was the rugged type, exactly the kind of man Rue had always avoided.

"Hello," Jonathan said. He started to offer his right hand, which was scarred, then shrugged, grinned sheepishly and eased his arm back to his side. Rue recalled Farley saying the doctor had been injured.

Bethie smiled and linked elbows with Rue, marching her double-time toward the house. "I want to hear everything," she told her cousin. *"Everything."*

They sat at the kitchen table, and Rue, hardly knowing where to begin, told the story. She explained that the search had begun after she'd read Elisabeth's amazing letters about traveling through time, and admitted she'd first thought her cousin needed professional help. Then she'd found the necklace on the floor of the upstairs hallway, she went on, and made the trip herself.

For some reason she didn't fully understand—under normal circumstances Rue would have told Bethie *anything*—she didn't mention the passion she'd developed for Farley Haynes.

Elisabeth told Rue about her honeymoon, blushing intermittently and looking impossibly happy, and explained how Jonathan had hurt his hand. A fire had broken out and, while Farley had dragged Elisabeth out, Jon and Trista had been trapped upstairs. Jon had had the necklace in his possession and he'd escaped with the little girl over the threshold into 1992. The flow of time did not run parallel on both sides of the threshold, as Rue had already discovered, and when Dr. Fortner and his child finally managed to return, they'd found Elisabeth on trial for their murder.

Jon had made a dramatic entrance, Elisabeth said, eyes glowing with the memory, thus exonerating her of all charges, and they'd been married that day.

With help from Rue and Trista, Elisabeth began preparing dinner. She did it as naturally as if she'd been born in the nineteenth century instead of the twentieth.

By then, the cousins had begun to speculate about the necklace. Although she couldn't explain why, Elisabeth believed the pendant's magic was different, depending on whose hands it fell into. She cautioned Rue to be careful about her choices.

Lanterns were lit as twilight tumbled silently down around the house and rose past the windows, and Jonathan moved, whistling, between the house and the barn.

"You truly do belong here," Rue marveled to her cousin later that night, when Jonathan had gone out to check on his regular patients and Trista was tucked away in one of the upstairs bedrooms.

Elisabeth nodded, lifting a kerosene lamp from the center of the table and leading the way into the parlor. A cozy fire crackled on the hearth and one other light burned on the mantelpiece. "I never knew it was possible for a woman to love a man the way I love Jonathan," she said softly, and there was a dreamy, faraway expression in her eyes as she gazed out the window toward the barn and the orchard and the covered bridge beyond. "It's like I was never whole before I came here. I felt like the odd woman out in some game of musical chairs—there was never a place for me to sit in that other world. The place is like a dream to me now, and I might even have convinced myself I'd imagined it all if it hadn't been for your appearance."

Rue thought of Farley and wondered if he was worried about her or if he'd even noticed she wasn't around. She sighed. "Don't you ever get scared? I mean, if a thing like this can happen, it changes everything. We're like players in some game, and none of us knows the rules."

Elisabeth turned to meet Rue's eyes. "They say that

realizing how little we truly understand is the beginning of wisdom. But I've got a handle on this much—when you love with everything that's inside you, you take a terrible risk. I'm vulnerable in a way I never was before I knew Jonathan and Trista, and, yes, that scares me."

Reaching into her pocket, Rue found the necklace and brought it out, dangling it from her fingers. "Here's your ticket out," she said. "If you don't want to be vulnerable, all you have to do is go back home."

Elisabeth actually recoiled, her blue-green eyes round. "*This* is home," she said. "For heaven's sake, put that thing away before something awful happens."

Rue smiled and hurriedly dropped the pendant back into her pocket. After her experience in the jailhouse at lunchtime, when she'd seen one world taking shape on top of another, she was still a little shy about holding it for too long.

"Then I guess you've decided the risk is worth taking," she said, taking a place on a settee, resting one elbow on the arm and propping her chin in her hand. "Don't you miss it, Bethie? Don't you ever wish you could see a movie or eat frozen yogurt in a mall?"

Elisabeth moved to the fireplace and stood looking down at the fire on the hearth. "I miss hot baths," she said, "and supermarkets and books on tape. I *don't* miss traffic jams, jangling telephones and the probability of one marriage out of two biting the proverbial dust."

"Would you want to go back if it weren't for Jonathan and Trista?"

Bethie thought for a long time before answering, "I'm not sure. Things are difficult here—the old saying about a woman's work never being done certainly holds true—but there's an intensity to life, a *texture,* that I

never found in the twentieth century. I feel as though
I've come home from some long journey of the soul."

Rue sighed. "Well, I guess this completes my mission," she said. "I can go home now."

Elisabeth looked alarmed. "Oh, please say you'll stay
for a few days, at least. After all, once you leave…"
She paused, lowered her head for a moment, then finished bravely, "Once you leave, we may never see each
other again."

"I can't stay," Rue said miserably. She reminded
Elisabeth how the power of the necklace seemed to be
changing, how she no longer needed to step over the
threshold to return to her own century, how she'd seen
images of the orchard in the middle of Farley's office
that day.

In typical Victorian fashion, Elisabeth laid spread fingers to her bosom. "You're right," she said. "You mustn't
take the risk. Do you suppose it's possible for a person
to end up in another time period entirely, or another
place? Say, medieval England, or Boston during Revo-
lutionary days?"

"I'm the wrong person to ask, Bethie," Rue answered. Her heart was aching at the prospect of leaving her cousin and, she could almost admit it to herself,
of leaving Farley. "I don't have any idea what laws gov-
ern this crazy situation, or even if there are any. Maybe
it's covered by Einstein's Theory of Relativity or something."

Elisabeth's beautiful eyes were glazed with tears.
"A day won't go by that I don't think of you," she said.
"Oh, Rue, I want you to be as happy as I am. Will you
try to go back tonight?"

Rue thought of Farley. "Yes, but there's something

I have to do first," she said. She glanced at the clock on the mantel, then at the darkened windows. "Oh, my gosh! I forgot I was supposed to get married!"

"What?"

Rue was hurrying toward the front door. "I wasn't really going to marry Marshal Haynes," she babbled. "He just thought we should because we've slept together and everything." She pulled open the door and would have bolted out into the starry night if Elisabeth hadn't caught her firmly by the arm.

"Now just a minute!" Rue's cousin protested. "You can't just go traipsing off to town through the dark of night! And what's this about your sleeping with Farley?"

Rue sagged against the doorjamb, heedless of the biting chill of the November night, and she began to cry. "I'm in love with him," she whispered brokenly, then sniffled. Her eyes found Elisabeth's worried face in the dim light of the moon and the glow of lanterns from the parlor. "I'm not like you, Elisabeth. I can't stay here—I can't be happy in a place where there's no UPS, no PBS, no CNN!"

Elisabeth laughed and put an arm around Rue's shoulders. "Come in and sit by the fire. I'll brew us a pot of tea and we'll work out this whole problem."

When Jonathan returned an hour later, Elisabeth and Rue were no closer to a solution. However, the doctor had brought a surprise along with him, a coldly angry Farley Haynes.

"The justice of the peace came and went," Farley said when Jonathan had taken Elisabeth's hand and led her out of the room so that Rue and the marshal were alone. He rested his hands on the sides of her chair, effectively pinning her between his arms.

Rue studied Farley's craggy, handsome face fondly, trying to make a memory that would last for all time. "I'm sorry, Farley," she said, touching his beard-stubbled cheek with one hand. "But I'm not the girl for you, and you wouldn't be happy with me."

Farley set his hands on either side of her waist, stepped back and hauled Rue unceremoniously to her feet. The necklace slipped to the floor, with a *chink* that seemed to echo throughout eternity, and she bent to grab for it. The marshal's hand tightened around her upper arm, as though he thought she might try to escape his hold, and then it happened.

There was a wild spinning effect, as if the parlor were a merry-go-round gone berserk. Colors and shapes collided and meshed. Rue, hurled to the floor, wrapped both arms around Farley's right leg and held on with all her strength to keep from being flung into the void.

"Jumpin' Juniper," Farley said when the wild ride subsided.

Rue couldn't let go of his leg, but she did look around, seeing that while they were still in that same parlor, the furniture was different. There was a TV in the corner with a VCR on top.

"What the hell just happened here?" Farley whispered. Rue had to admire his cool. She was trembling as she shinnied up his thigh and finally stood on her own two feet.

She wanted to laugh, hysterically, joyously. She was home, and Farley was with her. On the other hand, she would probably never see Elisabeth again, and that made her want to weep.

"You've just aged almost a hundred years," Rue said, resting her forehead against Farley's shoulder and almost automatically slipping her hands around his waist. "I've got a lot to show you, Marshal Haynes, but first I'd better give you a little time to absorb the shock."

Farley went to the television set and touched one of the buttons. The head and shoulders of a late-night talk-show host appeared on the screen in an instantaneous flash of light and color.

The marshal recoiled, though only slightly, his wonderful, weathered face crumpled into a frown. "Where's the rest of that fellow?" he demanded. Before Rue could reply, he tapped the screen with his knuckles. "I'll be damned. It's a picture."

Rue set the necklace on the mantelpiece. Suddenly, she was filled with pizza lust and the yearning for a long, hot shower. She went to the telephone and punched out a number.

"One large pepperoni with extra cheese, sausage, green peppers and mushrooms," she said. Then she gave the address and hung up.

Farley had left the television to examine the phone. He picked up the receiver and put it to his ear, as Rue had done, then handed it back. "It's a telephone," she said. "A later version of those big wooden boxes with hand cranks and chrome bells." At his look of puzzlement, Rue added, "I'll explain later. Right now, I'm perishing for pizza." She looked down at her Victorian clothes. "I'd better change or the delivery person will spread a vicious rumor that we're having a costume party."

The marshal, who would certainly have carried off the prize for the most authentic getup at such a gathering, went over to one of the chairs and sank into it.

He looked pale beneath his deep tan, and understandably bewildered.

"Where are Mrs. Fortner and the doctor?" he asked. "What happened here?"

"Listen, Farley," Rue said, sitting on the arm of his chair and slipping one arm reassuringly around his shoulders, "it's all pretty complicated, though if you'll remember, I tried to tell you about it before. Anyway, it's going to take a while for you to absorb the fact that this is really happening, let alone process a whole new universe. We just jumped a hundred years, you and I. Technically, Bethie and Jonathan are long dead. On the other hand, they're alive and well on the other side of some kind of cosmic chasm we don't understand."

"Thanks, Rue. That made everything clear as creek water," Farley said wryly. He was clearly still unnerved, as anyone would have been, but that lethal intelligence of his was stirring, too. Rue could see it in his eyes, hungry, wanting to comprehend everything. "Am I losing my mind?"

"No more so than I am, or Elisabeth. You just crossed from one dimension to another, somehow. All I know is that it has to do with my necklace."

"Good God," Farley sighed, rubbing his chin.

"Now you know how I felt," Rue said, polishing his badge with the sleeve of her dress. After that, she stood again. "Since you're company," she teased, "you can have the first shower."

"The first what?"

Rue laughed and took his hand. "Come on. I'll show you." She led the befuddled lawman up the stairs, along the hallway and into the main bathroom, reserving the one off the master bedroom for herself. There, she gave

Farley soap and shampoo and showed him where to find the towels, then adjusted the shower spigots.

Farley's eyes went wide with puzzled amazement, but he was already starting to strip off his clothes when Rue slipped out of the room. She'd gotten only part-way down the hall when a shout of stunned annoyance echoed from behind the door.

Thinking she should have explained that one spigot brought forth hot water and one cold, Rue smiled. She hoped it was ice Farley had just doused himself with, and not fire.

In the master bedroom, where all her things were still in the drawers and the closet, Rue had an urge to kneel and kiss the floor. She didn't, however. She just laid out jeans, underwear, socks and a bulky, white sweater, then took a shower.

The doorbell was ringing when she reached the upper hallway, and she heard voices roll up the front stairs.

"Here's the pizza, sir," said a voice, teenage and masculine. "That'll be fifteen dollars and seventy-five cents."

"For one flat box?" Farley boomed. "You'd better take your wares someplace else, boy."

Grinning, Rue hurried down the stairs. Farley was wrapped in a pink chenille bedspread taken from one of the guest bedrooms, and his freshly washed hair was standing up on top of his head.

"It's okay," Rue said quickly. She paid the young man, took the pizza and closed the door. Then looking up at Farley, she started to laugh. With the bedspread draped around him, toga-style, all he needed was a wreath of laurel leaves on his head to make him a very convincing Roman. "Don't tell me, I know. A funny thing happened to you on the way to the forum."

Farley was clearly not amused. "I'm in no mood for any of your fancy double-talk, woman," he said, glowering.

Rue opened the lid on the pizza box. "Mellow out, Marshal. This will fix you up—prepare to experience one of the best things about modern life." She pried a gooey slice loose and handed it to him. "Go ahead," she urged. "Eat it."

He took a cautious bite, tightened his bedspread toga with a nervous gesture of one hand and took another.

"Good, isn't it?" Rue said, talking with her mouth full.

Farley answered by taking another piece.

Rue had waited too long for this pizza to stand on ceremony. They went into the parlor and sat cross-legged on the floor in front of the empty hearth.

"Bet none of the Pine River ladies ever brought you anything like this for dinner," Rue said smugly.

He lifted a slice to look under it. "Damnedest pancake I've ever seen," he said in all seriousness.

Rue's attention had shifted to the bedspread. "We're going to have to get you some clothes, big fella. I think you're the button-fly-jeans type."

"I've got clothes," Farley protested. Rue hoped he wasn't going to pick now, of all times, to get stubborn.

"Chenille bedspreads have been out of style for a long time," she said. For Farley, the situation was gravely confusing, Rue knew that, but she couldn't help being happy that the two of them hadn't been separated. She would face the lingering pain of saying goodbye to Elisabeth later, and begin learning to live with it. She sighed. "Life is very complicated, Farley."

He glared at her, probably thinking she was a witch or a creature from another planet, that she'd deliberately uprooted him from the world he knew.

"Okay, so maybe that was kind of an obvious statement," Rue conceded. "I can't explain what happened to you, for the simple reason that I don't have the first idea myself. The fact is, you're in the 1990s instead of the 1890s, and you can probably go back if you want to just by holding the necklace in one hand." She started to rise to get the pendant from the mantel, but Farley stopped her by grasping her arm.

"Will you go with me?" he asked hoarsely.

Rue hesitated, then shook her head. "I belong here," she said. If she hadn't realized that before, she reflected, traveling back to 1892 had certainly cleared the matter up for her. She had a suspicion Farley belonged, too, because of his insatiable mind and progressive attitudes, but he would have to discover that for himself. It was not something she could decide for him.

Farley swallowed hard, the last slice of pizza forgotten in his hand, and Rue knew he was making a costly decision.

"I ought to go back where I came from," he finally said. "There are things I left undone and people I need to say goodbye to. But, damn it, scared as I am, I want to see this place." Farley gestured toward the TV set. "I want to see what other machines there are and how they work." He reached out from where he sat and touched the dangling cord of a lamp. "And these lanterns. Does the kerosene come in through this wire?"

Rue kissed his forehead. "You've got quite an adventure ahead of you, cowboy."

Farley finished the pizza, thoughtfully examining Rue's jeans and sweater. "I guess women must dress like that here, then?" he inquired, and it was obvious that he didn't wholly approve of the look.

She nodded. "Chinese women have worn pants for centuries," she said. "Here in the United States, the style didn't really catch on until the Second World War."

"There was a war involving the whole world?" Farley's eyes were wide and haunted with the horrible images of such an event.

"There were two," Rue said. "And all of us are praying like crazy that there'll never be a third."

Awkwardly, Farley got to his feet, still carefully clutching the bedspread that preserved his modesty, and started toward the back of the house. "The privy still in the same place?"

Again, Rue laughed. "The outhouse was filled in sometime in the thirties, Farley." She wriggled her fingers to summon him to the downstairs bathroom, showed him how to flush. "There's another one upstairs. I guess you missed it when you took your shower."

He whistled. "That's one fine invention."

"Wait until you see what we can do with computers," she countered, leaving the room and closing the door. She hung up Farley's sheepskin coat, his badge still gleaming on the lapel, and gingerly set his gun belt on top of the highboy in the smaller parlor. Then she dropped his socks, trousers and shirt into the washer. He'd need something to wear while they shopped for contemporary clothes the next day.

By this time, Farley was standing behind her, wearing just a bath towel around his middle now. Obviously, he was feeling a little more comfortable in the circumstances.

"What is that thing doing?" he asked, frowning at the washer.

Rue explained, and Farley grinned at the wonderment of such a thing, flashing his white teeth. He lifted the washer's lid to look inside. The agitator promptly stopped.

Rue closed the lid again and patted the top of the washer's companion appliance. "This is the drier. I'll put your shirt and pants in here after the washer stops, and they'll be ready to wear in less than half an hour."

Farley looked mesmerized. "Will you teach me how to work these things?" he asked.

"Count on it," Rue agreed. She was a firm believer in training a man right in the first place. That way, maybe he wouldn't be dropping socks and wet towels on the bathroom floor and leaving dirty dishes in the kitchen sink.

Upstairs, she gave him a new toothbrush from the supply in the linen closet, along with a tube of paste. He was standing at the sink in the main bathroom, happily foaming at the mouth when Rue retired to the master bath.

When she came out, Farley was sitting on the edge of the bed, still clad in the towel. Which was almost worse than nothing, because it sent Rue's fertile imagination spinning.

He discovered the switch on the bedside lamp and flipped it on and off three or four times before he was apparently satisfied that the same thing would happen ad infinitum, until either the mechanism wore out or he did.

When Farley turned his eyes to Rue and ran them over her short, cotton nightgown, she knew he'd gone a long way toward adjusting to his situation. He smiled broadly and said, "Hope you don't mind sharing your bed. I'm scared of the dark, and, besides, this was supposed to be our wedding night."

Chapter 9

Rue hesitated in the doorway, fighting a disconcerting urge to fling herself at Farley in unqualified surrender. She'd always found other men highly resistible, no matter how famous or accomplished they might be, but this self-educated nineteenth-century marshal could send her pulse careening out of control with a look, a simple touch or a few audacious words.

"Are you sure it would be wise for us to sleep together?" she finally managed in a thin voice. "After all, we don't exactly know where our relationship is headed."

"Relationship," Farley repeated with a thoughtful frown, stretching out on the bed. At least *he* was comfortable. Rue was a mass of warm aches and quivering contradictions. "That's a peculiar-sounding word. If it means what I think it does, well, I don't believe all of that has to be worked out tonight. Do you?"

Rue ran the tip of her tongue nervously over dry lips. "No, but—"

Farley arched one eyebrow. "But...?" he prompted, not unkindly.

Rue hugged herself and unconsciously took a step closer. "I'm not sure you're going to understand this, being a man, but when we made love, I opened myself up to you in a way that I never had before. There was no place for me to hide, if you know what I mean, and intimacy of that kind—"

He rose, graceful in his bath towel, and came to stand directly in front of her. "Did I hurt you?" he asked.

Rue shook her head. "No," she croaked after a long moment of silence. "It's just that I felt so vulnerable."

Gently, Farley took Rue's hand, raised it to his mouth, brushed the knuckles with his lips. "I'll make you a bargain," he said. "If I'm loving you and you get scared, all you have to do is say stop, and I will. No questions, no arguments."

Gazing into Farley's eyes, Rue knew he was telling the truth. Color pooled in her cheeks. "You know as well as I do," she told him with a rickety smile, "that once you start kissing and touching me, stopping will be the last thing on my mind."

He eased her to the side of the bed, pulled the night-gown off over her head and tossed it aside. Then he feasted on her with his eyes, and that alone made Rue feel desirable and womanly.

Her breasts seemed to swell under Farley's admiring gaze, the nipples protruding, eager. Her thighs felt softer and warmer, as if preparing to cradle his hard weight, and the most secret reaches of her womanhood began a quiet, heated throbbing.

When Farley spread splayed fingers through her freshly combed hair and bent her head back for his kiss, Rue gave an involuntary whimper. She was terrified, and the sensation of his mouth against hers was something like hurtling down the face of Mount Rainier on a runaway toboggan.

Rue felt Farley's towel fall away as he gripped her bottom, raised her slightly and pressed her against him, never slackening the kiss. Most of her wits had already deserted her, but she knew somehow that Farley was afraid, too, as she had been when she'd suddenly found herself in an alien century. He needed her comfort as he might never need it again, and if Rue hadn't already been incredibly turned on, that knowledge alone would have done the trick.

Passion made her bold. Farley broke the kiss with a gasp of surprised pleasure when she closed her hand around his manhood and instinctively began a fiery massage. Finally, Rue knelt and took him into her mouth, and his fingers delved into her hair, frantic, worshiping. A low groan rolled beneath the washboard muscles of his stomach before escaping his throat.

Farley allowed Rue to attend him for a long time— it was amazing, but somehow he was still in charge of their lovemaking, even while she was subjecting him to exquisite rapture. Finally he stopped her, raised her to the bed and gently laid her there.

He said something to her in a low, rumbling voice, and then repaid her thoroughly for the sweet torment she'd given him. He did not bring her to the brink again and again, as Rue had done to him, however. Instead, Farley took her all the way, pursuing her relentlessly, until her heels dug deep into the mattress and her cries of satisfaction echoed off the ceiling.

When at last he took her, Rue didn't expect to have anything left to give. Her own instant, fevered response came as a shock to her, and so did the deep wells of sensation Farley plumbed with every thrust. He was exposing parts of her emotional life, places in her very soul, that had never seen the light.

Afterward, as before, he held Rue close, and her soaring heart returned from the heavens and settled itself inside her like a storm-ruffled bird that has finally found a roosting place. A tear brimmed the lower lashes of Rue's right eye and then zigzagged down her cheek, catching against the callused side of Farley's thumb.

Maybe he knew she didn't need consoling, that she was crying because life was life, because she was so grateful for the steady beat of her heart and the breath in her lungs. In any case, all Farley did was hold her a little tighter.

"It's strange," she said after a very long time, "to think that Elisabeth and Jonathan and Trista are in this house, too, even though we can't see or hear them."

Farley's hand moved idly against her hair, her temple, her cheek. "I'm still trying to figure out that thing you've got downstairs, the box with the pictures inside. There's no point in vexing my poor brain with how many people are traipsing around without us knowing about it."

Rue smiled, spreading her fingers over the coarse patch of hair on Farley's chest. "It's nice, though, to think Bethie and the others are so close by, that they're not actually dead but just in another dimension."

He reached over to cover her lips with an index finger.

"I'm not even going to ask what you mean by 'another dimension,'" he said, "because I'm afraid you'll tell me."

She turned over, resting her leg on top of his and curling her foot partway around his ankle. Then she gave one of his nipples a mischievous lick before smiling into his eyes. "There is so much I want to show you, Farley. Like my ranch, for instance."

"Your what?"

"You remember. I told you I had a ranch in Montana."

He chuckled. "I thought you were just pulling my leg about that. How did you come to have your own land?"

"I inherited it from my grandfather. Let's go there, Farley—tomorrow. As soon as we've bought you some new clothes."

Farley stiffened, and his tone, though as quiet as before, had an edge to it. "The duds I've got will do just fine."

Rue sighed. "This is no time to have a fit of male pride, Marshal. Times have changed, and if you go around in those clothes, people will think you're a refugee from a Wild West show."

"I don't accept what I haven't earned," he replied. He'd clamped his jaw with the last word, and even in the thin moonlight Rue could see that his eyes had gone hard as marbles.

"Good," Rue said. "I need a foreman at Ribbon Creek anyway; my lawyers have been complaining about the one I've got ever since Gramps died."

In the next few seconds, it was as though Farley's masculine pride and desire for a ranch had taken on substance even though they remained invisible. Rue could feel them doing battle right there in the room.

"What are you going to do if you don't work for me, Farley?" she pressed quietly. "You're one of the most intelligent men I've ever known, but believe me, you don't have the kind of job skills you'd need to make a decent living in this day and age."

He was quiet for such a long time that Rue feared he'd drifted off to sleep. Finally, however, Farley replied, "Let's go and have a look at this ranch of yours, then."

Rue laid her cheek against his chest, smiled and closed her eyes.

When she awakened in the morning, Farley was sitting in a chair next to the bed, wearing his regular clothes. Although there were pulled threads shriveling the fabric in places, and the pants looked an inch or two shorter, he was still handsome enough to make Rue's heart do a happy little spin.

"I was beginning to think you meant to lay there till the Resurrection," Farley grumbled, and Rue ascertained in that moment that, despite the fact that he'd gotten up comparatively early, the marshal was not a morning person.

"Low blood sugar," Rue diagnosed, tossing back the covers and sitting up. She'd put her nightgown back on during the night, so she didn't feel as self-conscious as she might have otherwise. "Don't let it bother you. I have the exact same problem. If I don't eat regularly—and junk food is worse than nothing—I get crabby, too."

Farley was already at the door. "I don't know what the hell you're talking about, but if you're saying I'm hungry, you're right. I was planning to make breakfast, and I took some wood from the basket by the parlor fireplace, but I'll be damned if I could figure out where to kindle the fire in that kitchen stove of yours."

Rue grinned and preceded him out of the bedroom and down the stairs. "It's not the kind of stove you're used to, Marshal. Remember the cords on the lamp? Most everything in the kitchen works the same way, by electricity." She'd explained the mysteries of that science as best she could the night before, but in a way it was like trying to illustrate their trip through time. Rue couldn't very well clarify things she barely understood herself. "Never fear," she finished. "There's a set of books at the ranch that covers that type of thing—Gramps had a penchant for knowing how things worked."

She crossed the kitchen and opened the refrigerator, knowing ahead of time what she'd find. Nothing edible, except for three green olives floating in a jar. The other stuff had been there when she arrived at the house days—weeks?—before.

Rue opened the freezer and took out a box of toaster waffles. "I'm afraid this will have to hold us until we can get to Steak Heaven out on Highway 18."

Farley watched in consternation as Rue opened the carton, pulled apart the inner wrapper and popped two waffles into the toaster. While they were warming, she scouted out syrup and put two cups of water into the microwave for instant coffee.

"How does this contraption work?" Farley asked, turning to the stove that had so confounded him earlier.

Rue checked the oven on a hunch and found kindling sticks neatly stacked on the middle rack. She struggled not to laugh as she removed them, thanking heaven all the while that Farley had not gone so far as to light a blaze.

"These knobs on the top control everything," she said when she could trust herself to speak. With one arm, she held the applewood while pointing out the dials with her free hand.

Farley listened earnestly to her explanation, then nodded with a grin. It was plain that he was a quick study; no doubt he would take in information as fast as it could be presented.

They breakfasted on the waffles and coffee, and then Rue hurriedly showered and dressed. She wasn't afraid of her Aunt Verity's house, even after all that had happened to her and to Elisabeth here; she could never have feared that benevolent place. Still, Rue felt an urgency to be gone, a particular fear she didn't like facing.

Perhaps away from here, the necklace would have no power. If it did, however, Farley could disappear at any moment.

Getting the marshal to leave his gun belt behind required some of the fastest talking Rue had ever done, but in the end, she succeeded by promising him access to the big collection of firearms that had belonged to her grandfather.

It was almost noon when she and Farley locked the house and set out. Rue had brought her laptop computer, clothes and personal things, but she'd deliberately left the necklace behind; in its own way, the thing was as dangerous as the marshal's Colt .45.

Farley was fascinated by the Land Rover. He walked around it three or four times before getting in.

Thinking her guest might be interested in seeing how Pine River had developed over the decades since he'd been its marshal, Rue drove him down Main Street, showed him the movie house and the library and the local police station. She avoided the churchyard without looking too closely at her reasons.

Farley was, of course, amazed by the changes, and would have insisted on getting out and exploring, Rue was sure, if he hadn't been so fascinated by their mode of transportation.

He spent the entire ride to Steak Heaven opening and closing the glove compartment, turning the dials on the radio, switching on the heat, then the air-conditioning, then the heat again.

"Soon as we get to Ribbon Creek," Rue promised from her position behind the wheel, "I'll teach you to drive."

Farley beamed at the prospect.

When they reached the restaurant, Farley turned his attention from the dashboard and stared in amazement at the crowded parking lot. "Jumpin' Juniper," he said. "Does everybody in this place have one of these new-fangled buggies?"

Rue smiled. "Almost," she answered, "but they come in all shapes, sizes and colors, as you can see."

Farley paused to inspect a pricey red sports car as they passed, giving a low whistle of appreciation. It only went to prove, Rue thought in amusement, that some things transcend time. Maybe men had always been fascinated by methods of transportation.

The noise and bustle of the inside of the restaurant made Farley visibly nervous. His face took on a grim expression, and Rue saw him touch his outer thigh once or twice while they waited to be seated. Probably he was unconsciously seeking reassurance that wasn't there—his gun.

"Smoking or nonsmoking?" a waitress asked pleasantly.

Farley's turquoise eyes widened as he took in the

girl's short skirt, and Rue realized he'd never seen a female show so much leg in public.

"Non," Rue answered, linking her arm with Farley's and propelling him between the crowded tables as the girl led the way.

"Tarnation," Farley muttered, looking around and seeing that not only other waitresses but customers were dressed in the same way. "If the Presbyterians saw this, they'd be spitting railroad spikes."

Rue chuckled. "Some of these people probably *are* Presbyterians, Farley. This is an accepted way for women to dress."

They reached their booth, and Farley slid into the seat across from Rue, still looking overwhelmed. His eyes narrowed. "It's bad enough to see a woman in pants," he whispered pointedly. "I hope you don't plan on parading around in one of these getups you call a dress, with your knees sticking out. I'm the only one who should see you like that."

Rue rested her plastic-coated menu against her forehead for a moment, hiding her face while she battled amusement and her natural tendency to protest his arbitrary words. Finally, she met his gaze over the steaming cups of coffee between them, and said, "Even if we were married, which we're not, I wouldn't let you tell me what to wear, Farley. That would be like allowing you to tell me how to vote."

He stared at her. "You can vote?"

She sighed and rolled her eyes heavenward. "I can see this is going to be quite a project, acclimatizing you to the twentieth century."

The waitress returned, and Rue ordered a club sandwich and a diet cola, since it was lunchtime. Farley, having read his own menu, asked for sausage and eggs. Plainly, the toaster waffles hadn't seemed like breakfast to him.

When the food came, he loaded it down with pepper, except for the toast, and consumed every bite, leaving nothing on his plate but a few streaks of egg yoke.

Rue paid the check with a credit card, and when the cashier handed it back, Farley intercepted and studied the card intently.

"This is money?" he asked, handing the card to Rue as they crossed the parking lot a few minutes later.

"The plastic variety," Rue affirmed with a nod. She stopped and looked up into Farley's wonderful eyes, feeling so much love for him that it was painful. "I know everything seems pretty bewildering," she said gently, "but you're a very intelligent man and you'll figure things out."

He looked the Land Rover over speculatively as they approached. "I'd like to drive now," he announced.

"No way," Rue answered, pulling her keys from the pocket of her jeans. "Cars move a whole lot faster than horses, Farley, and when they collide, people get killed."

Although the marshal looked disappointed, he didn't argue.

Where before his attention had been taken up by the gizmos on the dashboard, now Farley was intent on the other cars, the buildings, the power lines alongside the highway. As they drove toward Seattle, he asked a million questions about the pavement, the road signs, the cars and trucks in the other lanes.

When Seattle itself came into view, with its busy harbor and the picturesque Space Needle, Farley was apparently struck dumb by the sight. He stared intently, as though his eyes couldn't take in enough to suit him, and he kept turning in different directions.

Rue drove through the city, knowing Farley couldn't have absorbed explanations just then, and kept going until they reached a large mall.

She parked and they entered the concourse. Rue still didn't speak because Farley was so busy absorbing the sights and sounds that he probably wouldn't have heard her anyway.

He studied a colorful display in front of a bookstore with an attitude that seemed like reverence to Rue. She was touched by the depth of his wonder, knowing it must be something like what she felt when he made love to her.

Suddenly she wanted to give him the world, show him everything there was to see.

"I remember that you like reading," she said, her voice a little shaky. She proceeded into the store, located the instructional section and found a comprehensive volume on how things work. Then from another shelf, she took a novel set in the twenty-fifth century. It was the only way she could think of to prepare Farley for the fact that human beings could fly now, that a few brave souls had even visited the moon.

Farley watched as she paid. "You can buy books with plastic money?" he asked as they left.

"You can buy almost anything with plastic money," Rue replied, handing him the bag.

They went on to the men's department of one of the big chain stores, and Farley was soon outfitted with jeans, shirts, underwear and socks. He refused to part with his boots, and Rue didn't press the issue.

Soon they were on the freeway again, headed east.

Farley alternated between staring out the window and thumbing through the books Rue had bought for him. When he opened one and started to read, she protested.

"You shouldn't read in a moving car, Farley," she said, amazed at how silly she sounded even as she was saying the words. "It'll make you sick."

Farley wet the tip of an index finger, turned a page and read on. "If you can go around with your knees showing in one of those short skirts," he said without even glancing in her direction, "I can read whenever I want to. And I want to."

"Fine," Rue replied, because there was nothing else she could say. She was glad, in a way, that Farley hadn't given in, because his stubborn strength was one of the qualities she loved most. Without looking away from the road, she took a cassette tape from the box between the seats and shoved it into the slot below the radio.

Farley jumped and then lowered the book when Carly Simon's voice filled the Land Rover.

"I think the closest thing you had to this in 1892 was the music box," Rue said without smugness. She knew Farley's curiosity had to be almost overwhelming. "Or maybe a hand organ."

"I'm getting a powerful headache," Farley confessed, rubbing his eyes. "How could so much have happened in a hundred years?"

She didn't tell him about automatic-teller machines and laser surgery, out of simple courtesy. "There were many factors involved," she said gently. "A lot of historians think the nation turned a corner during the Civil War. There were other conflicts later. As wretched and horrible as war is, it forced science to advance, in both good ways and bad, because of the awesome needs it creates."

Farley sat up rigidly straight—clearly some dire thought had just occurred to him—and rasped, "The Union—it still stands, doesn't it?"

Rue nodded and reached out to pat his arm reassuringly. "Oh, yes," she said. "There are fifty states now, you know."

"Canada is a state?"

She laughed. "Hardly. Canada is still a great nation in her own right. I was talking about Arizona, Utah, New Mexico, Oklahoma, Alaska and Hawaii."

Farley was quiet.

That evening, they pulled in at a truck stop to buy gas and have supper. Rue showed Farley how to work the gas pump, and his pride in the simple task was touching.

In the bright, busy restaurant adjoining the filling station, Farley consumed a cheeseburger deluxe, fries and a chocolate milk shake. "Anything that good has got to be kissing cousin to original sin," he commented cheerfully, after making short work of the food.

Rue shrugged and smiled slightly. "Only too true," she agreed with regret, deciding to save the nutritional lectures for later.

Farley cleared his throat. "I suppose these folks have filled in their outhouse, too," he said seriously.

Rue laughed, pushed away the last of her own chef's salad, and slid out of the booth. "This way, cowboy," she said. She pointed out the men's room, which was at the end of a long hallway, and paid the bill for their supper.

Farley reappeared shortly, his thick hair damp and finger-combed.

They were cruising along the freeway toward Spokane, a star-dappled sky shining above, before he spoke again.

"I keep thinking I must have gotten hold of some locoweed or something," he said in a low, hoarse voice. "How could this be happening to me?"

Rue understood his feelings well, having experienced the same time-travel process, and she was sympathetic. "You're not crazy, Farley," she said, reaching over to touch his arm briefly. "That much I can promise you. There's something really strange going on here, though, and I owe you an apology for dragging you into it the way I did. I'm sorry."

He turned to her in apparent surprise. "It wasn't your fault."

Rue sighed, keeping a close eye on the road. "If I hadn't attached myself to your leg the way I did when the necklace started acting up again and the room was spinning, you probably wouldn't be here now."

Farley chuckled and gave a rueful shake of his head. "I'd be back there wondering just how a lady could be standing in front of me one moment and gone without a trace the next."

"I think the thing that bothers me the most about this whole situation is not knowing, not being able to pick up a thread of reason and follow it back to its spool, so to speak. I don't like mysteries."

Farley was going through Rue's collection of cassettes. "Speaking of mysteries," he marveled, turning a tape over in his hand. "This is the damnedest thing, the way you people can put a voice and a whole bunch of piano players and fiddlers into a little box like this. Back there at that place where we ate, they were selling these things."

"Tapes are available almost everywhere. They don't just have music on them, either—you can listen to books and to all sorts of instructional stuff."

Farley grinned. "I saw one back at the truck stop that interested me," he said. "It was called, *Red-hot Mamas on Wheels.*"

Again, Rue laughed. "I didn't say it was all literature, Farley."

"What exactly is a red-hot mama?"

"I'll tell you when you're older."

"I'm thirty-six!"

"And then some," Rue agreed, and this time it was Farley who laughed.

Several hours later, they reached Spokane, and Rue stopped at a large motel, knowing Farley would be uncomfortable with the formality of a city hotel. As it happened, he was pretty Victorian when it came to the subject of sharing rooms.

"It didn't bother you last night!" Rue whispered impatiently. She'd asked for a double, and Farley had immediately objected, wanting two singles. The clerk waited in silence for a decision to be made, fingers poised over the keyboard of his computer, eyebrows raised.

Farley took Rue's hand and hauled her away from the desk. They were partially hidden behind a gigantic jade tree, which only made matters worse, as far as Rue was concerned.

"We're not married!" he ground out.

"Now there's a flash," Rue said, her hands on her hips. "We weren't married *last* night, either!"

"That was different. This is a public place."

Rue sighed. "Like the beds are in the lobby or something." But then she conceded, "Okay, you win. Explaining this is obviously going to be a monumental task, and I'm too tired to tackle the job. We'll compromise." She went back to the desk, credit card in hand, and asked for adjoining rooms.

Her quarters and Farley's were on the second floor, along an outside balcony.

"Good night," she said tightly, after showing Farley how to unlock his door with the plastic card that served as a key. There was an inner door connecting the two rooms, but Rue had promised herself she wouldn't use it. "Don't eat the peanuts or drink the whiskey in the little refrigerator," she warned. "Everything costs about four times what it would anywhere else."

Farley's tired blue eyes were twinkling with humor. "I'm only looking out for your reputation as a lady," he said, plainly referring to their earlier row over shared accommodation.

"I have a reputation as a reporter," Rue replied, folding her arms. "Nobody ever accused me of being a lady."

Farley put down her suitcase and curled his fingers under the waistband of her jeans, pulling her against him with an unceremonious jerk. "Somebody's accusing you of it right now," he argued throatily, and then he gave Rue a long, thorough, lingering kiss that left her trembling. "You're all woman, fiery as a red-hot branding iron, and the way you fuss when I have you, everybody in this place would know what was happening. I don't want that—those gasps and cries and whimpers you give belong to me and me alone."

Rue's face was crimson by that time. She'd heard much blunter statements—while traveling with other journalists and camera crews, for instance—but this was intimate; it was personal. "Good night," she said again, trying to wrench free of Farley's grasp.

He held on to her waistband, the backs of his fingers teasing the tender flesh of her abdomen, and he kissed her again. When he finally drew back, her knees were so weak, she feared she might have to *crawl* into her room.

"Good night," Farley said. Then he went into his room and closed the door.

Chapter 10

That night, Farley experienced a kind of weariness he'd never had to endure before—not after forced marches in the army or herding cattle across three states or tracking outlaws through the worst kind of terrain. No, it wasn't his body that was worn out—he hadn't done a lick of honest work all day long—it was his mind. His spirit. There was so much to understand, to absorb, and he was bewildered by the onslaught of information that had been coming down on him in a continuous cascade ever since his abrupt arrival in the 1990s.

He moved to toss his hat onto the bed, with its brown striped spread, and stopped himself at the last second. Where he came from, to do that was to invite ill fortune. In this strange place where everything was bigger, brighter and more intense, he hated to think what plain, old, sorry luck might have developed into.

After a little thought, he went to the wardrobe, which was built into the wall, and put his hat on the shelf. The conveniences were right next to that, and he couldn't help marveling at the sleek and shiny bathtub, the sink and commode, the supply of thick, fluffy towels.

Except for Rue, who was just beyond a puny inside door, he was most attracted by the box on the bureau facing the bed. Rue had called the machine a TV, describing it as a shirttail relation to the camera, and Farley found the device wonderfully mystifying.

Facing it, he bent to squint at the buttons arrayed down one side, then touched the one that said Power.

Immediately, a black man with hair as flat as the top of a windswept mesa appeared, smiling in a mighty friendly way. He said something Farley didn't quite catch, and a lot of unseen people laughed.

Farley punched another button and found an imposing-looking fellow standing behind the biggest pulpit he'd ever seen in his life. Beginning to catch on to the system, the marshal pressed still another button.

A lady wearing one of those skimpy dresses appeared, pushing something that might have been a carpet sweeper. There was a block in one side of the window, listing several different figures.

Farley proceeded to the next button, and this time he got a faceful of a bad-natured galoot with a long, red mustache and six-guns as big as he was. He was moving and talking, this noisy little desperado, and yet he wasn't real, like the other TV people had been. He was a *drawing*.

Farley sat down on the end of the mattress, enthralled. Next came a rabbit who walked upright, jabbered like an eager spinster and would do damn near anything for a carrot.

Finally, Farley turned off the machine, removed his boots and stretched out on the bed with a sigh. This century was enough to terrify a body, though he couldn't rightly admit that out loud, being a United States marshal and all.

On the other side of the wall, he heard a deep voice say, "This is CNN," and smiled. A month ago, even a day ago, he'd have torn the place apart, hearing that. He'd have been convinced there was a man in Rue's room, bothering her. Now he knew she was only watching the TV machine.

He imagined her getting ready for bed, brushing her teeth, washing her face, maybe padding around in one of those thin excuses for a nightdress that made his whole body go hard all at once. He could have been in there with her—it was torture knowing that—but he didn't want anybody thinking less of her because she'd shared a room with a man who wasn't her husband. She was too fine for that, too special.

Farley got up after a time, stripped off his clothes and ran himself a bath in the fancy room with the tiles that not only covered the floor but climbed most of the way up the wall. When the tub was full, he tested the steaming water with a toe, yelped in pain, and studied the spigots, belatedly recalling that *H* meant hot and *C* meant cold.

He had scrubbed himself from head to foot and settled into bed with one of the books Rue had bought for him when the ugly contraption on the bedside stand started to make a jangling noise. Farley frowned, staring as though to intimidate it into silence. Then, remembering the brief lecture Rue had given him at her house, he recognized it as a telephone.

He picked up the removable part and heard Rue's voice, tinny and small, saying, "Farley? Farley, are you there?"

He put the device to his ear, decided the cord wasn't supposed to dangle over his eye and cheek, and turned it around. "Rue?"

"Who else would it be?" she teased. "Did I wake you?"

He glowered at the contrivance, part of which still sat on the bedside table. If the TV machine was family to the camera, this thing must be kin to the telegraph. Now that he thought about it, the conclusion seemed obvious. "No," he said. "I wasn't sleeping." Farley liked talking to Rue this way, there was a strange intimacy to it, but he surely would have preferred to have her there in the bed with him. "I was watching that TV box a little while ago."

There was a smile in her voice, though not the kind meant to make a man feel smaller than he should be. "What did you see?"

Farley shook his head, still marveling. "Pictures— drawings—that moved and talked. One was supposed to be a person, but it wasn't."

Rue was quiet for a moment, then she said, again without a trace of condescension in her voice, "That was a cartoon. Artists draw and paint figures, and then they're brought to life by a process called animation. I'll tell you more about it tomorrow."

Farley wasn't sure he was really that interested, not when there were so many other things to puzzle through, but he didn't want to hurt Rue's feelings, so he would listen when the time came. They talked for a few minutes more, then said good-night, and Farley put the talking part of the telephone back where he'd found it.

He'd mastered light switches—to his way of thinking it was diabolical how the damn things were in a different place on every lamp—so he twisted a bit of brass between his fingers and the room became comparatively dark.

He was as exhausted as before, maybe more so, and he yearned, body and soul, for the comfort Rue could give him. He closed his eyes, thinking he surely wouldn't be able to sleep, and he promptly lost consciousness.

He must have rested undisturbed for a few hours, but then the dream was upon him, and it was so real that he felt the texture of the sheets change beneath him, the firmness of the mattress. Indeed, Farley felt the air itself alter, become thinner, harder to breathe.

The traffic sounds from the nearby highway turned to the twangy notes of saloon pianos, the nickering of horses, the squeaks and moans of wagon wheels.

Farley was back in his own lifetime.

Without Rue.

He let out a bellow, a primitive mixture of shock and protest, and sat bolt upright in bed. His skin was drenched with sweat, and he was gasping for breath, as though he'd been under water the length of the dream.

The dream. Farley wanted to weep with relief, but that, too, was something unbefitting a United States marshal. There was an anxious knock at the door separating his room from Rue's, and then, just as Farley switched on the lamp, Rue burst in.

"Good grief, Farley, are you all right? It sounded like you were being scalped!"

He was embarrassed at being caught in the aftermath of a nightmare, and that made him a little angry. "Do you always barge in on people like that?"

Rue was wearing a white cotton nightdress that barely reached the top of her thighs. Her eyes were narrowed, and her hands were resting on her hips. "I seem to recall asking you a similar question," she said, "when I woke up in the master bedroom at Pine River a hundred years ago and found you standing there staring at me." She paused, drew a deep breath and went on, a fetching pink color rising in her cheeks. "Your virtue is in no danger, Farley. I just wanted to make sure you were okay. I mean, you could have slipped in the bathtub or something."

He arched one eyebrow after casting an eye over her nightclothes—there were little bloomers underneath the skimpy gown, with ruffles around the legs—and then her long, slender legs. Lordy, she looked as sweet as a sun-warmed peach.

"Suppose I *had* fallen in the bathtub," he responded huskily, leaning back against the padded headboard and pulling the sheets up to his armpits. One of them had to be modest, and it sure as hell wasn't going to be Rue, not in the getup she had on. "How would you have known?"

She ran impudent eyes over the length of his frame. "The walls are thin here, Marshal. And you would have made quite a crash." She folded her arms, thus raising the nightdress higher. "Stop trying to evade the subject and tell me what made you let out a yell like that."

Farley sighed. Now that he'd stalled long enough

to regain most of his composure, he figured he could talk about what happened without breaking into a cold sweat. "I dreamed I was back in 1892, that's all," he said.

Rue came and sat on the foot of the bed, cross-legged. "Was I there?"

Farley hoped the tremendous vulnerability he was feeling wasn't audible in his voice. "No," he said. "Don't you have a dressing gown you can put on? I can't concentrate with you wearing that skimpy little nightgown."

She gave him a teasing grin. "You'll just have to suffer."

He fussed with his covers for a few moments. He was suffering, all right; it felt like he had a chunk of firewood between his legs. He changed the subject.

"Can one or the other of us be sent back even if that damn necklace is nowhere around?"

Rue's smile faded. She bit her lower lip for a moment. "I don't know, Farley," she said quietly. "When I first found the necklace, I had to be wearing or holding it to travel through time, and I had to pass through a certain doorway in the upstairs hall of my aunt's house. It was the same for Elisabeth. Later, it was as though the two time periods were meshing somehow, and I no longer had to go over the threshold to reach 1892."

"But you always had the necklace?"

She nodded. "Things are obviously changing, though. It seems to me that if people can step backward or forward in time, anything can happen."

Farley had another chill, though this was only a shadow of the one that had gripped him during the nightmare. Maybe he wouldn't be allowed to stay in this crazy, mixed-up century, with this crazy, mixed-up woman. The idea was shattering.

Rue was as vital to him as the blood flowing through his veins, and there was so much he wanted to see, so much he wanted to know.

He moved over and tossed back the covers to make room for her. He hadn't changed his mind about the impropriety of sharing a bed in a public inn, but he needed to sleep with his arms around her.

She switched off the lamp and crawled in beside him, all warm and soft and fragrant. When she snuggled close, Farley let out an involuntary groan.

Rue smoothed the hair on his chest with a palm. "Let's hope we don't do any time traveling while we're making love," she teased. "We could make an embarrassing landing, like in the horse trough in front of the feed and grain, or on one of the pool tables at the Hang-Dog Saloon. I don't mind telling you, Marshal, the Society would be livid!"

Farley laughed, rolled onto his side and gathered her close with one arm. There was no use in trying to resist her; she was too delicious, too funny, too sweet.

"What am I going to do with you?" he asked in mock despair.

Rue started nibbling at his neck, and murmured, "I have a few suggestions."

When Rue awoke the next morning, Farley was already up. He'd showered and dressed in some of his starchy new clothes, and he was sitting at the requisite round table by the windows, reading *USA Today*. "It seems to me that politicians haven't changed much," he commented without lowering the newspaper.

Rue smiled. She was hypersensitive, but in a pleasant way; the feel of Farley's hands and mouth still lingered on her lips, her throat, her breasts and stomach. "Some things stay the same no matter how much time passes," she replied, sitting up and wrapping her arms around her knees.

He peered at her over the colorful masthead. "I agree," he said solemnly, folding the paper and setting it aside. Having done that, Farley shoved one hand through his gleaming brown hair. "It's wrong for us to—to do what we did last night, Rue. That's something that should be confined to marriage."

Rue would have rolled her eyes if she hadn't known Farley was dead serious. She reached for the telephone and punched the button for room service. "Are you trying to tell me that you were married to every woman you ever slept with?" she inquired reasonably.

"No, ma'am," replied the youthful masculine voice at the other end of the line.

Hot color surged into Rue's face, and she would have hung up in mortification if she hadn't wanted coffee so much. "I wasn't talking to you," she told the room-service clerk with as much dignity as she could manage. Farley had clearly figured out what had happened, and he was chuckling.

Rue glared at him, then spoke into the receiver again, giving the room number and asking for a pot of coffee, fresh fruit and toast.

The moment she hung up, Farley gave a chortle of amusement.

"Well?" Rue demanded, not to be deterred. "*Were* you married to everyone you've ever made love with?"

Farley cleared his throat and reddened slightly.

"Of course not. But this is different. A nice woman doesn't—"

Rue interrupted with an imperious upward thrust of one finger and, "Don't you dare say it, Farley Haynes!" She stabbed her own chest with that same digit. "*I* slept with you, and I'm one of the 'nicest women' you'll ever hope to meet!"

"You only did it because I took advantage of you."

"What a crock," Rue muttered, flinging back the covers and standing. "Did I act like I was being taken advantage of?"

"You should have just stayed in your own room," Farley grumbled.

"So now it's my fault?"

The marshal sighed. "I think it would probably be easier to change General Custer's mind about strategy than win an argument with you. Damn it, Rue, what I'm trying to say is, I think we should be married."

Rue sat down on the edge of the bed again. She loved Farley, and she hadn't agreed to marry him in 1892 because she'd known she didn't want to stay in that dark and distant century. This proposal, however, was quite another matter.

"It might be difficult getting a marriage license," she said awkwardly after a long time. "Considering that you have no legal identity."

While Farley was still puzzling that one out, the food arrived. Rue wrapped herself in one of the big shirts they'd bought the day before to let the room-service waiter in and sign the check.

Once they were alone again, she sat at the round table, feet propped on the edge of the chair, and alternately sipped coffee and nibbled at a banana.

"What do you mean, I don't have a legal identity?" Farley wanted to know. He added two packets of sugar to his coffee and stirred it with a clatter of spoon and china. "Is there a gravestone with my name on it somewhere back there in the long ago?"

A chill made Rue shiver and reach to refill her coffee cup. "I can show you where Elisabeth and Jonathan are buried," she said, not looking at him. "But that's different, because they stayed in the past. You came here."

"So if we find my marker, say around Pine River someplace, that'll mean I'm going back. It would have to."

Rue's head was spinning, but she understood Farley's meaning only too well. Elisabeth had a grave in the present because she'd returned to the past and lived out her life. Coming across Farley's burial place would mean he wasn't going to stay with her, in the here and now, that he was destined to return.

"You're right," she blurted, "we should get married."

A slow smile spread across Farley's rugged face. "What are we going to do about my identity?"

Rue bit her lip, thinking. "We'll have to invent one for you. I know a guy who used to work with the Witness Protection Program—those people can come up with an entire history."

After giving the inevitable explanations, Rue finished her breakfast and took a shower. Farley brought her things from the room next door, so she was able to dress and apply light makeup right away.

They were checked out of the motel and on the road to Montana while the morning was still new.

As they passed out of eastern Washington into Idaho and then Montana, the scenery became steadily more majestic. There were snow-capped mountains, their slopes thick with pine and fir trees, and the sheer expanse of the sky was awe inspiring.

"They call Montana the 'Big Sky Country,'" Rue said, touched by Farley's obvious relief to be back in the kind of unspoiled territory he knew and understood. She'd have to tell him about pollution and the greenhouse effect sooner or later, but this wasn't the time for it.

"Are we almost there? At your ranch, I mean?"

Rue shook her head. "Ribbon Creek is still a few hours away."

They stopped for an early lunch at one of those mom-and-pop hamburger places, and Farley said very little during the meal. He was clearly preoccupied.

"We should have stopped at the cemetery in Pine River" was the first thing he said, much later, when they were rolling down the highway again.

Just thinking of standing in some graveyard reading Farley's name on a tombstone made Rue's eyes burn. "I'll call the church office and ask if you're listed in the registry for the cemetery," she said. Even as Rue spoke the words, she knew—she who had never been a procrastinator—that this was a task she would put off as long as possible.

In the late afternoon, when the sun was about to plunge beneath the western horizon in a grand and glorious splash of crimson and gold, Rue's spirits began to lift.

Roughly forty-five minutes later, the Land Rover was speeding down the long, washboard driveway that led to the ranch house.

Farley had opened the door and gotten out almost before the vehicle came to a stop. Rue knew he was tired of being confined, and he was probably yearning for the sight of something familiar, too.

Soldier, a black-and-white sheepdog, met them in the dooryard, yipping delightedly at Rue's heels and giving Farley the occasional suspicious growl. There were lights gleaming in the kitchen of the big but unpretentious house, and Rue had a sweet, familiar sensation of being drawn into an embrace.

The screen door at the side of the house squeaked, and so did the old voice that called, "Who's that?"

"Wilbur, it's me," Rue answered happily, opening the gate and hurrying along the little flagstone walk that wound around to the big screen porch off the kitchen. "Rue."

Wilbur, who had worked for Rue's grandfather ever since both were young men, gave a cackle of delight. Now that he was elderly, he had the honorary title of caretaker, but he wasn't expected to do any real work. "I'll be ding danged," he said, limping Walter Brennan-style along the walk to stand facing Rue in the glow of the porch light. His rheumy blue eyes found Farley and climbed suspiciously to a face hidden by the shadow of the marshal's hat brim.

"Who might this be?" Wilbur wanted to know and, to his credit, he didn't sound in the least bit intimidated by Farley's size or the aura of strength that seemed to radiate from the core of his being.

"Farley Haynes," the marshal answered, taking off the hat respectfully and offering one hand.

Wilbur studied Farley's face for a long moment, then the still-extended hand. Finally, he put his own palm out for a shake. "Since it ain't none of my business," the old man said, "I won't ask who you are or what your errand is. If Miss Rue here says you're welcome at Ribbon Creek, then you are."

"Thank you," Farley said with that old-fashioned note of courtliness Rue found nearly irresistible. Then he turned and went back to the Land Rover for their things, having learned to open and close the tailgate when they left the motel that morning.

"He gonna be foreman now that Steenbock done quit?" Wilbur inquired in a confidential whisper that probably carried clear to the chicken coop.

Rue looked back at Farley, wishing they could have arrived before sunset. When he got a good look at the ranch, the marshal would think he'd been carried off by angels. "Mr. Haynes is going to be my husband," she said with quiet, incredulous joy. "That means he'll be part owner of the place."

The inside of the house smelled stale and musty, but it was still the same beautiful, homey place Rue remembered. On the ground floor were two parlors—they'd been her grandmother's pride—along with a study, a big, formal dining room, two bathrooms and an enormous kitchen boasting both a wood stove and the modern electric one. Upstairs, above the wide curving staircase, there were five bedrooms, one of which was huge, each with its own bath.

"This looks more like a palace than a ranch house," Farley said a little grimly when they'd made the tour and returned to the kitchen.

Rue took two steaks from the freezer in the big utility room and set them in the microwave to thaw. "This is a working ranch, complete with cattle and horses and the whole bit," she said. "Tomorrow, I'll show you what I mean."

Farley shoved a hand through already-rumpled hair. "What about you? What are you going to do way out here?"

"What I do best," Rue said, taking two big potatoes from a bin and carrying them to the sink. "Write for magazines and newspapers. Of course, I'll have to travel sometimes, but you'll be so busy straightening this place out that you won't even notice I'm gone."

When she looked back over one shoulder and saw Farley's face, Rue regretted speaking flippantly. It was plain that the idea of a traveling wife was not sitting well with the marshal.

She busied herself arranging the thick steaks under the broiler. After that, she stabbed the potatoes with a fork so they wouldn't explode and set them in the microwave.

"Farley, you must have already guessed that I have plenty of money," she said reasonably, bringing plates to the table. "I'm not going to be rushing out of here on assignment before the ink's dry on our marriage license. But I have a career, and eventually I'll want to return to it."

Farley pushed back his chair, found the silverware by a lucky guess and put a place setting by each of the plates. He was a Victorian male in the truest sense of the word, but he didn't seem to be above tasks usually regarded as women's work. Rue had high hopes for him.

"Farley?" She stood behind one of her grandmother's pressed-oak chairs, waiting for his response. Quietly demanding it.

His wonderful turquoise eyes linked with hers, looking weary and baffled. "What if we have a baby?" he asked hoarsely. "A little one needs a mother."

Rue smiled because he'd spoken gently and because the picture filled her with such joy. "I quite agree, Mr. Haynes," she said, yearning to throw her arms around Farley's neck and kiss him soundly. "When we have a child, we'll take care of him or her together," she assured him.

She turned the steaks and wrapped the microwaved potatoes in foil. Soon, Rue and Farley were sitting at the table, like any married couple at the end of a long day, sharing a late supper. Farley ate hungrily of the potatoes and steak, but he politely ignored the canned asparagus Rue had heated on the stove. To him, the vegetable probably looked as though it had been boiled to death.

When they'd finished, they cleaned up the kitchen together.

"Sleepy?" she asked.

Farley's wind-weathered cheeks blushed a dull red. He was going to get stubborn about the marriage thing again, she could tell.

"Look," Rue said with a sigh, "you can have your own room until after the wedding. After that, there will be no more of this Victorian-virgin stuff, understand?"

Farley stared at her for a moment, then smiled. "Absolutely," he agreed, his voice throaty and low.

Rue led the way upstairs. On the second floor, she paused in front of an electrical panel and switched off the downstairs lights. "This will be our room eventually," she said, opening the door to the large master suite with its fireplace and marble hot tub, "so you might as well get used to sleeping here. I'll be just down the hall."

Farley's throat worked visibly as he swallowed and

nodded his agreement. Rue wanted him to sleep alone in the big bed, to imagine her sharing that wonderful room with him.

She stood on tiptoe to kiss the cleft in his stubbly chin. "Good night," she said.

"Good night," he replied. The words were rough, grating against each other like rusty hinges.

Rue went down the hall to her own room, whistling softly.

It was comforting to be back where she had sometimes slept as a child. When she was small, she'd spent a lot of time at the ranch, but later, her mother and grandfather had had some sort of falling out. That was why she'd ended up at Aunt Verity's when her parents had finally been divorced.

She unpacked, took a quick bath and climbed into bed. For a long time, Rue lay in the darkness, letting her eyes adjust, remembering. Once, a long time ago, she'd dreamed of living out her whole life on this ranch, marrying, raising her children here. Now it seemed that fantasy was about to come true.

Not that Farley wasn't going to have a hard time adjusting to the idea of having a working wife. He was fiercely proud, and he might never regard the ranch as a true home.

"Stop borrowing trouble," Rue scolded herself in a sleepy whisper. "Farley's always wanted a ranch. You know that."

She tossed restlessly from one side to the other. Then she lay flat on her back and spread her hands over her stomach. *Let there be a baby,* she thought. *Oh, please, let there be a baby.*

Imagining a child with turquoise eyes and unruly

brown hair like Farley's made her smile, but her pleasure faded as she remembered his terrible dream the night before. He'd been flung back to his own time without her.

Rue squeezed her eyes closed, trying to shut out the frightening possibilities that had stalked her into this quiet place. It was hopeless; she knew Farley could disappear at any time, maybe without any help from the necklace. And if that was going to happen, there was a grave somewhere, maybe unmarked, maybe lost, and he would have to lie there eventually, like a vampire hiding from the light.

A tear trickled over Rue's cheekbone to wet the linen pillowcase. Okay, she reasoned, love was a risk. *Life* was a risk, not just for her and Farley, but for everyone. The only thing to do was ante up her heart and play the hand she'd been dealt with as much panache as possible.

Chapter 11

Rue was out of bed with the first crow of Wilbur's pet rooster, but when she reached the kitchen, wearing boots, jeans and a chambray work shirt left behind on her last visit, Farley was already there. He'd built a fire in the wood cookstove and had used Gramps's old enamel pot to brew coffee. He was reading intently from his how-things-work book.

She decided to demonstrate the automatic coffee-maker another time; Farley would have enough to think about, between grasping the ways ranching had changed since the 1890s and dealing with the cowboys. He would not be given their respect and allegiance simply because he was the foreman; he would have to earn them.

Rue kissed the marshal's cleanly shaved cheek and glanced again at the book he was devouring with such serious concentration. He was studying the inner workings of the combustion engine, and she could almost hear his brain cataloging and sorting the new information.

"'Morning," he said without looking up from the diagram that spanned two pages.

Rue got a cup and went to the stove for coffee. The warmth of the wood fire seemed cozier, somehow, than the kind that flowed through the heat vents from the oil furnace. "Good morning, Mr. Ford."

"Mmm-hmm," Farley said.

Rue was gazing out the window over the sink, watching as big, wispy flakes of November snow began to drift down past the yard light from a gray-shrouded sky. Silently, she marveled that she'd stayed away from the land so long, loving it the way she did. She'd let things go where the ranch was concerned, having her accountants go over the books, but never examining them herself, hiring one foreman after another by long-distance telephone without meeting them, sizing them up.

Sorry, Gramps, she said silently.

Wilbur had bacon and eggs in the refrigerator—he had spent the night in the bunkhouse with the other men now that Rue was back—so she made a high-fat, high-cholesterol and totally delicious breakfast. "We'll have to go into town and stock up on groceries," she said, serving the food. "Then I'll introduce you to the men, and you can choose a horse."

By that time, Farley had finished reading about car engine motors, but he looked sort of absentminded, as if he was still digesting facts and sorting ideas. A light went on in his eyes, though. "A horse?" he echoed.

Rue grinned, a slice of crisp bacon in one hand. "Horses are still fundamental to ranching," she said.

"Is this a big spread?"

She told him the acreage, and he whistled in exclamation.

"You raise mostly cattle?"

Rue nodded. "Some horses, too. I'd like to pursue that further, start breeding show stock." She got up and pulled a newspaper clipping she'd spotted earlier from the bulletin board. Wilbur had a habit of saving unusual accounts. "As you can see," she went on, placing the picture of a miniature pony and its trainer next to Farley's plate, "horses come in all shapes and sizes these days."

Farley frowned, studying the photograph. "Tarnation. That little cayoose doesn't even reach the man's belt buckle. Can't be more than two feet high at the withers."

"People breed miniature ponies to show and sell," Rue said, reaching for her coffee. She was prattling, but she didn't care. She enjoyed talking to Farley about anything. "Horses used to be about the size of house cats back in prehistoric times. Did you know that?"

"What good is a two foot horse?" Farley asked practically, letting the history lecture pass without comment. "I don't imagine you could housebreak them like an old lady's pet dog."

Rue laughed. "True enough. And just imagine what it would be like if they jumped up in your lap, the way a cat or a puppy might do." Seeing Farley's consternation, she spoke seriously. "I know in your time every animal had to have a distinct function. Nowadays, people raise all kinds of creatures just because they enjoy it. I know of a woman who raises llamas, for instance, and a man who keeps a little pig as a pet. It even rides in his car."

"You know some strange people," Farley said, and he clearly wasn't kidding.

Rue smiled. "Yes," she agreed. "And the strangest one of all is a United States marshal from 1892."

Farley smiled back, but he was obviously a little tense. He probably felt nervous about meeting the ranch hands; after all, up until then, Rue had been the only twentieth-century person he'd had any real dealings with. Now he would have to integrate himself into a world he'd only begun to understand.

Rue touched his hand. "Everything will be fine," she promised. "Hurry up and finish your breakfast, please. I'll show you the horse barn, and then I want to get the grocery shopping out of the way."

After giving her a humorously ironic look, Farley carried his plate to the sink. "Don't nag me, woman," he teased.

Widening her eyes in feigned innocence, Rue chirped, "Me? Nag? Never!"

With a lift of one eyebrow, Farley put on his hat and the canvas coat he'd been wearing when he and Rue were suddenly hurled into the latter part of the twentieth century. Rue put on a heavy jacket, gloves and a stocking cap, knowing the wind would be ferocious.

The sun had yet to rise, the snow was still coming down, and the cold was keen enough to bite, but Rue's heart brimmed with happiness all the same. Although she hadn't consciously realized the fact before, this ranch was home, and Farley was the man she wanted to share it with.

When they reached the horse barn, the lights were on and one of the hands was helping Wilbur feed and water the valuable geldings and mares. Soldier, the sheepdog, was overseeing the project, and he ran over to bark out a progress report when Rue and Farley appeared.

Farley grinned and affectionately ruffled the animal's ears, one of which was white, the other black. "Good boy," he said.

Rue proceeded along the center of the barn until she came to the stall that held her own mare, Buttermilk. It had been too long since she'd seen the small, yellow horse, and she longed to ride, but there were other things that had to be done first.

She went on to meet Wilbur, who was hobbling toward her.

"Where is that stallion you wrote me about? The one we bought six months ago?"

Wilbur ran his fingers through hair that existed only in his memory. "That would be Lobo. His stall is on the other side of the concrete wall. Had to keep him away from the mares, of course, or he'd tear the place apart."

"Lobo," Rue repeated, well aware of Farley towering behind her. "That's a silly name. You've been watching too many cowboy movies, Wilbur."

The old man winked, not at Rue, but past her right shoulder, at Farley. Obviously Wilbur had pegged the marshal as a kindred soul. "No such thing as too many cowboy movies," he decreed. "Ain't possible. Hell, when the Duke died, those Hollywood folks just stopped making good Westerns altogether."

Rue could feel Farley's questions and his effort to contain them until they were alone again.

"Movies," she said as they rounded the concrete wall Wilbur had mentioned, headed for Lobo's private suite, "are pictures, like on TV, put together to make a story."

"Who's this Duke Wilbur was talking about? I thought we didn't have royalty in America."

Rue grinned, working the heavy latch on the door to

the inner stable. "There was a very popular actor called John Wayne. His nickname was the Duke."

Inside his fancy stall, the stallion kicked up a minor fuss. Rue supposed it was some kind of macho thing, a way of letting everybody know he was king of the stables.

"Easy, Lobo," she said automatically.

Farley let out a long, low whistle of admiration as he looked at the magnificent animal through the heavy metal slats of the stall door. "You broke to ride, fella?" he asked, stepping closer.

Rue had been around horses a lot, but she felt as nervous then as she would have if Farley had stood on the threshold of that mysterious doorway in Aunt Verity's house with the necklace in his hand. Either way, he'd have been tempting fate.

"Sure is," Wilbur replied from behind them, before Rue had a chance to answer.

She looked at the horse and then at Farley. "I don't think—"

"Where can I find a saddle?" Farley broke in. The line of his jaw and the expression in his eyes told Rue he would not be dissuaded from riding the stallion.

Wilbur produced the requested tack, along with a bridle and saddle blanket, and Farley opened the stall door and stepped inside, talking quietly to Lobo. Beyond the windows, the snow continued to tumble through the first gray light of morning.

Rue bit her lip and backed up, knowing Farley would never forgive her if she protested further. He was a grown man, he'd probably ridden horses most of his life, and he didn't need mothering.

Wilbur stood back, too, watching closely as Farley

slipped the bridle over Lobo's gleaming, ebony head, then saddled the horse with an expertise that made a lump of pride gather in Rue's throat. Finally, he led the animal from the stall and through the outer doorway into the paddock.

Lobo was fitful, nickering and tossing his head and prancing to one side.

"You're sure that stallion is broken to ride?" Rue asked Wilbur, watching as Farley planted one booted foot in the stirrup and swung himself into the saddle.

"Pretty much," Wilbur answered laconically.

Lobo gave a shriek of outrage at the feel of a man's weight on his back. He set his hind legs, and his coal black flanks quivered as he prepared to rebel. Several of the ranch hands had gathered along the paddock fence to watch.

"Damn it," Rue ground out, "this isn't funny!" She was about to walk up to Lobo and grab hold of his bridle when Wilbur reached out and caught hold of her arm.

"Let the man show what he's made of," he said, and Rue could have sworn those words came not from the mischievous old man beside her, but from her grandfather.

"That's stupid," Rue protested in a furious whisper, even though she knew Wilbur was absolutely right.

Lobo had finished deliberating. He "came unwrapped," as Rue's grandfather used to say, bucking as if he had a twenty pound tomcat burying its claws in his hide.

Farley looked cool and calm. He even spurred the stallion once or twice, just to let Lobo know who was running the show.

Finally, with a disgruntled nicker, the stallion settled

down, and permitted Farley to ride him around the paddock once at a trot. The watching ranch hands cheered and whistled, and Rue knew Farley had taken the first step toward making a place for himself at Ribbon Creek.

Farley rode over to the fence and spoke to the men who remained there, and soon he was bending from Lobo's back to shake hands.

Rue gave Wilbur a look fit to scorch steel, then crossed the paddock to speak to Farley. She smiled so that no one, least of all the marshal himself, would get the idea she was trying to boss him around.

"I guess we'd better be getting to town if we're going to get our business done," she said.

Farley nodded and rode toward the stables without protest, dismounting to lead Lobo through the doorway.

The cowboys at the fence greeted Rue pleasantly and then went on about their own tasks. When she stepped inside the stable, Farley had already unsaddled Lobo and was praising the horse in a low voice as he curried him.

"That was some fancy riding, Marshal," she said.

Farley didn't look away from the horse. "This is some pretty fancy stallion," he replied.

Rue nodded and wedged her hands into the pockets of her jacket. "The men seem to like you. I guess you know they'll play some pranks and bait you a little, to see if they can get a rise out of you."

"I know about ranch hands, Rue," he said with gentle amusement in his voice. "Don't worry yourself. The boys and I will get on just fine."

Rue sighed. "Maybe I'm like Wilbur," she said. "Maybe I've seen too many Westerns on TV."

He looked back at her over one shoulder, grinned and shook his head.

"In the movies, the new arrival on the ranch always has to prove himself by showing that he's got the hardest fists and the quickest draw," Rue said a little defensively.

Farley ran those saucy eyes of his over her in a searing sweep. "I haven't seen anybody around this place I couldn't handle," he said. He gave the horse a last wistful look before joining Rue to walk toward the house.

She put a hand on his arm. "Don't worry, Marshal. You'll be back here and in the saddle before you know it."

Since it was a two-mile stretch to the main highway, Rue let Farley drive on the first leg of the journey to town. He swerved right off the road once, and sent the Land Rover barrelling through the creek that had given the ranch its name, whooping like a Rebel soldier leading a raid.

Rue decided he was better at riding horses.

The drive into town took another half an hour. By the time they arrived, the community's one supermarket was open for business.

Even though he'd been to the mall outside Seattle and had driven across three states with Rue, Farley was still stricken mute with amazement when he walked into the market and saw the wide aisles and the colorful, complicated displays of boxes and cans and bottles. He jumped when the sprayers came on over the produce, and his eyes widened when he saw the pyramids of red apples and plump oranges. In the meat department, he stood watching a mechanized cardboard turkey until Rue finally grabbed his sleeve and pulled him away.

When they finally returned to the parking lot to load

two bulging cartfuls of food into the back of the Land Rover, the marshal was looking a little dazed. All during the ride home, he kept turning around in the passenger seat and plundering products from the bags. He read the boxes and labels letter by letter, it seemed to Rue, frowning in consternation.

"No wonder you women are getting into so much trouble with your short dresses and all," he finally remarked when they were turning off the highway onto the ranch. "Everything can be cooked in five or ten minutes, and you've got all sorts of contraptions besides, like that washing machine. You've got too much free time."

Rue smiled. "I'm going to let you get by with that chauvinistic observation just this once, since for all practical intents and purposes, you're new in town."

"Chauvinistic?" Farley looked puzzled, but certainly not intimidated.

"It's another word for a hardheaded cowboy from 1892," Rue replied. Then she proceeded to explain the finer points of the definition.

Farley sighed when it was over. "I still think you've got too much free time," he said. He was gazing out at the snow-dusted plains of the ranch, and the longing to escape the confines of the Land Rover was clearly visible in his face.

"I guess you'll want to saddle one of the horses and look the place over on your own," Rue observed, pulling to a stop in front of the house.

He grinned with both relief and anticipation, and the moment they'd taken the grocery bags into the house, he headed for the barn.

Knowing Farley needed private time to acclimatize

himself, Rue put away the food, then retired to the study to make some calls. Farley's old-fashioned insistence that they needed to be married had never been far from her mind and, due to her wide travels, she had contacts in virtually every walk of life.

It wasn't long before she'd arranged a legal identity for Farley, complete with a birth certificate, Social Security number, S.A.T. scores and even transcripts from a midwestern college. All the necessary paperwork was on its way by express courier.

Farley hadn't returned by noon, when a new snow began to powder the ground, so Rue made a single serving of vegetable-beef soup and sat by the big, stone fireplace in the parlor, her feet resting on a needlepoint hassock.

Once she was finished eating, Rue immediately became bored. She went to the woodshed and split a pile of pine and fir for the fireplace. She was carrying the first armload into the house when Farley appeared, striding toward her from the direction of the barn.

His smile was as dazzling as sunlight on ice-crusted snow as he wrested the wood from Rue's arms and carefully wiped his feet on the mat outside the back door. Obviously the ride had lifted his spirits and settled some things in his mind, and she found herself envying him the fresh air and freedom.

"At least you haven't come up with a machine to chop wood," he said good-naturedly, carrying his burden through the kitchen after seeing that the box by the cast-iron cookstove was full.

Rue followed, marveling at the intensity of her reactions to his impressive height, the broad strength of his shoulders, the muscular grace of his arms and legs.

"We can get married in a few days," she said, feeling slightly foolish for her eagerness. "The system recognizes you as a real, flesh-and-blood person."

Farley laid the wood on the parlor hearth, pulled aside the screen and squatted to feed the fire. "That sounds like good news," he commented wryly, "though I've got to admit, I can't say I'm entirely sure."

Rue smiled. "Trust me," she said. "The news is good. Are you hungry?"

Farley closed the fireplace screen and stood. "Yes, but I can see to my own stomach, thank you." He went into the kitchen, with Rue right behind him, and took a frozen entrée from the fridge.

Rue watched with amusement as Farley read the instructions, then set the dish inside the microwave and stood staring at the buttons. She showed him how to set the timer and turn on the oven.

He took bread from the old-fashioned metal box on the counter, and his expression was plainly disapproving as he opened the bag and pulled out two slices. "If a man tried to butter *air*, it would hold up better than this stuff," he remarked scornfully, evidently wanting to let Rue know that not everything about the twentieth century was an improvement over the nineteenth. He held up a slice and peered at Rue through a hole next to the crust. "It's amazing you people aren't downright puny, the way you eat."

Rue laughed and startled Farley by jumping up and flinging her arms around his neck. "I never get tired of listening to you talk, lawman," she said, and her voice came out sounding husky. "Tell me you won't ever change, that you're always going to be Farley Haynes, U.S. Marshal."

He set the bread aside and cupped her chin in one hand. "Everybody changes, Rue," he said quietly, but there was a light in his eyes. She knew he was going to kiss her, and the anticipation was so intense that she felt unsteady and interlocked her fingers at his nape to anchor herself.

The bell on the microwave chimed, and hunger prevailed over passion. Farley stepped gracefully out of Rue's embrace and took his food from the oven.

It was a curious thing, being moved emotionally and spiritually by the plain sight of a man eating spaghetti and meatballs from a cardboard plate, but that was exactly what happened to Rue. Every time she thought she'd explored the depths of her love for this man, she tumbled into some deeper chasm not yet charted, and she was amazed to find that the inner universe was just as vast as the outer one.

Shaken, she tossed her hair back over one shoulder and stood with her hands resting on her hips. "I'm really in trouble here, Farley," she said, only half in jest. "It seems I want to cook for you and wash your clothes and have your babies. We're talking rapid retrograde, as far as women's rights are concerned."

Farley smiled and stabbed a meatball with his fork. "I imagine you'll be able to hold your own just fine," he said, and Rue wondered if he knew how damnably appealing he was, if his charm was deliberate.

That afternoon, while Farley was out somewhere with Wilbur and the dog, Rue dusted off her grandmother's old cookbooks and hunted down a recipe for bread. When the marshal returned, the dough was rising in a big crockery bowl, and the air was still clouded with tiny, white particles.

Farley's turquoise eyes danced as he hung up his hat and gunslinger coat. "Somebody dynamite the flour bin?"

Rue was covered in white dust from head to foot, but, by heaven, those Presbyterians back in 1892 Pine River had nothing on her. As soon as the dough had puffed up for the second time, she would set it in the oven to bake, and Farley would have the kind of bread he was used to eating.

Sort of.

She thought of the vast differences between them, and the very real danger that they might be parted by forces they could neither understand nor control. All the rigors of past days caught up with her…all of a sudden, and Rue felt some barrier give way inside her.

She was stricken with what women of Farley's generation would have called "melancholia," she guessed, or maybe she was pregnant. The only thing she was certain of was that for the next little while, she wasn't going to be her usual, strong self.

Rue let out a wail of despair, covered her floury face with her floury hands and sobbed. Out on the utility porch, Soldier whined in unison.

Smelling of soap and clean, country snow, Farley came to her and gently pulled her hands down. His mouth quirked at one corner, and his eyes were still shining with humor.

"Stop that crying," he scolded huskily, wiping a tear from her cheekbone with the side of one thumb. "You're going to paste your eyelids together."

"I don't…even know…why I'm…acting like this!" Rue babbled.

Farley kissed her forehead, no doubt leaving lip

prints. "You've been through a whole lot lately, and you're all tired out," he said. Then he led her into one of the downstairs bathrooms, ran warm water into the sink and tenderly, carefully washed her face.

The experience in no way resembled lovemaking, and yet the effect was just as profound.

After that, Farley carried her into the parlor, laid her on the big leather sofa and covered her with the lovely plaid throw she'd brought home from a trip to Scotland. She lay sniffling while Farley went to build up the fire.

"This is really unlike me," she whimpered.

"I know," he answered, his voice low and laced with humor. "Just close your eyes and rest awhile, Rue. I'll look after you."

Rue was used to taking care of herself, for the most part. Aunt Verity and Elisabeth had coddled her when she came down with a head cold or the flu, but having a man's sympathy was an entirely new experience. The sensation was decadently delicious, but it was frightening, too. She was afraid that if she laid down her sword even for a little while, it would prove too heavy to lift when the time came to fight new battles.

Chapter 12

Rue hadn't suffered through her bread-baking crisis for nothing. After she'd enjoyed the crackling parlor fire and Farley's pampering for half an hour, she returned to the kitchen and tackled the remainder of the job.

While the loaves were baking, filling the room with a very promising fragrance, Rue put game hens on the portable rotisserie, washed some russet potatoes for baking in the microwave and poured a can of cooked carrots into a saucepan to heat.

Farley had gone out to help with the evening chores, and when he returned, Rue had set the kitchen table with her grandmother's favorite china and silver. She'd exchanged her flour-covered clothes for a set of black lounging pajamas with metallic silver stripes, put on a little makeup and swept up her hair.

When the cold Montana wind blew Farley in, he

stood staring at her, at the same time trying unsuccessfully to hang his hat on the peg next to the door. "How soon did you say we'd be getting married?" he asked.

Rue smiled, pleased, and lifted one shoulder. "Three or four days from now, if all goes well." She sighed. "Too bad you're such a prude. Montana nights can get very cold, and it would be nice to have somebody to snuggle with."

Farley was unbuttoning his coat. "Seems to me Montana nights can turn hot even in the middle of a snowstorm," he retorted hoarsely. He walked to the sink, rolling up the sleeves of his shirt as he went, and washed his hands as thoroughly as any surgeon would have done.

Proudly, Rue served the dinner she'd made, and Farley made it obvious that he enjoyed the fare, and even though the bread was a little on the heavy side, he didn't comment.

After eating, they washed and dried the dishes together—Rue never mentioned the shiny, perfectly efficient built-in dishwasher—and they went into the parlor. Rue had hoped for a romantic interlude in front of the fire, but Farley, having apparently absorbed everything in his how-things-work book, had gone to Gramps's bookshelf for another volume. This time, it seemed, he'd decided to investigate the secrets of indoor plumbing.

Resigned, Rue got out her laptop computer, and soon her fingers were flying over the keyboard. It seemed more important than ever to record what had happened to Elisabeth, and to her and Farley because of the strange antique necklace Aunt Verity had left as a legacy.

Rue had written several pages when she realized Farley was watching her. She glanced at him over her shoulder. He was next to her on the couch, holding his place in his book with a thumb. He'd already read nearly half the volume, which was incredible, given the technical nature of the material.

She smiled, reading the questions from his eyes and the furrows in his brow. "This is a computer, Farley. If I were you, I'd make that my next reading project. The modern world runs on these handy little gadgets."

Farley had seen the laptop before, of course, but never while it was running. "Light," he marveled. "You're writing words with *light* instead of ink."

As usual, his wonderment touched Rue deeply. He'd made such a profound difference in her life simply by being who he was, and even though she had been happy and fulfilled before she'd met him, Rue cherished the special texture and substance he gave to her world.

She showed him how to work the keyboard, and she watched with delight as he read from the screen.

All in all, it was a wonderful evening.

In the morning, Farley was up and gone before Rue even opened her eyes. She stumbled in and out of the shower, dressed warmly and went down to the kitchen for coffee. Since Soldier was whimpering on the back porch, she let him in to lie contentedly on the hooked rug in front of the old cookstove.

Farley had left a note on the table, and Rue read it while the water for her instant coffee was heating in the microwave.

Rue,
It might be a long day. The snow is getting deeper, and Wilbur and the others think some of the cattle may be in trouble out on the range. Stay close

to the house; folks have been lost in weather like this. Warm regards,
F.H.

"'Warm regards,'" Rue scoffed, turning to the dog, who lifted a single ear—the black one—in polite inquiry. "I give the man my body, and he signs notes 'warm regards.' And this command to stay in the house! What does he think I am? A child? A greenhorn? Next he'll be tying a rope between the back porch and the chicken coop so I don't get lost in the blizzard when I gather the eggs!"

Soldier whimpered and lowered his muzzle to his outstretched paws, eyeing Rue balefully.

"Oh, you're right," she conceded, though not in a generous way. "I'm being silly. Farley is a man of the 1890s, and it's perfectly natural that he sees things from a very different angle."

She went to the window and felt a vague sense of alarm at the depth of the snow. The drifts reached halfway up the fences and mounded on the sills, and shimmering, pristine flakes were still whirling down from a fitful sky.

Rue drank her coffee, poured herself a bowlful of cereal and began to pace. She was an active person, used to a hectic schedule, and the sense of being trapped in the house made her feel claustrophobic.

She went upstairs and made her bed, and even though she tried to resist, she couldn't. Rue opened the door to the master suite, intending to make Farley's bed, as well, and stopped cold on the threshold.

Farley had already taken care of the task, but that wasn't what troubled Rue so much. A golden chain lay on the bedside table, shimmering in the thin, winter light, and she knew without taking a single step closer it was *the* necklace, the magical, deadly, ticket-through-time necklace she'd purposely left on Aunt Verity's parlor mantel.

Rue sagged against the doorjamb for a moment, one hand cupped over her mouth. The discovery had been as startling as a sudden earthquake, and the implications crashed down on her head with all the weight of timbers shaken loose from their fittings.

Farley knew about the pendant, knew about its power. He could only have brought it along for one reason: he didn't intend to stay in the twentieth century with Rue, despite all his pretty talk about their getting married. This was only a cosmic field trip to him; he planned to return to 1892, to his jailhouse and his horse and women who never wore pants!

She started toward the necklace, possessed by a strange, tender spite, fully intending to carry the thing into the master bathroom and flush it. In the end, though, she retreated into the hallway, afraid to touch the pendant for fear that it might send her spiralling into some other period in time.

The distant toot of a horn distracted her, and she was grateful. She ran down the main staircase, one hand trailing along the banister, and bounded out onto the porch without bothering to put on her coat.

A white van had labored up the road from the highway. The logo of an express-courier company was painted brightly on its side, and the driver came cheerfully through the gate in the picket fence and up the unshoveled walk.

"Rue Claridge?" he inquired.

Rue nodded, hugging herself against the cold, her thoughts still on the necklace.

The courier handed her a package and pointed out a line for her signature. "Sure is a nasty day," he said.

Rue had long ago made a personal pledge to fight inanity wherever she encountered it, but she was too distracted to do battle that day. "Yes," she muttered, scrawling her name. "Thank you."

She fled into the house a moment later and tore open the packet. Inside were the papers her somewhat shady acquaintance had assembled for Farley.

Tears filled her eyes, and her throat thickened. Maybe he didn't intend to marry her at all. Or perhaps he'd planned to go through with the ceremony and then blithely return to 1892, leaving his bride behind to cope as best she could....

Soldier was in the kitchen, and he suddenly started to bark. Grateful for the distraction, Rue headed in that direction, the express packet still in her hand.

Through the window in the back door, she saw Wilbur standing on the porch, smiling at her from beneath the brim of his hat. She was surprised, having gotten the impression from Farley's note that the old man had gone out to help with the cattle.

Rue opened the door. "Hi, Wilbur. Got time for a cup of coffee?"

Her grandfather's old friend looked a little wan. "It isn't often that I turn down the opportunity for a chat with a pretty lady," he said, "but the truth is that I'm under the weather today. I wondered if you could pick up my prescription for me, if you were going to town or anything."

Rue took a closer look at the old man. "You come in

here and sit down this instant," she ordered in a firm but friendly tone. "Of course, I'll get your medicine, but why didn't you have the store deliver it?"

"Costs extry," said Wilbur, hanging up his hat and slowly working the buttons on his ancient coat. He took a chair at the kitchen table and accepted the coffee Rue brought to him with a philosophical sigh.

"For heaven's sake," she scolded good-naturedly, sitting down with her coffee, "you're not poor, Wilbur." She knew that was true; Gramps had provided well for the faithful employee in his will. "Besides, you can't take it with you."

Wilbur smiled, but his hand trembled as he lifted his cup to his mouth. "You young people gotta spend a nickel or it burns a hole in your pocket."

Rue leaned forward, frowning. "What kind of medicine are you taking, anyway?"

"Just some stuff that jump starts the old ticker," he replied with a sort of blithe weariness.

In the next instant, as quickly and unexpectedly as Rue and Farley had been thrust from the nineteenth century into the twentieth, Wilbur's coffee clattered to the table. Brown liquid stained the cloth, and the old man clutched at his chest, a look of helpless bewilderment contorting his face.

"Oh, my God," Rue gasped, jumping up, rushing to him and grabbing his shoulders. "Wilbur, don't you do this to me! Don't you dare have a heart attack in my kitchen!" Even as she spoke the words, she knew how inane they were, but she couldn't help saying them.

He started to fall forward, making a choking sound in his throat. Soldier hovered nearby, whimpering in concern. Rue gently lowered her friend to the floor and loosened the collar of his shirt—a handmade one, Western cut with pearl snaps—that was probably older than she was.

"Hold on," she said urgently. "I'll have some help out here right away. Just hold on!"

She stumbled to the phone on the wall, punched out 911. Wilbur lay moaning on the floor, while Soldier helpfully licked his face.

"This is Rue Claridge out at Ribbon Creek," she told the young man who answered her call. "A man has collapsed, and I think he's having a heart attack."

"Is he conscious? Breathing?"

Rue glanced nervously toward her patient. "Yes. I think he's in extreme pain."

The operator was reassuringly calm. "We're on our way, Miss Claridge, but the roads are bad and the trip is bound to take some time. Are you trained to administer CPR?"

Rue nodded, then realized that was no help and blurted out, "Yes. Tell the paramedics to hurry, will you? We're in the kitchen of the main house."

"Would you like me to stay on the line with you?"

She looked at Wilbur, and her eyes filled with tears at his fragility. "I'd appreciate that—I think I'd better put some blankets over him, though."

"I'll be right here waiting," the dispatcher answered, and the unruffled normalcy of his tone gave Rue a badly needed dose of courage.

She quickly snatched thick woolen blankets from a chest in one of the downstairs bedrooms and rushed back to the kitchen to cover Wilbur, then rushed back to the phone.

"Should I give him water?"

"No" was the brisk and immediate response on the other end of the line. "Can the patient speak?"

Rue rushed back to the old man's side. He was looking up at her with glassy, frightened eyes, and she found herself smoothing his thin hair back from his forehead. "You'll be all right, Wilbur," she said. "Help is on the way. Can you talk?"

He grimaced with effort, but only an incoherent, helpless sound came from his lips. His hands were still pressed, fingers splayed and clutching, against his chest.

Rue spent the next half hour running back and forth between the telephone and the place where Wilbur lay, but it seemed like much longer to her. When she heard a siren in the distance, she felt like sobbing with relief.

"The cavalry's just about to come over the rise," she told Wilbur. "Hold on."

Farley and the others must have heard the siren, too, for the paramedics had just finished loading their charge into the ambulance when the whole yard seemed to be crowded with horses.

"What happened?" Farley asked, reaching Rue's side first. He was gazing speculatively at the vehicle with the spinning red light. "Is this what was making all that racket?"

Rue linked her arm through his and let her head rest against the outside of his shoulder. She hadn't forgotten that he'd brought the necklace to Ribbon Creek, knowing full well what could happen, but she was still in the throes of the current crisis and unable to pursue the point.

Yet.

"Wilbur came by to ask me to pick up his prescription if I went to town," she said. "After a few minutes, he grabbed his chest—" Emotion overcame her, and Farley held her close against his side.

Life was so uncertain, so damn dangerous, she thought. Here today, gone tomorrow. No guarantees. Catch as catch can.

One of the paramedics slammed the rear doors of the ambulance, then the vehicle was reeling away through the ever-worsening weather. The light flung splashes of crimson onto the snow, and the sound of the siren was like big needles being pushed through Rue's eardrums.

With Farley holding her close, Rue's heart was mended, if only briefly, and she could almost believe he hadn't planned to desert and betray her.

She forced herself to look up into his wonderful, rugged, unreadable face. "Are the cattle all right?"

He nodded, this man she loved, this man she'd hoped to spend her life with. "For the moment. Let's get you back in the house before you start sprouting icicles." With that, he ushered her away toward the warmth and light of the kitchen.

And the danger of the necklace.

Perhaps because she was used to crises, Rue quickly regained her composure. There was no point in worrying about Wilbur until she'd heard something from the hospital, and she wasn't sure how to broach the subject of the antique pendant.

"We can get married now," she said with only a slight tremor in her voice, after showing him the paperwork. They were in the parlor, by the fire, sitting on the raised hearth and drinking hot coffee laced with Irish cream. She watched him closely after making the announcement.

"Today? Tomorrow?"

Rue was heartened by his response, but only a little. "I think there's a three-day waiting period and, of course, it would be foolish to try to get into town today."

Farley grinned. "We could make it if we went on horseback."

Rue's heartbeat quickened, but she sternly reminded herself how sneaky men could be. Words were cheap; it was what a person *did* that counted. "Okay, cowboy," she said testily, thrusting out her chin. "You're on."

Farley looked at his feet and the gleaming hardwood floor immediately surrounding them. "On what?"

"I'm accepting your challenge. We're going to put the Land Rover into four-wheel drive and head for town. Just don't blame me if we get stuck and freeze to death!"

The marshal narrowed his eyes, not in hostility, but in confusion. "Wilbur was just saying the other day that women are odd creatures, and he was right. What the devil's gotten into you, Rue?"

"You kept the necklace!" she cried, surprising herself as much as Farley. "How could you do that? How could you pretend that I meant something to you, that you were planning to stay here with me, when all the time you intended to go back!"

Farley gripped her shoulders and lifted her onto her toes. While the gesture was in no way painful, it was certainly intimidating. "I thought you'd forgotten the damn thing," he said, his eyes darkening from turquoise to an intense blue. "I was trying to help."

Rue longed to believe him, and she felt herself wavering. "Sure," she threw out. "That's why you didn't mention it."

He closed his eyes for a moment, jawline clamped down tight, and if he wasn't feeling pure frustration, he was doing a good job of projecting that emotion. "It's not every day a man jumps a hundred years like a square on a checkerboard, Rue. I've been thinking about electricity and gasoline engines and computers and supermarkets and shopping malls—and how much I want to sleep with you again. There just wasn't room in my head for that blasted necklace!"

Rue felt herself sagging, on the inside at least. She wondered, not for the first time, whether this man sapped her strength or nurtured it. She let her forehead rest against his shoulder, and he slipped his arms lightly around her waist and kissed the top of her head.

"Let's hitch up your Land Rover," he said with a smile in his voice. "I think I'd better hurry up and marry you before you decide Wilbur's the man for you."

Rue laughed and cried and finally dried her eyes.

Then she grabbed the false papers proving Farley was a real person, smiling at the irony of that, and the two of them headed for town. The conditions were bad, but the snowplows and gravel trucks were out, and the Land Rover moved easily over the slippery highways.

At the courthouse in Pigeon Ridge, Farley and Rue applied for a marriage license, then went to the town's only restaurant to celebrate. The establishment was called the Roost, to Rue's amusement.

She called the hospital in the next town, while Farley's cheeseburger and her nachos were being made, and asked about Wilbur. He had arrived, the nurse told her, but was still in the emergency room.

Farley was poking the buttons on the fifties-style jukebox at their table, frowning the way he always did when something puzzled him.

Rue smiled, fished a couple of coins out of her wallet and dropped them into the slot. "Push a button," she said.

Farley complied, and a scratchy sound followed, then music. A country-western ballad filled the diner, an old song that would, of course, be totally new to the marshal. He grinned. "Cassette tapes," he said triumphantly.

"Close," Rue replied, fearing the strength of the love she felt for this man, the depth and height and breadth of it. She explained about 45-r.p.m. records and jukeboxes while they ate. After the meal, she called the hospital again.

Farley was having a second cup of coffee when she returned. "How is Wilbur?" he asked.

Rue sighed and slid back into the booth. "He's going to make it, thank God. He definitely had a heart attack, but he could live a long time yet, if he takes care of himself. I mean to see that he does."

"If Wilbur were a younger man, I'd be jealous."

Rue smiled at Farley's teasing, knowing he was trying to help her over a slick place, so to speak. "You should be. A guy like Wilbur can drive a woman mad with passion."

"Can we see him?"

She shook her head. "Not today. He needs to rest."

The trip back to the ranch was even more treacherous than the journey into town. Even with four-wheel drive, the Land Rover fishtailed on the icy highway, and finally Farley braced both hands against the dashboard and let out an involuntary yelp of alarm.

"For heaven's sake, Farley," Rue snapped, managing the steering wheel with a skill her grandfather had taught her, "get a grip!"

He thrust himself backward in the seat and pushed

his hat down over his eyes, and Rue knew for certain that it wasn't because he wanted to sleep.

She spared one hand from the wheel just long enough to thump Farley hard in the shoulder. "I suppose you think you could do better!"

He pushed the hat back and glared at her. "Lady, I *know* I could do better."

"This superior, know-it-all attitude is one of the many things I don't like about men!" Rue yelled. She wasn't sure *why* she was yelling; maybe it was the stress inherent in the day's events, the tension of driving on such dangerous roads or frustration because it would be three days before she and Farley could be married and he had suddenly decided he had to be a virgin groom. Then again, it could have been because she'd thought she'd escaped the power of Aunt Verity's necklace, only to find that it had followed her.

Very carefully, she pulled to the side of the road.

"All right, wise guy," she challenged, "you can drive the rest of the way home. But when we're both in the emergency room, shot full of painkillers and wrapped in surgical tape and looking like a couple of fugitives from the King Tut exhibit, don't say I didn't warn you!"

Farley had already unfastened his seat belt, and he was opening the door before Rue even finished speaking. "I don't have the first idea what you're talking about," he said evenly, "but I know a dare when I hear one and, furthermore, I don't care for your tone of voice."

They traded places, Rue grimly certain they'd end up in the ditch before they'd traveled a mile, Farley quiet and determined. Much to Rue's relief and, though she wouldn't admit it, her disappointment, they reached the ranch without incident, and Soldier met them in the yard.

"There's a blizzard blowing in," Farley announced, looking up at the sky before he wrapped one arm around Rue and shuffled her toward the house. Even though the gesture was protective, there was something arrogant and proprietary about it, too.

Within an hour, the power had gone off. Farley built up the fire in the kitchen stove, and Rue lit a couple of kerosene lamps she'd found on the top shelf of the pantry. While she read the book she'd started earlier, Farley went over the account books for the ranch. He made notes, paused periodically to slip into deep thought, then went back to the study for more reports and files.

If Rue hadn't known better, she'd have sworn he was auditing her income tax return.

"I'm sorry," she said.

"About what?" Farley asked without looking up. He was making notes on a pad of paper, and every once in a while, he stopped to touch the tip of the pencil to his tongue.

"For yelling before. It's just that—well—it's the necklace. It's really bugging me."

That made him lay down the pencil and regard her somberly. "'Bugging' you?"

"Troubling. Irritating. Farley, this is no time for a lesson in twentieth-century vocabulary. I love you, and I'm afraid. That necklace has the power to separate us."

Farley reached across the table and took her hand in his. For a moment, she really thought he was going to say he loved her, too, she believed she saw the words forming in the motion of his vocal cords. In the end, though, he simply replied, "We're going to be married. I don't know how to make my intentions any plainer, Rue."

She traced his large knuckles with the pad of her

thumb. When Farley declared his love, it had to be by his own choice and not because she'd goaded him into it. She suspected, too, that men of his time had an even more difficult time talking about their feelings than the contemporary variety did.

"Okay," she finally responded, "but I'm still scared."

Farley gripped her hand and gently but firmly steered her out of her chair and around the table, then into his lap. "Don't be," he muttered, his lips almost touching hers. "Nothing and no one will hurt you as long as the blood in my veins is still warm."

Rue could certainly vouch for the warmth of the blood in *her* veins. She ached with the need to give pleasure to Farley, and to take it, and when he kissed her, tentatively at first and then with the audacity of a plundering pirate, her whole body caught fire.

"Just tell me," she pleaded breathlessly when Farley finally freed her mouth, "that you won't go back to 1892 without me."

The stillness descended on the room suddenly, with all the slicing, bitter impact of a mountain snowslide. Farley thrust Rue firmly off his lap and onto her feet. "I can't promise that," he said.

Chapter 13

Rue clenched her hands into fists and stood beside the table, staring down into Farley's stubborn, guileless face. "What do you mean, you can't promise you won't go back without me?" The question was a whispery hiss, like the sound of water spilling onto a red-hot griddle.

Farley reached out and pulled her back onto his lap. He splayed his fingers between her shoulder blades, offering slight and awkward comfort. "Rue, I was the marshal of Pine River, and I had responsibilities. People trusted me. One day, I just vanished without a fare-thee-well to anybody. Sooner or later, I have to find a way to let those folks know I'm not lying in some gully with a bullet through my head, that I didn't just ride out one day and desert them. I can't make a new life with you until I've made things right back there."

Rue looked away, but she didn't have the strength

to escape his embrace again. The day had been long and stressful, and she was drained. "So I was right in the first place," she said miserably. It wasn't often that Rue wanted to be wrong, but this time she would have given her overdraft privileges at the bank for it. "You brought the necklace to Ribbon Creek because you knew you were going back, just like I said. When you claimed you thought I'd forgotten it, well, that was just a smoke screen."

Farley paused, obviously stuck on the term "smoke screen," then he met Rue's gaze squarely. "I'm not the kind of man the Presbyterians entirely approve of," he confessed in a grave tone of voice, "but there's one thing I'm definitely not, and that's a liar. And if you'll search your memory, you'll find that I never promised to stay here."

Rue was aghast. "We took out a marriage license today," she whispered. "Didn't that mean anything to you? Was it just something to do?"

He laid his strong hands to either side of her face, forcing her to look at him, making her listen. "There's nothing I want more than to be your husband," he said evenly. "Unless you change your mind and call off the wedding, we *will* be married. We'll fill this big house with children, and I think I can even set aside my pride long enough to accept the fact that my place at Ribbon Creek came to me by marriage instead of honest effort. But the longer I talk, the more certain I get that I can't leave that other life unfinished."

Rue was exasperated, even though she could see the merit in his theory only too well. "What are you going to do, Farley?" she demanded, and something in her tone made Soldier whimper fretfully from his place on the hooked rug by the stove. "Grab the necklace, click your heels together, make a dramatic landing in 1892 and tell everybody you're a time traveler now?"

He shook his head. "I wouldn't talk about what really happened with anybody but Jon Fortner or your cousin Elisabeth." He frowned, his brows knitting. "You don't suppose they're in any sort of trouble over our being gone all of a sudden like that, do you? After all, we were in their parlor when we disappeared."

Rue was ashamed to realize that the possibility had never crossed her mind. "I imagine the townspeople think I spirited you away to some den of never-ending iniquity. Besides, Jon and Bethie had no motive for foul play. Jon is—was—your friend, and everybody knew—knows."

Farley didn't look reassured, and Rue was almost sorry she'd ever confronted him about the necklace. It was plain that if he'd had any intention of using the pendant to escape her and an admittedly hectic modern world, he hadn't been consciously aware of the fact. No, the marshal had only begun to seriously consider returning to 1892 to tie up loose ends *after* Rue had reminded him that such a thing was possible.

She laid her head against his shoulder. "Don't try to send me off to bed alone tonight, Marshal, because I'm not stepping out of reaching distance. If I have to attach myself to you like one sticky spoon behind another, I'll do it. And I don't give a damn about your silly ideas about keeping up appearances, either. Everybody within a fifty-mile radius of this ranch thinks we're making mad, passionate love every chance we get."

Farley kissed her forehead. "We'll be married soon enough," he said.

The house was cooling off rapidly, since the furnace wasn't working, and the kitchen was the only logical place to sleep. Rue took one of the lamps and went in search of sleeping bags, making a point of going nowhere near the necklace. She returned sometime later to find Farley still absorbed in paperwork. He reminded her of Abraham Lincoln, sitting there in the light of a single lantern, reading with such solemn concentration.

She built up the fire in the wood stove and spread the sleeping bags within the warm aura surrounding it. "What are you doing?" she asked, sitting cross-legged on the floor to watch him.

He scribbled something onto a yellow legal pad and then glanced at her distractedly. "Doing? Oh, well, I'm just writing up some changes we could make—in the way the ranch is being run, I mean."

Rue was heartened that he was thinking of the ranch from a long-range perspective, but her fear of being abandoned hadn't abated. Afraid or not, though, she was tired, and after brushing her teeth and washing her face, she stripped to her T-shirt and stretched out on one of the sleeping bags.

The power outage wasn't bothering Farley a bit; lantern light and wood fires were normal to him. Rue wasn't above wishing he were a little spooked by the encroaching darkness and the incessant howl of the wind; she would have liked for him to join her in front of the stove. With his arms around her, she might have been able to pretend there was no danger, just for a little while.

She yawned and closed her eyes. Sleeping on the kitchen floor reminded her of other nights, long ago, when Aunt Verity had sometimes allowed Rue and Elis-

abeth to "camp out" on the rug in front of the parlor fire.
They had turned out all the lights, munched popcorn
and scared each other silly with made-up stories about
ghosts and vampires and rampaging maniacs—never
dreaming that something with equally mysterious pow-
ers, an old-fashioned pendant on a gold chain, lay hidden away among their aunt's belongings.

Waiting.

Farley continued to read and work on the rough outline of his plans for the ranch, but every once in a while,
his gaze strayed to Rue, who lay sleeping in a bedroll
in front of the cookstove. Looking at her tightened his
loins and made barbs catch in the tenderest parts of his
heart, but he wouldn't let himself approach her.

He sighed and took a cold, bitter sip from his mug,
rather than pass Rue to get fresh coffee from the pot on
the stove. If he got too close, he knew he'd end up pulling that peculiar-looking nightdress off over her head
and making love to her until the sun came up.

The lights flared on just as dawn was about to break,
and Farley switched them off so Rue wouldn't be disturbed, then he went upstairs to shower and change
clothes. After last night's storm, there would be plenty
to do.

As he entered the room he would soon be sharing
with Rue, Farley looked at the big, welcoming bed and
wondered if he was losing his mind. Rue was so beautiful, and he wanted her so much. Refusing to sleep with
her now was like putting the lid back on the bin after
the mice had gotten to the potatoes, and he knew she
was right in believing that her reputation was long gone.

Still, he wanted to offer her a tribute of some sort, and honor was all he had.

The necklace glittered on the nightstand, as if to attract his attention, and he reached for it, then drew back his hand. He'd be returning to 1892, all right, but only long enough to put his affairs in order. Then he would come straight back to Rue. He didn't intend to go before he'd married her, at any rate, nor would he leave without saying goodbye.

He made his way into the bathroom, kicked off his boots and peeled away his clothes. By then he'd figured out the plumbing system, thanks to one of the books he'd found in the study, and when there was no hot water, he knew it was going to take a while for the big heater downstairs to return to the proper temperature.

Resigned, Farley went back to the bed, crawled under the covers because he was naked and the room was still frigidly cold, and immediately felt the fool for being afraid of a little geegaw like that necklace. He reached out and closed his hand over it and, in the next instant, the room rocked from side to side. It was as though somebody had grabbed the earth and yanked it out from under the house like a rug.

Farley felt the firm mattress go feathery soft beneath him, and he bolted upright with a shout. "Rue!" He was sweating, and he could feel his heart thundering against his breastbone, as if seeking a way to escape.

He knew immediately that he was in a different room, in a different house. He could make out blue wallpaper, and the bed, an old four-poster with a tattered canopy, faced in another direction. And those things were the least of his problems.

Not only had Farley landed in a strange bed, there

was someone sharing it. At his shout, a plump middle-
aged woman in a nightcap let out a shriek loud enough
to hasten the Resurrection, bounced off the mattress and
snatched up a poker from the nearby hearth.

She continued to scream while Farley frantically
clutched the necklace and willed himself back to the
1990s and Rue. The poker was coming toward his head
when the mattress turned hard again and the wallpaper changed to paneling. He hadn't had more than two
seconds to acclimatize himself when the bedroom door
flew open and Rue burst in. She hurled herself over the
foot of the bed and scrambled the rest of the way to Farley on her knees, throwing her arms around his neck
when she reached him.

"I heard you yell. You saw something, didn't you?
Something happened."

Farley tossed the necklace aside and embraced Rue.
She was real and solid, thank God. "Yes," he finally
rasped when his breathing had slowed to the point
where speech was possible. "Yes."

"What?"

"I don't know. A woman with a poker in her hand—"

Rue drew back, her hands resting on the sides of
his face, her eyes full of questions. "You're sure you
weren't dreaming?"

Farley laughed, though amusement was about the last
thing he felt. "I wasn't dreaming. That woman was as
real as you are, and she wasn't pleased to find a naked
cowboy in her bed, I can tell you that. Another second
and she would have changed the shape of my skull."

Rue turned her head, looking at the necklace lying a
few feet away on the carpet. "Farley, let's throw the pendant away before something terrible—and irrevocable—

happens. Surely the good people of Pine River hired a new marshal, and Jonathan and Elisabeth *must* have found a way to explain your disappearance."

Farley gathered Rue close and held her, taking comfort from the soft, fragrant, womanly substance of her. "We can't do that, Rue," he reasoned after a long time. "There's no way of predicting what the consequences might be. Suppose somebody found it, a child maybe? No, we've got to hide that pendant and make damn sure it stays put."

She buried her face in his chest, that was all, but the surface of Farley's skin quivered in response, and he felt himself come to attention. "I'm scared," she said, her voice muffled by his flesh.

Farley wanted Rue more than ever, having been separated from her by a wall of time, but he was strong and stubborn, and so were his convictions. The next time he made love to Rue, she would bear his name as well as the weight of his body.

Her hand trailed slowly down over his chest and belly, leaving a sparkling trail of stardust in its wake. Then she captured him boldly.

He groaned in glorious despair. "Damn it, Rue, let go."

She did not obey. "You're bigger and stronger," she teased in a whimpery voice. "But I declare, Marshal, I don't see you trying to wrest yourself free of my sinful attentions."

Farley fully intended to pull her fingers away, but his hands went instead to the sides of her head. With a strangled cry, he kissed her, his tongue invading her mouth, plundering. And still she worked him mercilessly with her hand.

He broke away from the kiss, gasping. "Oh, God, *Rue*—"

She teased his navel with the tip of her tongue. "You promised not to make love to me again until we were married," she said, and he trembled in anticipation, knowing what was going to happen. "I, on the other hand, never said anything of the kind."

Farley felt her moving downward and groaned, but he could not make himself stop her. When Rue took him, he gave a raspy cry of relief and surrendered to her.

Later, Farley left the bed, showered and went about the business of running a ranch. Rue took a pair of tweezers from her makeup case, picked up the necklace, which was still lying on the floor where Farley had thrown it after his unscheduled flight into history, and dropped it gingerly into a big envelope.

She held the envelope by a corner, carrying it downstairs and laying it on the desk in the study. She opened the safe hidden behind her grandmother's bad painting of a bowl of grapes, expecting to find it empty since she had long since gone through all her grandfather's papers. To her surprise, however, there was a thin envelope of white vellum inside, and when she pulled it out, a chill went through her.

The handwriting on the front was old and faded and very familiar, and it read, "Miss Rue Claridge, Ribbon Creek, Montana." There was even a zip code, a fact that might have made Rue smile if she hadn't been so shaken. The date on the postmark was 1892.

She let the other envelope, containing the necklace, drop forgotten to the floor and sank into a chair, her heart stuffed into her throat.

Apparently the letter had been delivered to Gramps, and he'd saved it for her, probably never noticing the postmark or the antiquated ink.

Rue drew in a deep breath and sat up very straight. If the letter had been delivered to the ranch, why hadn't she found it before, when she'd settled Gramps's affairs? Come to that, why was any of this happening at all?

The only explanation Rue could think of was that Farley was going back to 1892 in the near future, if he hadn't done so already. And this was the only way he could contact her, by writing a letter that would be misplaced and passed from person to person for a hundred years.

Fingers trembling, Rue opened the envelope and pulled out a single, thin page. Stinging tears came instantly to her eyes. These words had been written a century before by a man she'd brazenly made love to only that morning.

My Dearest Rue,
I'm writing this to say goodbye, even though I know my words will be confusing to you when and if you ever lay eyes on them. Maybe you'll not see this page at all, but I don't mind admitting I take some comfort from the writing of it. I never meant to leave you forever, Rue, especially not on our wedding day; I want you to know that. My love for you is as constant as my breath and my heartbeat, and I will carry that adoration with me into the next world, where the angels will surely envy it.

I have every confidence that if a child is born of our union, you will raise our son or daughter to be strong and full of honor.

I'm staying here at the Pine River house, having been shot last week when there was a robbery at the bank. Oftentimes, I wonder if you're in another room somewhere, just beyond the reach of my eyes and ears.

When last I saw your cousin Lizzie, which was just a little while ago when she came to change my bandages, she was well. She saw that I was writing you and promised to help me think of a way to get the letter to you, and she asked me to give you her deepest regards.

I offer mine as well.

With love forever,

Farley.

Rue folded the letter carefully and tucked it back into the envelope, even though there was a wild fury of panic storming within her. She wanted to scream, to sob, to refuse to accept this fate, but she knew it would be useless.

Farley was going back; the letter was tangible proof of that. And he was dying from the wounds he'd received during the robbery. He hadn't come right out and said that, but she had read the truth between the lines.

She pushed the envelope under the blotter on the desk. She wanted to confront Farley with what she'd discovered, but she couldn't. For one thing, he hadn't done anything wrong; it was his life, and if he wanted to go back to 1892 and throw it away in a gunfight with a pack of outlaws, that was his prerogative. No, Farley wasn't the only one with integrity; Rue had it, too, and in those moments, the quality was her greatest curse.

Rue paced. She could warn him. Maybe if she did

that, he would at least avoid stumbling into that bank at the wrong moment and getting himself killed.

Finally she remembered the registry at the graveyard in Pine River, got the number from information and put a call through. After half an hour and a string of hassles that heightened her frustration to new levels, a clerk in the church office finally unearthed an old record book and found Farley's name in it.

"Yes, he's listed here," the woman said pleasantly. "His grave would be out in the old section, under the oak tree. I hope that helps. It might be hard to find otherwise. Not everyone had a stone, you know, and a wooden marker would be long gone."

Rue squeezed her eyes shut, almost overwhelmed by the images that were filling her mind. "Does the record list a cause of death?" she asked, her voice thin.

"Gunshot wound to the chest," the clerk replied after a pause. "He was attended by Dr. Jonathan Fortner, a man who played quite an important part in the history of Pine River—"

"Thank you," Rue said, unable to bear another word, even though it meant cutting the woman off in the middle of a sentence. Her eyes were awash in tears when she hung up the receiver. Soldier came and leaned against her leg, whining in sympathy.

Rue knew it might be hours until Farley returned, and she couldn't stand to stay in the house, so she went out to the woodshed and split enough firewood to last through a second ice age. When that was done, she started up the Land Rover, Soldier happily occupying the passenger seat, and headed out over roads of glaring ice.

It took an hour to reach the hospital in the next town over from Pigeon Ridge. Leaving the dog in the Land

Rover, Rue went inside and bought a card in the small gift shop, then asked to see Wilbur.

He'd spent the night and most of the day in intensive care, a nurse told her, but she supposed one visit would be all right if Rue kept her stay brief.

She found him in Room 447, and although there were three other beds, they were all empty. Wilbur looked small and forlorn, with tubes running into his nose and the veins of both his wrists.

"Hello, Wilbur." Rue set the card on his nightstand, then bent to kiss his forehead.

He looked surprised at his misfortune, and helpless.

Rue blinked back tears and patted his arm. "That's all right, I know you can't talk right now. I just wanted to stop by and to say hello and tell you not to worry about Soldier. I'm taking good care of him. In fact, he's out in the car right now—it was as close as the nurses would let him get."

Wilbur made a funny noise low in his throat that might have been a chuckle.

"I'd better go," Rue said. "I know you need to rest and, besides, you won't want me hanging around when all your girlfriends come in." She touched his shoulder, then left the room. In a glance backward, she saw him reach awkwardly up to catch hold of the get-well card she'd brought.

For all her activity, Rue had not forgotten Farley's letter for a moment. She circled the thought the way a she wolf might move around a campfire, fascinated but afraid to get too close.

The sun was out when Rue returned to the Land Rover, and the ice seemed to be thawing, but it still took forever to get home, because there were so many accidents along the way. When she and Soldier arrived, Farley and the other men were driving several hundred head of cattle into the big pasture west of the house, where a mountain of hay and troughs of fresh water awaited.

Rue started toward Farley, fully intending to tell him about the letter she'd found in the safe, but the closer she got, the more convinced she became that it would be impossible. She could barely think of being parted from him, let alone talk about it.

She stopped at the fence, listening to the bawling of the cattle, the yelling and swearing of the cowboys, the neighs and nickers of the horses. In those moments as she stood watching Farley work, she realized how simple the solution really was.

All she had to do was destroy the necklace. Once that was done, there would be no way for Farley to return to 1892 and get himself shot.

He rode over to look down at her, his face reddened by the cold and his mustache fringed with snow. His smile practically set her back on her heels.

"Where have you been?" he asked. He didn't sound annoyed, just curious.

"I went in to see Wilbur at the hospital. He's doing all right." The words brought an image of a wounded Farley to mind, a man dying in another time and place, close enough to touch and yet so far away that even science couldn't measure the distance.

Farley shook his head. "You've got no business driving on these roads."

Rue wanted to weep, but she smiled instead. "Are you jealous, Farley?" she teased, stepping close to Lobo and running a finger down the inside of the marshal's thigh. "Think I'm paying Wilbur too much attention?"

Farley shivered, but Rue knew it wasn't from the cold. He'd loved the game they'd played that morning, and her attempt to remind him of it had been successful. He bent down and exclaimed in a low voice, "You little wanton. I ought to haul you off to the woodshed and blister your bustle!"

"Very kinky," she said, her eyes twinkling even as tears burned at their edges. Then, before he could ask for the inevitable definition, she turned and walked toward the house.

That night, the power stayed on and the wind didn't blow. Rue and Farley curled up together on the couch in the big parlor and watched television. At least, Farley watched—Rue alternated between thinking about the necklace and about the letter hidden beneath the desk blotter.

Although they didn't make love, Farley seemed to know Rue would not be separated from him, and they shared the large bed in the master bedroom. He held her and for the time being that was enough.

Contrary to her expectations, she slept, and the next thing she knew, Farley was kissing her awake.

"Get up," he said, his breath scented with toothpaste. "Today is our wedding day."

Some words from the letter he didn't know he'd written echoed in Rue's heart. "I never meant to leave you forever, especially not on our wedding day." Unless she did something and soon, she would become Farley's wife and his widow without turning a single page of the calendar in between.

"I love you," she said, because those were the only safe words.

He kissed her lightly and quoted a mouthwash commercial they'd seen the night before. One thing about television, it had an immediate impact.

Rue got out of bed, passed into the bathroom and brushed her teeth. When she came back, Farley was gone.

Panic seized her. With another man, she would only have thought he'd left the room, or maybe the house. Farley might have left the century.

Dressed in jeans and a warm woolen shirt, she raced into the hallway and down the stairs. "Farley!"

He was in the kitchen, calmly sipping coffee, and he smiled at Rue with his eyes as he took in her furious expression. "A body would almost think you'd been left at the altar, the way you carry on when I get out of sight."

Looking up at him, Rue ached. Why did it all have to be so complicated? Other people had problems, sure, but not the kind that would have made an episode on *Tales from the Crypt.* "Farley, the necklace—"

"I know where it is," he said calmly. "The safe, behind that painting of the fruit."

Rue paled. "But you couldn't have known the combination."

He had noticed her terror by then, and he reached out with his free hand to caress her jaw. "I found it when I went through the ranch records, Rue," he said quietly. "I checked the safe to see if there were any more reports to go over."

Rue closed her eyes, swayed slightly and was steadied by Farley's firm grip. "But the necklace is still there?" she asked evenly, reasonably. "You didn't move it, did you?"

"No," he answered. "But I want your promise that you won't move it again, either. I need to know where it is, Rue. Now, for the moment, all I want you thinking about is becoming my wife." He bent his head, bewitched her with a soft kiss. "I hope you're planning to wear something pretty, though. I draw the line at a bride wearing trousers."

Chapter 14

Rue struggled to maintain her composure; in all her travels as a reporter, she'd never faced a greater challenge than this one. "Farley," she began reasonably, "you've got to listen. If you go back to 1892, you'll die."

He touched her face. "Everybody dies, darlin'," he answered gently. "Considering that I was born in 1856, I've outlived a number of folks already."

She stepped back, raised her fingertips to her temples. It sounded as if Farley knew what was going to happen to him if he went back to 1892 and that he'd resigned himself to that fate. "You found the letter, too."

"By accident," he said. "I spilled a cup of coffee on the desk, and when I moved the blotter, I came across an envelope with my own handwriting on it. I would have put it aside if it hadn't been for that."

Rue sagged into one of the kitchen chairs. "You'd

go back, knowing you were going to be shot by a bank robber and die of the wounds?"

"I have to settle my affairs, Rue. I told you that. And I'm still the marshal of Pine River, as far as I know. God knows, it wasn't a job the town council would be able to foist off on somebody else without a fight. If there's a holdup, I'll have to do whatever I can to intervene. Besides, I've been warned—I'll just be more careful than usual."

Rue felt sick. This was supposed to be one of the happiest days of her life. And she *was* happy, because she wanted the legal and spiritual bond with Farley no matter what lay ahead—or behind—but she was terrified, as well.

Apparently nothing would shake his determination to return to 1892. That left only one avenue open to his distraught bride-to-be.

"I'm going with you, then."

"Rue—"

"I mean, it, Farley," she interrupted, rising so fast that her chair toppled over backward behind her. She didn't pick it up. "I'm not marrying you so we can be apart. We belong together."

He looked at her for a long time, then sighed. "All right," he agreed reluctantly. He kissed her, then left the house without breakfast.

Rue was still inwardly frantic, but fortunately for her, she had things to do. She called the hospital for a progress report on Wilbur, who was doing well, then wired her mother, who had no doubt moved on from the spa to one of several favorite ski resorts.

Giving the credit-card number to pay for the wire

took longer than dictating the telegram itself, a fact that seemed ironic to Rue.

"Mother," it read, "I'm marrying at last, so stop telling your friends I'm an old maid. His name is Farley Haynes, and I adore him. Love, Rue."

The message to Rue's father, who might have been anywhere in the world, but could be counted on to check with his answering service in New York on occasion, was even more succinct. "Dad. By the time you get this, I'll be married. Rue."

With those two tasks out of the way, Rue turned all her concentration to the upcoming wedding. She hadn't brought anything suitable for the ceremony—in fact, she didn't *own* anything suitable. But she remembered the line of trunks in the attic, filled with things from all phases of her grandmother's life. When she was younger, she'd worn those lovely, antique garments to play solitary games of dress-up during long visits.

Naturally, the room at the top of the house was dusty, and the thin winter sunlight barely found its way through the dirty panes of glass in the only window. Rue flipped the light switch and the single bulb dangling in the middle of the ceiling flared to life.

This was a friendly place, though cold and a little musty smelling, and Rue smiled as she entered. If there were ghosts here, they were merry ones come to wish the bride well on her wedding day.

After a few moments of standing still, feeling a reverence for the old times and wondering if her grandmother might not be here after all, young and pretty and just beyond the reach of Rue's senses, she approached the row of trunks.

The sturdy old chests had metal trim, tarnished to

a dead-brass dullness by the passing of time, and the stickers plastered to their sides were peeling and colorless. Still, Rue could make out the names of a few places—Istanbul, Prague, Bora Bora.

She smiled. Grammie had been quite the traveler in her youth. What had it been like for such an adventurous woman to settle on a remote ranch in Montana?

Rue knelt in front of the first trunk and laid her palms on its dusty lid. She didn't remember her grandmother, though Gramps and Rue's own mother had spoken of her in only the most glowing terms.

She lifted the lid and right on top, wrapped tightly in yellowed tissue paper, was a beautiful pink satin dress. Rue took a few minutes to admire it, to hold the gown to her front and speculate as to whether or not it would fit, then carefully rewrapped it and returned it to the chest.

Time blew past like the wind flying low over the prairies, and Rue was barely aware of its passing. Going through the things her grandmother had so carefully packed away, she found a lovely calf-length dress of ecru lace, with a modest but enticing neckline, a pearl choker, pale satin slippers that were only slightly too small and a lovely, sweeping straw picture hat with a wide rose-colored ribbon for a band and a nosegay of pink and blue flowers for decoration.

Because the chests were lined with camphor, the fragile old clothes smelled only faintly musty. Totally charmed, the threat of Aunt Verity's necklace held at bay for just a little while, Rue carried the treasures down from the attic and hung the dress on the screen porch to air.

Upstairs again, she gave herself a facial, washed her hair and then took a long, hot bath. She was back in the kitchen sipping from a cup of noodle soup, a towel wrapped around her head turban-fashion, when Farley came in.

"Are you hungry?" Rue asked, lowering her eyes. She'd said and done outrageous things in this man's arms, and it wasn't as if he hadn't seen her in considerably less than a bathrobe, but suddenly she felt shy.

"Yes," he answered with a smile in his voice. "But I'm still planning to wait until after some preacher has said the words that make it all right."

Rue blushed. "I was talking about food."

"I wasn't," Farley replied. "Are we getting hitched here, or do we have to go into town?"

She felt another stream of color rush into her cheeks, but since the previous flood probably hadn't subsided yet, it wouldn't be so obvious. She hoped.

"I arranged for a justice of the peace to come out. It was the same day we got our license."

"Where was I?" Farley hung up his hat and coat, then crossed to the refrigerator and opened the door. It was an ordinary thing, and yet Rue pressed the image into her mind like a cherished photograph. Just in case.

She smiled. "You were playing with the drinking fountain," she said.

Farley took the milk carton out, opened it and started to raise it to his mouth. He went to the cupboard for a glass when he saw Rue's warning glare. "I don't have a ring," he said worriedly, "or a fancy suit."

"You're still going to be the best-looking groom who ever said 'I do,'" Rue retorted, taking the carton from his hand.

He squeezed her bottom through the thick terry cloth of her robe when she bent over to return the milk to the fridge. "And after I've said 'I do,'" he teased huskily, "you can bet that I will."

The justice of the peace, who ran a little bait shop at Ponderosa Lake in the summertime, arrived an hour later.

By then, Farley had showered and changed into clean clothes, and Rue had put on makeup, arranged her hair in a loose Gibson-girl style and donned the lovely, gauzy lace dress and the pearl choker.

A couple of the ranch hands came in to serve as witnesses, wearing shiny, ill-fitting suits that had probably been in and out of style several times. One of the old-timers, Charlie, brought along his relic of a camera, which had a flash attachment the size of a satellite dish, fully prepared to record the event.

Rue didn't allow herself to think beyond the now; she wanted to cherish every second for its own sake.

Being a civil ceremony, the wedding itself was short. Even though Rue was trying to measure out the moments and make them last, the whole thing didn't take more than five minutes. When Farley kissed her, the hat tumbled off her head and the flash of Charlie's camera glowed red through her closed eyelids.

Rue would have been content to go right on kissing her husband, but, of course, they weren't alone, so that was impossible. Hope overflowed her heart as she looked up into Farley's tender eyes, and in those golden moments, she found it impossible to believe that time or trouble or even death could ever separate them.

The justice of the peace left as soon as he'd been paid, but the ranch hands stayed for refreshments, since festive occasions were such a rare treat. Sara Lee provided the wedding cake, which had to be thawed out in the microwave, and coffee and soda completed the menu.

When Charlie wasn't eating, he was taking pictures.

Finally, however, one of the other hands elbowed him in the ribs, then cleared his throat pointedly and suggested that they get back to the bunkhouse and change into their working duds. Some of the cowboys started to protest, then caught on and pushed back their chairs, beaming.

Time was more precious now than ever, so Rue didn't urge the hands to stay. Despite her insistence that Farley take her with him when he went back to 1892, she hadn't forgotten that his letter said he'd gone alone—on their wedding day. She was glad when she and her new husband were finally by themselves.

She unbuttoned the top two buttons of Farley's shirt. "No more virginal protests, Farley," she said, sliding her hand under the soft chambray to find and caress a taut masculine nipple. "You're my husband now, and I demand my rights as a wife."

He chuckled, but the sound was raw with other emotions besides amusement. No doubt he, too, was wondering how much of their destiny could be changed, if any. He swept Rue up into his arms and mastered her with a thorough kiss, then carried her to the bedroom.

"You look so beautiful in that dress," he said after setting her on her feet at the foot of the massive bed. "I almost hate to take it off you."

For Rue time no longer stretched into the past and the future, forming a tapestry with no beginning and no end. Nothing and no one existed beyond the walls of that room, and their union would be eternal.

She didn't speak, but simply began unfastening the pearl buttons at the front of her gown, her chin at a high, proud angle, her eyes locked with Farley's, challenging him to resist her.

He couldn't; sweet defeat was plain in his face, and the knowledge made her jubilant.

The dress fell over her hips, and Rue hung it over the back of a chair, then kicked off the tight slippers. She kept stripping until all that was left was the wide, pearl choker at her throat.

Farley's throat worked visibly as he swallowed, looking at her as if he'd never seen a naked woman before. When Rue lifted her arms to unclasp the choker, Farley rasped, "No. Leave it," and she obeyed him.

He began taking off his own clothes, starting with his boots, setting them aside with a neatness that made Rue impatient. She watched with brazen desire as he removed his shirt, unfastened his belt, stepped out of his jeans.

Finally, Farley stood before her wearing only his skin, and he was as incorrigibly, magnificently male as a wild stallion.

He held out a hand to Rue. "Come here, Mrs. Haynes," he said.

It wasn't the time to say she meant to hyphenate both surnames into one; in that bedroom, alone with her mate, no title suited her better than Mrs. Haynes. Rue yearned to give herself to Farley totally.

She went to him and he drew her upward into his kiss, a tall shaman working his treacherous magic. Rue trembled as she felt his hand cup her breast, and she moaned into his mouth as his fingers lightly shaped the nipple.

As Rue's body was pleasured, so was her soul. There was a joy in the depths of her being that overruled all her fears and doubts and furies. She was, while Farley loved her, in step with a dancing universe.

He continued to worship her with words and kisses and caresses while she stood with her head back, lost in glorious surrender. When he knelt to pay the most intimate homage, she gave a soft, throaty sob and burrowed her fingers in his thick hair, holding him close, stroking the back of his head.

Their lovemaking was woven of silver linings plucked from dark clouds, golden ribbons of sunset and lengths of braided rainbow, formed at once of eternity itself and the most fleeting of moments. Farley's and Rue's souls became one spirit and did not exist apart from each other, and this joining sanctified their marriage in a way an official's words could never have done.

There was no room in Rue for any emotions other than soaring happiness and the most intense pleasure, not while she and Farley were still celebrating their wedding. Finally, however, she dropped off to sleep, exhausted, perspiration cooling on her warm flesh.

Farley held Rue for a long time. He'd heard other men talk about love, but he'd never imagined it could be the way it was for him with this woman.

He kissed the top of her head, even though he knew she wasn't awake to feel the touch of his lips, and his eyes stung. Returning to 1892 wasn't really his choice, as he'd implied to Rue earlier, but it was his fate—he knew that in his bones. The letter, penned in his own handwriting, was irrefutable proof of that.

Farley grew restless. If he managed to circumvent destiny, somehow, and stay in the twentieth century with Rue, would the letter stop existing? Would his fate, or anyone's, be altered?

The room was filling with gray twilight, and Farley felt a chill. He eased himself apart from Rue and went into the bathroom, where he took a shower. Then he put on the same clothes he'd worn earlier, because he'd been married in them and because they'd borne a vague hint of Rue's scent. He stood beside the bed for a long time, memorizing the shape of her face, the meter of her breathing, knowing his heart was beating in rhythm with hers, even though he could hear neither.

"I love you," he whispered raggedly. He knew he should wake her, since any parting could be a permanent one, but he turned away. If he looked into her eyes, he would see the reflection of his own despair, and the pain would be beyond bearing.

Downstairs, Farley put on his coat, took the necklace from the safe, left the house and strode toward the barn. Most of the men were in the bunkhouse, since the day's work was over, but he found Charlie puttering around in the barn.

Farley touched the brim of his hat as he passed the man, but he didn't trust himself to speak. He needed to ride, cold as it was, and let the fresh air clear his mind. Maybe then he could figure out some way to change things.

He entered the separate part of the barn where Lobo was stabled, led the big stallion out of his stall and saddled him. The animal nickered and tossed his head, as eager for the open spaces as Farley was, and it was then that a profound, almost mystical bond took shape between the man and the horse.

Farley led Lobo outside, under a full but icy moon, and swung up into the saddle.

"Everything all right, boss?" Charlie inquired. He was leaning against the paddock fence, Soldier at his side, both of them lonely for Wilbur.

Farley looked around him at the land, the kind of land that could soak up a man's blood and sweat and still make him happy. In his mind the ranch would always be Rue's, even if he managed to keep himself from getting shot back in 1892 and found his way home to her. One day, though, the land on either side of Ribbon Creek would belong to their child, if he'd been fortunate enough to sire one, and Farley wanted to guard the place and make it grow almost as much as he wanted to stay with Rue.

He looked toward the big house, adjusted his hat and finally answered the ranch hand's question. In a way. "You'll look out for her if something happens to me?"

"Exactly what is it you're expectin' to happen to you, Mr. Haynes?"

Farley lifted a shoulder. "Maybe nothing." He reined an impatient Lobo toward the south, where the moon spread silver over the snow.

He rode until neither he nor the horse could travel any farther, until he wasn't even sure he was still within the borders of the ranch. He pulled off his gloves and reached into his coat pocket for the thin cigars he loved, but instead of the package, he felt a cold, fragile chain between his fingers.

He'd tried to forget he was carrying the necklace.

"Go on," he muttered hoarsely, glad nobody was there to hear him talking to a trinket. "Do your worst and get it over with!"

Farley held the pendant up, watched the moonlight do a twinkling dance along the length of the chain. He considered flinging it aside into the snow, but he knew now that that would do no good. A force he did not begin to understand had brought the necklace into his life, for good or evil, and that force would not be denied. He had to tie up the loose ends of his old life so that he could live the new one to the fullest.

"Rue." Her name was a ragged, broken whisper on his lips. Once again, his vision blurred, and he wasn't sure whether the necklace was working its bitter magic or if he was finally giving way to the grief dammed up inside him.

Five minutes passed, then ten, while the stallion rested and Farley waited.

When the transition occurred just as the sun came up, it was a subtle one. There was a roaring in Farley's ears, and Lobo fretted and sidestepped beneath him. The power lines and the distant gray ribbon of the highway dissolved into nothingness.

Farley knew without consulting a calendar that he and the horse were back in his own century, and it was a long way back to Pine River from the Big Sky Country.

Still, he dropped the necklace into his pocket and rode back to the place where the house should have been, where Rue should have been drinking coffee in a warm kitchen and Soldier should have been barking. There was nothing except for an abandoned cabin and a single grave marked with a wooden cross.

Farley took off his hat for a moment, his throat thick with misery, his heart full of the kind of loneliness that can drive a person to do stupid, reckless things. He lowered his head for a few moments, struggling with his emotions, and then turned Lobo west, toward his destiny.

Rue stirred in her marriage bed, dreaming. She saw Farley riding alone through a winter dawn, his horse's gleaming onyx coat contrasting starkly with the pristine snow. Knowing she could never catch up with her husband, she struggled to awaken instead.

The instant Rue opened her eyes, however, she knew the nightmare was real and she hadn't escaped it. She and Farley had said their vows and consummated them, and now he was gone.

A frantic sob tore itself from her throat and she covered her face with both hands, trying hard to get a grip on her emotions. Farley was probably downstairs, reading one of his how-to books with one eye and watching his favorite TV program with the other.

She jumped out of bed, found her robe, pulled it on and dashed downstairs.

"Farley?"

The parlor fire was out, and the TV screen was blank.

Rue hurried into the study, but she knew before she reached it that Farley wouldn't be there. His presence had a substance, an impact all its own, and she felt nothing except a rising numbness.

"Oh, God," she prayed, unable to go farther, stumbling through the darkening house to the kitchen.

No fire in the cookstove, no coffee brewing, no Farley reading at the table.

Rue was still in shock, but she could feel her emotions moving underneath the hard layer of control. Soon they would break through and panic would reign.

She continued to entreat heaven as she ran back up

the stairs to shower quickly and dress. Her hair was still damp when she followed Farley's boot prints along the path that led to the barn. She nearly collided with Charlie at the gate.

"He's gone," she choked out miserably when the aging man gripped her shoulders to steady her.

"He took Lobo out hours ago," Charlie said, his craggy, ancient face looking worried in the light of the moon. "I'm going to wake the other men so we can saddle up and start lookin' for him soon as the sun's up."

"I'm going with you," Rue insisted, as if anyone had given her cause to argue. "I think we should start right now."

"Mr. Haynes made me swear to look after you," Charlie said stubbornly. "And lettin' you ride out in the dark of night over dangerous ground ain't my idea of keepin' my promise."

Rue's heart stopped for a moment, and she felt her eyes widen. "Farley asked you to take care of me?" The certainty came to her then that they weren't going to find her husband, no matter how long or how thoroughly they searched, but since the realization wasn't one Rue was ready to accept, she pushed it to the back of her mind.

"That's right," Charlie responded with a nod. "Now, you just go back in that house and mind your p's and q's until we can head out. Remember this, too—you won't be a damn bit of good to the man if you've worked yourself up into a tizzy."

Doing fierce battle with a flock of instincts that bade her to do otherwise, Rue obeyed. She walked stiff legged into the house, brewed coffee, drank a cup and then ran to the bathroom to throw up.

That ruled out the idea of breakfast—she would only have been going through the motions anyway—and her knees were too shaky for effective pacing. She took a chair at the kitchen table and laid her head on her arms.

The shrill ringing of the wall phone made her jump a good six inches off her chair, and she snatched the receiver off the hook and yelled, "Hello! Farley?" before she realized he wasn't very likely to call.

Even in the face of logic, however, Rue's disappointment was keen when an operator announced that she had a telegram for Ms. Rue Claridge.

She closed her eyes. "Read it, please," she whispered.

"'A set of sterling is on its way. What do you know about this man? Is he a fortune hunter? Have they found poor Elisabeth yet? Do write. Love, Mummy.'"

"Thanks," Rue muttered when she was certain the operator had finished. Under other circumstances, the message would have embarrassed her, but she was too distraught over Farley to feel anything so mundane.

"Will there be an answer?"

"Not one you could send over a public-communications system," Rue answered with wooden sweetness. Then she hung up the receiver. At least the annoyance of her mother's passionate disinterest had put some starch in her knees and she was able to pace for a while.

Rue even drank another cup of coffee, but that proved to be a foolish choice. She was back in the bathroom, in the midst of violent illness, when she heard the back door open and close.

Quickly, Rue rinsed her mouth and washed her face, but when she hurtled into the kitchen, Farley wasn't there. Charlie was, and he stood, hat in hand, looking worried and authoritative, obviously trying to do and say the things Wilbur would have. The crisis had made him younger and stronger, if only for a little while.

Rue didn't speak. She just put on her winter gear and followed him outside. Her mare, Buttermilk, had been saddled, and all the hands were mounted and ready to ride out.

Lobo had left a trail of hoofprints in the hard snow, and they followed it for several miles, their breaths and those of the horses making white clouds in the bitterly cold air.

The tracks led to the middle of a vast clearing, and there they stopped. Rue, who had been riding in front, alongside Charlie and a younger man called Bill, closed her eyes, absorbing the shattering reality that Farley was gone.

Without her.

Recalling the words of Farley's letter, written from his deathbed, Rue reminded herself that he had left her reluctantly. It was that damn code-of-honor thing, the need to finish all his business before he took up something new.

He was gone, and he surely had the necklace, so there was no way to follow him.

The hands were circled around the pattern of tracks in the snow, exclaiming. Naturally, they'd never seen anything like that before. One even speculated that both Farley and his horse had been abducted by aliens, and Rue wondered disconsolately if that theory was really any stranger than the truth.

Reining Buttermilk toward the house, feeling too broken inside even to cry, Rue let the animal take her home. She was aware of the men riding with her, although she didn't look at them even once.

"I'll get the sheriff out here quick as I can, Mrs. Haynes," said one. "Don't you worry. We'll find your bridegroom."

Tears glittered in Rue's eyes, but she kept her chin high. "They won't find him," she managed to say. "Nobody could find him."

"You don't believe that crackpot idea of Buster's about the spaceship and the little green men, do you?" Bill asked.

Rue meant to laugh, but a sob came out inside. "Right now," she said when she could speak, "I don't know what I believe, but I'm sure of one thing—wherever Farley is, that's where I want to be."

The sheriff came, and he called in the state police. They summoned the FBI, and all the ruckus attracted reporters from the tabloids. A week passed, and no trace of Farley or the horse was found, and in every supermarket check-out line in the country, the front page of the *National Scoop* screamed, UFO SNATCHES MAN AND STALLION, STATE OF MONTANA ON RED ALERT.

If Rue hadn't been in mourning, she would have thought it was all a wonderful joke.

Chapter 15

It took Farley a full week, riding hard, to reach Pine River. Having no money and no gun, he'd lived on what he could scavenge, which wasn't much, considering there was snow on the ground. Lobo, once fat from his winter confinement in the stables at Ribbon Creek, was now sleeker and leaner, the kind of horse a man could depend on.

Folks shouted from the sidewalks and waved from the windows as Farley rode through the center of town, but he not only didn't stop to talk, he didn't even acknowledge them. His whole being was focused on a single objective: getting back to Rue.

As he came abreast of Jon Fortner's office, Farley saw his friend waiting by the hitching rail out front, his arms folded, his gaze steady.

"That's a fine-looking horse, Farley," the doctor said.

The marshal drew back on the reins, dismounted and tethered the stallion to the rail. He needed to talk with Jon, but he feared to start because his emotions were so raw and sore and so close to the surface.

Jonathan came down the steps and laid a reassuring hand to Farley's shoulder. "I've been there, too, remember?" he said, keeping his voice low so the gawking townspeople wouldn't hear. "Come on inside, and I'll pour you a cup of my special medicinal coffee."

For the first time in more than a week, Farley smiled, though he knew the effort was probably somewhat on the puny side. "How about just giving me a cup of medicine with a little coffee in it?"

Rue was lying in bed one night, a month after Farley's dramatic disappearance, when the memory invaded her mind, three-dimensional and in full color.

She saw herself in Pine River, at the churchyard, talking with a dark-haired young man. Michael Blake, that was his name, and he'd said Elisabeth and Jonathan Fortner had been his great-great-grandparents.

Now her heart was pounding like some primitive engine, and the fog of pain and confusion was finally lifting. She heard the young man say cordially, *My grandmother would really like to meet you, since you're a shirttail relation and everything. She lives with my mom and dad in Seattle. Why don't you give her a call sometime?*

Rue threw back the covers and leapt out of bed. Michael had written a name and telephone number on a page from a pocket-size notebook. She squeezed her eyes shut. Where had she put that piece of paper?

At the same time she was pulling on clothes, Rue was ransacking her memory. Whenever someone handed her a business card or anything like that, she always slipped it into her pocket, and she'd been wearing a Windbreaker jacket that day....

Her stomach clenched into a painful knot as she struggled to pursue the recollection further. It was like trying to chase a rabbit through a blackberry thicket, but Rue followed tenaciously, because finding Farley and saving him from the bank robber's bullet was so critically important to her.

"My purse!" she yelled, flipping on the overhead lights. She snatched her bag from the bureau top and upended it over the bed, sending pennies and gum wrappers, credit-card receipts and scruffy tissue all over. After a feverish search, however, she unzipped the change pocket and found the paper folded inside.

On it, Michael had written a name, Mrs. Elisabeth R. Blake, and a telephone number.

Rue reached for the bedside telephone, then caught sight of the alarm clock and realized it was four o'clock in the morning, and just three in Seattle.

"Hell," she muttered, wondering how she could contain herself until a decent hour. Maybe Mrs. Blake was one of those old ladies who have trouble sleeping, and she was sitting up, working a crossword puzzle or watching one of the cable channels.

Rue's speculations changed nothing. Michael had said his grandmother lived with his parents, and *they* were probably sleeping, with no clue of what a mystery their existence really was.

She went downstairs and made herself a cup of tea, since she could no longer tolerate coffee, a drink she'd once loved. She felt dizzy sometimes, too, and she was cranky as a bear recovering from a root canal, but she attributed these symptoms to the stress she'd been under for nearly a month. Pregnancy was both too wonderful and too terrible a prospect to consider.

Soldier, who had been sleeping on the hooked rug in front of the cookstove, as usual, traipsed over to give Rue a friendly lick on the forearm. Idly, she patted his head and went right on sipping her tea.

Perhaps this delay was a good thing. Rue didn't have any idea what to say to Mrs. Blake once she reached her, but she knew the woman was her only link with Elisabeth and Farley, now that the necklace was gone.

Slowly, the icy gray light grew brighter at the windows. Rue fed Soldier, let him out and wandered back to the study.

The photographs taken at the wedding were there, tucked into a place of honor in a drawer of her grandfather's cherrywood desk. Although it always did her injury to look at them, Rue could no more have ignored those pictures than she could have given up breathing or stilled the meter of her heartbeat.

She flipped through them, smiling even as tears pricked her eyes. Farley with coconut frosting all over his mouth. Herself wearing the gauzy dress from the attic. The bride and groom kissing right after the justice of the peace had pronounced them man and wife....

Rue carefully returned the photos to their envelope, then put on her coat and boots and made her way to the woodshed. She brought back an armload of pitchy pine logs, feeling better because of the effort of wielding the ax.

She made a fire and watched an early-morning news show in the study. When eight o'clock came around, Rue simply could not wait any longer. She sat down at the desk, pulled the telephone close and carefully punched out the number Michael had given her that day in the graveyard.

There were a few vague thumps on the line, then a long ring, then another.

"Blake residence," a pleasant male voice answered.

"My name is Rue Claridge-Haynes," Rue blurted. "I'd like to speak with Mrs. Blake—the senior Mrs. Blake— about some genealogy research I've been doing."

"That would be my mother," the man said. "If you'll wait just a moment...." There was a thumping sound as he laid the receiver down, and Rue chewed a fingernail while she waited.

After what seemed like a long time, though it was probably not more than a minute or two, a woman's voice came on the line, almost drowned out by the racket of an extension being hung up.

"Rue Claridge?"

Rue shoved a hand through her hair. "Yes. Mrs. Blake, I'm calling about—"

"I know what you're calling about," the old lady interrupted, crisply but not unkindly. "I've been waiting all my life for this moment."

"I beg your pardon?"

"My grandmother, Elisabeth Fortner, left something for you under the flyleaf of her Bible."

Rue's heart was hammering. This, she realized, was what she had been subconsciously hoping for. Elisabeth had found a way to reach across a hundred years, to send word about herself or Farley.

"Miss Claridge? Are you there?"

"My name is Claridge-Haynes now," Rue said. It sounded totally inane, she knew, but she was in shock.

"I'm married." She paused, cleared her throat. "Mrs. Blake, what did my cous—your grandmother leave for me?"

"It's an envelope," Bethie's descendant answered. "A letter, I suppose. I didn't look because Grandmother's instructions said I mustn't. No one but you is to open the packet, and I cannot send it through the mail or by messenger. The note on the front specifically says that you will contact me when the time is right and that I must insist on your coming for it in person."

Rue was practically dizzy with excitement and suspense. "I'm in Montana, Mrs. Blake," Rue said. "But I'll be there as soon as I can."

Mrs. Blake gave Rue an address and told her to call the moment she arrived in Seattle, no matter what time it was. "I'll be waiting by the phone," she finished.

Rue immediately called the nearest airport, but there were no planes available, charter or otherwise, because of the weather. Rue accepted that disappointment. She told Wilbur, who was recuperating at the ranch house under the care of a nurse, that she was leaving and he was boss until further notice, then threw her suitcases into the back of the Land Rover and left.

The storm started out as a light, picturesque skiff of snow, but by the time Rue reached Spokane, it had reached blizzard proportions. She stopped there and forced down a hearty dinner while a man at a service station across the street put chains on her rear tires.

"You shouldn't drive in this, ma'am," he said, when Rue returned from the restaurant and was settling up the bill. "It's a long way to Seattle, and you've gotta go over the mountains. Snoqualmie Pass is probably closed anyway...."

Rue smiled, nodded, got behind the wheel and went right on.

Hours later, she reached the high mountain pass that connected the eastern and western parts of Washington state. Sure enough, traffic was backed up for miles, but the road was closed only to people who didn't have chains on their tires.

On the other side of the mountain range, there was hardly any snow, and a warm, drizzling rain was washing that away.

Just over an hour after that, Rue pulled into the parking lot of a convenience store in the suburbs of Seattle. She called Mrs. Blake, who was awake and waiting, as promised.

After washing her face, combing her hair and brushing her teeth in the rest room, Rue bought a tall cup of hot chocolate and went on.

She found the Blake house with relative ease, but even though her exhausted state made her feel slightly bewitched, Rue wouldn't let herself attribute the fact to anything mystical. She had always had a good sense of direction.

A white-haired old woman with a sweet smile and soft blue eyes came to the door only an instant after Rue rang the bell.

"Rue," she said, and something in the very warp and woof of the woman reminded Rue of Elisabeth and filled her with an aching sense of nostalgia. Bethie's *granddaughter*—how impossible that seemed. "Come in."

"I hope I haven't awakened anyone...."

"Mercy, no," Mrs. Blake said, linking her thin, age-spotted arm with Rue's and ushering her into a large, tastefully decorated room to the left. "Phillip, my son, is a surgeon, and he's been up and gone for hours. Nadine, my daughter-in-law, is at the health club, swimming, and, of course, Michael lives in one of the dorms at the university now. I pretty much have the place to myself, except for the maid. Won't you sit down?"

Even though she felt sure she would faint any moment, Rue was so tired, she was almost painfully tense. She sat in a graceful Queen Anne chair, upholstered in a pretty blue-and-white floral pattern, and tried to keep calm.

"Would you care for some coffee?" Mrs. Blake inquired, taking a chair facing Rue's and gesturing gracefully toward the silver service on the cocktail table.

Rue shook her head. "No, thank you," she said, and then bit down hard on her lower lip to keep from demanding the envelope Elisabeth had left for her.

"Well, then, there's no sense in dragging this out, even if it is the biggest thing to happen around here since Nadine's friend Phyllis crawled out on the roof during last year's Christmas party and made a world-class fool of herself. She sang twenty-two different show tunes before the fire department got her down, you know, and every note was off key."

Rue smiled and nodded and tapped the arm of the chair with her fingertips.

Mrs. Blake flushed slightly. "I'm sorry, I do get to running on." She pulled a battered blue vellum envelope from her bag, which was resting on the marble-topped table beside her chair, and held it out to Rue.

Rue forced herself not to snatch it out of Mrs. Blake's fingers. She must have looked calm on the outside, but inside, Rue was suffering an agony of hope. If this was nothing more than a cosmic postcard—"How are you? I am fine. Wish you were here"—the disappointment would be beyond tolerance.

Rue made herself read the faded but familiar lettering on the front of the envelope, and tears filled her eyes. Elisabeth's cryptic instructions were all there, just as Mrs. Blake had relayed them.

Finally, like a child opening a fascinating, fragile present found under the Christmas tree, Rue broke the old wax seal and pulled a single page from inside the envelope.

The necklace did not tumble to her lap, as Rue had hoped it would, but she'd mourn that oversight later. Now, she would read words that had waited a hundred years for her attention.

My Dearest Rue,

I know you probably expected to find the necklace folded inside this letter, so that you could return here to find Mr. Haynes, but, of course, once you think about it, you'll realize that I couldn't take a chance like that. You and I know only too well what magic Aunt Verity's pendant is capable of.

If you must find it, I can only tell you to remember that rainy afternoon when we were thirteen and we decided to make a time capsule.

I hate writing this part, knowing what an awful impact it's going to have, but you married Farley, and I think you have a right to the truth, so you can get on with your life. Rue, Farley was shot ten days ago while stopping a robbery, and last night he died of his wounds.

Rue stopped there, fighting to hold on to consciousness while the gracious room swayed around her, then forced herself to go on reading.

"There are no words I can say to console you, except that I know Farley loved you desperately, and that his greatest wish was to return to you.

Rue, I told you where to find the necklace because I know I don't have the right to withhold a choice that rightfully belongs to you, but I beg you not to try to return. The power of that pendant is unpredictable, we know that if hardly anything else, and it's dangerous. Anything could happen.

I love you, Cousin, with my whole heart, and I'm depending on you to do your grieving, then pull yourself together and go on.

Forever, and with a new understanding of the word,

Beth

When Rue let the letter crumple to her lap, Mrs. Blake was ready with a glass of cool water.

"Here, dear, drink this. You look as waxen as a ghost."

Rue might have smiled under other circumstances. As it was, she only reached out a trembling hand for the glass and drank with desperate thirst. Once she felt a little steadier, she thanked Mrs. Blake, carefully folded Bethie's letter and tucked it into her purse.

"I can't share it," she confessed softly. "I hope you understand."

Mrs. Blake's smile was reminiscent of Elisabeth's. "I won't say I'm not curious, dear," she replied, "but I understand. There are mysteries aplenty in this life, and I've learned to accept the fact."

Rue kissed the old lady's cheek lightly. "Thank you again, Mrs. Blake. And goodbye."

Barely an hour later, Rue was back in Pine River, her eyes puffy and sore. Alone in the Land Rover, insulated from a world that couldn't have comprehended her pain, Rue had screamed in rage and grief over her husband's unfair death. Tears had left acid trails on her cheeks, and her throat was so constricted, she could barely breathe.

Instead of heading for Aunt Verity's house, Rue stopped at the churchyard. She found Farley's grave, under the old oak tree as the clerk in the church office had told her. If there had ever been a stone or a wooden marker, no trace remained.

Rue was mourning a man who'd been dead a century, and there wasn't even a monument to honor his memory.

The cemetery was cold on that grim winter day, and Rue's strength was almost gone. She turned—she would visit Elisabeth's and Aunt Verity's graves some other day—and made her way back to the muddy Land Rover.

Moving like a person in a voodoo documentary, Rue bought soup and soap and tea and other supplies at Pine River's state-of-the-art supermarket, then drove to the house where all her adventures had begun.

The mail was knee-deep in front of the slot in the door, and there were so many messages on the answering machine that the tape had run out. Rue didn't play them back. She just put away her groceries, made a bowl of tomato soup and ate without actually tasting a single spoonful.

After rinsing the bowl, she went upstairs, put fresh

sheets on one of the beds, took a shower and collapsed. She slept for fourteen hours straight, got up and made herself another bowl of soup, then went back to sleep for another seven.

When she awakened, rested at last, but still numb with sorrow, Rue took Elisabeth's earlier letters from their hiding place in the rolltop desk in the parlor and read them again.

Her heart began to thump. Time did not necessarily run parallel between then and now, she remembered, with growing excitement. If she found a way back—and the whereabouts of the necklace was teasing the edges of her consciousness even then—she would probably arrive after Farley's shooting. But she could also get there before it happened.

Maybe she could intercede.

She ran to find her purse—she'd discarded it on the floor of the downstairs hallway when she first returned—pulled out the letter Mrs. Blake had kept for her and scanned it.

Her gaze snagged on one particular sentence. "...I can only tell you to remember that rainy afternoon when we were thirteen and we decided to make a time capsule."

Rue yelped in frustration and began to pace. Her memory wasn't good when it came to things like that, though she could reel off statistics and stock prices and phone numbers until her voice gave out.

"Time capsule, time capsule, time capsule." She repeated the words like a litany, hoping they would trigger some rusty catch deep down in her mind.

Suddenly, gloriously, the memory was there.

Rain on a leaky roof. The smell of dam dust and

moldy hay. Two adolescent girls, herself and Elisabeth, in the barn loft, talking about the distant future. They'd wanted posterity to know about their lives, so they'd swiped a lidded plastic bowl from Aunt Verity's kitchen and put in things they considered representative of Planet Earth in the 1970s. Lip gloss. Pictures of their favorite rock group, carefully snipped from fan magazines. A candy bar with peanuts and caramel....

Rue hurried through the house and outside, crossing the dead winter grass in long strides. The barn was old and flimsy and should have been torn down years before, but safety was the last thing on Rue's mind as she went inside.

She did test the ladder leading up to the loft, but only in a quick and cursory way. The boards under her feet swayed a little when she reached the top, but that didn't stop her, either. She and Elisabeth had put their time capsule into the creaky framework where the floor and wall met with great ceremony.

"X marks the spot," she said breathlessly when she found the hiding place and knelt to wrench back a board. The whole loft seemed to shimmy at the intrusion, but again Rue was undaunted.

Behind the filthy, weathered board was a dirty plastic container riddled with the tooth marks of some creature that could probably qualify for top billing in a horror movie. Rue tossed the bowl aside without lifting the lid to look inside and peered into the crevice behind it.

At first, she could see nothing but darkness, dirt and spider webs, but after a few moments her vision seemed to sharpen. Well behind the place where her and Elisabeth's treasures had been hidden, a solid-looking shadow lurked in the gloom.

Rue grimaced, reached deep into the unknown and closed her hand around the object. Having found what she sought, she drew back so fast that a splinter or the tip of a nail made a long, shallow gash in her arm.

She paid no attention to the wound; all she could see was the round, rusted tin she held. Once it had held salve, and the distinct possibility that it was nothing more than a stray piece of trash raised panic into Rue's throat like bile.

"Please," she whispered, and it was at once the most sincere and the most succinct prayer she had ever said.

It was hard, and she broke a couple of fingernails, but Rue finally managed to pry off the lid of the tin. Inside, dusty and tarnished and as full of mystery as ever, lay the necklace.

Rue's eyes filled with tears of relief, and she clutched the pendant to her chest. Now, if only the magic would work again.

Nothing happened, so Rue carefully tucked the necklace into the pocket of her jacket. Only then did she notice that the bit of paper lining the salve tin had writing on it.

Carefully, Rue lifted it to the thin light coming in through one of the wide cracks in the barn wall. "I knew you wouldn't listen!" Elisabeth had scrawled.

Rue smiled, dried her eyes with the back of one hand and climbed cautiously down the ladder again.

Inside the house, she laid the necklace on the drainboard beside the kitchen sink and washed it with cotton balls, mild soap and water. When the pendant was clean, she patted it dry with a soft paper towel, draped the chain around her neck and carefully closed the clasp.

She shut her eyes, gripped the edge of the counter and waited. Hoped.

At first, nothing happened, but then a humming sound filled Rue's ears, rising steadily in pitch. The floor buckled and rolled under her feet, and it seemed that she could feel the spin of the earth itself.

Someone screamed and something crashed to the floor.

Rue opened her eyes to see Bethie's housekeeper standing there, aghast and staring, a shattered crockery bowl at her feet. Its contents covered the length of the woman's calico skirts.

"Ellen, for heaven's sake..." a familiar voice complained, and then Elisabeth appeared in the doorway leading to the main parlor. When she saw her cousin, her blue-green eyes widened and her face lit up with a dazzling smile. "Rue!"

"She just came out of nowhere, missus," Ellen blathered. "I'm telling you, I don't know about the goings-on in this house. I just don't know. And now I've got myself a sick headache."

"You'd better go and lie down," Elisabeth told her gently, but she didn't look at the housekeeper again. She gave Rue a gentle hug.

"Is he dead?" Rue whispered, unable to bear the agony of wondering for another moment.

"Who?" Bethie asked, and her look of puzzlement raised Rue's spirits considerably.

"Farley. Farley Haynes, the marshal." For the first time, the thought occurred to Rue that she might have come back not only before her husband's death, but before he knew her.

"Well, he hasn't been very happy about being separated from you," Elisabeth said with a fond smile, "but people don't usually die of a broken heart. They just *wish* they could."

Farley was alive, and he would know her. Rue's knees literally went slack with relief, and she might have collapsed if Elisabeth hadn't steadied her.

"I've got to go to him right now," she said after a few deep breaths.

"But you're shaken—you need to sit down and have a cup of tea—"

"I need to find my husband!" Rue said. "Is there a horse I can borrow?"

Elisabeth offered no further argument; she knew her cousin too well. "There's a chestnut mare in the barn. Her name is Maisie, and she prefers to be ridden bareback."

Rue hugged her cousin, bade her a good life with Jonathan and raced out the back door, nearly tripping because the steps were different from the ones she was used to. The barn that had been a teetering disaster the last time she entered it was sturdy now, and well maintained.

Quickly, Rue bridled the small mare and swung up onto its back. A woman in pants, riding astride no less, was going to come as yet another shock to the fine people of Pine River, but that could not be helped. The necklace had slipped beneath her shirt; it felt warm against her collarbone, and she was filled with a new and terrifying sense of urgency.

She'd gotten back in time, but just barely. There wasn't a second to lose.

Sure enough, Rue heard the shots just as she and Maisie hit the foot of the town's main street. Rue spurred the animal through the uproar and confusion—everybody was trying to take cover—weaving her way around wagons and buggies and other horses.

Undaunted, Rue rode hell-bent for the bank. If she had to, she would catch that outlaw's bullet herself before she let it strike Farley.

Two men ran out of the bank, their faces, except for their eyes and foreheads, covered by dirty bandannas. It was just like a scene in a John Wayne movie, except that here the bullets were real.

Rue looked frantically for Farley, which was why she was caught completely unprepared when an arm as hard as iron wrenched her off the mare's back and onto another horse. After that, everything was a dizzying blur.

Either she was dreaming, or she was sitting sidesaddle behind Farley, clutching his canvas duster with both hands. The magnificent animal carrying them both was Lobo. She felt the swift, skilled movement of the marshal's arm as he drew his .45. Then she heard two shots in rapid succession and felt the recoil in the muscles between Farley's shoulder blades, where her cheek rested. The air seemed thick with the smells of horse manure and burned powder, and Rue figured if she survived this, the first thing she was going to do was vomit.

In that moment, of all moments, she realized she was definitely pregnant.

A brief silence followed. Rue clung to Farley, soaking in the hard strength of his body in front of her. He was alive, and so was she.

He turned his head to look back at her, and although a muscle in his jaw jumped in irritation, Rue could see joy in his eyes. "That was a damn fool thing to do," he bit out. "You could have been killed."

The necklace was searing Rue's skin. She locked her hands together in front of his stomach, determined that even a brand new Big Bang wouldn't blast her loose. "I love you, too, Farley Haynes," she said.

The magic was beginning again; the air was filled with a vibrant silence so noisy that Rue could hear nothing besides her own voice and Farley's heartbeat. She threw back her head and shouted for joy, at the same time tearing the necklace from her throat and flinging it away.

They might land in heaven or in hell. Either way, the die was cast.

"Tarnation," Farley marveled when the spiritual storm subsided. The marshal, Rue and Lobo were square in the middle of the deserted parking lot at Pine River High School. It was twilight, and the wind was chilly, but to Rue, the sky had never looked brighter nor had the air felt warmer.

Farley turned, his beautiful teeth showing in a broad grin. "Well, Mrs. Haynes," he asked, just before he kissed her, "what do we do now?"

It was a long moment before Rue caught her breath. "That's easy, Mr. Haynes," she replied. "We ride off into the sunset."

* * * * *

Visit the Author Profile page
at Harlequin.com for more titles.

LASSOED

B.J. Daniels

The one thing no one told me was how many good writer friends I would make on this journey. This one is for Amanda Stevens, who is always there when I need her. I should add, she is also the scariest person I know, and if you don't believe it, wait until you read her Graveyard series.

Chapter 1

The lights came out of the darkness like an oasis in the desert. Billie Rae glanced at the gas gauge on the old pickup, then in her rearview mirror.

She hadn't seen a vehicle behind her for miles now, but she didn't slow down, didn't dare. The pickup engine roared loudly, the speedometer clocked at over a hundred, but it was the gas gauge that had her worried.

She was almost out of fuel. Which meant she was also out of luck.

At the speed she was traveling, the lights ahead were coming up fast. At first she thought it was a small town. She hadn't seen one for more than fifty miles. But as she sped toward the glittering lights, she realized it wasn't a town. It appeared to be a fairgrounds aglow with lights.

Suddenly fireworks shot up from the horizon, bursting in the huge ebony sky stretched over this vast Mon-

tana prairie. She stared in surprise, realizing with a
start what day it was. July 2. Two days away from the
Fourth. She let the pickup slow to eighty as the boom-
ing fireworks burst around her, momentarily blinding
her. The engine coughed. She glanced at the gas gauge.
The pickup was running on fumes.

In her headlights she caught sight of the sign to
the Whitehorse fairgrounds and another sign that announced Rodeo July 2–4. As the pickup engine coughed
again, Billie Rae knew she'd just run out of options as
well as gas.

She turned onto the dirt road that had a handmade
sign that read Rodeo Parking and let the pickup coast
in past dozens of trucks and horse trailers parked in the
field around the rodeo arena. Just as the engine died,
she pulled the truck into a spot between two pickups
and turned off the headlights.

The highway she'd just come down had been nothing but blackness in her rearview mirror. Now, though,
she wasn't surprised to see a set of headlights in the far
distance. She'd known she didn't have much of a head
start. Just as she'd known nothing short of dying would
keep him from coming after her.

Billie Rae sat for a moment fighting tears. Her chest
ached from the sudden loss of hope. Without gas she
wasn't going any farther—as if she really believed she
could ever go far enough to get away from Duane. She
slumped over the steering wheel.

She'd left the house with only the clothes on her back,
and now it was just a matter of minutes before he found
her. Duane was no fool. He'd know the pickup would be
running low on gas by now and that she hadn't stopped
to fill it up since she had no money. She'd had to leave

her purse behind—not that there was any money in it, thanks to Duane. He had kept her a virtual prisoner since their wedding six months ago.

None of that mattered now, though. She should never have run. Duane was right. There was no getting away from him. He'd get a good laugh out of her thinking she could. Hadn't he said he would follow her to the ends of the earth?

But it was what else he'd said when she'd told him she wanted out of the marriage that made her now begin to tremble in the dark cab of the pickup.

He had grabbed her by the throat and thrown her down on the bed. "You ever leave me and I will hunt you down like a mad dog and hurt you in ways you can't even imagine."

Her heart began to pound now with both fear and outrage. Duane had been so sweet, so loving, so caring before the wedding. Her mother had just died and she'd needed someone strong to lean on. Duane had provided the broad shoulder. He'd helped her through a tough time.

And then she'd made the mistake of marrying him. It wasn't that he'd suddenly changed. It was that once he put that ring on her finger, he'd finally revealed who he really was—a bully, a bastard, a batterer.

Her hands were shaking as she let go of the steering wheel. Her fingers ached from gripping it so tightly. Was she just going to sit here and wait for him to find her? He'd done his best to beat her down, but there was still a little fight left in her. She'd left him, hadn't she? That proved she had more courage than she'd thought and certainly more than Duane had thought.

She wasn't going back. Nor was she going to let

Duane kill her. She had been a young, foolish, enam-
ored woman when she'd married him, but once she'd
seen behind the mask to the monster, there was no going
back after that. She wasn't one of those women who
thought their husbands would change. Or that it was her
fault when her husband took out his bad moods on her.

But there was no denying she was in trouble.

Opening the door, Billie Rae climbed out of the
pickup, surprised how weak her knees felt. Between
booms of fireworks she heard a vehicle slowing on the
highway before the small community fairgrounds. She
didn't dare look and what was the point? She knew
who it was.

She quickly worked her way through the pickups
and horse trailers, following the sound of the oohs and
aahs of the audience in the stands as the fireworks continued to explode over her head. The fireworks were
going off closer together. One huge boom rattled in her
chest after another. Soon the crowd would be dispersing and leaving.

She felt all her bravado leave as well. Soon everyone
would be gone. Maybe she could find a place to hide
where Duane wouldn't… Who was she kidding? Duane
was going to find her, and when he did…

Glancing back through the parked vehicles, she
caught a glimpse of a large black car driving slowly into
the lot. Duane. He'd find the old classic Chevy pickup
that had been his father's pride and joy. He'd find her.

She raced behind the grandstand in blind panic,
knowing what he would do when he found her. She
shouldn't have tried to leave him. She should have
waited until she had a plan. But when Duane had
come home earlier and she'd seen the rage building in

him, she'd known how the evening would end and she couldn't let him hurt her again.

Billie Rae ran, blinded by tears and terror. If she could reach the stands, maybe she could disappear into the crowd—at least temporarily. Eventually, though, the stands would clear out and all that would be left would be her—and Duane.

As she came around the end of the grandstand, she collided with a tall cowboy. She'd been running for her life, glancing back over her shoulder and not looking where she was going, so she was hit hard, with her breath knocked out of her and her feet out from under her. If he hadn't caught her, she would have fallen to the ground.

"Easy," the cowboy said, his big hands gripping her shoulders to steady her. Tears continued to spill and she couldn't quit trembling. She opened her mouth to speak but nothing came out as she looked up into the man's handsome face.

He was dressed in boots, jeans and a fancy Western shirt. A gray Stetson was tilted back on his dark head. But it was the kindness in his brown eyes that had her riveted as the fireworks' grand finale continued.

Huge booms reverberated through her as brilliant colors showered the sky around the two of them in breathtaking beauty. For a few moments, it seemed they were the only two people in the world. As if this show was only for them alone. The cowboy smiled down at her and she felt a hitch in her chest.

The fireworks show ended in hushed dark silence, then the large lights of the fairgrounds blinked on and Billie Rae heard the crunch of gravel under a boot heel at the other end of the large grandstand.

As if coming out of a dream, she swung her gaze to where a dark figure was heading their way. Duane. She would recognize that arrogant gait anywhere.

She tried to pull away from the cowboy, needing to run, but he held on tight to her as the crowd suddenly swarmed around them.

Tanner Chisholm would have scoffed at even the idea of love at first sight—until a few moments ago. When the woman had come running out of the darkness behind the grandstand and into his arms in a shower of fireworks, noise and beautiful lights, he'd taken one look at her face and fallen.

Time froze with fireworks going off all around them. When she'd crashed into him he felt as if his whole life had been leading up to that moment. He'd known in an instant that it was no accident that this woman had run into his arms on this warm summer night.

He stared into her wide brown eyes, as her dark curly hair floated around her shoulders. He saw the terror etched in her tear-streaked face, felt her trembling and realized that come hell or high water, he'd do his damnedest to move heaven and earth for this woman.

It was crazy, wonderful and totally out of character. He wasn't the kind of man who fell in love in a split second. But any man would have seen that this woman was running for her life.

"What's wrong?" he asked as she fought to pull away from him and run. He saw her look behind him again. A man was headed in their direction, fighting the crowd to get to them in a way that left no doubt the man was furious—and coming after the woman in Tanner's arms.

"Come with me." Tanner took her hand and pulled

her through the crowd. He knew these rodeo grounds like the back of his hand because he'd grown up here, played under these grandstands, ridden in junior rodeo and had later ridden bucking broncs out in the arena.

The woman resisted for only a moment before she let him lead her through the crowd and the darkness toward the shadowy fairground buildings beyond the rodeo arena. From the way she was still trembling, he suspected that the man chasing her meant to hurt her. Or at least she thought so. The fact that she was more afraid of the man than a complete stranger told him the woman was desperate.

As he drew her between two of the fair buildings, he spotted the man fighting his way through the rodeo crowd. Tanner caught the man's expression under one of the large lights. The heightened fury he saw on the man's face made him worry he might have made things worse for the woman by trying to protect her.

Too late now. Whatever had the man all riled up, he wasn't going to be taking it out on this woman. Not tonight, anyway.

Tanner led her between two more buildings, weaving his way through the maze of dark structures, until he reached one he knew would be unlocked. Pulling the door open, he drew her inside, closed the door and turned the lock.

"Who is that out there?" he whispered, still holding her hand in the blackness inside the building.

Silence, then a hoarsely whispered, "My husband."

Tanner mentally gave himself a swift kick. He really had stepped in it this time. Only a fool jumped into a domestic argument. "Why's he so angry?"

She started to answer but he felt her freeze as she

heard the same sound he did. Someone was running in this direction on the wooden boardwalk in front of the buildings. He didn't have to tell her to be quiet. He knew she was holding her breath.

The footfalls came to a stop outside the building, the last along the row. Past it was a line of huge cottonwoods cloaked in darkness. With luck, the man would think that was where they had gone.

Tanner could hear the man's heavy breathing and cursing, then his angry voice as he muttered, "You may have gotten away this time, Billie Rae, but this isn't over. When I find you, I'm going to make you wish you were dead. That's if I don't kill you with my bare hands."

The man stood outside the door panting hard, then his footfalls ebbed away back the way he'd come. The woman he'd called Billie Rae let go of Tanner's hand, and he could hear her fumbling with the door lock.

"Not so fast," Tanner said, reaching around her to turn on the light. They were both blinded for a moment by the sudden light. "I think you'd better tell me what's going on, because you heard what he just said. That man plans to hurt you. If he hasn't already," Tanner added as he saw the fading bruise around her left eye.

What Billie Rae had heard her husband say wasn't anything new. He'd threatened her plenty of times before, and the threats, she'd learned the hard way, weren't empty ones.

"I appreciate what you did for me, but I can't involve you in this," she said, finally finding her voice.

The cowboy let out a humorless laugh. "I'm already

involved up to my hat. Do you have someplace you can go? Family? Friends?"

Billie Rae opened her mouth to lie. Duane had moved her away from what little family and friends she'd had right after the wedding. She'd lost contact over the past six months. Duane had made sure of that. Just as he had thrown a fit when she'd suggested going back to work.

"Your work is in this house, taking care of me. That's your work."

"You don't have anyone you can call, do you?" the cowboy said. "Don't worry. It's going to be all right. I know a place you can stay where you will be safe."

Billie Rae wanted desperately to take the cowboy up on his offer but realized she couldn't. It had been bad enough when Duane had been after her alone. Now he would be looking for the cowboy he'd seen her with. "No, you don't understand. Duane will come after *you* now. I'm so sorry. I should never have put you in this position."

"You didn't. I'm the one who dragged you in here," he said as he pulled out his cell phone.

She tried to protest to whatever he was about to do, but he shushed her.

"I need a ride," he said into the phone.

She heard laughter on the other end.

"I need you to bring me my pickup. That's right, it's parked right where we left it before the rodeo. No, I can't come get it myself, Marshall, or I wouldn't have called you. The keys are in it. I'm in the last fairground building. There will be two of us. Make it quick, okay?" He snapped off the phone and gave her a reassuring smile.

Billie Rae wondered if she'd just jumped from the skillet into the fire. But there was something about this man that made her feel safe. It wasn't just the kindness she saw in his brown eyes.

There was a softness to his voice and his movements that belied his size and the strength she could see in his broad shoulders, muscled arms and callused hands.

This was a man who did manual labor—not one who either sat behind a desk or rode around all day in a car.

"I'm Tanner Chisholm," he said and held out his hand.

"Billie Rae Johnson." She realized she'd given him her maiden name instead of her married one.

"My brother Marshall is coming to pick us up in my truck, then we'll go out to the ranch where my step-mother, Emma, will make you feel at home. She'll insist you have something to eat. She does that to everyone. Humor her; it is much easier in the long run." He smiled. "You'll like Emma. Everyone does."

"I couldn't possibly impose—"

"Trust me, it is impossible to impose at the Chisholm ranch. If anything, Emma and my father, Hoyt, will want to adopt you."

She felt tears well and quickly brushed them away. "Why are you being so nice to me? You don't know me."

"I know you're in trouble and I'm a sucker for a woman who needs my help," he joked. "Seriously, what-ever is going on, you need someplace to stay tonight at least and to give your husband a chance to calm down."

As if Duane was going to calm down, she thought with a grimace. All of this would have him foaming at the mouth with fury.

"I assume you drove to the rodeo?"

"A pickup. It's out of gas. But—"

"My brother and I will see to it tomorrow. It will be safe here tonight."

Maybe the truck would be safe but the brothers wouldn't be if they came to fetch it tomorrow. Duane would be watching it and waiting.

She had to stop this now. She knew Duane, knew what he would do to this cowboy. "You have to let me go," she said as she reached for the doorknob again. "You don't know my husband. He'll come after you—"

"I think I *do* know your husband," Tanner said and gently touched her cheek under her left eye with his fingertips. She flinched, not because her bruised cheek still hurt, but because she'd forgotten about her healing black eye and now this kind cowboy knew her hidden shame.

At the sound of a truck pulling up outside the building, Tanner said, "That will be Marshall." He opened the door a crack and looked out as if checking to make sure the coast was clear. "I come from a large ranch family that sticks together. I have five brothers. Your husband isn't going to take on the six of us, trust me."

Before she could argue, he quickly ushered her out to a large ranch truck. She noticed the sign printed on the side: Chisholm Cattle Company. Tanner opened the truck door, then taking her waist in both of his large hands, lifted her in before sliding into the bench seat next to her.

"Marshall, meet Billie Rae. Billie Rae, my big brother Marshall."

The cowboy behind the wheel grinned. Like his brother, Marshall had dark hair and brown eyes reflecting his Native American ancestry. Both men were very handsome but there was also something kind and comforting in their faces.

"I'd appreciate it if you got this truck moving," Tanner said, glancing in his side mirror. He turned back to Billie Rae, plucked a cowboy hat from the gun rack behind her and dropped it onto her long, dark, curly hair.

Marshall laughed. "So you got yourself into some kind of trouble and apparently involved this pretty little lady in the midst of it, huh?" He shook his head, but he got the truck moving.

As they drove out the back way of the fairgrounds, Billie Rae stared through the windshield from under the brim of the hat, afraid she'd see Duane in the dispersing crowd. Or worse, Duane would see her—and the name of the ranch painted on the side of the truck.

Chapter 2

Duane Rasmussen leaned against his father's pickup, arms crossed over his chest, his heart pounding with both anger and anticipation.

The fairgrounds were still clearing out. His head hurt from searching the crowd and waiting to see Billie Rae's contrite face.

She would come crawling back, apologizing and saying how sorry she was. She'd be a lot sorrier when he got through with her. The thought kicked up his pulse to a nice familiar throb he could feel in his thick neck.

As his daddy used to say, "A man who can't control his woman is no man at all."

He used to think his old man was a mean SOB. But Duane hadn't understood what his father had to contend with when it came to living with a woman. Sometimes just opening the door and seeing Billie Rae with that look on her face…

Duane couldn't describe it any other way than as a deer-in-the-headlights look. It made him want to wipe it off her face. He hated it when she acted as if she had to fear him.

He had told her repeatedly that he loved her and that the only reason he had to get tough with her sometimes was because she made him mad. Or when she acted like she was walking around on eggshells, treating him as if she thought he might go off at any moment and slap her.

Didn't he realize how that would make him even angrier with her?

Duane shook his head now. He'd never be able to understand his wife.

Like this little trick she'd just pulled, taking off on him. What the hell was she thinking? She'd been so sweet and compliant when they were dating. She'd liked it when he took care of her, told her what was best for her, didn't bother her with making any of the decisions.

He couldn't understand what had changed her. It was a mystery to him especially since he'd given the woman everything—she didn't even have to work outside the home.

He'd squashed all talk of her looking for a job after they'd moved. No wife of his was working. Every man knew that working outside the home ruined a woman. They got all kinds of strange ideas into their heads. Let a woman be too independent and you were just asking for trouble.

With a curse, he saw that the parking area was almost empty. Only a few stragglers wandered out from the direction of the rodeo grandstands. The rodeo cowboys had loaded up their stock and taken off. The parking lot in the field next to the fairgrounds was empty.

A sliver of worry burrowed under his skin. Where was Billie Rae? Still hiding in those trees to the west of the fairgrounds? The night air was cooling quickly. She wasn't dressed for spending the night in the woods, not this far north in Montana.

That was another thing that puzzled him, the way she'd taken off. She hadn't planned this as far as he could tell. He'd found her purse and her house key. She hadn't even taken a decent jacket, and it appeared she'd left with nothing more than the clothes on her back. How stupid was that?

He settled in to wait. When she got cold and hungry she'd come back to the pickup. She'd know he would be waiting for her, so she'd come with her tail between her legs. He smiled at the thought. Of course Billie Rae would come back. Where else could she go?

Emma Chisholm took one look at the woman her stepson had brought home from the rodeo and recognized herself—thirty years ago. It gave her a start to have a reminder show up at her front door after all these years.

All of it was too familiar, the terror in the young woman's eyes, the fading bruises, the insecurity and indecision in her movements and the panic and pain etched in her face.

The worst part, Emma knew, was the memory of the tearful promises that would be forgotten in an instant the next time. But it was those tender moments that gave every battered woman hope that this time, her lover really would never do it again. They called it the honeymoon period. It came right before the next beating— and that beating was always worse than the one before.

It made her heart ache just to look at the woman.

A part of Emma wanted to distance herself, deny that she had been this young woman, but if there was one thing she'd learned, it was that all things circled back at you for a reason.

"This is Billie Rae Johnson," Tanner said. "Her car broke down at the rodeo. I told her we had plenty of room and that we'd get her fixed up in the morning."

Emma smiled and held out her hand to the young woman. "I'm Emma. We are delighted to have you stay with us as long as you'd like." Her gaze shifted to Tanner.

He'd never been one to exaggerate or lie, but she didn't believe his story for a moment. Billie Rae was on the run. Emma knew the look, remembered it only too well. Her heart went out to Billie Rae.

"I don't want to be an imposition." Billie Rae was a beauty, but Emma knew that her stepson had seen beyond that. Tanner was like his father, who brought home those in need. Was that one reason Hoyt had fallen in love with her? Because he'd seen the need in Emma herself?

"I promise you it is no imposition," Emma said. "I love having guests, especially female ones. I'm so outnumbered around here."

"Thank you," Billie Rae said. She looked exhausted. No doubt she'd been running on adrenaline and fear for hours and was about to crash.

"Why don't I show you up to one of our many guest rooms?" Emma said quickly. "Since all six of the boys have their own places now, we have more empty bedrooms than you can shake a stick at. Then I'll get you a snack. It always helps me sleep."

Billie Rae glanced at Tanner, who smiled and nodded, then she followed Emma without a word.

"You have this whole wing to yourself," Emma said when they reached one of the rooms that was always made up for guests. "So please, make yourself at home and if there is anything you need, don't hesitate to ask."

"I won't be here more than tonight."

Emma smiled. "Get some rest. Sometimes it takes more than a night. You are welcome to stay as long as you need. You're safe here."

Billie Rae nodded, tears coming to her eyes. "You're very kind."

"No, I've been where you are right now." Admitting it was easier than she'd thought it would be.

For a moment, the young woman looked as if she was going to deny it or pretend she didn't know what Emma was talking about.

"I was with a man who kicked the hell out of me on a regular basis," Emma said, surprised how easily too the anger came back. "Oh sure, he was always sorry. It was for my own good. He loved me. It took me a while to realize it wasn't for my own good, just as it wasn't my fault and that nothing I did or could do would change him. He didn't love me. He didn't know what love was."

Tears spilled over Billie Rae's cheeks. "I'm just so embarrassed."

Emma took her hand and they sat down on the edge of the bed. "Embarrassed? Oh, sweetie, you have done nothing to be embarrassed about."

"I married the wrong man. He…fooled me."

She nodded. "But you got smart and left him."

"He told me he'll kill me and I don't doubt it," Billie Rae said, brushing angrily at her tears.

Emma shook her head. "He isn't going to find you here. Tomorrow you can decide what to do next."

"You don't know Duane. I'm afraid he'll find out that you all helped me and do something terrible to you."

"Honey, that's why there's a shotgun in this house. Trust Tanner. He's a good man." She studied the young woman for a moment. "I don't know if you believe in fate or not, but I can tell you this. Tanner finding you and bringing you here was no accident."

As Duane sat in the empty fairgrounds in the dark, he knew where he'd made his mistake. If he'd gotten Billie Rae pregnant right away, none of this would be happening. But instead he'd listened to his wife, who'd wanted to wait until they were "settled in as a couple," as she called it.

With a surge of angry resentment, he realized she just wanted to make sure the marriage was to her liking. That *he* was to her liking.

Duane swore under his breath. Wait until he got his hands on her. He'd show her. She would never pull a stunt like this again. He'd kill her if she did. That was if he didn't end up killing her this time. He flushed, embarrassed to be put in this position, as the scent of fried food still drifted on the breeze coming through the open window of his Lincoln.

The last of the lights of the rodeo vehicles had dimmed away to darkness in the distance, all headed west. From the faint glow on the horizon, Duane figured the closest Montana town had to be up the highway. He was hungry and tired and even his anger couldn't keep him going much longer.

Duane looked around. It was just his car now and his father's pickup.

Where the hell was Billie Rae?

He waited until the night air cooled to a chill before he put up his car window, started the engine and drove down to park by the pickup. Billie Rae would be coming back soon and he didn't want to miss her.

A thought struck him like a blow. Unless she'd left with someone.

That cowboy he'd seen her with?

He couldn't get his mind around that. But then he'd thought he'd made it clear to Billie Rae what would happen to her if she ever tried to leave him—or to anyone who helped her. She'd made a friend who thought she could come between them. That friend was no longer anywhere around, now, was she?

Duane had thought Billie Rae had learned her lesson that time. But apparently that hadn't stopped her from "befriending" someone else who thought they could interfere in his marriage to her.

None of this was like Billie Rae, he thought as the hours wore on, and he felt an uncertainty that rattled him. For the first time, he wasn't sure he knew his wife as well as he thought he did.

After her talk with Emma Chisholm, Billie Rae showered, slipped into the cotton nightgown left for her on the huge bed and slid between the sheets that smelled like fresh air.

Emma had also left her a glass of milk and a plate of sliced homemade banana bread. Billie Rae had eaten all of it. She hadn't realized how hungry she was or that she hadn't eaten since breakfast that morning.

For the first time in a long time, she felt as if she could breathe as she got up to brush her teeth with the new toothbrush Emma had set out for her. The cool night air blew in through the open window next to her bed as she crawled back under the covers. The breeze billowed the sheer white curtains. She could see the outline of mountains in the distance, smell sage and hay beyond the fresh clean scent of the line-dried linens on the bed.

But it was the sweet scent of freedom that she gulped in as if she was a drowning woman finally coming up for air. She was still half-afraid to believe it, but lying here in this house, she was filled with a sense of peace like none she had felt since she'd married Duane.

Don't rest too easy. I'm still out here looking for you. And when I find you—

She took another deep breath, chasing away the sound of Duane's voice. Like Scarlett O'Hara, she wouldn't think about tomorrow. For tonight, she was alive and safe, and that was more than she had hoped for.

At a tap at her door, she said, "Come in," thinking it would be Emma.

"I just wanted to check on you and make sure you have everything you need," Tanner said, peeking around the door.

"I'm fine." More than fine. "Thank you."

"I'll see you in the morning, then," he said. "I'll be just down the hall."

She couldn't help her surprise. Emma said that all the Chisholm sons had their own places now. "I thought—"

"I decided to stay here tonight." He shrugged, looking a little embarrassed. "In case you…"

"Needed anything," she finished for him, smiling.

"Good night, then," he said and closed the door.

Billie Rae lay in the bed still smiling, remembering what Emma had said. Trust Tanner. She did. She closed her eyes, dead tired, aching for sleep, but quickly opened them as Duane's image appeared as if waiting to taunt her in a nightmare.

Trust Tanner? Do you really think that cowboy or his whole damned family can save you?

She touched her diamond engagement ring in the darkness, the thick band of white gold next to it a reminder of who she was. Mrs. Duane Rasmussen, as if she could forget it.

Were you listening to that preacher? Till death do us part, Billie Rae. And that, sweetheart, is the way it is going to be, come hell or high water. You understand me, or am I going to have to refresh your memory?

As she spun the band in a circle, she thought about what Emma had said about fate. Did she believe in fate? Tanner had saved her tonight, he'd brought her to this house, to his stepmother, Emma, who had known instinctively what Billie Rae was going through.

Maybe fate had brought her together with this family tonight, but Billie Rae knew she had to run again come morning.

Slowly she took off the rings to set them on the bedside table. The diamond winked at her in the light of the star-filled night coming in through the sheer, billowing curtains.

You really think it's that easy to be rid of me?

She got up, stood in the middle of the room, unsure what to do with the rings. Her first impulse was to throw them away, but common sense won out. The rings were worth money and she was going to need some if she hoped to stay free of Duane. She put them in the pocket of her slacks.

As she climbed back into the bed and pulled the covers up, she felt stronger than she had since she married Duane. It had been fate that she'd met Tanner Chisholm and that he'd brought her to this house. She'd been ready to give up and go back to Duane, believing she had no choice.

But now she felt as if she could do this. She *would* do this. She had let Duane Rasmussen bully her for too long.

This time when she closed her eyes she pictured Tanner Chisholm's face. But she didn't kid herself that Duane wouldn't be nearby waiting to ruin her sleep.

Tanner woke to screaming. He bolted upright in bed, confused for a moment where he was. As everything came back in a rush, he swung his legs over the side of the bed, pulled on his jeans and ran barefoot down the hall.

His conscious mind told him it was impossible that Billie Rae's husband had found her here. That there was no way the man could be in the house. Worse, that he could have found the bedroom where she slept and—

He shoved open the door. Faint light shone through the sheer curtains at the large window next to her bed. A shaft of light from the hallway shot across the floor, making a path into the room. Tanner felt his heart break at the sounds coming from the bed. He rushed to Billie Rae.

She came out of the dream swinging her arms wildly. He didn't have to guess who she was trying to fight off.

"It's me, Billie Rae. Tanner. Tanner Chisholm."

Her eyes were wild with panic. She blinked at the sound of his voice and slowly focused on his face in the dim light before bursting into tears.

"You had a bad dream, but you're all right," he said as he sat down on the bed and pulled her into his arms. As he stroked her hair, he whispered, "It's all right. You're safe. You're all right."

She clung to him, sobbing, her breathing ragged. He could feel her damp cotton nightgown against his bare chest. She was shivering uncontrollably from the cold, from whatever horror still clung to her from the nightmare.

He held her close, continuing to stroke her hair and whisper words of comfort while all the time he wanted to kill the man who'd hurt this woman.

"Your nightgown is damp with sweat," he said after her breathing became more normal. Shadows played on the walls, the breeze whipped the sheer curtains and outside the window, a branch scraped against the house.

As he started to pull away, she cried, "Please, don't leave me."

"I'll be right back. I'm just going to get you something warm and dry to sleep in." He hurried to his room, rummaged through a drawer where he'd left some of his old clothing. He found a large soft-worn T-shirt and hurried back to Billie Rae's room.

She was sitting up in the bed, clutching the covers to her chest. He sat down on the edge of the bed next to her again. "Here, take off the nightgown and put this on." He turned his back. He heard her behind him struggling to get out of the damp nightgown and knew she was still trembling from her nightmare.

What had her husband done to her to make her so

frightened? He recalled what he'd heard the man say outside the door at the fairgrounds. But he'd thought them merely angry words. It wasn't until he'd seen the bruised area around Billie Rae's eye that he'd realized why she was so afraid of her husband.

Now he heard her pull on the T-shirt and lay back against the headboard.

He turned to look at her, jolted again by that strong emotion he'd felt under the lights of the exploding fireworks. Her face was lovely in the faint starlight. He couldn't imagine her ever looking more beautiful or desirable. Or vulnerable.

"Do you think you'll be able to sleep now?" he asked, starting to get to his feet, knowing what could happen if he stayed.

Her hand shot out and grabbed his wrist. He slowly sat back down.

There was a pleading in her brown eyes, along with flecks of gold.

"You want me to stay?"

She swallowed and he could see the battle going on inside her reflected in those big eyes. As he looked down, he saw that she'd taken off her wedding rings. There was a wide white mark where they had been.

He raised his gaze to her eyes again. "Slide over. I'll hold you until you fall asleep."

He saw relief, gratitude and something he didn't dare think about too long in those eyes.

She slid over and he lay down next to her. She moved closer as if desperately needing to know he was still there. He put his arms around her and drew her to him. She fit against him perfectly. He nestled his head against the pillow of her dark, luxurious hair and breathed in her scent. She smelled of soap and summer. He closed his eyes, feeling the steady beat of his heart in sync with hers.

"Thank you," she whispered. "I'm sorry that I—"

"Shh," he whispered. "I'll be here as long as you need me."

Billie Rae woke in the wee hours of the morning from a wonderful dream. She lay very still, keeping her eyes closed as she tried to get back into the dream. But it stayed just out of reach, slipping further away, and she finally opened her eyes.

She thought she was at home, so when the horrible dread she always woke with settled over her, she closed her eyes again, pleading silently for the dream and the man in it who had made her feel so loved. Like in the dream, the arms around her didn't hold her as tightly as Duane's did. Tanner held her gently, not as if he feared she would get away, but more like he wanted to keep her safe.

With a start, she came fully awake. She *had* gotten away from Duane.

Tanner shifted in his sleep and for a moment she feared he would let her go. She had never met anyone like him. She hadn't dated all that much before she met Duane. In college, she'd had to get good grades to keep her scholarships and still help her mother, who had by then been diagnosed with cancer, so she'd had no time for a social life.

She'd never been held this tenderly, never felt this safe and secure, never felt…the emotions she was experiencing at this moment—not even the first time she'd gone to bed with Duane. He'd been disappointed she wasn't a virgin and that had spoiled their lovemaking for both of them. After that, he was always much rougher as if he was punishing her for losing her virginity to the boy she'd dated all through high school and thought she was in love with.

Scott had been a nice boy, but just that—a boy. After high school, they'd gone to different colleges. They'd stayed in touch for a while, but had grown apart. Billie Rae had been thankful for that since she'd known by then that Scott wasn't the person she wanted to spend the rest of her life with.

She'd met Duane right after her mother died. Looking back, she saw that he had taken advantage of the vulnerable state she'd been in. She'd needed someone to lean on and Duane had made sure he was there, taking over her life, running it.

The problem was that when she no longer needed him in that way or wanted him to run her life, it was too late. By then, she'd needed and wanted something different from him. But Duane wasn't a giving, loving man. Nor was he going to let her go. He'd whisked her off to Vegas for a quickie marriage, selling it as romantic.

Hadn't she known that night, standing in a gaudy wedding chapel on the strip in front of a justice of the peace and his wife, that she was making a mistake? She remembered feeling as if she might faint. Duane had told her she just needed food and that he would feed her right after the ceremony.

Instead, they'd flown straight home as the sun came up and he'd sprung the news on her. They were moving to North Dakota.

Tanner shifted again in his sleep. Billie Rae held her

breath, afraid he would awaken and leave her. A part of the dream returned, startling her because there was no doubt that the man in it had been Tanner Chisholm.

She sensed him coming awake and turned in his arms to face him. It was still dark out. In the faint starlight, she could see his bare chest, a light sprinkling of dark hair that formed a V disappear into the waistband of his jeans.

She met his gaze and felt a bubble form in her chest. Her heart began to beat faster.

He started to pull away, but she cupped his jaw and he froze. "Billie Rae—"

Her thumb moved to his lips and she shook her head, her gaze holding his. She hadn't felt desire in a long time. It felt raw and powerful and urgent. Under normal circumstances she would have never acted upon it with a man she hardly knew.

She brushed a lock of dark hair back from Tanner's wonderful face, feeling as if she knew him soul-deep. Her fingers tingled at the touch. By the time the sun set tomorrow there was a good chance Duane would have caught up with her and, if not killed her, definitely hurt her.

There were some things she couldn't live with. Duane was one of them. The other was not acting on what she was feeling at this moment, knowing it might be her last day alive.

Slowly, she leaned toward Tanner and brushed a kiss over his lips. Her pulse thundered in her ears as he gently drew her to him. His kiss was light as the summer breeze coming through the window. His hands came up to cup her face in his warm, callused palms.

Desire burned through her veins like a runaway train

on a downhill track. As the kiss deepened, his fingers burrowed into her wild mane of hair. She shoved back the covers, needing to feel the warmth of his body against her, desperate for his human touch after months of flinching whenever Duane reached for her.

Tanner drew her to him, rolling over on his back and pulling her on top of him. "Are you sure about this?" he whispered.

She kissed him, sat up and then grabbing the hem of the large T-shirt, she pulled it up over her head and tossed it away. She heard Tanner moan, and then his hands were cupping her breasts, his thumbs gently teasing her nipples, which were already hard as marbles.

He drew her down again, kissing her softly. She rolled off him and wriggled out of her panties, desperately needing to feel his warm flesh against hers. She heard him slip out of his jeans and then he was pulling her into his arms. He brushed a tendril of hair back from her cheek.

Their eyes locked as he slowly and sweetly began to make love to her.

Chapter 3

Duane woke in his car, cramped and out of sorts. He couldn't believe he'd had to spend the entire night in a fairgrounds parking lot in the middle of nowhere.

As he climbed out, he looked into the front seat of his father's classic pickup, expecting to see Billie Rae curled up there. He'd been so sure she would return, probably with some cowboy with a can of gas for the pickup and some romantic ideas for her.

But he hadn't heard a sound all night and the pickup front seat was empty. No Billie Rae. With a curse, Duane realized he was going to have to call his boss and ask for some time off.

As for his wife, he didn't know what to do. First, he supposed, he would search for her himself. Someone had to have seen her. If that failed… Well, he might have to contact a couple of associates he'd met through his work. The nice thing about his job was that he met people who could and would do things for him that he'd rather not do himself. A little pressure here, a little pressure there, and people knew better than to say no to him.

He pulled out his cell phone, swearing under his breath as he punched in the number and asked for his boss. The last thing he'd do was admit the truth. He didn't want anyone to know what the bitch had done, how she'd made him look like a fool, let alone that he couldn't handle his own wife. He'd never live it down if his buddies found out about this. Other men lost respect for a man whose wife ran off on him.

No, he would take care of this himself and no one back home would be the wiser. That is, as long as he found Billie Rae fast. And one way or the other, he'd have to convince her never to pull something like this again. Either that or his lovely wife would end up dead, a terrible accident that would leave him a grieving widower—and free to find him a wife who knew her place.

He came up with a lame excuse, but his boss seemed to buy it. As he hung up, he told himself it was now time to deal with the mess Billie Rae had made. Walking around to the driver's side, Duane unlocked the pickup with his key and stared into it for a long moment, thinking about Billie Rae taking it. The truck had been his father's, purchased new almost fifty years before. His old man had loved this pickup and cared for it like a baby.

Hell, Duane had never even gotten to drive it until the old man died. His mother had been the one to give it to him—had his father known he was going to fall over dead with a heart attack he would have made other arrangements for his beloved classic pickup.

But Duane's mother hated the truck and resented the

time and money and care the old man had put into it. She'd given it to Duane out of spite, knowing his father was now rolling over in his grave to think that his son had the truck. Which made Duane even angrier that Billie Rae had the impudence to take it. The woman must be crazy. No one drove this pickup but him.

As he slid behind the wheel, he saw that she'd left the key in the ignition and swore. Her lack of respect… He couldn't wait to get his hands on her.

He reached to turn the key and saw that it was the spare he kept locked up. She'd broken into his desk? He hadn't even been aware she knew where he kept the spare key.

Duane felt that strange chill creep over him again. Billie Rae had been watching him, paying more attention than he'd thought.

He turned the key. The engine refused to turn over. That's when he saw the gas gauge. She'd run out of gas. That's why she'd stopped here.

The tap on his side window startled him. For an instant, he'd expected to see Billie Rae standing there instead of some old guy in a plaid shirt and a baseball cap.

"Trouble getting her started?" the old man asked.

Duane realized the man must be the caretaker in charge of the fairgrounds. He hadn't heard him drive up. Duane climbed out, pocketing the truck key. "The wife. She didn't check the gas gauge before she headed to the rodeo."

The old man laughed and shook his head. "I'm surprised you let her drive this. A 1962 Chevy Fleetside Shortbed with a Vortec 350, right?"

Duane nodded as he watched the caretaker run his

hand over the hood. His old man had to be turning flips in his casket. He'd never let anyone touch his truck.

"You don't happen to have a few gallons of gas I could buy from you to get her into town, do you?" Duane asked.

"I haven't seen her around town," the man said frowning, still talking about the pickup. "You new to Whitehorse?"

So Whitehorse must be the closest town. "You could say that. If I had a hose, I could siphon some gas out of my car," Duane said impatiently.

"No need for that. I keep some extra gas for the lawnmower."

Duane followed the man back to a shed, waited while he unlocked the padlock on the door and went inside, returning with a small gas can that felt about half full.

"I'll bring this right back," he said, hoping the man wouldn't come with him. He hurried off, returning shortly, and handed the man the gas can and a twenty-dollar bill. "Thanks for your help." He had a thought. "Hey, is there any chance I could leave the pickup in one of your barns out here. My wife is tied up and I need to get back to her. I can't come back to get the truck for a while."

"No problem. You can just pull it in that one," the old man said pointing at the closest barn. "It will be plenty safe there until you can pick her up."

"Great," he started to turn away telling himself he had no choice since he couldn't drive two vehicles and who knew when he'd find Billie Rae. Nor did he want anyone else driving the truck.

"You're going to have to teach your wife to watch

that gas gauge," the old man called after him with a chuckle.

He was going to have to teach his wife a lot of things when he found her.

"Good morning," Billie Rae said shyly from the kitchen doorway.

Tanner looked up. He'd been sitting at the kitchen table having a cup of coffee with Emma, who'd been chastising him.

He knew she was right. He'd fallen for a woman who was not just married—but in a very vulnerable state right now. He *should* have known better than to get more involved with her for not just his sake but hers as well.

When he met her gaze now, he was afraid he would see regret in her eyes. The morning light brought out the gold flecks in those eyes. With relief, he saw that they were free of regret. Their eyes locked and, after a moment, a slight flush came to her cheeks before she looked away.

They'd made love and fallen back to sleep in each other's arms. When he'd awakened this morning, she'd looked so beautiful and so serene lying there, he hadn't wanted to wake her.

He looked down into his coffee cup now, checking his expression as he felt Emma's watchful gaze on him. She'd already given him hell, telling him that she couldn't bear to see him get his heart broken and Billie Rae wasn't ready for another relationship.

"Sleep well?" Emma asked smiling as she handed Billie Rae a mug of coffee.

"Yes, thank you," Billie Rae said dropping her gaze

and blushing as she took the mug and sat down in a chair across from Tanner.

Tanner smiled across the table at her. She looked a hundred percent better than she had last night at the rodeo. There was no longer that deer-in-the-headlights look in her eyes. Her long dark hair was still damp from her shower. He caught a whiff of her now too-familiar scent. She smelled heavenly. He couldn't help but think about their lovemaking and wish he had awakened her this morning.

Emma refilled his coffee cup, giving him another of her knowing looks. This one held a warning he couldn't ignore. He knew making love with Billie Rae shouldn't have happened. Legally, she was a married woman. But to his way of thinking, Duane had broken the vows, destroying that fragile thing that made a marriage.

He knew Emma was worried about him getting too close to Billie Rae and getting his heart broken. But he wondered if it wasn't already too late. Damned if he would ever regret what had happened between them, no matter what today brought. He didn't kid himself. He knew that Duane was still out there looking for Billie Rae—and that she knew it as well. Whatever was going to transpire between them, it wasn't over yet.

Emma kept up a cheerful chatter as she and the cook, Celeste, served homemade pancakes with huckleberry syrup. Tanner watched Billie Rae put away a dozen of the silver-dollar-sized cakes, smiling to himself. A good appetite was a sure sign that she was bouncing back.

"She doesn't want to hear any of this," Tanner said after Emma told a particularly funny story she'd heard about him as a boy. Billie Rae was smiling, looking relaxed, looking as if she belonged in this kitchen.

"I wish you'd gotten a chance to meet my husband Hoyt," Emma was saying. "He could tell you some stories about his boys. But Hoyt's off digging fence post holes with Tanner's brothers."

Hoyt hadn't been home last night when Tanner and Marshall returned from the rodeo with Billie Rae. Tanner's father, according to Emma, had been at a ranchers' association meeting about some rustlers operating across the border in Wyoming.

It was odd, though, that Hoyt had already taken off so early this morning. Tanner hadn't even seen him before he left. His father had been putting in long hours recently, almost as if avoiding home.

He frowned at the thought and hoped everything was all right between his father and Emma. He and his brothers hadn't been happy when their father had sprung a new wife on them. But once they'd been around Emma for five minutes, they too had fallen in love with her.

Tanner was told she was nothing like Hoyt's other wives. He'd been too young to remember Laura, his father's first wife. She'd drowned in a boating accident. Tasha, his father's second wife, Tanner had heard was killed by a runaway horse.

A third wife, Krystal, had disappeared shortly after Hoyt had brought her to the ranch. Tanner vaguely remembered her. After all that tragedy, his father had gone years without a woman in his life.

Then, out of the blue, he'd come home with Emma. She was older, closer to Hoyt's age, more full-figured, redheaded and had a fiery temper that had earned her respect from all of the men in the family. She'd changed things around here, but in a good way. And Tanner had never seen his father happier. Until recently, when he seemed to be avoiding being home.

"What would you like to do first this morning?" he asked Billie Rae after breakfast.

"Is there a pawnshop or jewelry store in White-horse?"

Tanner shook his head. "But there are several in Havre. I'd be happy to drive you."

"No, I couldn't possibly ask you—"

"You didn't ask. I'm volunteering, unless you need to go back to the fairgrounds for your vehicle?"

"The pickup I was driving isn't mine."

"Then I guess we don't need to worry about it."

She nodded but he saw the dark cloud move over her eyes. She had a lot to worry about. They both did. She was worried about Duane, and Tanner was worried that this woman who had come crashing into his life would leave it just as suddenly.

"It's a nice drive to Havre," he said. "We'll have lunch and shop for whatever you need. I could use the day off, but don't tell my stepmother."

Emma swatted him as she passed.

Billie Rae nodded, tears in her eyes. "You have all been so kind. I really wish—"

"No regrets." Emma stopped next to her chair to lay a hand on her shoulder. "No tears, either, not on such a beautiful morning," she said. "You two best get goin'. Make sure Billie Rae gets whatever she needs in Havre." Emma pressed a wad of cash into Tanner's hand along with another silent warning look.

He was to make sure nothing happened to Billie Rae and that he didn't make things worse for her—as if he hadn't already.

"We'll be fine," he told his stepmother. He had a shotgun in his pickup, and this morning he'd put a pistol under the seat. He wasn't taking any chances—he'd already done that last night.

Sheriff McCall Crawford looked up to find a young woman standing in front of her desk.

"There wasn't anyone out front," the teenager said, looking nervous. She was slightly built, though tall and regal in appearance. Her straight shoulder-length hair was white blond, her eyes a clear, disarming blue. She had a pretty face that belied how young she really was, since on closer inspection McCall realized she was no more than a girl, probably not even out of high school.

"Can I help you?" McCall asked the girl.

"*You're* the sheriff?" She glanced at the open door and the name stenciled on it. "I thought the sheriff's name was Winchester?"

"I recently got married." It had been more than a year and a half, but McCall was wondering why she'd bothered to change her name, since everyone in town still called her Sheriff Winchester. "Why don't you have a seat and tell me what seems to be the problem."

"It's my aunt, Aggie Wells," the girl said as she pulled up one of the orange plastic chairs across from McCall's desk and sat down. "She's missing."

"How long has she been missing?"

"Several weeks now."

Several weeks? "Why have you waited this long to report her missing, Miss…? I'm sorry, I didn't catch your name."

"Cindy Ross. My aunt is gone a lot with her job. But this time she didn't call or come home."

"Where is home?"

"Phoenix, Arizona. That's where I live with my father."

"And your aunt?"

"She stays with us when she's in town. Like I said, she travels a lot but she calls me every few days from wherever she is and always calls on Sunday."

"So you haven't heard from her since…"

"The second week of May, that Sunday. She called to say she would be flying home that afternoon."

"Called from…?"

"Here. Whitehorse. She said she was driving to Billings, leaving her rental car and would be coming in on the last flight. I was to pick her up but she wasn't on the plane."

"And there has been no word?"

"No. My dad said something must have come up with her job." The girl looked down in her lap. "But when I called her office, they said she'd been fired a long time ago." She looked up, tears in her eyes. "I'm afraid something has happened to her."

"What does your father think?" The girl met her gaze, but didn't respond. "He doesn't know you're here, does he?"

"He says Aggie can take care of herself and that she'll turn up. But I have a bad feeling…"

McCall didn't like the sound of any of this. She picked up her pen. "Your aunt's name is Aggie Wells?"

"Agatha, but she's always gone by Aggie. She's an insurance investigator. That is, she was."

"What was she doing in Whitehorse?"

"She said she was trying to prove that some man murdered all three of his wives."

McCall's head shot up from taking notes.

The girl nodded knowingly. "I thought you might know about the cases. The man's name is Hoyt Chisholm. Aggie told me that he killed his first three wives and now he has married again. Her last appointment was with him and his new wife. She said they'd invited her out to their house for supper."

McCall was unable to hide her surprise. Everyone in town knew about the deaths of Hoyt's first two wives, and the disappearance of the third one.

The recent scuttlebutt throughout the county was about his new wife. McCall had heard that some residents were taking odds over at Whitehorse Café, betting how long this wife would be alive.

"My aunt told me that if anything happened to her, I was to make sure that Hoyt Chisholm didn't get away with another murder." The girl burst into tears. "I know he killed her."

Billie Rae found herself enjoying more than the ride to Havre. Tanner pointed out landmarks and told her stories. She knew he was trying to keep her entertained, to distract her from thinking about her life and Duane.

But the one thing she couldn't stop thinking about, sitting this close to Tanner, was last night. He had been so tender, so heartbreakingly sweet. She had cried after they'd made love.

"What is it?" Tanner had asked, sounding stricken.

How could she tell him that she felt she'd ruined her life by marrying Duane? That she'd lost her chance to be with someone like Tanner. Duane was going to kill her. Or at the very least, have her living in fear and on the run the rest of her life.

She could never be with Tanner again. As it was, she feared she had already put him and his family in danger.

"I forgot what happiness feels like," she had finally choked out. He'd held her and she'd spooned against him, relishing the warmth of his body and the way this man made her feel, dreading when the sun would come up and she would have to leave him.

"That's the town of Wagner down there," Tanner said now, pointing at the few buildings left. It appeared most of the towns along the Hi-Line were shrinking, some little more than a sign and a couple of old buildings.

"Butch Cassidy and the Sundance Kid held up a train not far from here," he said. "It was allegedly their last robbery before they headed to South America."

The day had dawned clear blue, sunny and warm. The land was a brilliant spring-green and, with the windows down, the air blowing in smelled of summer. It was the kind of day she remembered from when she was a girl and still had her illusions about life.

Billie Rae breathed in the sweet scents, catching a hint of Tanner's masculine one. When she was with him, she felt her strength coming back. Duane had done his best to beat it out of her. She was almost surprised that she could feel like her old self. But Tanner reminded her of who she'd been. Who she could be again—except for Duane who was determined to kill every ounce of independence in her.

She tried not to think about where he was or what he was doing. She knew he would be furious wherever he was. Just as she knew he would be frantically looking for her and wouldn't stop until he found her.

She shuddered at the thought.

"Warm enough?" Tanner asked, noticing.

"Someone just walked over my grave." She regretted the quick retort immediately. "You know what I mean."

"I do," he said and quickly pointed out an old Spanish mission on the road ahead. She was glad he didn't mention Duane, but neither of them had forgotten about him, she knew. She'd caught Tanner checking the rearview mirror occasionally—just as she had been doing in the side mirror.

Duane would not give up. She just had to make sure he never found her—or learned that Tanner Chisholm had been the one who'd saved her last night.

Hopefully Duane would also never learn about this trip to Havre. She hated involving Tanner Chisholm in the mess she'd made of her life any more than she already had. But she needed to sell the rings. Hopefully she could get enough to buy an old car and enough gas to put a whole lot more distance between herself and Duane before she found a job.

"You're going to have to deal with him, you know," Tanner said as if realizing she hadn't been listening about the old mission they'd just passed.

Billie Rae nodded. "I'm sorry. I just can't help thinking about him."

"How long have you been married?"

"Six months. We met in Oklahoma, where I was teaching kindergarten. Right after we eloped, Duane sprung it on me that he'd gotten a job in Williston, North Dakota, and we had to move at once. I didn't even get to finish the school year."

"You had friends in Oklahoma?"

She nodded. "I lost track of them once we got to North Dakota. Duane made sure of that. It's hard to accept that I'm the classic case. The abused wife. But

Duane wasn't like this when we were dating. He was…" She let her voice trail off. "That's not true. The signs were there. He was controlling but I wanted to believe it was because he cared and just wanted what was best for me, like he said." She laughed at that. "I was such a fool."

"We've all been fools," Tanner said. "Myself included. But you realized your mistake and got away from him."

If only it were that simple.

"You don't know my husb… Duane," she said. She couldn't bear to call him her husband anymore. She hadn't only left him, hadn't merely taken off her wedding rings. In her heart she was no longer Duane Rasmussen's wife, and last night with Tanner she'd felt like a free woman, even though she'd only been kidding herself.

Under the law, she was still Duane Rasmussen's wife. Only technically, she thought, because there was no love in her heart for him. When had she stopped loving him? She didn't know. Just as she didn't know when she'd begun to hate him.

"He's…dangerous," she said, thinking that was putting it mildly.

Tanner let out a dismissive sound. "Only to a woman who can't fight back."

She shook her head. "He carries a gun, he kills people." And when he caught her, she wouldn't be the first person he killed in a rage. "Duane's a cop."

Chapter 4

It hadn't taken long for Sheriff McCall Crawford to verify what Cindy Ross had told her. Agatha "Aggie" Wells hadn't used her plane ticket—nor had she returned her rental car—a white SUV. Aggie had also been fired from the insurance company seven years ago.

"Can I be honest with you, Sheriff?" Wells's supervisor asked.

"Please."

"Aggie was one of our best. She was relentless. But something happened with this Chisholm case. Once she found out another of his other wives had died and a third had disappeared, she became obsessed. I'm afraid that for her the case became almost…well, personal."

"Personal in what way?"

The supervisor cleared his throat. "I know this is going to sound crazy, but at one point I thought she had fallen in love with Hoyt Chisholm. See what I mean? Crazy, huh? It made no sense. If she really believed he'd killed his first two wives for the insurance money, and possibly the third wife who disappeared, then she wouldn't fall for the guy, right?"

McCall knew that crazier things had happened.

"Aggie just got so worked up when she talked about him, and even when she was pulled off the case, she continued to work on it in her spare time. Now, that's… scary."

Yes, McCall thought. And possibly dangerous.

"I take it she was never able to find any evidence that Mr. Chisholm had anything to do with the deaths or disappearance of his wives?" she asked.

"No evidence at all. Maybe that's what drove her so crazy. I finally had to let her go. May I ask why you're inquiring about her?"

"Apparently she hasn't given up on proving that Mr. Chisholm's guilty," McCall said. "She was in White-horse a couple of weeks ago and she met with the Chisholms."

"Chisholms?"

"Mr. Chisholm has remarried." McCall heard the heavy silence on the other end of the line and felt her concern growing.

"I have to tell you, I am very disturbed she is still apparently looking into this, and now with a new wife…"

"If you know something—"

"I probably shouldn't have said as much as I have," the supervisor said, clearly backpedaling. "Like I said, it was just a feeling. Aggie took her job very seriously. Quite frankly, I think she might…no, never mind."

"If there is something else you need to tell me, please

do. It's important that I know everything. The reason I called you is because Aggie Wells has disappeared. She had called her niece to pick her up at the airport the day after she had dinner with the Chisholms, but never arrived. Nor has she used her plane ticket or returned her rental car."

"Let me guess. Aggie told her niece that if anything happened to her to contact law enforcement because Hoyt Chisholm would have killed her, right?"

"Yes, as a matter of fact."

"She insisted the same memo be put in her employee file here," the supervisor said. "We all thought she was just being paranoid, but what if Aggie was right? What if Hoyt Chisholm killed his three other wives and now plans to kill the fourth one as well?"

The rings brought less money than Billie Rae had hoped.

"The diamond is flawed," one jeweler told her.

She had argued that Duane had told her how much he paid.

"I'm sorry but there isn't any way your husband paid that kind of money for this," the last pawnbroker said handing back the ring.

Tanner had driven her to all of the jewelry stores and pawnshops in town. He had waited in his pickup while she'd gone inside, as she'd asked him to. For that she was thankful because the experience had been humiliating. They'd all told her the same thing.

Duane had lied about what he'd spent on the rings. She realized he'd probably picked them up from a pawnshop to begin with or gotten them from one of the criminal types he loved to intimidate. Duane enjoyed the benefits that came with being a cop—those being throwing his weight around and flashing his badge to get what he wanted.

"What will you give me for the rings?" she asked the owner of the last place in town. When he told her, she had nodded, fighting tears of both discouragement and anger. Duane had lied to her from day one.

She knew that shouldn't have come as a surprise, the way their married life had turned out. But by the time she pocketed the small amount of cash she could get for the rings, she no longer had any illusions about the man she'd married.

"You all right?" Tanner asked as she slid into the truck seat next to him.

She gave him the best smile she could muster.

He laughed. "Stupid question. Let's get some lunch. There's a great Chinese food place here in the mall. You like Chinese?"

She knew she shouldn't spend any more time with him. While she couldn't imagine how Duane could have somehow followed them to Havre, she knew the longer she was around Tanner, the more she was putting him in danger.

"You have to eat," he said as if seeing her hesitation.

She nodded, hating the thought of the time that would come when she would have to tell him goodbye. "And then can we see if we can find me a used vehicle?" she asked as he started the truck and pulled out into the traffic.

He glanced over at her, but said nothing.

They ate at the Chinese buffet, finishing up with the fried donuts. Tanner was amusing during their lunch, telling stories about growing up on the ranch with five brothers.

Billie Rae looked around the restaurant. It had been so long since she'd felt normal. Sitting across from Tanner, she was able to eat without her stomach knotting up in fear that she would say the wrong thing and ruin it. With Duane she was seldom able to finish a meal without him getting upset and upsetting her in return.

"I saw you looking at that guy over there," Duane would say under his breath.

"What guy? Duane—"

"If you do it again, I'm going to go over there and punch him in the face, you understand?"

Tears welled in her eyes now at the memory of those horrible nights they would leave a restaurant, her in tears and Duane becoming more worked up by the minute. Billie Rae had known what was going to happen long before they got home, and she was never wrong.

Tanner reached across the table and put his hand over hers. "Billie Rae?"

She swallowed and wiped at her eyes with her free hand. "I'm sorry."

"He can't find you here. He has no idea where you are."

She nodded. Tanner didn't remove his hand. She didn't, either. She loved the feel of his large, callused hands. In his long fingers she felt a wonderful strength that seemed to flow into her. She thought of those hands exploring her naked body last night and remembered that feeling of both pleasure and sadness.

Billie Rae knew she would forever ache for his touch. As she looked across the table at this wonderful cowboy, her regret was that she would never see him again after today, let alone make love with him again. It was a regret she thought she couldn't bear to live with.

She realized Tanner was waiting for her to say more. He actually wanted to hear what she was feeling? "I was just thinking how nice this is, having lunch with you."

"I was thinking the same thing," he said and squeezed her hand gently before letting go.

She felt that well of happiness that she'd experienced last night after they made love. She was happy. The word almost seemed alien to her because she hadn't let herself admit how unhappy she'd been for so long.

Billie Rae had gone into marriage believing it really was until death do you part. She just hadn't known that those words had a totally different meaning for the man she married.

"I love hearing the stories about you growing up on the ranch," she said.

"Where did you grow up?"

She told him about being an only child, her father dying when he was young and her mother raising her in a small house in Oklahoma City.

"My life was very dull compared to yours," she said. "I wish I'd had brothers who tried to talk me into jumping off the barn roof."

"Sure you do," he said with a laugh.

"So you're all adopted?" She loved listening to him talk about his big family. Billie Rae had always dreamed of a large family as a girl. She wanted the noise, the activity, the feeling at night of all of them under the same roof.

"Yep, Dad likes kids. He adopted three when his first wife was alive. When three more kids needed a home, he was right there to take us. He would have taken more if he'd had better luck with wives." Tanner seemed to realize what he'd said. He stammered, "What I meant was—"

"It's all right."

"No, you need to understand. Two of his wives died. Another…disappeared. Emma, well, he married her recently after being alone for years. He's had a rough time of it. But I've never seen him happier."

"You're trying to tell me there is life after marriage?"

"Yep. And there is no shame in getting it wrong— and getting out."

She smiled across the table at him. He had no idea how impossible Duane would make that. There was only one way she feared she would be leaving Duane and that, as he told her many times, would be in a body bag.

"Emma is wonderful," she said, refusing to let Duane ruin this lunch. "I'm happy for your father. If he is anything like you…" Billie Rae ducked her head, embarrassed because she'd again thought of lying in his arms last night. But talking to Tanner was so easy. She could be honest with him without fear that what she said would set him off.

This closeness she felt with this man both warmed— and frightened her. It was too tempting to take him up on his offer to stay at the ranch and try to handle the Duane problem through legal channels.

But Billie Rae had already tried that. Tanner didn't know what Duane was capable of. She did.

After lunch, they stopped at one of the few used car lots in town and Billie Rae realized quickly that she wasn't going to get much of a vehicle and still have gas money to leave town.

"You can't run far enough, if that's what you're thinking," Tanner said as they walked around the last lot. "Sometimes you have to draw a line in the sand and fight. Come back to the ranch with me. I'll help you. You'll be safe. You shouldn't have to do this alone. I promise. I won't let anything happen to you."

He reached over and took her hand, squeezing it gently, and she was reminded of last night when he had pulled her through the rodeo crowd and kept Duane from catching up to them.

Tanner pulled her to a stop and turned her to face him. "There is something I have to tell you. Last night when I saw you," he said as if he too had been remembering when they'd met. "You're going to think I'm crazy, but it was love at first sight. It wasn't that I saw this beautiful woman and fell in love. I felt this strong connection as if you were some missing part of me, and when I saw you it was like this jolt…" He stopped and looked embarrassed.

She cupped his strong jaw with her free hand and smiled as she looked into his eyes. "I don't think you're crazy. I felt it too."

"Then come back with me—"

"I can't. If you knew Duane you would understand. I have to go. I have no choice." Her heart ached at the thought of never seeing him again. But if she wanted to protect him, she *had* to leave. Whatever had happened between them, she couldn't put Tanner and his family in jeopardy any more than she already had because of her bad decision to marry Duane and then make a wild run across the Hi-Line.

"At least think about it?"

She'd nodded, but she knew she couldn't change her mind—even as much as she wanted to.

At the cheapest car lot, Billie Rae bought a small

beat-up old car that seemed to run fine and got good gas mileage. She paid cash but the owner of the lot still needed her to fill out paperwork—all traceable when you have a cop on your tail.

"I'm going to need some identification," he said as he pushed the papers across the desk toward her. "Your driver's license," he said when she gave him what he took for a blank look. "I need to make a copy of it."

"I lost my purse," she said.

"Then I can't sell you the car until I have—"

"Put the car in my name," Tanner said and placed a hand on Billie Rae's shoulder before she could stop him. "It's better that way," he said to her after the owner had gone to make copies of Tanner's driver's license. "Duane won't know, right?"

She nodded numbly, thinking this would make what she had to do all that more difficult. Tanner had saved her last night in more ways than she wanted to admit and now here he was saving a woman he didn't really know again.

Billie Rae said as much to him and he laughed.

"I feel as if I've always known you," he said, and she thought he might be right. Sometimes she caught him looking at her as if he could see into her soul.

They *had* connected last night at the rodeo. She'd felt it and yet even now she denied the feelings for so many reasons. How could she trust her emotions right now? She couldn't. Not to mention she was on the run from her husband.

But Billie Rae knew the real reason she had to ignore what she was feeling was because it scared her. Tanner was the man she'd dreamed of marrying. She'd loved being on the ranch with his family. It only made her feel worse about marrying Duane. She'd ruined her life and now the best she felt she could expect was to keep her husband from killing her.

"I can't go back with you to the ranch," she told Tanner as they walked out to the car she'd bought. "I won't put your family in any more danger than I already have. I got myself into this. I'll get myself out."

"Billie Rae—"

She put a finger to his lips and felt a frisson of pleasure course through her from just touching those lips. She shook her head, afraid of what she might say. Or worse, do. If only she could just lose herself in him again. To be in his arms…

He leaned in and kissed her, and it took all of her strength not to throw her arms around his neck and let him take her back to the ranch, back to a life she had only dreamed possible, where she was safe and loved.

"I wish there was something I could say or do to keep you from doing this," he said as he drew back. "But I wouldn't force you even if I could. If you ever need me, though…"

Billie Rae had to fight tears. "Thank you for everything."

He pulled her to him, hugging her quickly as he whispered, "Be safe, Billie Rae." He stepped back. "Chisholm ranch will always be here if you're ever passing through again."

She realized then that he'd known she wouldn't be going back to the ranch with him. As she drove away, she tried not to look back. When she did, though, she saw Tanner standing beside the ranch truck watching her.

The look on his face seemed to say he knew there was little chance he would see her again. At least not alive.

Chapter 5

Emma Chisholm looked up to see the sheriff's SUV pull into the yard. At first she thought it was her stepson Colton's fiancée, Deputy Halley Robinson, stopping by, but the woman who climbed out wasn't familiar.

Going to the front door, she pushed open the screen and stepped out onto the porch. She hadn't been locking the doors for almost a week now—not since she finally felt confident Aggie Wells wouldn't be coming back.

Emma had just started feeling safe again. She'd noticed that Hoyt, though, was keeping his distance as if he really believed there was a curse on him and that Emma was doomed to die as well.

She couldn't bear the thought that he might regret marrying her. They'd been so happy. She thought of Hoyt tempting her up into the hayloft of the barn and their lovemaking. They'd proven that age didn't matter when it came to love and desire. Emma ached for her husband and had been determined to be patient with him. Once he realized that Aggie Wells was gone and that there was no stupid curse…or worse, that she might think for a moment he had anything to do with his wives' deaths…

Now, though, Emma felt her heart drop as she saw that the woman was the local sheriff. She'd heard that Whitehorse had a woman sheriff, but she hadn't heard how young and beautiful she was.

"Good afternoon, Sheriff," she said brightly as the woman flashed her credentials.

"I'm Sheriff McCall Crawford. You must be Emma."

"I am." Emma took her hand, amused by the surprise she'd seen on the young woman's face. Apparently the sheriff had been expecting Hoyt's new wife to be a trophy wife—not a short, plump redhead.

"I'd like to talk to you. Is your husband home?"

"No." Emma felt the first inkling of real anxiety. "Is something wrong?"

"I just need to ask you a few questions. When do you expect Mr. Chisholm to return?"

"He's working on the other side of the ranch. I don't expect him until late tonight. You know summer, with all this daylight, the men work late."

Emma realized she was doing too much explaining, giving away just how nervous she was. "Won't you come in, Sheriff? As they say, coffee is always on at any decent rancher's house. Why don't you join me for a cup back in the kitchen?"

The sheriff followed her to the kitchen and took a seat at the table while Emma set about getting the coffee and dishing up some of her freshly baked oatmeal cake that was still warm.

"Mrs. Chisholm—"

"Please, call me Emma," she said as she placed a brimming mug of coffee and a plate of warm cake in front of the sheriff. "Cream, Sheriff?"

"No, thank you."

Emma sat down across the table from the sheriff and, lifting her mug of coffee, studied the woman through the steam as she tried to still her raging nerves. "Something tells me this isn't a social call."

"Actually, I'm looking for Aggie Wells."

She knew the sheriff was also looking for a reaction and hoped to give her one she wasn't expecting. "A delightful woman. We had her to supper a couple of weeks ago."

"I heard that."

"Oh? Aggie told you, then." So the woman hadn't left town as Emma had hoped. Then why hadn't they heard from her? Because Aggie had been waiting until she had enough evidence to involve the sheriff?

"No, actually, her niece mentioned it. Apparently Ms. Wells is missing."

Emma put down her mug very carefully. The feeling of finally being safe evaporated like sun-kissed dew on the morning grass. "I'm sorry to hear that."

"I was hoping you might have heard from her."

"No, but then I didn't expect to."

McCall raised a brow. "Your business was completed with Ms. Wells?"

Emma laughed and helped herself to the cake. "I wouldn't say we had business together. I'm sure you know that Aggie Wells used to work for an insurance company. Apparently once she started a case, she had a hard time quitting until she was completely satisfied."

"And was she finally satisfied?" the sheriff asked.

"I think she was." Emma took a bite of the cake, closed her eyes and let it melt in her mouth. "Mmm." She opened her eyes and chuckled. "Sorry, but I do love this cake when it is still warm."

"You baked it?" McCall asked, glancing around the kitchen. "You don't have help?"

"Oh, yes, but I can't stay out of the kitchen. I love to cook and bake. It's a flaw." She felt the sheriff studying her, no doubt wondering about her other flaws. "The cook won't come in until later. It's the housekeeper's day off."

"When was the last time you saw Aggie Wells?"

"The night she came here for supper," Emma said, her heart in her throat. The sheriff wouldn't be here unless something had happened to Aggie. She couldn't help but think about her first reaction to the woman. She'd thought they could have been friends under other circumstances.

"Did she say where she was going when she left your house?"

"No. But since we didn't hear from her again, we assumed she'd left town."

"Do you know where Ms. Wells was staying?"

"No. I met her for a drink, though, out at Sleeping Buffalo." Emma could see that the sheriff was taken aback by how forthcoming she was being.

"Did anyone see you there together?"

She studied the sheriff for a moment, wondering if she didn't believe her—or if she was just looking for someone who might know how to find Aggie Wells.

"Just the bartender. A female." She described the woman, and the sheriff nodded as if she knew her.

"Mind if I ask what you talked about?"

"She informed me of her suspicions concerning my husband."

McCall had been in the middle of sipping her coffee but quickly put it down. "You weren't aware of your husband's past before then?"

"No, actually. I hadn't cared. I knew he'd been married and that he'd lost several wives. I love my husband, Sheriff. I trust him and I know he couldn't kill anyone."

McCall had just gotten back to her office and was sitting at her desk when she looked up to find a large man standing in her doorway.

His expression quickly changed from a slight frown to a smile as she greeted him.

"Sheriff Crawford," he said, stepping forward to extend his hand. His handshake was a little too firm, his smile a little too bright.

McCall instantly didn't trust him.

"My name is Officer Duane Rasmussen." He flashed his badge.

"May I see that?" she asked as he started to put it away. She could tell he didn't like being questioned even for something like this as he slowly handed her his shield.

She studied it and handed it back. "What brings a police officer from Williston, North Dakota, to Whitehorse, Montana?"

"It's a delicate matter," the cop said as he closed the door, pulled out a chair and sat down without being invited to. He leaned toward her, the smile this time self-deprecating.

He was good looking in the way a lot of ex high school football players are. She took him for a college linebacker who'd managed to stay in good shape, probably through hours in a gym.

"I'm looking for someone," he said.

She waited, knowing that if this was a professional investigation he would have come through normal channels and she would already be aware of the suspect through a bulletin.

This cop was off the leash.

"This is embarrassing," he said and did his best to look bashful. "It's my wife. She's not well. I'm worried about her. She took off without even her purse."

"What makes you think she's in Whitehorse?"

"I found my pickup at the fairgrounds where she'd run out of gas."

McCall lifted a brow. "She didn't take her own car?"

Some of his smooth veneer fell away. "She doesn't have her own car. She doesn't like to drive."

Alarms were going off all over the place for McCall. She didn't like this guy, was suspicious of his entire story and could see that he knew it.

"I was just hoping that you might have heard something that would help me find her," he said, looking as if he wished he hadn't come by to talk to her.

"What is your wife's name?"

"Billie Rae Rasmussen. But she could be going by her maiden name, Johnson."

McCall nodded and took down the cop's name and his wife's. "I'm sorry. I haven't heard anything, but I will keep an eye out for your wife. I'm surprised, if you're that worried about her, that you haven't put out an APB on her."

"I was hoping that wouldn't be necessary since I don't want to upset her. I just want to get her help. We've been trying to have a baby. I'm afraid she went a little berserk after this last disappointment."

"I'll need a description of your wife."

He pulled her picture from his shirt pocket.

McCall looked at the studio shot of the woman standing next to the man sitting across from her. The woman was small and pretty with a wild mane of dark curly hair and warm brown eyes. The sheriff asked for a more detailed description, jotted it down and handed the photo back.

"You have a number I can reach you?" McCall asked.

He gave her his cell phone number. "My wife is in a very…fragile state. I hate the thought of her out there somewhere…"

McCall nodded, wondering about the pretty dark-haired young woman in the photograph he'd shown her. There'd been something in the woman's eyes….

He rose to his feet. She could tell he hadn't got whatever he'd come here for and doubted it was information about his wife. "Thanks for your time, Sheriff." He said the last word with just enough emphasis to let her know what he thought of a woman sheriff.

She watched him leave, worried about his wife. McCall had come across his type before. But in this one, she sensed fury below the surface. This was a dangerous man, and she suspected the wife knew it and that's why she'd run.

After Officer Duane Rasmussen left her office, Mc-

Call told her deputies to be on the lookout for Billie Rae Johnson Rasmussen.

Now she had two missing women—one of them the wife of a cop, the other an obsessed insurance investigator after a man she believed had committed three murders.

McCall was thinking about that when her phone rang. "Sheriff Crawford," she said distractedly.

"I just found that vehicle you put the alert out on, the white SUV rental the missing woman was driving," a local highway patrolman told her. "It's down in the trees beside the Milk River, about ten miles north of town on River Road."

The same road as the one that went to the Chisholm Cattle Company ranch.

"The driver's side door is standing open, the keys are still in the ignition and there's a purse, the contents spilled on the ground nearby," the officer was saying. "No sign of the occupant."

"I'll be right there," McCall said and headed for her patrol car.

Billie Rae filled up the car with gas, bought a map of Montana and tried to anticipate what Duane would do once he realized she wasn't coming back to his dad's old pickup.

From Havre, she had few options. She couldn't head north to Canada. Even if Duane didn't have the border patrol looking for her, he could find out if she'd crossed. She could head southwest to Great Falls. Or she could keep going west across the Montana Hi-Line toward Glacier Park. Either way she chose would be two-lane blacktop for miles.

Nor could she catch a commercial flight even if she had the money until she reached a much larger city, which would be several hours away minimum.

She still wasn't sure what she was going to do until she reached the junction on the outskirts of Havre and found herself turning south toward Great Falls.

Billie Rae had to fight the feeling that no matter which way she went, Duane would find her and it would all end the same way. So why run at all? Why not just turn around and go back?

Just the thought of Tanner kept her going down the highway. For so long she'd devalued herself, thinking she deserved everything Duane was dishing out. But Tanner Chisholm had made her feel whole again.

She prayed that Duane would never learn that Tanner and his family had helped her. She'd actually considered leaving some kind of trail so Duane would follow her and leave them alone.

This made her laugh. Duane didn't need a trail of breadcrumbs to find her. He could get the help of any law enforcement department. That's if he couldn't find her himself.

When she glanced in the rearview mirror, her heart lodged in her throat. No need to leave a trail. Duane had already found her.

A large black car came racing up behind her. She couldn't see the driver's face behind the glare on the dark windshield, and the car was too close for her to see the license plate. But her thundering pulse told her it was Duane.

She turned back to her driving. With growing panic, she saw that she was partway off the highway and headed for the ditch. She swerved back into her lane and glanced back again.

The driver of the black car swerved around her, sitting on the horn as the car zoomed past. She caught only a glimpse of the irate woman behind the wheel.

Billie Rae tried to catch her breath. Her heart was pounding and she felt sick to her stomach. That *could* have been Duane.

But it hadn't been. She was still free. Still safe. But for how long?

As she drove through the wide-open country, finally picking up the Missouri River as it cut a deep path through the state, she knew she had to come up with a plan.

She'd go as far as she could on what little money she had, then she would find a job, get an apartment and work until she had enough money to move on.

The hardest part would be establishing a new identity. She needed a social security number to go with that new identity. Or a job where she was paid cash and no questions were asked.

But she was determined. Tanner Chisholm had shown her what her life could be like with a loving, caring man. She desperately wanted that. The thought made her ache because she knew there was only one Tanner Chisholm and she'd just left him.

As the miles whizzed past and no sign of Duane's large black car coming up fast behind her, she was almost starting to relax a little when the right back tire blew.

Chapter 6

Stopping by the local sheriff's office had been a mistake. Duane had expected some country sheriff who would sympathize with his dilemma. If he'd known Whitehorse had a female sheriff he wouldn't have bothered.

Bitches always stuck together.

He'd driven into Whitehorse, which was the closest town to the fairgrounds, so he assumed that was where Billie Rae had gone. One of the locals had to have given her a ride. It stuck in his craw that someone had helped her. Maybe a woman. He swore under his breath. More than likely, though, it had been a man—possibly that cowboy he'd seen with his wife at the rodeo.

Whitehorse had turned out to be one of those small Western towns that dotted the Hi-Line of Montana. The towns had sprung up when the railroad came through.

Many of them, like Whitehorse, had a main drag of brick buildings facing the tracks. Apparently in Whitehorse, though, they'd recently had a fire, because there was a gaping hole between two of the buildings.

After talking to the sheriff, Duane knew he now had to find Billie Rae before the local law did. Billie Rae couldn't have gotten far—not without any money or wheels.

But someone had helped her. Where would she have spent the night? In a local church? Do-gooders often put up the poor, helpless sorts who arrived in town without a car or food or money.

He was counting on her still being in Whitehorse. Sure, someone would be nice enough to give her a ride that far, but no farther since the closest towns were Glasgow, an hour away to the east back toward Williston and North Dakota, and Havre, an hour-and-a-half away to the west. The only other option was Canada, about fifty miles to the north.

He couldn't see her heading back the way she'd come, toward North Dakota. If she'd left town, she would either go north toward Canada or west toward Glacier Park.

But he still thought she hadn't gotten that far yet. Even if she'd talked someone into giving her a ride, this was a small town. Somebody would have seen her. All he had to do was ask the right people.

Tanner had gotten back from Havre too late. By the time he'd reached the fairgrounds, there was no sign of the old pickup Billie Rae said she'd escaped from her husband in—nor of the black Lincoln she'd said her husband had been driving.

"I should have gone out there first thing this morning," Tanner had told his brother Marshall when he'd called him after leaving the fairgrounds.

"That would have been a boneheaded thing to do," Marshall said. "Didn't you say this guy is a cop?"

Now back at the ranch, he found his family sitting around the dining room table eating an early supper. It was clear that Marshall had told them what Tanner had been up to.

"The man's abusing his wife," he said, angry at the reproach he saw not only in his father's gaze but in Emma's as well. "I saw her black eye and the bruise on her cheek, but more than that, I saw her fear. Last night she was running for her life."

"Then she should have gone to the sheriff," his father said.

Tanner shook his head. "It would be her cop husband's word against hers. Even if he was arrested, he would get out on bail and be even more dangerous than he is now." Billie Rae was afraid of law enforcement and he could understand why, given she was married to a cop. "I tried to get her to stay. I told her I would help her," he said voicing his frustration.

"This woman really got to you, didn't she?" Emma said.

"I can't explain it. I saw her last night and…" He realized what he was saying and shut up. Emma, he suspected, would understand, but not his brothers. Unless anyone had felt something like that….

"She wasn't ready for your help," Emma said. "There really is nothing you can do until she's ready."

"But Billie Rae wants out. Otherwise, why would she have run when he told her he would kill her if she did?"

Hoyt shook his head. "Most of the time, the woman goes back. Better the devil you know than the devil you don't. A smart man never gets in the middle of a domestic dispute, especially for a woman he doesn't really know."

"Tanner is no smart man," Marshall joked. "He's determined to save this woman—even from herself."

"You aren't going looking for this husband again, are you?" his father asked.

"I drove out to the fairgrounds when I got back from Havre, but he wasn't there," Tanner said.

"I told him it was a stupid thing to do," Marshall said and shrugged when Tanner sent him a withering look.

"She's afraid he's going to kill her," Tanner said. "He threatened to if she left him and she did. She needs help. Why can't you see that?"

"We do see it," Emma said. "But she didn't want yours or she would have stayed."

"She's afraid she put us all in jeopardy by letting me bring her here last night," Tanner said.

"Son, by now she could be headed back to her husband, for all you know," Hoyt said. "You can't save a woman who doesn't want to be saved. I ought to know."

Tanner knew his father was talking about his third wife, Krystal. He'd saved her from an abusive situation, only to have her disappear shortly after they were wed.

"Did Krystal go back to her abusive boyfriend?" Tanner asked, ignoring his brother's warning look not to.

"Yeah, she did and he was only her boyfriend. This woman you think you rescued is *married*. Let it go, son," his father said, laying a protective hand on his shoulder as he got up from the table. "We've got fence posts to set before it gets dark. Come on, work is the best medicine for what's ailing you. That, too, I know from experience."

"Your father only wants to help. He's worried about you," Emma said after the others had gone outside. "But Tanner, trust what you feel and pray. She's going to need it."

Sheriff McCall Crawford found the patrolman waiting for her at the spot along the Milk River where he'd discovered Aggie Wells's rental vehicle.

As she walked toward the stand of cottonwoods where the white SUV had been abandoned, there was no doubt in her mind that whoever had left it there had been trying to hide it. Law enforcement had been looking for Aggie's vehicle since the niece had reported her aunt missing.

She felt her heart beat a little faster as she neared the officer and saw his expression. "You found a body?"

He quickly shook his head. "But it appears we might be dealing with foul play. There is blood on the driver's seat." He handed her a flashlight so she could look into the tree-shaded vehicle.

She shone the beam into the rental, quickly taking in what appeared to be blood on the driver's seat; two open suitcases in the back, with clothes strewn around; a purse on the ground, the contents dumped as if someone had gone through her belongings. Or had hoped to make this look like a robbery.

"Have you checked the area yet?" she asked the patrolman.

"Just the immediate area."

McCall looked into the deep shadows under the cottonwoods. She could see the gleam of the river's dark surface through the low branches. The water looked murky. She felt a sudden chill as she remembered watching her father's pickup being pulled from an old stock pond where it had been buried in the mud for twenty-seven years.

At least whoever had hidden this car hadn't opted to sink it in the river where it might not have been found for years—or ever.

That thought gave her pause. Why hadn't the last person to drive this car done exactly that? Because they'd wanted the car to be found?

She glanced around. Maybe the person had been in a hurry. Possibly someone had been waiting for them up on the road, so they hadn't taken the time to do more than try to hide the car.

Too many possibilities, McCall thought. "Let's call in some help and broaden our search, and if we don't find her we're going to have to drag the river for her body."

As she reached for her phone, the question was still the same one she'd been asking herself since the niece had walked into her office. Where was Aggie Wells?

Duane decided that his best approach when he questioned the good people of Whitehorse, Montana, wasn't to admit that Billie Rae was his uncontrollable wife on the lam. That might garner unwanted sympathy for Billie Rae from the kind of people who took in strays and just felt the need to do good all the time—like whoever had given her a ride last night after the rodeo, the someone who just didn't know any better.

So it made sense that his best approach was to make

her a dangerous felon and to flash his badge and put enough pressure on this town that someone came up with some answers. He figured if he moved fast, the local female sheriff wouldn't get wind of it.

He began to hit the churches, which were notorious for taking in stranded motorists and people passing through town. There were a half dozen in the small town, more churches than bars. When he struck out there he tried the motels, thinking the good Samaritan had put her up in one for the night.

Striking out again, Duane was tired and hungry and losing his patience. He considered repeating the story he'd told the local sheriff to some of his friends in law enforcement. If he put an all-points bulletin out on Billie Rae, everyone in the northwest would be looking for her. With luck, some good ol' boy would find her and—

With a start he realized that Sheriff McCall Crawford could have already done that. Someone could have already found his wife. But then, wouldn't the sheriff have called him? Probably not, he thought with a curse. Not until she talked to Billie Rae herself.

Duane realized it was time to put in a call to a couple of buddies he'd met who worked for the Montana state highway patrol department. They were good ol' boys. He gave them the same story he'd told the sheriff. It didn't matter if they believed it or not. They'd see that he got his wife back.

Then he found a small café on the edge of town and ordered a cheeseburger, fries and a chocolate milk shake for a late lunch, telling himself it would be his word against his wife's. After all, he was a cop. And Billie Rae was…just his wife.

As he ate, he listened to the locals talking. He'd

found you could learn a lot about a community by listening to the old guys talk in the local café. There was always a table or two of them and Whitehorse was no different. The talk was about range, cattle, water, weather and finally the rodeo.

Duane finished his meal, pushed the plate away and rose to go over to the table. "Gentlemen, sorry to bother you, but I heard you mention the rodeo." He took out his badge, flashed it and quickly put it away. He didn't need any smart rancher telling him he had no jurisdiction here. "I'm looking for a dangerous felon whose pickup was found at the rodeo last night. I was hoping you might have seen her."

"Her?" one of the old-timers said with a snort. Another one of them laughed as Duane handed him the photo he'd removed from his pocket of Billie Rae.

"You say this woman is a dangerous felon?" the man asked, disbelieving.

"The sweeter they look, often the more dangerous they are," Duane said, thinking how true that was. This woman was going to be the death of him, he thought.

"What's she wanted for?" another man at the table asked as the photo was passed to him.

"She killed her three children, ages eleven months, two and four years," Duane said without batting an eye. "Drowned them in the bathtub. The four-year-old fought for his life."

The men at the table wagged their heads in shock and horror, and quickly passed the photo back to him, wanting nothing to do with such a woman.

"I was hoping you might have seen her," Duane said solemnly. "As far as I can figure, she caught a ride with someone from the fairgrounds into town."

The waitress had come up beside him. She'd obviously been listening. He let her steal a look at Billie Rae's photo before he put it back in his shirt pocket.

"Rachel might have seen her," the waitress said and hollered at the cook to come out. "She was telling me about some woman she saw right as the fireworks were over."

Duane felt a surge of hope as a heavyset cook came out of the back. He showed her the snapshot of Billie Rae.

"I can't say for positive," Rachel said, handing the photo back. "But I think it might be her."

Duane had been a cop long enough to know that often people liked to be a part of the drama by saying they saw something they didn't.

"Where did you see her?" he asked.

"By the grandstands."

"There must have been a lot of people there last night," Duane said. "What was it about her that made her stand out in your memory?"

She seemed to think for a moment. "I guess the reason I noticed her was because she was going the wrong way. We were all trying to leave and she was heading back in as if she'd lost something, you know."

"She looked upset?" he said.

The cook nodded. "She was crying. I thought maybe she'd misplaced one of her kids or something, and I was about to ask her if I could help, when I saw she already had help."

Duane felt his stomach roil. "She was with someone?"

"One of Hoyt Chisholm's sons."

Chapter 7

Billie Rae gripped the steering wheel as the car rocked, the flat tire flopping loudly on the pavement as she tried to keep control of it. She finally got it pulled over to the side of the road and climbed out to see how much damage had been done.

There hadn't been a lot of traffic along the two-lane, but now several semis passed blowing up a cloud of dust and dirt. Covering her eyes, she waited until they passed before she opened the trunk.

A motor home blew past as she looked in the trunk for what she would need to change the tire. She'd changed a tire once, but it had been a long time ago. Since Duane didn't let her drive and had sold her car right after they got married—

It made her angry how she'd let him make all the decisions in her life since they got married. But she'd learned early on not to argue with him. It was just easier—and safer—to go along with whatever he wanted than to argue, which always led to a fight.

She heard another vehicle coming and braced herself as she pulled out the bag of tools and waited for a truck pulling a trailer to roar past. Tanner, bless his heart, had made sure she had tools and the spare had air and some tread on it.

As she reached for the spare, she heard the sound of a vehicle slowing, then pulling up behind her. She turned to see a man in uniform climb out of a Montana highway patrol car.

One of Hoyt Chisholm's sons? Turned out there were six of them and they were grown men anywhere from their late twenties to their early thirties, and all six had been adopted by some big rancher to the north of Whitehorse.

Duane had gotten the information from the group gathered in the café.

"So what's the story on the Chisholms?" Duane had asked.

The waitress, not surprisingly, had turned out to be the most talkative. She told him about Hoyt Chisholm's four wives, two dead, one missing and one a newlywed, then about the six adopted sons.

"So you think he killed the other three wives?" he'd asked, not really giving a damn. All he really cared about was finding one of the man's sons—the bastard who'd apparently taken his wife away from the fairgrounds last night.

"There's this insurance investigator who thinks he did. Now she's up and disappeared. I heard they found her car by the river." She lowered her voice. "My good friend works as a dispatcher at the sheriff's department."

Great. "So all six of his sons live on this big, old ranch of his?" he asked, trying to keep the woman on the subject he *was* interested in.

"Nah, I think they've all moved out. He keeps buying up ranches and the sons move into the houses that come with them."

"This guy must have money."

"Insurance money from those three wives," the waitress said under her breath. "Everyone is wondering how long it will be before he kills the fourth wife."

"So which one of them was at the rodeo last night with the woman I'm after?" he asked the cook, whom he had talked into sitting down at a booth with him and the waitress since the place was dead right now.

"It didn't really register when I saw him with her," Rachel said. "I was mostly looking at her. But later..." she added quickly as she must have seen him getting upset. "As we were driving out, we passed the Chisholm Cattle Company ranch truck and I noticed there were three people in the cab." She looked a little uncomfortable and Duane tried not to show how frustrated he was getting.

"I was still wondering if the woman had found her child or if she was upset about something else," the cook said.

Duane nodded, wishing to hell she would get on with it, but knowing better than to push her again.

"I saw the woman was sitting in the middle and Marshall Chisholm was driving. There was another brother riding shotgun, but I didn't get a good look at him before my husband went flying around them." She realized she'd just told a cop that her husband had been speeding. "He slowed down after that, but Marshall had already turned off, so I didn't see them again."

"You wouldn't happen to know where Marshall Chisholm lives, do you?"

Duane tipped the cook and the waitress more than either deserved and left with directions to Marshall Chisholm's house. Apparently it was a good distance from any other ranch house and miles north of town.

The perfect place to hide a woman who didn't want to be found.

Billie Rae was surprised Duane hadn't called the law on her sooner, she thought as she watched the highway patrolman get out of his car. He'd always told her not to bother calling the cops on him because they all stuck together.

She'd learned that the hard way the one time she'd tried to get help from the police. But how had he known what she was driving? The car was in Tanner's name. Unless...

Her heart began to pound harder. She felt faint at the thought that Duane had found Tanner and what he had done to him to make Tanner talk.

The patrolman was a big man with an angular face. He wore mirrored shades and touched his nightstick as he walked up to her, his face stern.

She leaned against the back of the car, her legs suddenly weak as water.

"Looks like you could use a little help," the officer said and picked up the bag of tools from the ground where she'd laid them. "Why don't you get off the road and I'll take care of this. Won't take but a few minutes."

Billy Rae licked her dry lips, her mouth like cotton. "Thank you," she said, choking out the words.

She stepped off the road as he went to work on the tire. He was right, it didn't take him long. She'd watched him, telling herself this was all there was to him stopping. Duane hadn't put the word out on her. She had nothing to fear.

But as she watched the highway patrolman she was suddenly aware of how little traffic there was on the highway. She was alone out here in the middle of nowhere with a man in uniform—and she had learned not to trust a badge of any kind.

The highway patrolman put the blown tire in the trunk along with the tools and slammed the lid shut. "There, you should be fine now. I'd suggest, though, that you get that tire fixed or buy another one. Where are you headed?"

"Great Falls." It was the only town she could remember on the map.

"Good, it's not far up the highway. I'll follow you to make sure you don't have any more trouble."

"That's not necessary, really." She was trying hard not to let him see how upset his suggestion made her. The last thing she wanted to do was make him suspicious.

"It's not a problem," he said. "I'm headed that way, anyway."

All she could do was nod and thank him again.

Climbing behind the wheel, it took her a few moments to get the car started, her hands were shaking so badly. He hadn't asked for her driver's license. Because he knew who she was, knew she didn't have it with her?

Billie Rae drove across the high bench for what seemed forever, the highway patrolman a couple of car lengths behind her. Finally the highway dropped down to the river and into the city of Great Falls. She pulled into the first gas station she came to and put down her window to let in fresh air as she tried to breathe.

What happened now? Would the patrolman detain her until Duane got here? She didn't think the man would hurt her, because he'd had the perfect opportunity out in the middle of nowhere if that's what he had planned.

When she looked, she saw the highway patrolman give her a friendly wave, turn around and leave.

Billie Rae couldn't believe it. Her relief was so intense, she had to fight tears. Was it possible Duane hadn't put the word out on her? He'd always told her he had friends all over the country and that there was nowhere she could hide from him.

"Can I help you?"

Startled, she jumped and turned to find a young gas station attendant standing next to her open car window. It took a moment before she could speak. "I blew a tire. I was hoping—"

"Pop your trunk and I'll take a look at your tire." A moment later, the young man came back to the window carrying the tire. "You picked up a nail. I can patch it. Shouldn't take long."

She heard a cell phone ring.

The attendant looked at her as it rang again. "I think that's yours," he said as he took the flat tire and headed for one of the bays in the garage. On the third ring, she realized the sound was coming from inside the glove box of her car.

As she opened it, she saw the cell phone lying inside.

For just an instant she had the crazy, insane suspicion that Duane had put it there. Or the highway patrolman when she wasn't looking. But that was impossible. Only one person could have put it there, she realized as she snatched up the phone.

"Hello?"

"I see you found the phone," Tanner Chisholm said. "Look, I'm sorry. I was worried about you. You wouldn't take my other offers but I thought at least you'd have a phone if you needed it."

She was so touched that for a moment she couldn't speak. "Thank you."

"Where are you?"

"Great Falls. I had a flat, or I would have been a lot farther down the road."

He was quiet for a moment. "I wish you'd stayed. It's not too late to change your mind."

She wished she could. She remembered the views from the ranch, the feeling of peace and solitude and freedom. She remembered what it felt like to be in Tanner's strong arms, to sit at the table with some of his family and feel safe.

The attendant came back out with her tire and loaded it into the trunk.

"I should go," she said.

"I bought another cell phone. You have the number now since I called you. Be careful and, when you get to where you're going, give me a call if you want to."

"I will," she promised and snapped the phone shut. As she started to put it back in the glove box, she saw the money Tanner had left for her and felt tears burn her eyes.

* * *

Emma had been expecting the sheriff since the moment she'd heard about Aggie Wells's white SUV being found abandoned down by the river. The news had traveled like wildfire on the Whitehorse grapevine, not that Emma was on it since she was apparently too new in town, but Hoyt's ranch housekeeper had heard the news.

The moment she'd seen Mae Sutter's face when she'd come to work late that afternoon, Emma had known there was fresh gossip about the Chisholms.

"Spill it," she'd said to Mae, who'd looked surprised. But Emma was tired of beating around the bush with the cook and housekeeper. She'd tried to get close to them for weeks and they'd held her off as if she had a communicable disease.

Mae was a tiny thing. Emma had thought that a good gust of wind would blow the woman away. But Mae had turned out to be a lot stronger and more solid than she looked. She was also a good worker.

"I don't know what you're—"

"Save your breath, Mae. What's happened? And don't give me that innocent look of yours," she said to the housekeeper.

Mae straightened to her full height, all of five feet with her sturdy work shoes on, and tried to look indignant, but Emma could tell she was dying to tell everyone she knew—even her boss—who was involved.

"That woman who had dinner here the other night—"

"Aggie Wells," Emma said, trying to keep the tremor out of her voice. "What about her?"

"The sheriff questioned me about her," Mae said.

No surprise there. Emma put her hands on her hips

and gave the housekeeper an impatient look, knowing there was a whole lot more to it than that.

"They found her car abandoned by the river," Mae blurted out. "There was blood on the driver's seat. They're dragging the river for her body."

Emma had always been proud of her ironclad composure, but she felt all the blood drain from her face and had to sit down.

Mae got her a glass of cold water. "Are you all right?"

She nodded, knowing that Mae must be champing at the bit to tell everyone in the county about her reaction. Emma didn't care right now. "I liked Aggie," she said, tears in her eyes as she grasped the housekeeper's hand. "I know it sounds crazy, but I really liked her. I hope nothing happened to her."

Mae didn't look convinced. Nor was Mae surprised any more than Emma was when a few minutes later the sheriff drove up in the yard.

"I'll take care of this," Emma said, pulling herself together as she went to open the screen door and step out on the porch.

"Good afternoon, Sheriff," she said as McCall climbed out of her patrol SUV. "I thought we'd sit out here and talk, if that's all right. Would you like coffee or lemonade?"

The sheriff shook her head. "I need to speak with your husband."

Emma hadn't mentioned to Hoyt the sheriff's earlier visit when he and his sons had surprised her and come home for lunch. She hadn't wanted to upset him. She told the sheriff what she'd told her before. Hoyt wasn't expected back until late.

"You've heard," the sheriff said as she studied Emma still standing at the top of the steps.

Emma nodded, not up to playing games. She was still shaking inside and felt light-headed. "Have you found her?"

"No, not yet. When you hear from your husband, would you tell him to contact me as soon as possible?"

"Of course." She didn't need to ask why. Of course Hoyt would be the number one suspect, with her falling in at a close second.

The sheriff seemed to hesitate. "Did either of you leave the house that night after supper with Agatha Wells?"

"No. We were here the rest of the night." But she knew that wouldn't clear them. Hoyt had gotten up early the next morning and left. Emma didn't know where he'd gone, had just assumed it had something to do with the ranch.

She, herself, had gone into town that morning and didn't have an alibi for her whereabouts as she had taken a ride south to the Little Rockies to clear her head. The truth was, she hadn't wanted to stay around the house. She'd been too antsy, afraid of what Aggie Wells would do next.

When Aggie had left, her last words had been a warning that Hoyt Chisholm was dangerous, that he'd killed all three of his former wives and that Emma would be next.

Emma had hoped that having Aggie out to dinner would change her mind about Hoyt. It had been a foolish idea. At dinner Aggie had seemed to enjoy Hoyt's company, but later she was more convinced that Emma was living with a killer.

"Are you sure you wouldn't like some coffee or lemonade?" Emma asked the sheriff, hating the fear she heard in her voice.

"Thank you, but I need to get going," the sheriff said, turning to leave. "Do you know where your husband is working today on the ranch?"

Emma didn't. Hoyt had said they were putting in a new fence, but she had no idea where. He hadn't confided in her much about the ranch and his work lately. She'd told herself he had a lot on his mind, just as she told herself he hadn't been avoiding her. The thought that she'd been lying to herself about a lot of things scared her more than she wanted to admit.

After all this had come out about the deaths of two of his wives and the disappearance of the third, he had begged her to leave him. She had refused. It was after that that Hoyt had made himself scarce, as if he feared just being around her might put her in mortal danger.

"I assume you already tried to reach him by cell phone," Emma said.

The sheriff nodded. "It went straight to voice mail. I left him a message. It's important I speak with him as soon as possible."

"I'll tell him. And you'll let me know what you find out about Aggie?" Emma called from the porch.

The sheriff had reached her patrol SUV. She glanced back at her and nodded.

What was Emma thinking? If Aggie's body was found, she and Hoyt could expect to see the sheriff at their door—probably with an arrest warrant for at least one of them.

Duane found Marshall Chisholm's farmhouse without any trouble. It was off the county road, back in a quarter mile and sheltered by a large stand of old cottonwoods.

He drove up to the two-story house, noting there were no vehicles parked in front. The large old barn out back had a tractor and some rusted farm equipment around it but nothing inside. The perfect place to hide a vehicle.

He pulled his car into the back of the barn deep in the shadows, then taking the tire iron from the back, went to have a look in the house. While he didn't believe Marshall was home, he couldn't be sure Billie Rae wasn't hiding inside.

He was only a little surprised to find the back door unlocked. People in this part of Montana were awful trusting. Duane let himself in.

The kitchen linoleum was worn and dated just like the appliances and cabinets, but everything was clean. Duane couldn't imagine living alone and wondered about a man who could. No wonder the man had jumped at the chance to pick up a woman like Billie Rae.

The living room was neat as well, even though the furniture was also dated. It would seem that the son, even an adopted son, of a rich rancher could afford better furniture.

He climbed the stairs to find two bedrooms, one empty, the other with an antique metal bed frame and antique dressers that had probably come with the house.

Duane moved to the bed, pulled back the quilt and smelled the sheets. Billie Rae hadn't slept here. In the bathroom, he also found no sign that Billie Rae had ever been there.

Maybe she hadn't spent the night here, but Marshall

Chisholm still had to know where Billy Rae had gone last night after he'd given her a ride to Whitehorse.

Duane settled in to wait for Marshall Chisholm to come home.

"Any news?" McCall asked when she reached her husband. As a local game warden, Luke Crawford was often involved with any law enforcement in the county. Since he'd been in the area checking fishing licenses and had a boat, he was now involved in the search for Agatha Wells's body.

"Nothing so far. We're dragging the river."

"I just spoke with Emma Chisholm again. After she and her husband, Hoyt, had Aggie out to supper the night she disappeared, Emma says neither of them left the house after that."

"You believe her?"

The sheriff thought about the new Mrs. Chisholm. She liked her and wanted to believe her. "Not sure. She's scared, which makes me think her husband wasn't in the house all of that time."

"From what you told me," Luke said, "Hoyt Chisholm has the most to gain by this woman's death."

"I spoke with the insurance company that Agatha Wells worked for. She was fired. Her boss said she became obsessed with the Chisholm case, convinced that Hoyt killed all three of his wives, including the third one who disappeared. I found out that he only recently had her declared dead."

"And now he's remarried. Wouldn't that explain the fear you saw in Emma Chisholm? I know that would scare me if your last three husbands met with accidents or just plain disappeared."

McCall chuckled. "I scare you already."

"True." She heard the soft, seductive tone in his voice and felt a small shiver. Could she love this man anymore? Not likely.

"I just needed to hear your voice," she said truthfully.

"Always glad to oblige. See you later?"

"Absolutely." She disconnected, and following a feeling she hadn't been able to shake all day, she put out an all-points bulletin on Billie Rae Johnson Rasmussen.

By the time Billie Rae got something to eat from a fast-food place, filled the car up with gas and looked at a map to decide which way to go next, it was getting dark.

The emotional roller coaster of the past forty-eight hours had taken its toll on her. She felt wrung out and knew she wasn't up to driving much farther. The next large town was hours down the road and she didn't trust staying in the smaller Montana towns, feeling it would be too easy for Duane to find her.

She could almost feel him breathing down her neck. He wouldn't give up. It wasn't in his nature—not when he would feel justified for whatever he did to her. He would be driven and nothing and no one could stop him.

At least Great Falls was large enough that she should be able to find a motel, pay cash and get some sleep with some assurance she would be safe. At least for tonight.

She thought about changing her appearance, bleaching her dark hair, cutting it, getting a pair of glasses at the dime store. Instead, she picked up a baseball cap at a convenience store and stuffed her long hair up under it.

When she found a motel downtown, though, she ran into the same thing she had when she purchased the car. No identification.

"I'm sorry, we need a credit card or some kind of identification," the older male clerk behind the desk told her.

"My purse was stolen," Billie Rae said. "I'm just trying to get home."

"Where's home?"

"Spokane." She picked the name out of thin air.

The clerk studied her. She was still wearing the blouse and slacks she'd been wearing when she'd made the run for it. She must look a mess. Tomorrow she had to buy some more clothing. Thanks to Tanner, she could afford a few items.

Billie Rae also realized that her "disguise" had been a mistake and quickly took off her baseball cap. Her long curly dark hair spilled around her shoulders.

Duane had told her she looked too young, that she should try to look older; people thought he'd robbed the cradle worse than he had. As it was, he was seven years her senior—him nearly forty.

She knew it bothered him, turning forty, and that was part of the problem. While he had begun to gray around the temples, Billie Rae could still pass for her early twenties, although she tried to dress and act older to please Duane.

"Well, I suppose it will be all right this time," the clerk said now.

She started to fill out the registration card as he watched her. She was so nervous she wrote down her first name without thinking, then unable to quickly think of a second name, wrote down Chisholm. After all, the car was registered to Tanner Chisholm.

"Billie Rae Chisholm," the man said reading the

card. She'd done better on making up an address in Spokane, Washington, but didn't dare make up the zip code.

"You don't know your zip code?"

"I keep forgetting it. We just moved there."

He nodded and put the registration card away as if he didn't believe anything she said but no longer cared. He gave her the key and told her how to get to her room.

By the time she reached the motel room, she was trembling all over and furious with herself. If Duane started calling motels in Great Falls, he would have no trouble finding her since she'd already made the clerk suspicious.

She thought about just leaving, hitting the road, trying to drive to another town or even another motel in Great Falls. But it would be the same thing all over again. Exhaustion overtook her. She plopped down on the bed, telling herself she would only rest for a few minutes before leaving, and fell into the sleep of the dead.

Duane saw the lights coming up the road. One vehicle. Good, Marshall Chisholm was alone. Unless he'd brought a girlfriend, but Duane was pretty sure that wasn't the case or he wouldn't have picked up Billy Rae last night.

He smiled when he saw the cowboy climb out of his truck alone. Duane loved being right.

Marshall Chisholm was good sized. Duane wasn't all that sure he could beat him in a fair fight, but then there was no chance of that.

He waited until Chisholm opened the door and stepped in before hitting him from behind, knocking him to his knees.

The idea was to disarm him—not to knock him out. While he'd love to beat the hell out of the man who'd interfered in his marriage, he needed to know where Billie Rae was first.

"What the hell?" the dazed cowboy said when Duane stepped in front of him.

"Where is Billie Rae?"

The cowboy was on his feet before Duane could get a good swing with the tire iron. The blow didn't even stun him. Marshall Chisholm grabbed the tire iron before Duane could hit him again.

Seeing how this was going down, Duane pulled the gun just so the cowboy knew who was boss here. "Where is my wife?"

Marshall Chisholm took a step back at the sight of the gun. He rubbed a hand over his jaw, and his eyes widened just enough that Duane knew they were finally on the same page.

"Now you *remember?*" he said with a laugh. "Where is she?"

"You're the cop," Marshall said as if trying to get up to speed. Or maybe he was just reminding himself that he'd just slugged an officer of the law.

"That's right," Duane said, brandishing the gun. "And you're the son of a bitch who picked up my wife last night at the rodeo." He took a threatening step toward Marshall. "Now put down the tire iron and tell me what you did with her and where she is now." He fired a shot next to the cowboy's head. Wood splintered, the boom echoing through the house. "I suggest you start talking."

Chapter 8

Tanner woke to an unfamiliar sound. It took him a moment to realize it was his landline ringing. After he'd put his cell phone in Billie Rae's car, he'd picked up another cell phone and had his number changed, but no one but Billie Rae had the number.

He'd slept badly last night and now felt groggy as he glanced at the clock. It wasn't even daylight yet.

As he reached for the phone, he realized it might be Billie Rae calling. He knew he shouldn't have called her yesterday evening, but he'd needed to hear her voice, needed to know she was all right, needed to be sure she hadn't changed her mind and gone back to her abusive husband. He'd also wanted to make sure she found the phone—and the money—he'd left her.

"Hello?" He heard the hope in his voice that it was Billie Rae and that she'd changed her mind and was coming back. He should have known that no call this time of the morning was going to be good news.

"Son, it's Dad."

"What's wrong?" Tanner sat up, now fully awake. Had Hoyt heard something about Billie Rae? Was that why he was calling?

"It's your brother Marshall. He's in the hospital."

"What happened?" All Tanner could think was a car accident.

"He's been beaten up pretty badly, but the doctor says he's going to be all right. He's asking to see you."

Beaten up? How could he have gotten into a *fight*? Last night Marshall said he was heading home after they finished work late, that he was tired and going home to his house.

"He asked to see all of the family?" Tanner asked in alarm. Maybe his father was wrong and Marshall was worse off than they thought.

"Just you."

Thirty minutes later, Tanner found his brother sitting on a gurney in the emergency room of the hospital, Hoyt and Emma standing nearby. Marshall's head was bandaged and he had a dark row of stitches along his jaw.

When he saw Tanner, he asked their father and stepmother to give them a moment alone.

"Come on, Emma," Hoyt said, shooting Tanner a look that spoke volumes. He was responsible for this?

With a curse he realized who had done this to his brother. "I'll kill the son of a bitch," Tanner swore again, seeing red. He'd gotten in the middle of Billie Rae's marriage to a cop, of all things, and now he had gotten his brother almost killed. How could this situation be any worse?

Marshall shook his head. "I'm fine. But we have to find Billie Rae before he does."

The anger fled in an instant at the sound of her name, leaving him clearheaded. "You told him where she'd gone," Tanner said, no judgment in his tone. His brother had taken a beating because of him.

"Not on your life. I sent him north to the Canadian border to buy us time," Marshall said, sliding off the gurney.

"Sir, the doctor hasn't released you," the nurse said, rushing toward them. "He wants to keep you overnight. You have a concussion."

"She's right," Tanner said, putting a hand on his brother's arm. "I can handle this."

Marshall met his gaze as though assessing if he thought his brother was too emotionally involved, then he slumped back against the gurney.

"I'm so sorry," Tanner said as he and the nurse helped Marshall back up onto the gurney.

"This isn't your fault. I know what would have happened to Billie Rae if we hadn't helped her last night and so do you, but he's a cop, little brother. You can't kill a cop, even a bad one, and if you tangle with him you'll get yourself killed."

"I can handle this."

His brother shook his head. "Even when he pulled the gun on me, I wanted to go for the bastard's throat. I'm afraid that's exactly what you would have done and he would have killed you. I'm telling you, Tanner, this dude is dangerous. Just make sure he doesn't find Billie Rae until you can get her some kind of protection from this psychopath."

* * *

Sheriff McCall Crawford got the call before breakfast. Luke had left early since he was overseeing the dragging of the river. She had wanted to go with him but got held up with a phone call.

She had just hung up when the phone rang again. It was her deputy.

"We just found a grave not far from where Aggie Wells's car was abandoned by the Milk River," he said. "It's not our missing vic, though," he added. "These remains have been here for a lot longer than a few weeks."

By the time McCall reached the scene, Coroner George Murphy was crouched beside an open hole in the side of the riverbank.

"Looks like whoever killed her dug into the side of the bank, shoved the tarp-wrapped body in, then let the soft dirt slide down and cover her." He motioned to the bones lying on what was left of an old canvas tarp.

"Her?" McCall asked.

"Definitely a woman. I'd say in her late twenties."

McCall glanced at the gaping hole in the side of the bank. "How was it again that you found the grave?" She remembered finding her father's. It had been like opening Pandora's box and she suspected this grave would be no different.

"Apparently another dirt slide unearthed it—or maybe one of the searchers inadvertently did," the coroner said. "This morning I happened to spot a bone and a piece of the tarp sticking out."

"That was handy, wasn't it?" she said, never comfortable with coincidence. "Or maybe someone wanted us to find it. Any chance of matching dental records?"

"She's had some dental done," George said slowly,

then met her gaze. "I think you might get luckier with her medical records. She had an abnormal amount of broken bones for a woman her age."

"Are you suggesting some medical reason for that?" McCall asked.

"Maybe. More than likely this woman was seriously abused in her twenties, I would say."

"You can tell all that from her skeleton?"

"It's the type of breaks. Facial, wrists, arms, ribs…" George looked a little green around the gills. He always did when things got ugly. For a man who didn't like knowing about the evil things humans did to one another, it was amazing the EMT was still willing to act as the county coroner.

"How long would you estimate that the remains have been there?"

George sighed. "Hard to say, but given the amount of decomposition… I'd guess, and remember this is just a guess, twenty-five years. Maybe less, maybe more." He launched into a speech about all the factors that made a body deteriorate, a speech she'd heard many times before.

"Let's get her ID'd as quickly as possible," McCall said and glanced through the trees where she could see Aggie Wells's vehicle. The wrecker was coming today to take it to the sheriff department's storage unit as evidence.

They'd been searching for Aggie Wells's body and now another woman's had turned up? And still no sign of Aggie.

McCall didn't like what she was thinking and was surprised when the very person she was thinking about called.

"Sheriff Crawford here," she said into the phone. She listened as Hoyt Chisholm told her why she needed to come down to the hospital, then said, "I'll be right there."

Duane sat in his car down the street from the small town hospital. He knew Marshall would warn whoever had been in the pickup that night with Billie Rae after the rodeo. All he had to do was wait and see who showed up.

Duane wasn't surprised at all when a cowboy drove up shortly after the father and stepmother had arrived. He recognized him from the high school yearbooks he'd found at the library.

Tanner was a big cowboy like his brother, but as Duane had always said, "The bigger they are, the harder they fall." And this one was going down.

He smiled to himself as he waited for a few minutes to see if anyone else would show up. When no one did, he climbed out of his car and walked down the deserted street to the pickup the brother had arrived in. It had Chisholm Cattle Company printed on the side, Duane noted as he slipped under it and secured the tracking device.

Another benefit of being a cop, he was able to get all the toys that went with the job, along with anything else he wanted from the sleazebags he came in contact with on the streets.

Slipping out from under the pickup, he moseyed back to his car and checked it on his cell phone. "Modern technology," he said in admiration, pleased with himself, as he looked at the small screen. Now wherever Tanner Chisholm went Duane was sure to follow, and he had no doubt that this cowboy was going to lead him straight to Billie Rae.

"It's just a matter of time now, Billie Rae," he said to himself, then swore as he spotted a sheriff's department vehicle coming up the street. He slid down in his seat, swearing profusely as the patrol car pulled into the hospital parking lot.

He'd told Marshall Chisholm not to call the law or he would come back and finish him. Apparently the hick hadn't taken his threat seriously. Duane rubbed his jaw where the cowboy had got in a good punch. First Marshall had lied to him about where Billie Rae had gone. Duane had believed that under the threat of death the cowboy had told him the truth. But one call to the border after he'd left Marshall and he'd verified that Billie Rae hadn't been anywhere near the crossing.

Duane told himself he should have known better than to believe that she'd head for Canada. Billie Rae was proving she wasn't as stupid as he'd once thought. Obviously she'd known how easily he could find out if she'd crossed into Canada, so she'd probably gone in another direction. What he needed to know, though, was *which* direction—and how she was getting wherever the hell she thought she was going.

These Chisholm cowboys had been playing him. They really had no idea what a mistake that was yet. But they would soon.

As he watched the woman sheriff being met at the door by the parents of Marshall Chisholm, Duane knew it was time to get out of town. Apparently that was what Billie Rae had already done.

Wherever she was, he was counting on Tanner Chisholm leading him right to her.

* * *

Tanner called Billie Rae the moment he left his brother's hospital room. The cell phone rang four times. A shaft of icy fear made his stomach roil at the thought that she'd dumped the cell phone, afraid her husband would somehow be able to follow her because of it.

Billie Rae answered on the fifth ring.

"It's Tanner. Are you all right?"

"What's wrong?" She sounded as if she'd been asleep. He'd forgotten how early in the morning it was.

"Tell me where you are."

"No, I—"

"Duane beat up my brother Marshall. He's in the hospital."

"Oh, no." He heard what sounded like her crying softly. "Is he all right?"

"He'll live but he's worried about you. He sent me to find you and make sure you were safe until something can be done about your situation." Tanner could hear her moving around.

"If Duane found out your brother was with us that night at the rodeo, then…oh, Tanner, he'll come after you next. He won't stop with your brother. You're in terrible danger. The rest of your family might be as well."

"You just worry about yourself right now."

Billie Rae let out a choked laugh. "I'm the one who put your brother in the hospital, the one who has put you all in danger."

"Listen to me, Billie Rae. None of this is your fault."

"You're the one who said I needed to draw a line in the sand."

"That was before I saw what Duane did to my brother."

"He's capable of doing much worse. But you were right the first time, I can't keep running. He will go after anyone who helps me."

"My brother has filed charges against him," Tanner said. "The only place he's going is jail."

"No, you don't understand. Even if the sheriff finds him and arrests him, he'll be out within hours and even more furious. Tell your brother not to press charges."

"Billie Rae, it's too late. If you come back to White-horse—"

"And what? Get a restraining order against Duane?" She let out a humorless laugh. "Do you really think that would do any good? Tanner, I know about battered women whose husbands threaten to kill them. The husbands find a way to get to them no matter what and do exactly what they said they would."

Tanner wanted to argue, but he'd seen too many examples of women in the news who'd been killed by their husbands or boyfriends—or lived in fear of them even with their abusers behind bars.

"Then I will get you enough money so that you can disappear and Duane will never be able to find you," he said even as he realized it would mean he would never see her again, either. The thought hurt. But all that mattered right now was keeping her safe.

"Tanner, do you really think there is that much money in the world?" she asked. "Even if I could accept your too generous offer, I can't live like that, always looking over my shoulder. This was the reason I hadn't tried to leave Duane before. And now I've gotten your brother hurt—"

"He's going to be all right. He told Duane you were headed for the border in one of our old trucks."

She groaned. "Once he finds out that your brother lied to him—"

"He isn't going after my brother again. The sheriff is putting a deputy outside his room until he is released. There is an APB out on Duane. Everyone will be looking for him. I'm betting he will get out of Whitehorse and not come back. It's you I'm worried about. Come back to the ranch. I'll make sure he never hurts you again."

"Tanner..." she said with a sigh.

"I know. You don't even know me."

"That's the amazing part. I feel as if I have always known you. This closeness I feel..." Her voice broke off.

"I feel the same way. I can't explain what happened the moment I saw you, but I don't want to let you go."

"And I can't let him hurt you or your family simply because you helped me."

Tanner heard something in her voice that scared him. "You can't go back to him. You know it will be worse for you. That's if he doesn't end up killing you. You can't go back because of me. Please, I can't let that happen."

"I can't run, either. You were right. I have to take a stand."

"*No,* I was wrong. Billie Rae—"

"Make sure you and your family are safe."

"My father and brothers will see to that. Billie Rae, I'm leaving right now headed for Great Falls. Meet me halfway between Whitehorse and Great Falls. There's an Indian casino called Northern Winds just outside of Havre. I'll be waiting for you in the parking lot." He heard her open the motel room door; he could hear traffic outside. He knew he was losing her. "And if you're still determined to go back to him after we talk, then—"

"Thank you, Tanner. I wish we'd met under different circumstances."

"Billie Rae. Billie Rae?" The line had gone dead. He called back but it went straight to voice mail.

Swearing, he started his pickup. If she was headed back this way, then he would see her on the highway. He would do whatever he had to do to stop her. He couldn't let her go back to that madman because of him.

All he could hope was that after she hit the road on the way back that she would change her mind and meet him at the casino. He said a silent prayer that she would be waiting for him when he reached Northern Winds as he pulled away from the Whitehorse hospital and headed west.

Tanner hadn't gone far when he checked his rearview mirror. He couldn't take the chance that Duane was still in town, waiting for him to lead him to Billie Rae.

But there were no other vehicles behind him as he turned onto Highway 2 and headed west toward Great Falls. Wherever Duane Rasmussen was, he wasn't behind him. Breathing a sigh of relief, Tanner settled in for the long drive, thinking about Billie Rae and fate and how he was going to stop her.

Billie Rae couldn't breathe. Wasn't this what she'd feared? She choked back a sob and closed the motel room door behind her. She'd never felt such pain—not even when Duane had hit her. The woman she'd been—before Duane Rasmussen—never dreamed she would find herself in this position.

Her heart ached and she felt sick to her stomach. She'd only made it worse by making love with Tanner the night before. What if Duane found out? She told herself there was no way that would ever happen. But they hadn't used protection. Last night she'd told herself it wouldn't matter. Duane was going to find her and kill her before she'd even know if she was pregnant.

But what if she was? She touched her stomach. Just the thought of having Tanner's child sent a wave of excitement through her. Then instant regret that she had now possibly endangered yet another life. What was she going to do?

You should never have left me. This is on your head. You forced me to hurt someone else. You deserve everything you're going to get.

She slid behind the wheel of the car and sat, trying to pull herself together. Since she'd realized the mistake she'd made marrying Duane, Billie Rae had been desperate to get out—but she hadn't known what to do. Duane had made it clear that leaving him was out of the question. The fact that he was a cop made it all the more impossible.

She'd felt trapped with no way out and no one to turn to. Early on in their marriage, she'd had a friend she'd met at the small market within walking distance of their home. The friend had noticed Billie Rae's bruises and had tried to help her.

Not long after that, the friend had suddenly moved away without a word.

Billie Rae had inquired about her through a mutual acquaintance at the market and found out that a policeman had come around the night before her friend had left. Duane. After that Billie Rae hadn't let anyone get close, knowing the price they would have to pay if Duane found out.

Now she had involved the Chisholm family and it

had gotten Marshall injured. She didn't want to think about what Duane would do to Tanner if he knew how much he'd helped her. And yet Tanner hadn't backed down for a moment. He was still ready to help her—even knowing now what Duane was capable of.

She felt such a well of emotion at the thought. Tanner was the kind of man Duane would call a fool. Duane would scoff at anything that smacked of chivalry. No doubt because he could never measure up and he knew it. That was why he resented men like Tanner Chisholm so much.

Thinking of Tanner reminded her of his smile, the warmth in his brown eyes, that spark that had brought the old Billie Rae back to life when he touched her. Tanner had already saved her in ways he couldn't imagine. But she couldn't let him get in any deeper.

After a few minutes, she could breathe again. She picked up the map, remembering something she'd noticed on it yesterday. It was a dangerous plan. A desperate plan. But for the first time in months, she felt she was finally thinking clearly. She almost felt like her old self—the strong, independent woman Duane had done his best to destroy.

For so long she thought she deserved what she got because she was the one who'd married Duane. *You made your bed, now lie in it,* her mother used to say.

No more. Anger boiled up from deep inside her. No more. She *didn't* deserve this. Nor did the Chisholms who had helped her. Tanner had been right. It was time to draw a line in the sand and fight.

It was time she took her life back.

Or lose it.

But at least she wouldn't go down without a fight,

and if she was lucky she'd take Duane with her. Taking a deep breath, she braced herself, opened her phone and tapped in his number. Her hand was barely shaking as the phone at the other end began to ring.

"Hello?" He hadn't recognized the cell number. Tanner had blocked the ID on it. She could hear Duane's car stereo in the background and wondered where he was. He turned down the music and repeated, "Hello? Who is this?"

Just the sound of his voice brought it all back. Fear knifed through her, and for a moment her courage faltered. She drew on the memory of the woman she had been in Tanner's arms, the woman Tanner Chisholm had seen in her, the woman he was bound and determined to save even if it meant risking his own life.

"It's me," she said.

The soft chuckle that came over the line sent a chill through her. "I wondered when I'd be hearing from you." Duane's words were clipped. Anyone else might not have heard the fury behind them. But she heard it and, if she hadn't known before, she knew now that he would beat her to death this time if she gave him a chance.

Terror gripped her and she couldn't breathe, couldn't speak, couldn't think for a moment. Then she reminded herself that Duane had been systematically killing her for months. He'd tried to suffocate her in a loveless marriage, beat her down, make her question herself, especially her strengths, and he'd hurt her in more ways than she wanted to admit.

"So you're ready to come home." His tone made it clear he couldn't wait to get his hands on her.

And that was exactly what she was depending on.

Chapter 9

Aₛ Emma and Hoyt left the hospital, she saw her husband stop to take a call on his cell phone. He turned his back to her and she felt her heart drop—just as it had weeks ago when she'd feared her husband was having an affair. Instead the woman who he had been talking to back then was Aggie Wells, the former insurance investigator determined to see Hoyt hang for murder.

Hoyt hadn't wanted her to know that Aggie was not only back in town—but also that she was more determined than ever to see him go to prison for murder.

"Who was that?" Emma asked now as he put his phone away and joined her. She was half afraid it was Aggie. And at the same time, almost hoping it was. No one wanted Aggie Wells to turn up alive more than her.

Hoyt hesitated, then sighed. She'd made him promise there would be no more secrets. She still felt guilty about that because she had things she'd never told her husband, things she wanted to hide as well.

"It was Tanner. He wanted to tell me he was going after Billie Rae."

"He's his father's son," she said, not at all surprised—even after what had happened to Marshall, or because of it, Tanner would be all the more determined to protect the woman.

"He's a fool," Hoyt said as he led the way to the ranch pickup. The doctor was keeping Marshall in the hospital for observation even though her stepson had only a minor concussion. She'd seen how upset her husband had been after their visit with Marshall in the hospital and knew he feared that another son would be injured—or dead—before this was over.

She noticed how Hoyt glanced around the hospital parking lot. He was looking for Billie Rae's husband—or at least anyone who might fit that bill since the only description they had of him was what Sheriff Crawford had given them.

"Tanner's worried the husband might come after us, isn't he?" Emma said as she climbed into the pickup next to Hoyt.

He shot her look. "The man sounds crazy. It is cause for concern since his wife involved us in her troubles."

"Hoyt," Emma snapped as he started the engine and headed toward the ranch. "How can you say such a thing? The poor woman was running for her life. The man is an animal. Can you imagine what he'll do to Billie Rae if he finds her?"

Hoyt swung his head around to look at her. "Can you imagine what he'll do to Tanner if he finds him with his wife? And what will have been the point? Women like that go back to the men who abuse them."

"Women like *what?*" Emma demanded, shocked by his last statement. She too was worried about Tanner. But she was also worried about Billie Rae. And her husband had hit a nerve. He didn't know she used to be one of those women. But like Billie Rae, she hadn't stayed— nor had she gone back in the way he meant, anyway.

"You know what I mean," he said. "I'm worried about my boys and now Tanner is going after the woman."

"You raised your sons to help those in need. The only reason Billie Rae would go back to her husband is to protect your boys, who by the way, are men. Are you going to let that happen?"

"What would you like me to do?" Hoyt demanded.

"This attitude of yours is all because you're so certain that your third wife went back to her abusive boyfriend." He'd told her about Krystal, a woman he'd tried to help by foolishly marrying her.

"She *did* go back. I hired a private detective. Krystal went back because she missed the drama, especially the honeymoon period, after he's beaten her up, when he pleads for her forgiveness, treats her like she's rare crystal, buys her things, promises never to hurt her again until he does and the cycle starts all over again. She was hooked on it and life with me was just too damned dull for her."

All Emma heard was the part where Hoyt said he'd had proof that Krystal went back to her boyfriend. "You hired a private investigator who had proof and you didn't give that information to Aggie?"

He stared straight ahead, ignoring her as he drove.

"No, you didn't give Aggie the information because

you wanted to save face, because of your damned male
ego. You'd rather have people believe you're a murderer." She was furious with this man she'd come to
love more than life.

"Aggie Wells already believed I killed at least one
of my wives," Hoyt snapped. "What could another one
hurt? Anyway, you wouldn't understand."

"Oh, I understand just fine, Hoyt Chisholm. If Aggie
had known about any of this—"

"She would still believe I killed Krystal. Don't you
get it? She would think I couldn't stand my wife leaving me and that I went after her and killed her. Maybe
killed the boyfriend too because shortly after that, both
of them disappeared and not even the private detective
I hired could find them."

This news took the wind out of Emma's sails. Hoyt
was right. He would still look guilty, maybe even guilt-
ier than he had.

He glanced over at her. "I'm not as stupid as I look.
After I calmed down, I told the P.I. to get proof that
Krystal was alive to give to Aggie. I thought maybe then
she'd believe that I didn't have anything to do with my
first wife's drowning or Tasha's accident. But by then,
both Krystal and her abusive boyfriend had vanished."

Emma fell silent as Hoyt turned onto the road to the
ranch. "I'm sorry. You could have told me."

"I just did. It proves nothing." He reached over and
took her hand, all the frustration leaving his voice.
"This crazy cop husband aside, I'm still worried as
hell about you. I'm so afraid something is going to happen to you."

"I'm fine as long as I'm with you."

He squeezed her hand. "How did I get so lucky as

to find you? Maybe that's what scares me. I feel like I'm tempting fate."

"Don't be silly. I'm hard enough to get along with that maybe *I'm* your punishment."

He laughed softly, but didn't disagree.

"I saw the sheriff talking to you. What was that about?"

"She wanted to know the last time I saw Aggie Wells. If I knew where she'd been staying. If she happened to mention where she was going or what she was doing. The usual."

Emma realized he'd been questioned by the sheriff on numerous occasions before. But those times it had been about his wives. Her heart went out to him and for a moment, she hated Aggie Wells for making him have to relive this all over again.

"So you told her the last time you saw Aggie was that night at dinner?" Emma said.

He shot her a look. "Are you asking me when was the last time I saw her?"

"No, I—"

"I didn't kill her, if that's what you're asking."

"I know you didn't kill her. I just thought—"

"That I might have met her the next morning?" He shook his head. "I never saw her again after that night at dinner and I hope to hell I never see her again. Any more questions?"

Emma shook her head, wishing she'd kept her mouth shut, but that was so not like her. Had she really believed Hoyt would meet Aggie the next morning?

"I have no idea where she is or what happened to her."

Emma could hear the fear in her husband's voice.

It matched her own. Since Aggie's car had been found with, according to the scuttlebutt around town, her purse and suitcase, and blood on the driver's seat, the sheriff's department had been searching for her body along the riverbank.

"The sheriff asked where she could find me and I told her we were headed back to the ranch," Hoyt was saying. "I intend to stay with you until this cop who beat up Marshall is caught."

That sounded just fine with Emma. She'd missed her husband. Ahead she could see the main house at Chisholm Cattle Company. All Emma wanted to do was get home, go upstairs with her husband and make love. She said as much to Hoyt.

He swore under his breath. She thought that was his reply to her suggestion. Instead he was staring at the house as he pulled into the yard.

Emma turned to see that the front door was standing open, no other vehicles around and since Marshall's brothers, other than Tanner, were now all at the hospital…

"Stay in the pickup," Hoyt ordered as he pulled down the shotgun from the rack behind the pickup seat. Grabbing a handful of shells, he carefully closed the truck door and hurried toward the house and the open doorway.

Emma, who had never been good at taking orders, especially from a man, was hot on his heels. As she hurried up the steps and crossed the porch, she heard Hoyt moving cautiously through the rooms.

She would have followed him farther into the house, but she stopped just inside the door pole axed, her heart pounding as she breathed in the familiar scent of Aggie Wells's perfume.

The insurance investigator was no longer missing.

She'd been in this house again, which meant she was alive even though her car had been found abandoned and the sheriff suspected foul play.

But it was the second realization that panicked Emma. Aggie Wells was still determined to prove Hoyt Chisholm a murderer—even if it was her own "murder" he went to prison for.

"Billie Rae?" There was now a sharp edge to Duane's voice.

"I'm still here," she said into the phone. She told herself to just breathe. She could do this.

"Right, and where exactly is *here?*" he asked as if she was a disobedient child. It was the same tone he'd used with her since she'd said, "I do."

"I'm broke down near a town called Fort Benton."

He swore. "Of course you are and now you need my help." There was smug satisfaction in his voice. She knew he was smiling and that, she'd learned, was when he was his most dangerous.

"How long will it take you to reach me?" she asked, needing to know where he was and how much time she had to prepare.

"I'm leaving Whitehorse now." She heard him put down his car window. A moment later a siren came on. He'd put the portable cruiser cherry light on the roof. "Give me the directions."

She told him how to get to the dead-end river road she'd seen on the map.

"How could you be so stupid as to go down a dead-end road?" he demanded, but didn't wait for an answer. "Never mind. The two to three hours you're going to have to wait for me will give you time to think about what you've done and how you intend to make it up to me." He hung up.

Billie Rae snapped the cell closed with trembling fingers, then went back inside the motel room for the phone book. She found the first address she needed, then checked the Great Falls map at the front and started the car.

She shuddered at the thought of facing Duane and feared she wouldn't have the courage to carry through with her plan. But she knew that if she showed any sign of weakness, she was a dead woman.

What sustained her was the knowledge that if she didn't make her plan work, Duane wouldn't end it there. He would still go after Tanner. In his mind, Tanner would be to blame for all of this.

Pushing the thought away, she concentrated on what she had to do. Tanner would be waiting for her at Northern Winds casino. He should be safe there. Just thinking about him made her feel stronger as she drove to the first shop on her list.

Sheriff McCall Crawford was just leaving the hospital after putting out a warrant on Duane Rasmussen when her cell phone rang.

"We have a positive identification on the remains found buried out by the river," Coroner George Murphy said.

McCall braced herself because she had a bad feeling she already knew.

"The remains are those of Krystal Blake Chisholm," George said.

Hoyt Chisholm's third wife, the one who disappeared almost thirty years ago.

"Cause of death?" she asked.

"A blow to the back of the head, according to the crime lab doctor who did the autopsy. It's all in the report, but I know you can never wait for the report, so I called you."

McCall smiled. "You know me too well. Thanks." Krystal Chisholm's murder cast a whole new light on the deaths of Hoyt Chisholm's other two wives who had died under questionable circumstances—and now insurance investigator Aggie Wells's disappearance.

"We found something among the remains in the tarp I think you're going to want to see," George said.

"I'll be right there."

As she walked into the autopsy room a few minutes later, she pulled on latex gloves and stepped over to where the box of weather-rotted scraps of canvas tarp and the remains had been placed on a gurney.

George handed McCall a piece of silver jewelry.

"The victim's?" she asked, wondering why he'd wanted her to see this.

He shook his head. "My best guess? It's part of a men's bolo tie." A lot of western-dressed men in this part of the country wore a bolo tie. It was as dressed up as they ever got. The tie consisted of two thin cords that formed a loop with the ends dangling down from some sort of decorative clasp that held the tie together.

"How would it have ended up with the body?" she asked just wanting his take on it. She already had her own theory.

"The killer has the woman down, she reaches up and grabs the bolo tie, the silver clasp slides off."

Her thought as well. "Wouldn't the silver be more

tarnished, though, if it had been with the body for the past twenty-five to thirty years?"

"Silver reacts badly to just about everything, latex gloves, ammonia, chlorinated water, air pollution, perfumes, hair sprays, even some foods like onions and eggs, anything salty unless the silver is plated with a thin layer of metal protection, which older jewelry wasn't," George said and then seemed to notice her looking at him sideways. "My sister works for a jeweler."

"Sorry, as you were saying…"

"Humidity alone can cause silver to tarnish."

McCall nodded. "So who knows how tarnished it would be, is that what you're saying?"

"Something like that," George said. "What do you think of the design?"

While he was squeamish about the violence of murder and what it did to the human body, he seemed to be getting into the investigation part of his job a lot more than when he first started, she thought.

She'd been turning the piece of silver in her fingers. If you turned it one way it appeared to be three tiny silver horseshoes welded together.

If you turned it the other way, it looked like three small C's.

She held it up. "One of a kind, I'd say." She was waiting for George's opinion, which she knew he was dying to give her. "Probably someone had it specially made at a jewelry store. Could be tiny horseshoes or—"

"We both know that it is three C's and that those three C's are for Chisholm Cattle Company," George said, losing his patience with her.

She laughed. "Why do I get the feeling you have

something to back up that statement?" George was all about facts.

"In fact I do," he said stepping over to the laptop computer on a nearby desk, "I thought I'd seen Hoyt Chisholm wearing this very piece of jewelry and I was right."

McCall stepped over to look at a photograph of the cattleman taken at Whitehorse Days twenty-seven years before. Hoyt was wearing the bolo tie with the silver clasp, and he was with a woman. The cutline under the photo identified the woman as Krystal Chisholm.

Duane had forgotten about Tanner Chisholm after Billie Rae's call. He'd been so excited at the prospect of getting to his wife that Tanner Chisholm had been the last thing on his mind.

That was, until he heard the soft beep from the tracking device on the seat next to him.

"What the hell?" he said as he saw Tanner's location. "The son of a bitch is following *me?*"

He almost ran off the road he was so busy staring at his cell phone screen. How was this possible? The cowboy had left Whitehorse before him. He must have stopped for gas or something. How else could Duane explain it?

Unless he was right and the bastard was actually *following* him.

All he had been thinking about after Billie Rae's call was getting to her. It was so like her to call—after she'd gotten herself into a pickle. Just the sound of her voice had gotten his blood boiling.

He chewed at his cheek for a moment now, giving this change of events some thought. Did he really give a damn about this cowboy? Wasn't getting to Billie Rae and settling this all he should concern himself with?

As anxious as he was to reach Billie Rae—there was always the possibility that she would get some wild idea to take off again—especially if someone encouraged her. He realized he couldn't let the cowboy follow him to her.

Another thought breezed past. What if Billie Rae had also called her cowboy savior, covering all her bets?

Duane swore. He was going to have to take care of Tanner. He watched the highway ahead looking for the perfect place to wait in ambush.

Chapter 10

All it took was a couple of calls to jewelers in Glasgow and Havre. McCall hit paydirt on her second try.

"Chisholm, sure, I know him well," the elderly sounding jeweler said.

She described the clasp for the bolo tie.

"Yep, I made that, but not for Hoyt. It was an anniversary present I made for his wife to give to him," the jeweler said.

"His wife?"

"What was her name? Just a minute. I can look it up. I keep records back to when I started this business." She heard him digging in a file. A moment later he came back on the line. "Just as I remembered. An anniversary present, the clasp for the bolo tie and a set of cufflinks. Three tiny silver C's for Chisholm Cattle Company. I made them for Krystal Chisholm, October 16, 1984."

Twenty-seven years ago. Just about the time that Hoyt had married Krystal, McCall thought.

She asked if the jeweler could fax her a copy of that order, thanked him and hung up.

Earlier at the hospital, Hoyt Chisholm had assured her he knew nothing about Aggie Wells's disappearance. He'd sworn he hadn't seen her since the night she'd come out to the ranch to have dinner.

But given what she knew now, she wondered how long it would be before they found her body as well.

McCall sat for a moment before she placed the call to the county attorney. It was time to bring in Hoyt Chisholm before another wife ended up dead.

"Aggie was here," Emma said when Hoyt returned to where his wife was still rooted just inside the door.

"There's no one in the house. The front door probably blew open," he said as if he didn't hear her. He started toward her to put his shotgun back into his pickup.

"Did you hear what I just said to you?" she demanded. "Aggie was in the house again."

He stopped in front of her and frowned. "Emma—"

"Didn't you smell her perfume when you entered the house?"

He looked at her, shook his head and swore under his breath. "Where are you going with this?"

Did he think she was making it up? Imagining it? "I know what I'm talking about. Don't you see what she's doing? She's trying to frame you for murder."

"She's been doing that for years," he said as he tried to step past Emma.

"Hoyt, I'm telling you she set this whole thing up, her disappearance, her car being found, the blood on the seat, the whole thing to make it look as if you killed her."

He shook his head. "I really don't want to talk about this." He pushed past her and headed for his truck.

"Hoyt Chisholm, do not treat me like I am imagining things," she said following him as far as the porch. "I smelled her perfume. She's been in our house again while we were gone. It's as if she knew we were all going to be at the hospital and—"

"And what, Emma?" he demanded as he turned from hanging up his shotgun on the rack behind the seats. He slammed the pickup door before he turned back to her. "Emma, why would she be sneaking around our house? For what possible reason?"

"She did it before."

"Yes, no doubt to let me know she hadn't given up sending me to prison." He swore under his breath. "Aggie Wells is the last person I'm concerned with right now."

"I smelled her perfume. She was in this house again." But she was talking to his back for he had turned and was headed out to the barn where he always went when he was upset—or didn't want to hear what she had to say.

As she started after him, Emma saw the sheriff's patrol car coming up the road toward the house.

Tanner knew he was driving too fast. He'd made good time. Even after his stop at the bank to get more money for Billie Rae and gas in the pickup in Havre, he was going to beat Billie Rae to the casino parking lot.

The casino wasn't far ahead. Just the thought of seeing Billie Rae again had his heart pounding with anticipation. He thought about the first time he'd laid eyes on her at the rodeo grounds.

He still couldn't describe the effect she'd had on him. Love at first sight? How was it possible to fall in love with a complete stranger in a nanosecond? It was easier to believe they'd been together in a past life and had found each other again in this one.

Whatever it had been, it had happened. In that instant, Billie Rae's face had lit up in a burst of fireworks and he'd felt his heart skyrocket. The fireworks had showered down from Montana's big night sky, the air smelling of summer and rodeo concession stand food. Music had played against the boom of the rockets exploding over their heads and he'd lost his heart.

That moment was frozen in time forever for him.

But as odd as it sounded, maybe it had been luck that brought them together. That is, if they could stop this maniac after her.

Ahead, Tanner saw a large black car parked at the edge of the road. His heart lodged in his throat. Had Duane somehow found out where Billie Rae was going to meet him?

The black car pulled out, turned in his direction and headed down the highway toward him. Past it Tanner could see the casino in the distance. His gaze shifted from the black car approaching him to the casino parking lot.

He didn't see Billie Rae's small red car. He hoped that meant she hadn't arrived yet—and not that Duane had already stopped her.

His gaze shifted quickly back to the black car as it increased speed on the other side of the highway coming in his direction. The car was big and black, possibly a Lincoln like the one Duane drove, just as Billie Rae had described it and it was gaining speed quickly.

Tanner tried to see the face behind the steering wheel as it neared, but the sun was glinting off the windshield. He felt himself tense. He gripped the wheel tighter, bracing himself because he feared the driver of the black car was planning to swerve into his lane.

At the sped the car was coming, it would probably kill both of them if Tanner couldn't avoid the crash, but then Duane Rasmussen was a psychopath, wasn't he?

The car was within yards of him, still on the other side of the road. And then it was roaring by in a blur, throwing up dust and gravel on the edge of the highway. Tanner caught a glimpse of an elderly man behind the wheel with a shock of white hair as the car sped past.

Tanner had to hit his brakes to make the casino turnoff. As he fishtailed into the parking lot, his blood was still hammering in his ears. He'd been so sure the driver of the black car was Duane on a suicide mission that was going to take them both out.

Now as he brought the pickup to a stop in the parking lot, he had to take a minute to catch his breath. He glanced around the lot. Billie Rae wasn't here yet. He hoped that meant she was still safe. Police officer Duane Rasmussen was probably still back in Whitehorse. Or maybe already in jail.

Tanner tried to reassure himself that everything was going to be all right. Billie Rae would be here soon. He would talk her out of going anywhere near her husband. Somehow it had to work out because he couldn't bear the thought that he might never see her again. Or worse, that Duane would find her.

* * *

Duane swore as he stared at the GPS screen. Tanner Chisholm had been right behind him, then he suddenly stopped when Duane had found the perfect place to finish the bastard for good?

He tapped the screen on his cell phone and looked down the highway in the direction Tanner had been heading until a few minutes ago. No sign of a Chisholm Cattle Company pickup headed this way. Instead it appeared the pickup had left the highway and was no longer moving. Why would he pull off?

Duane looked at his watch. Turn back and find him? Or wait? Or keep going and take care of Billie Rae and then worry about Tanner Chisholm?

He tapped the screen again, thinking something was wrong with the tracking device. Maybe it had fallen off the cowboy's rig. The tiny icon representing the Chisholm Cattle Company pickup still hadn't moved. The location appeared to not be that far back up the highway.

What if Billie Rae's call had been bogus? What if she was meeting the cowboy back down the road? Duane tried to remember if there'd been a place back up the highway where Tanner and Billie Rae might have planned to meet.

With a jolt he remember seeing a large building set off the highway. A Native American casino.

Duane slammed the car into gear and, with tires throwing gravel, flipped the Lincoln around and headed back down the highway. If he was wrong about Billie Rae being with Tanner right now, he'd have to make this fast, which annoyed him to no end. He'd wanted to make the cowboy suffer enough that he wouldn't be stupid like his brother and call the law on him.

On impulse, Duane called the cell phone number Billie Rae had called him from this morning. It went straight to voice mail.

"What the hell?" he said tossing the phone on the passenger seat as he floored the Lincoln.

He was driving so fast he almost missed the turn into the casino. The Chisholm Cattle Company pickup was sitting in the lot away from the few other vehicles, the cab empty.

Duane hadn't taken Tanner Chisholm for a gambler, but then he'd gambled with his life when he'd helped Billie Rae, hadn't he?

Parking next to a large motorhome out of sight of the cowboy's pickup, he sat for a moment considering his options. He didn't have the patience to wait for Tanner to come out. He was too anxious to get to Billie Rae.

But then again, she might be inside the casino with the cowboy right now.

The problem was he would have to be careful once inside. If he made a scene, he could end up in a Native American jail cell. He got out of his car. He didn't think walking into the casino wearing his shoulder holster would be the smartest idea, either. While he didn't have jurisdiction in Montana, he really didn't on the reservation.

But he also wasn't going in the place unarmed. He took off the holster, tossed it on the seat and removing the Glock, tucked the gun into the waistband of his slacks. The tail of his shirt covered it well enough. If this place was like most casinos, it would be fairly dark inside.

Duane locked his car and walked toward the front door, hoping he didn't find the cowboy and his wife together gambling when Billie Rae had convinced him he needed to save her at the end of some dead-end road up the highway.

If that happened, Duane wasn't making any promises about what he would do. But as it happened, Duane didn't have to go inside the casino.

Billie Rae looked at the pile of supplies she'd put in the car trunk, glanced at her watch and slammed the lid. Fortunately she didn't have far to drive, she thought as she slid behind the wheel.

She repeated the mantra that had been echoing in her head since Tanner's call. *Desperate times called for desperate measures.* She wondered, though, if Duane rationalized his behavior with the same kind of catch phrases.

The cell phone rang on the seat where she'd laid it. She checked to see who was calling as she drove out of Great Falls. Tanner. She wanted to answer just to hear his voice and take some comfort in it. But there was nothing more to say. She let it go to voice mail. If he knew about her plan he would try to stop her.

She couldn't let that happen.

Billie Rae knew how dangerous her plan was. So much could go wrong she didn't want to think about it. But she felt she had no choice. She had to stop Duane from hurting anyone else and if that meant sacrificing herself in the process, then so be it.

Ahead she saw the sign for the dead-end road she'd seen on the map. Turning off the main highway, she drove down the narrow dirt road until it dropped precariously toward the river gorge below.

Billie Rae hit the brakes and sat for a moment gripping the steering wheel. Where was the road she'd seen on the map? What if it had washed out?

Setting the emergency brake, she climbed out of the car and walked to the edge. The wind whipped her hair around her face. She brushed it back and looked down. Her stomach knotted at what she saw. Far below was the river, a green snake of rock and rushing water.

The road she'd seen on the map was little more than a rocky two-rut path that had been cut into the side of the mountain high above the river gorge. Getting to it would require her to drive off this steep edge to reach it.

She couldn't do it. She took a step back, glanced at her watch. Time was running out. Duane would be here in the next thirty minutes, maybe sooner.

That's when she saw it. The swinging foot bridge across the narrow gorge. It was at the end of the road just like it had shown on the map. Billie Rae stared at it for a long moment, surprised that it was just as she'd envisioned it—except even from here, she could see it swinging in the wind.

This was pure suicide, she thought as she looked from the swinging footbridge high over the river gorge to the road that ended at the bridge. The map had failed to give her any idea of just how narrow or how rough the road was. Add to that the large sign that prohibited anyone from going past this point unless for authorized use only.

She'd always been so law-abiding she actually hesitated, then reminded herself given what she planned this was a pretty minor infraction.

Taking a deep breath, she eyed the road for a moment, then gathering her courage, she got back into the car, released the emergency brake and, riding her foot brake, let the car drop over the rim into the river gorge.

Tanner felt as if he'd suddenly been dropped in Las Vegas. From the carpet to the noise and flashing lights of the gambling machines, it took a moment to get his equilibrium once he'd stepped inside the casino.

The place was huge and nearly empty, which made the beeps and dings echo through the large room giving it an end-of-the-world feeling as he walked through.

He couldn't help searching for Billie Rae among the few patrons and employees even though he didn't think she could have been here yet unless like him, she'd driven too fast. He wasn't all that sure that she could get that kind of speed out of the car she'd purchased—not to mention the fact that her car hadn't been in the lot.

But to be safe, he found the rear exit and checked to see if there was a back lot. No Billie Rae.

He found the men's room on his way back through the casino. He kept telling himself that once he had a chance to talk some sense into Billie Rae, she would come back to the ranch with him.

Hell, maybe by now the sheriff had already picked up Duane. Even if she couldn't hold him long before the cop made bail, at least Duane wouldn't be stupid enough to get into any more trouble in Whitehorse.

As he walked back to his pickup to wait, Tanner hoped Billie Rae would be here soon. He couldn't wait to see her. He glanced down the highway in the direction of Great Falls looking for her small red car.

He was almost to his pickup when Duane Rasmussen came out from behind a van and jumped him.

***

Emma couldn't look at her husband for fear she would burst out crying. She had taken his hand the moment they'd all sat down at the kitchen table and now gripped it tightly, afraid of what would happen if she didn't hang on for dear life.

As she looked across the table at the sheriff, she told herself this wasn't happening. "Are you sure I can't get us some coffee? Maybe some of that cake…" Hoyt squeezed her hand making the rest of her words dissolve in her mouth.

"You're sure it's Krystal," Hoyt asked the sheriff. He hadn't seemed surprised when McCall had informed them that Krystal Blake Chisholm's remains had been found not far from the ranch.

Emma refused to read anything into that. Hoyt must have suspected his third wife was dead after she and her old boyfriend had both disappeared. But hadn't he said the old boyfriend lived down in Wyoming? So how did Krystal end up buried up here? And where was the boyfriend?

Emma's mind whirled with such thoughts as she tried to concentrate on what the sheriff was saying.

"We have matched both dental records and the DNA which you provided when she disappeared," McCall said.

"So it really is her?" he repeated as if in a fog. He seemed to have aged right before Emma's eyes.

"Where did you find her?" Emma asked.

The sheriff seemed to hesitate, but she had to know the news would be all over the grapevine, if it wasn't already. "Near where we found Aggie Wells's vehicle." She was looking at Hoyt, obviously hoping for a reaction.

Emma sat up straighter. She'd erroneously thought the remains had been found on the ranch. Why else would the sheriff be acting as if she was about to arrest Hoyt at any moment?

"Near where you found Aggie Wells's car?" she repeated.

Didn't anyone else see what was going on here?

"You haven't found Aggie's body, though, have you," Emma challenged. Hoyt squeezed her hand. She pulled it free. "And you're not going to find it because Aggie isn't dead."

"Emma—"

It was the sheriff who cut Hoyt off. "Where would you suggest we look?" she asked, her eyes narrowing as she turned her attention on Emma.

"Aggie staged her disappearance," Emma said and Hoyt groaned next to her. "She isn't dead. I know that because she was here earlier today."

"You saw her?" the sheriff asked.

"After we got back from the hospital, the front door was standing open—Hoyt began to search the house. I smelled her perfume the moment I stepped inside the house."

"Emma," Hoyt pleaded again.

"I smelled her perfume another time when she went through our things in our bedroom. Don't you see what is happening here?" Emma cried. "Aggie is trying to frame my husband. She is so determined to be right."

The sheriff looked uncomfortable.

"Emma, the sheriff isn't here about Aggie Wells," Hoyt said. "This is about Krystal."

Sheriff Crawford nodded solemnly and then Emma knew even before the woman reached into her pocket that there was more. They had found some kind of evidence at the scene.

"I need to ask you, Mr. Chisholm, if this is yours." Sheriff Crawford pushed a small plastic bag across the table. Emma caught sight of something discolored inside it. She recognized it at once—and so did Hoyt.

"Where did you get that?" Emma demanded.

"It was found with Krystal Chisholm's remains."

"That's not possible. Hoyt has his upstairs in his—" Emma was on her feet. She hurried up the stairs and opened the top drawer of Hoyt's bureau and rummaged through the wooden box. She knew she'd seen the bolo tie with the three C's on it in the box. It had to be there.

She found matching cufflinks but no bolo tie. She stood, trying to catch her breath from her panic, her fear, the run up the stairs. She'd been so sure the bolo tie had been in there even though she hadn't seen Hoyt ever wear it.

Returning downstairs, she found the sheriff and her husband waiting for her. Hoyt had his head down, looking like a guilty man. She wanted to snap at him, tell him to knock it off. She knew he was innocent. She knew that the reason he was behaving this way was that he felt responsible because he'd married Krystal, because he thought Aggie Wells had won, as if he'd always feared it was just a matter of time before he was arrested.

Three dead wives. Who wouldn't think he did it?

The sheriff didn't have to ask if Emma had found the bolo tie, but Emma still shook her head, her gaze going to her husband as she slid into the chair next to him and took his hand again.

"Mr. Chisholm?" The sheriff was looking at Hoyt. "Is this yours?"

He nodded, then glanced at the tape recorder she had turned on when the questioning began and said, "Yes, it's mine."

"When was the last time you saw it?" she asked.

He glanced at Emma, then shook his head. "It was part of a bolo tie I haven't worn in years."

"So you weren't aware it was missing?"

"No."

The sheriff rose to her feet. "Hoyt Chisholm? You are under arrest for the murder of Krystal Blake Chisholm."

Emma listened as the sheriff stated her husband his rights. "He didn't kill her," she cried as the sheriff pulled out her handcuffs. Hoyt pushed himself up from the table as if carrying the weight of the world on his broad shoulders. "I'm telling you he couldn't kill *anyone*."

Her husband turned, gave her a sad smile. "It's going to be all right."

The sheriff gave her a sympathetic look as she led Hoyt out the door. "You might want to call a lawyer for your husband."

Emma could only nod as she watched the sheriff escort Hoyt out to the patrol car, put him in the rear seat and drive away. She knew she should rush to the phone and call his lawyer and his sons, but what she really needed to do was find Aggie Wells.

Or maybe, she thought with a sudden chill as she looked out across the wide open country that was Chisholm Cattle Company, maybe Aggie was planning on finding her.

Chapter 11

Billie Rae drove the car down the impossibly narrow road cut into the side of the mountain wondering if she'd lost her mind. She had to creep along, dodging the rocks that would take out the oil pan, while at the same time avoiding the solid rock face of the side of the mountain—and the sheer drop off into the river gorge.

Once she'd turned onto the road, she'd also realized she couldn't change her mind. She would have to go to the end of the road. No way could she back up. She was committed.

"You should be *committed*—to the nut house," she said to herself. More and more she was realizing this was a suicide mission. Desperate times called for—

"Just drive."

She could hear the wind rushing down through the gorge. It whistled through the gap in her car window and whipped at what little vegetation grew between the boulders on the mountainside next to her. Ahead she could see the bridge and felt physically ill at the sight of it swaying wildly in the gale.

Billie Rae concentrated on the road and tried not to look—or think—too far ahead. There was literally no turning back now. Duane would be coming soon. She had to get ready. If he caught her now...

Ahead she saw where the road abruptly ended in a pile of rock and dirt. There was just enough room to park the car. She didn't try to turn it around. If her plan worked, she would worry about getting out of here then. It was such a long shot that she would be leaving here at all she wasn't about to take the time now to turn the car around.

Climbing out, she felt the full force of the wind as it roared through the canyon. For a moment she froze as she watched the footbridge swing back and forth high above the rocks and dark green water below. Could she do this? Or had she played right into Duane's hands and given him the perfect place to kill her? This would give him such an easy out. He could get away with her murder if things went wrong and never serve a day in jail for it.

But then, Billie Rae thought no matter where she met him, he would figure out a way to get away with what he planned to do to her anyway. He'd gotten away with murder before. All the odds had been stacked in his favor, they always were. But she promised herself that she would end it here. One way or another.

She glanced at her watch. She could feel time slipping through her fingers. She had to move. *Now!* If Duane caught her just standing here, everything he'd said about her would be true. And everyone knew what happened to cowards.

Billie Rae cautiously moved to the rear of the car, feeling as if she was hanging on the side of the mountain by the skin of her teeth. Opening the trunk, she pulled out the large jacket she'd purchased, then taking the knife, began to cut into the cloth.

This morning after Tanner's call she'd known she had to use her husband's Achilles heel if she hoped to still be alive by dark. She'd found out about Duane's weakness by accident—something Duane had never forgotten—or forgiven.

"Did you hear about your big, tough husband?" one of the other cops she'd only just met, had asked her after too many drinks. They had been at one of the few parties with his fellow boys in blue that Duane had allowed her to attend—and the last after that night.

"Shut up," Duane said under his breath, but either the cop didn't hear or ignored the warning.

"So here we are chasing a robbery suspect and he hightails it up a six-story fire escape," the cop continues. "Duane starts up after him, me behind him. Then all of a sudden Duane looks down and stops dead. I crash into him and say, 'What the hell?' The dumb bastard, it turns out, is scared of heights." The cop broke up in loud guffaws.

The cop hadn't been watching Duane, but Billie Rae had. His face had been flushed with anger, a vein throbbing in his neck, his hands fisted at his sides. She'd known Duane would never forgive the cop for telling that story—especially in front of her.

Two months later the cop was found shot to death in an alley. No suspect was ever found, but Billie Rae knew who'd killed him—and why. She also knew that had she told the police, no one would have believed her.

Just as no one had believed her the one time she'd tried to report the abuse.

"I'm going to give you some good advice," her husband's captain had told her after she'd taken a taxi down to the police station on a day she knew Duane would be on assignment away from the department. "Go home. Stop fighting with your husband. Work a little harder to make him happy."

Now she glanced again at the bridge hanging suspended over the gorge. She was about to take on the fight of her life with her cop husband. And how it ended would all depend on how badly he wanted to get his hands on her.

Tanner came to in the dark. He was immediately aware of the pain—and his surroundings. He was in the trunk of a fast-moving car. He could hear the whine of the tires on the highway and smell exhaust. His hands were bound in front of him and he felt cramped even in the roomy space of what he knew was the Lincoln's trunk.

He wiped something sticky and wet from his left eye and tried to sit up. His brother Marshall had been right. He had gone for Duane's throat, charging him after the ambush even though the cop had quickly pulled a gun from under his shirt.

Tanner had gotten in a few good punches, catching the cop off balance. Duane had thought the pistol he pointed at Tanner would deter him. It hadn't. Tanner hadn't thought Duane would shoot him in the casino parking lot but the furious cop had definitely *wanted* to pull the trigger.

Duane had gotten the final blow, though. Tanner hadn't seen the butt of the gun coming until it was too late. He tried to block the blow, but his head had taken the brunt of it.

That's all he remembered although he was sure Duane had kicked him a few times when he was down. His ribs hurt like hell and he felt as if he'd been used for a punching bag. From what he could tell, there was a cut over his left eye which was bleeding and his nose might be broken.

He had no idea how long he'd been out—or how far they had driven. All he remembered was Duane saying that Billie Rae was waiting for them up the road.

It was too dark to see if there was a latch, something that could get him out of the trunk when the time came. He felt around, trying not to move too much, but didn't find anything. He didn't want the cop to know he was awake. Not yet, anyway.

Tanner felt he had the best chance of survival by pretending to still be knocked out. The element of surprise might be his *only* chance, he thought, remembering the fury in the cop's face when he'd jumped him.

What confused Tanner was how Duane had known he would be at the casino. Billie Rae wouldn't have told him. Tanner swore as he realized how stupid he'd been. Duane was a cop. He probably put a tracking device on Tanner's pickup.

He tried to think of when Duane might have had access to the truck. When Tanner had gone to the hospital to see his brother? The bastard had probably been just waiting for him to lead him to Billie Rae.

* * *

Billie Rae put on the harness she'd purchased at the climbing store. She attached the rope the way the clerk had shown her, her fingers hardly shaking.

Don't think about all the things that can go wrong.

Don't think about Duane. Or the bridge. Or... Tanner.

Instead, she concentrated on what she had to do as she put the large jacket on over the climbing harness, coiled the rope she'd attached to the harness and put it in one large pocket of the jacket. The gun she put in the other pocket along with the extra cartridges. Hesitating, she took the gun from her pocket, lifted it to chest high and aimed it toward the bridge.

The weight of the weapon in her hands made her feel stronger than she really was, braver, almost invincible. She wondered if that was how Duane felt when he was armed. He spent hours cleaning his gun, handling it, holding it, aiming it. She shuddered at how often he had aimed it at her heart and threatened to blow a hole in her the size of a half dollar.

"You should learn to shoot," Duane said one night after a few beers.

"I don't like guns."

He'd laughed at that. "Only fools don't like guns. A gun can save your life."

"Or take it," she'd said.

He'd smiled at that. "I wouldn't waste a bullet on you, sweetheart. I'd kill you with my bare hands if you ever gave me reason."

The next afternoon, he'd come home early. "Come on," he'd said.

"Where are we going?" It wasn't like him to come home early. She feared something had happened at work and that they would be moving again. She'd only recently learned by overhearing Duane on the phone that something he did in Oklahoma was why he'd applied to the force in Williston, North Dakota. He'd told her it was because the job paid more but she'd found out that too had been a lie.

She'd later learned that he'd assaulted one of the suspects who'd said something to him that set him off. Two other policemen had been forced to pull him off the suspect. Unfortunately for Duane, some witness had gotten a little of it on his cell phone camera.

His fellow cops had covered for him so Duane had managed to get off with little more than a slap on the wrist, but the department was watching him—something Duane couldn't handle.

"We're going to the shooting range," he had announced the day he'd come home early. "No wife of mine is going to be afraid of guns."

"I'm not afraid, I just don't—"

"You're going to learn to shoot—and shoot well." She'd heard the warning in his tone and knew there was no arguing with Duane once he'd made up his mind.

Now she quickly slipped the gun into her jacket pocket again. Learning to shoot had been the one thing Duane had taught her that was finally going to come in handy.

The wind blew her hair into her eyes. She tied it back but still some tendrils escaped. Then she double-checked to make sure she had everything, before she glanced at her watch again. Duane could be here any minute. Slamming the trunk, she turned to look again at the bridge.

It was made of wooden slats that were no more than

four feet wide. They were bound together with what appeared to be rope. Two other ropes that stretched from bank to bank acted as handrails. Each of those was attached vertically to the bridge platform every four or five feet with more rope.

Two steel cables anchored in concrete on each side ran under the bridge to give it reinforced support. But the cables were slack enough to let the bridge move and, boy, was it moving.

From this angle, it swayed in the wind as hypnotically as a pendulum. Billie Rae couldn't imagine trying to walk out on it—or how she would get to the middle where she needed to be when Duane arrived. She just knew she had to take that first step—just as she'd taken the first step to be free of Duane.

This time, she let herself think of Tanner as she slipped down the steep rocky slope to the bridge entrance. She was terrified of what she was about to do. Thinking of Tanner Chisholm gave her strength. At the base of the footbridge, she had to climb up to get on it.

A chain had been stretched across the opening with another sign that warned that the bridge was for authorized personnel only. Violators would be prosecuted. Like so many signs she'd seen out west, this sign had been used for target practice. It was peppered with rusted gunshot holes.

The holes made it hard—but not impossible—to read the smaller print at the bottom of the sign: Danger: Do Not Cross In High Wind.

She watched the wind kick up dust from the other side of the mountain, a gust wildly rocking the bridge before it settled back into just swinging.

Gathering all her courage, Billie Rae ducked under the sign and crawled up onto the bridge.

Just the thought of Aggie Wells pulling their strings as if they were puppets made Emma angry. She had to calm down before she went back into the house after the sheriff left with Hoyt. She called the lawyer first, then each of her stepsons.

"Dad didn't kill anyone," said Dawson, the eldest of the brothers and the one they all agreed was the most responsible of the six. "Don't worry. We can take care of the ranch until we get him out. Have you called his lawyer?"

"Yes, he's headed down to the sheriff's department to see about getting Hoyt out on bail," Emma told him—just as she had the others.

That wasn't the problem—getting Hoyt out on bail, she thought after she hung up. It was finding Aggie Wells and getting at the truth. No way did Emma believe it was a coincidence that Aggie's car ended up abandoned near where Krystal's body was found. Or that the bolo tie clasp had ended up at the site.

Unless Hoyt is guilty.

The thought flew at her out of the darkness of her thoughts.

"My husband is not a killer," she said to the empty kitchen. Her voice echoed back at her and, with a chill, she realized how alone she was. The cook, Celeste, had called and made a lame excuse for why she couldn't make it today. Housekeeper Mae had called shortly after with an equally weak excuse. They were bailing off Chisholm Cattle Company as if it were a sinking ship.

She couldn't really blame them. Nor could she bear to

think of Hoyt locked up—let alone him going to prison for a murder, or murders he didn't commit. Aggie Wells had to be behind this.

And if that was the case… Emma let out a cry as a thought struck her. *Aggie killed Krystal. How else would she know where the woman was buried so she could implicate Hoyt by putting the silver bolo tie clasp at the scene?*

She started to reach for the phone to call the sheriff when she realized she had no proof. It was all conjecture. She couldn't prove the bolo tie had been in Hoyt's jewelry box and he didn't seem to remember if it had been there or not since he'd said he hadn't worn it in years.

"Hoyt didn't do it." She said it loud enough that if the house wanted to argue she was up for it. All she got was an echo and realized she was arguing with herself because she was scared.

She was convinced Aggie Wells was alive and behind this. But did she really believe the former insurance investigator had gone so far off the rails that she would murder Hoyt's third wife just to frame him? That did seem extreme.

But Aggie had already been investigating the deaths of Hoyt's first two wives. What if she'd become so frustrated for lack of proof that she'd decided to kill Krystal and make it look as if Hoyt had, just so she could frame him?

"And then wait almost thirty years before she made sure the woman's remains were found?" Emma demanded of the empty room.

She was glad she hadn't called the sheriff. Her theory sounded way too far-fetched.

Just the fact that she'd smelled the woman's perfume in the house twice hardly proved that Aggie Wells was alive. Which begged the question, why hadn't she turned up?

Emma poured herself a mug of coffee and cut a small piece of the oatmeal cake. After staring down at the small piece of a cake for a long moment, she cut herself a larger piece as a thought crossed her mind.

If she really believed in Hoyt's innocence—which she did—then she needed to figure out what Aggie had been doing in her house. She took a bite of the cake. She really did make the best oatmeal cake, she thought, as she swallowed and had a sip of coffee. She could feel her strength coming back as well as her senses.

The reason for Aggie coming to the house at least the first time came to her like a shot out of the dark.

Aggie took Hoyt's bolo tie to frame him.

Emma felt a chill as she realized that had to be it. All of their bureau drawers had been gone through including Emma's jewelry box. She hadn't thought to check Hoyt's because he'd glanced in and said he didn't think anything was missing.

The only clue had been that lingering scent the woman had left behind. Emma had recognized it when she'd met Aggie at the bar at Sleeping Buffalo. When she'd accused Aggie of snooping around their ranch house, Aggie hadn't denied it. She'd given Emma the impression that she had merely been curious—and concerned—about Emma, Hoyt's fourth wife, after what had apparently happened to the other three.

Sitting up straighter, Emma saw how foolish she had been not to see this before. Aggie was so determined to prove Hoyt had murdered his first wife that she had become obsessed with being right. It had apparently cost Aggie her job at the insurance company.

But if she had killed Krystal… Emma had a thought that felt so right it scared her. What if Aggie hadn't killed Krystal to frame Hoyt—but to get rid of the competition?

Hoyt was an incredibly handsome man—not to mention wealthy and respected, a great catch. If Aggie had fallen for him while investigating him…

It fit. She wished she could ask Hoyt how Aggie had acted after his third wife had disappeared. Of course Aggie would have investigated the disappearance. That meant she'd been in Whitehorse, probably had been out to the ranch to talk to Hoyt.

But Hoyt hadn't been interested. He'd sworn off women all those years until he'd met Emma—and Aggie Wells had come back into his life. How would a jealous woman react to Hoyt getting married again after all those years?

Badly, Emma thought. So badly, though, that she would make sure Krystal's body turned up and that her own didn't? So obsessed that she had faked her own disappearance and made it look as if she too had been murdered?

Emma hugged herself as she realized just how obsessed that was. If she was right, then Aggie Wells was a very dangerous person with a very jealous streak.

She glanced toward the window, uneasy at the direction her thoughts had taken. The day was bright and sunny, the sky a brilliant blue, not a cloud in sight. Still she felt a chill wrap itself around her neck like a noose. Where was Aggie right now? Was she hiding in the hills, watching the house with binoculars? That seemed unlikely.

If Aggie wasn't hiding in the hills watching the house with a pair of binoculars then how had she known earlier that there was no one around so she could come back into the house again?

Emma took the last bite of cake and almost choked as the answer came to her.

Aggie Wells had bugged the house!

The moment Billie Rae stepped onto the bridge, she made her first mistake. Still on her hands and knees after slipping under the chain across the bridge entrance, she'd looked down. The rushing movement of the dark green water over the rocks far below threw her off balance.

She closed her eyes, held on to the wooden slats of the bridge beneath her and tried to regain not only her breath—but her courage.

After a few moments, she opened her eyes, this time focusing on the other side of the gorge as she got to her feet. This end of the bridge was attached to a concrete base set back into the side of the mountain so the bridge was fairly stable.

But the moment she took her first step, she felt the bridge move under her weight. She clutched the ropes that formed the handrail. They felt insubstantial. She didn't look through the gaping hole on each side between the rope or through the wooden slats of the bridge beneath her feet, but she was well aware of how easily it would be to fall between the bridge floor and the handrail rope uprights and drop the fifty feet to the river and rocks below.

She couldn't move for a moment. The wind blowing down the canyon buffeted her hair, sending tendrils into her eyes. She could hear the river and the wind and a semi shifting down on the highway off in the distance, but she couldn't take a step—just as she hadn't all those years ago.

She'd been eleven the first time she'd ever seen a bridge like this. A boy she'd liked had asked her to go on a picnic with his family. The bridge spanned across a creek only about fifteen feet above the water. Nor was the bridge very long.

The boy had scampered across it and turned to look back at her, daring her to cross. She hadn't liked the feel of it, the way the footbridge swayed with each step she took, or the way the boy was watching her intently.

She'd gotten halfway across when the boy had started making it rock violently. Instinctively, she'd dropped to her hands and knees and gripped the rough edges of the worn boards in her hands and couldn't move.

The boy had felt badly for scaring her, for making her cry. He'd stopped rocking the bridge and offered to help her up, but she'd wanted nothing to do with him or his help and ordered him to leave her alone.

His father had come and talked her off the bridge. She'd never forgotten being in the middle of that bridge on her hands and knees. She'd never felt so trapped and nakedly vulnerable—until she found herself married to an abusive cop who would rather see her dead than free her.

At the sound of a car engine, Billie Rae turned her head to look back toward the road down to the bridge. Duane's large black car came to a stop on the rim of the gorge.

She turned back to the bridge and with an urgency born of survival, she took a step, then another, desperately needing to reach the swaying middle before Duane came after her.

Bugged? Emma almost laughed at how ridiculous she sounded and yet she went straight to the computer and typed in: How to tell if a house is bugged?

To her amazement a list came up with not only inexpensive listening devices that could be purchased by anyone, but video surveillance devices as well. She'd had no idea how small or how high-tech the devices had become.

Just the thought that Aggie Wells could have been not only listening to their every word—but also watching them all this time—gave her more than a chill. As she read what to do about the problem, she realized that if Aggie was watching, Emma didn't want her to know that she was on to her.

Under the pretense of cleaning, she began to search the house for what the article called "conspicuous" places bugs or small video cameras could be hidden: lamps, picture frames, books, under tables and chairs, inside pots and vases. She hoped the sound of the vacuum would mask what she was up to—even if Aggie was watching her.

The devices were made to look like something else or hide in a plant or the edge of a frame on the wall, she'd read. Aggie could be watching her clean right now on a remote device as ordinary as a computer screen or even a cell phone. So Emma knew she had to be very careful if she didn't want to give herself away.

She discovered the first bug quite by accident. She

was vacuuming the rug next to the bed when she noticed tiny pieces of plaster. It wasn't the first time she'd seen them in the same spot. The last time she'd been too distracted to think much about it since the house was old and the plastered ceiling had small cracks where the house had shifted.

But now she froze and slowly looked up to the smoke alarm on the ceiling. Her heart began to pound. The smoke alarm was new. Why hadn't she noticed it before? It was small and round and nothing like the other smoke alarms in the house.

Emma knew she'd been staring at it for weeks since some nights she couldn't sleep and— With a shudder, she realized Aggie had been listening to everything Emma and Hoyt had said in this bedroom. In this bed.

Furious, she wanted to take the vacuum attachment and beat the device off the ceiling. She had to refrain from doing that, though, if she hoped to find Aggie. Somehow she had to use this in her favor.

Leaving the vacuum running, she dragged a chair over and climbed up on it to inspect the smoke alarm. It didn't appear to have video. That was a relief.

Taking the advice she'd picked up on the internet, she put on headphones, then using her radio dial, listened near the smoke alarm for uniform distortion. The bleeps and recurring patterns indicated the presence of a covert listening device—just as the directions had said.

She finished vacuuming up the flakes of plaster that installing the alarm had caused. Not just installing it, Emma thought. Aggie had come back to the house a second time and messed with the alarm. Had it not been working properly? She could only hope.

Moving through the rest of the house, this time

Emma knew what to look for and quickly found three more new smoke alarms. She could understand now why none of the family had noticed them. The devices were small and unobtrusive. The one in the kitchen was hidden on the other side of the overhead light, same with the ones in the dining room and living room.

Emma put the vacuum away, went back into the kitchen and poured herself a cup of coffee before sitting down at the table to plot the best way to draw Aggie Wells out into the open.

She had a feeling it wouldn't be necessary if Aggie thought she was alone at the house. Emma remembered how Aggie had repeatedly warned her that she would be the next wife of Hoyt Chisholm's to die.

She curled her fingers around the warmth of the mug. If Aggie had just been waiting for the time when Emma would be all alone in his big rambling ranch house, this was the time. No Hoyt. No stepsons. No cook or housekeeper. Just Emma, the fourth wife of Hoyt Chisholm.

Chapter 12

Duane could not believe what he was seeing. He'd turned off where Billie Rae had told him to, driven down the narrow dirt road, but when he'd come to where the road disappeared over the edge into the gorge, he'd thrown on his brakes with a curse thinking she'd meant to kill him.

Now as he stood next to the car, listening to the wind whistling down the river canyon, he hoped to hell he *was* seeing things. Billie Rae didn't really expect him to drive down that road cut into the side of the mountain, did she?

"What the hell were you thinking, woman?" he yelled. The wind blew his words back at him.

That's when he spotted her. She was standing at the entrance to a foot bridge that hung high above the river gorge. Who *was* this woman? Not the woman he'd married. Billie Rae had never been daring. He scoffed at even the idea. If anything he would have said his wife was timid. He thought of the way she often cowered away from him, which only made him more angry with her at the time.

So what had happened to her?

He frowned as he took in the small red compact car she apparently had been driving. Where the hell had she gotten that? From that cowboy? Or some other man she'd told her hard-luck story to? He ground his teeth at the thought that she'd told people about him. What went on between them was private. She had no business sharing anything personal with another person.

He watched Billie Rae start across the bridge.

"What are you doing?" he yelled again. She didn't seem to hear him as she took another step, then another.

He looked from her to the road. No way was he driving his car any farther down this road. He reached back inside the Lincoln, pulled on his shoulder holster and, on impulse grabbed the small unregistered handgun he'd taken off a drug dealer in Oklahoma. He stuffed it into the waistband of his slacks, covered it with his shirt, and slammed the car door.

As he walked away, he hit the automatic lock on his keys, heard it beep once, then pocketed his keys.

Billie Rae had stopped on the bridge. She was clinging to the rope rails. What was she doing out there in the first place? The damned fool woman must have changed her mind knowing he was going to be furious with her and now she was trying to get away from him by crossing the river?

He glanced to the other side and saw only a narrow trail that led to what appeared to be some kind of weather station box used by meteorologists. The trail ended abruptly. Billie Rae was only going to find herself at another dead end. The stupid damned woman.

Well, if she thought he was going out on that bridge after her, she was sadly mistaken. She could just figure out how to get back and when she did, he would be waiting for her.

The road was rocky and rough and the dress shoes he was wearing were all wrong for chasing his wife into a river gorge. Duane swore as he started down the road, telling himself he would make Billie Rae rue this day.

Tanner had felt the big car slow, then turn onto a bumpy road. Is this where the cop was meeting Billie Rae? Or was this where he was getting rid of the passenger in the trunk?

He'd listened. Earlier he'd heard stereo music and even at one point, Duane signing along. The man couldn't carry a tune.

Tanner had tried hard not to bounce around on the rough road. He was hoping that Duane, in his hurry to get to Billie Rae, had forgotten about him. At least he was driving slow now—no doubt to protect his car—not his passenger.

The Lincoln had finally come to a sudden stop, throwing Tanner hard against the trunk wall. He had lain dazed, blinking in the darkness as he heard Duane get out of the car.

He heard the wind and then the cop swear. Tanner thought he smelled the river. Or at least water. All his senses seemed more acute. He felt something against his hip and realized it was his cell phone. It had fallen out of his pocket. He hadn't even thought to check for it, just assuming Duane would have taken it.

Picking it up, he hit 911. When the operator came on, he whispered, "Someone is about to be murdered. I don't know where I am. I'm locked in the trunk of a black Lincoln with North Dakota plates, off the road, north of Great Falls. Hurry."

He disconnected as he heard Duane get back into the car and cut the engine. This must be where Billie Rae had told Duane to meet her. Was she outside the car? He listened but didn't hear her voice, but he'd heard Duane yelling earlier though he hadn't been able to make out what he'd been saying with the howling wind rocking the car.

Tanner felt an overwhelming need to call her, let her know the police were on their way, but he'd feared with the music and motor shut off, the cop would be able to hear him since he could hear the cop moving around in the front seat. The car shifted as Duane got out again, slamming the door.

Tanner held his breath, assuming Duane would be walking back to the trunk and that any moment the lid would swing open and— He heard a beep and the doors all lock. Then there was nothing but the sound of the wind outside the car.

Listening hard, Tanner tried now to gauge how much time had passed. He keyed in the number of his old cell phone and prayed Billie Rae would answer.

Billie Rae wasn't sure she could do this. She'd never been afraid of heights, but as she started across the swaying bridge, she felt motion sickness roil in her stomach.

She took another step, sliding her hand along the rope railing to where it connected with the lower part of the bridge, forcing herself to let go and reach for another section of rope. The bridge swayed beneath her like a writhing snake.

Don't look down.

She thought she'd heard Duane yelling something at her, but realized she may have only imagined his angry bellow.

Then she heard him. Duane was yelling at her, his voice closer. She couldn't look back. She wasn't even sure now if she could pull off her plan because it meant not only reaching the middle of the bridge, but also turning around.

She kept moving, one step, then another. The wind whipped her hair around her face, rocked the bridge and kicked up dust from the mountain on each side of the gorge. She didn't look back, couldn't. Just a little farther.

She stumbled on one of the boards that had bowed in the weather and almost fell. Tightening her grip on the rope on each side of her, she froze as she tried to catch her breath. Her heart was pounding so hard it hurt.

As she started to take another step, her cell phone rang. She'd stuck the phone in the pocket of her slacks earlier and had forgotten about it. The phone rang again.

She stopped moving across the bridge, willing herself not to look down. Gripping the ropes on each side of the narrow footbridge, she turned her head just enough that she could see the road cut into the side of the mountain. Duane was half way down the road, coming on foot. She squinted at the bright sun, the wind in her hair and the bridge swaying under her feet.

She'd thought it would be Duane calling her. But he

wasn't on his cell phone. That meant… Tanner was calling. A bubble rose in her chest. He would have reached the casino by now and be waiting for her. The phone rang again.

Billie Rae thought of him worrying about her. She knew it was foolish, what she was about to do. She needed to get to the middle of the bridge. Duane was coming. The man was crazy. Who knew what he would do?

But she also desperately needed to hear Tanner's voice right now. She was too aware that it was probably going to be the last time she heard it.

Letting go of one of the rope railings, she started to reach into her pocket. The bridge rocked wildly in a gust of wind and she lost her balance. She grabbed for the rope railing again, her fingers closing on it. Her heart lodged in her throat so tightly she could hardly draw a breath.

The phone rang again and she let out a cry of frustration and pain. She steadied herself, praying that Tanner wouldn't hang up before she could get the phone out of her pocket. She dug it out, balancing her weight on the bridge and trying hard not to think about Duane coming up the road toward her.

"Hello?" She had to raise her voice over the wind.

"Billie Rae, where are you?"

She couldn't speak; his voice filled her with sudden warmth and made her ache for what could have been.

"I called the police. They'll be here soon."

She felt her pulse begin to race. *"Here?"*

"I'm in the trunk of Duane's car. Tell me if he's far enough away that I can try to bust out."

She looked back toward Duane's car. "No," she said into the phone. "You shouldn't be here. Please don't—"

The bridge rocked in another gust of wind, throwing her off balance again. She dropped the phone. It hit at her feet, bounced once, then fell between the bridge slats.

She watched the cell phone drop to the deep green of the river and rocks far below as she grabbed wildly at the rope, missing it, then lurching for it again. Her fingers clamped over the line and she teetered between the two ropes, her pulse thundering in her ears as she fought to regain her balance again.

"What the hell are you doing?" Duane's angry bellow sounded as if he was right behind her. He must have run the last stretch and was now at the other end of the bridge.

She didn't dare look back for fear he would be racing along the bridge toward her. Concentrating on nothing but her next step, she slid her hands along the weathered ropes, letting go only to grab the next section.

"Billie Rae, you stupid bitch! Get back here now!" Out of the corner of her eyes, she caught glimpses of deep green through the gaps between the wooden slats of the bridge floor as she took a step—just enough to remind her what was at stake if she failed.

"If I have to come after you..."

She heard a creak, felt the rope railing on her right grow taut and knew without looking that Duane was on the bridge behind her.

Tanner felt an urgency like none he'd ever experienced before. Something in Billie Rae's voice. Where was she? Close by. He'd heard the sound of the wind and a creak of boards. But it was what he'd heard beneath her words that had him frantically shifting his body around so his feet were pointed at the back seat of the Lincoln.

He prayed that Duane was far enough from the car that he wouldn't hear the noise and come back, but he couldn't wait any longer.

He kicked the back seat, putting as much force as he could into it given how cramped his surroundings were. He kicked harder. He felt the seat give a little.

Repositioning himself, he braced against the wall of the trunk and kicked and pushed as hard as he could. He felt the seat give a little more.

He stopped to listen, afraid he would hear the beep of Duane unlocking the car doors—or worse, the trunk lid.

Hearing nothing but the wind, Tanner kicked again and again. The seat finally gave. He lay in the trunk breathing hard, then gave the seat a final push. He could see light coming in through the rear tinted windows.

Just a little more....

As he stepped out onto the bridge, Duane watched the water far below and felt the muscles in his legs begin to spasm. It was all he could do to keep standing. He clung to the rope rail, feeling sick to his stomach.

He couldn't move, couldn't breathe. Acrophobia. That's what the doctor had called it.

"It's not unusual," the mandatory police department psychiatrist had told him after the fire escape incident. "A large percentage of the population has the same problem."

"Acrophobia? What the hell is that?"

"It's an extreme or irrational fear of heights."

"Are you saying I'm irrational?" he'd demanded.

"It means that sufferers of acrophobia experience

panic attacks in high places and often become too agitated to get themselves down. Isn't that what happened to you, Officer?"

Duane raised his gaze to look down the swaying footbridge to where Billie Rae had stopped moving. Maybe she was coming back. At the thought, he felt a rush of relief, of gratitude, almost love. If she came back, he wouldn't be forced to go out any farther on this bridge.

Maybe he wouldn't kill her. He'd just make her wish she was dead.

"I'm glad to see you've come to your senses," he called to her. "If you'd made me come after you…"

You don't want me to have to come after you.

Duane was startled by the sound of his old man's voice echoing in his head.

So what's it going to be, sonny? You think you can get away from me? You want to try? Or are you going to take what's coming to you like a man?

He'd been six years old that day when he'd stood in the field, his father standing at the edge of the barn door with a thick leather strap dangling from one large hand.

You going to take your medicine like a man or am I going to have to come after you? I guess I don't have to tell you what's going to happen if I have to come after you, do I, Duane?

"Come on back now, Billie Rae," he called to her when she still hadn't moved. He could tell by the way she was balanced on the bridge, her head and shoulders slumped, that she'd scared herself. She didn't want to go any farther. She would come back now.

"You want me, Duane?" she called back over one

shoulder. "Then you're going to have to come get me. I can't move."

He swore under his breath. Hell, he'd just leave her there. She'd either starve or lose her balance and fall. Either way would work for him.

But his need to teach her a lesson with his hands pulled at him, taunting him. "Damn it, Billie Rae."

Duane looked back over his shoulder. It wasn't that far back to solid ground. If he turned around now... He started to, but then he saw Billie Rae glance back at him and remembered the night that dumb cop had told her he was afraid of heights. It was bad enough that she'd left him, bad enough that she'd put him through all of this, but now she was almost daring him to come out on the bridge.

Unless you're too afraid, you coward.

He stared at her, realizing she didn't think he could do it. She was planning on him getting scared and... what? Falling?

"You've made a big mistake," he called to her as he took a step toward her, then another. "You think I won't come get you?" His laugh echoed on the wind. "Oh, I'll come get you, Billie Rae. But you are going to wish to hell and gone that you hadn't done this."

Squirming around, Tanner worked his torso through the opening he'd made by kicking the back seat free. Now he just needed something to cut the plastic handcuffs. He managed to get the rear door open and dropped to his feet outside the car.

With a shock, he took in his surroundings. Duane had parked the car only feet from the edge of a precipice. Tanner stared at the river gorge for a moment wondering where the cop had gone. Was he really meeting Billie Rae here?

His stomach knotted at the thought.

He quickly reached into the car and unlatched the trunk. In the back, he found what he was looking for. A pair of pliers. He worked the pliers between his wrists, snapped the handles shut and snipped the plastic. The cuffs fell away.

For a few seconds, he searched through the tools to see if there was anything he could use as a weapon. He chose the tire iron, saw that it had what looked like dried blood on it, and quietly closed the trunk.

As he neared the rim of the river gorge, he peered over, saw the deep gorge, then looked upriver to where the narrow road that had been cut in the side of the mountain ended at a footbridge.

His heart dropping, he saw Billie Rae had stopped part way across the footbridge—the cop close behind.

Tanner began to run, the wind and dust blowing in his face, fear gripping him. He didn't want to think of what was going to happen when Duane caught up with her on the bridge.

Tanner wouldn't be able to reach Duane before he got to Billie Rae. The treacherous road made running at any speed almost impossible. Duane was now slowly moving across the bridge going after Billie Rae.

He could hear Duane yelling. So far, the cop hadn't seen him. Tanner had a feeling that Duane had forgotten about him. The wind howled in his ears. He could smell the river and the dust that kicked up along the steep bank of the gorge.

Billie Rae had started to move again, but the cop seemed to be gaining on her. Tanner ran up behind the car she'd bought. The cop still hadn't seen him apparently. He noticed that Duane was wearing a shoulder holster but he hadn't reached for his gun. Instead, he was holding onto both ropes suspended across the river gorge as if his life depended on it as he continued across the bridge after Billie Rae.

Tanner ran from behind the car over to the entrance of the bridge. A gust of wind whirled up dust around him and rocked the bridge wildly.

Billie Rae had reached the middle of the bridge. Suddenly she seemed to lose her balance. He felt panic seize his chest as he saw her drop to her hands and knees on the footbridge.

Duane was yelling obscenities at her as he clutched at the rope railing, the bridge swinging crazily. The cop was staring down at the river and rocks far below him. He wasn't looking at Billie Rae.

But Tanner was.

He saw her reach into the pocket of the large jacket she wore and attach what looked like a length of climbing rope to the steel cable that held the suspended footbridge in place.

Then she got to her feet again and turned around so she was facing Duane who was still yards away, the rope hidden behind her leg.

Tanner watched her hand sink into the pocket of the jacket again. He let out a silent groan, then said under his breath, "What are you doing, Billie Rae?" as he crawled up and onto the bridge behind Duane.

Billie Rae looked down the stretch of bridge swaying in the wind, estimating how many feet lay between her and Duane. He had stopped and now stood as if petrified and unable to move.

Unfortunately he hadn't come far enough out onto the bridge. She needed him to come at least another ten feet toward her—and the middle of the bridge.

Even from here she could see that his face was flushed, the large vessel in his neck bulging with fury and no doubt fear. It was a wonder he didn't give himself a heart attack, she thought.

"Get your ass back here, Billie Rae," he yelled, but his bellow had lost a lot of its bravado.

He didn't want to come out on the bridge. He was scared.

She saw how easily her plan could fail if he suddenly turned tail and rushed back toward the safety of the mountainside.

Worse, she realized with a start, Tanner had gotten out of the trunk of the Lincoln. A moment before he'd been behind her car, but now he had mounted the bridge and was coming up behind Duane.

If Duane turned now, he would see Tanner. She could see that Duane had on his shoulder holster. That meant he'd brought his Glock. She didn't doubt for a moment that he would shoot Tanner in a heartbeat.

"Duane," she called trying to sound as pathetic as he thought she was. She had to get him to come toward her another ten feet—six at the minimum. "I can't move..." Her voice broke. "I'm...scared."

He glared at her as if he thought she was mocking him. He stood with his feet spread apart as he tried to keep his balance, his hands gripping the ropes.

"Please," she cried. "You're going to have to help me."

"If I have to come out there, only one of us will be coming back," Duane yelled.

"You don't mean that."

"The hell I don't. It ends here, Billie Rae. I can't have a wife like you, don't you get it?"

She got it. "And I can't have a husband like you," she said under her breath. "Then just leave me here," she called back. "Divorce me."

He smiled, then let out a laugh. "You'd like that, wouldn't you?" The laugh died on his lips as they twisted into a snarl. "Over *your* dead body."

Her heart pounded as Duane took another step toward her, then another.

Come on, Duane. Just keep coming.

He stumbled on probably the same board she had and almost fell. He grabbed hold of the ropes, clinging to them. His face was livid with fury and fear. She could see the white of his knuckles on the rope and knew he was thinking about wrapping those fingers around her throat.

"We can stop this right now," she called to him. "You realize I'm not going to be your wife any longer—one way or the other."

"You got that right."

"Duane, I'm not going to let you hurt me again."

He laughed. "Then I suggest you jump."

He took another step toward her.

Billie Rae didn't dare look past him to where Tanner was cautiously moving along the bridge as to not let Duane know he was back there. She knew that she couldn't change her mind now. She'd come this far and if she wanted this to end, she knew there was no other way out.

That night after the day she'd stopped by the police station to report the abuse, Duane had almost killed her. She should have known Duane's boss would tell him that she had come down to the police station. She'd realized then that there was no restraining order or locked door that could protect her from the man she'd married.

And that was how they had ended up on this bridge, she thought. It had all come down to this moment.

Duane took another step toward her. She gauged the distance and reached into her other pocket and carefully closed her hand around the grip of the gun.

"It will be extremely effective at from four to seven feet. Seven to ten feet is optimum," the sales clerk had told her.

Billie Rae knew she couldn't let Duane get too close. If he lunged for her—

"It doesn't have to be this way," she called to him. "There is no shame in divorce."

The word shame seemed to strike a nerve. Duane swore and took another step toward her and another. Billie Rae watched him, gauging the distance.

She could see that he was perspiring heavily. He was fighting looking down, gripping the ropes. Each step was costing him dearly.

"The hell you will shame me, you stupid bitch," he spat as he lurched toward her.

Billie Rae felt a tremor inside her. Duane was closing the distance between them quicker than she'd thought he would—or could.

Had she really believed he would let her go, agree to a divorce, stop this craziness?

He had left her no choice, she told herself as he advanced. As if she'd ever had a choice from the day she'd married him.

Duane lumbered forward, grabbing the rope in his big fists, lurching on the wildly swinging footbridge. His anger had trumped his fear. He was too blind with rage to even realize he was suspended fifty feet over a rocky gorge on nothing more than a few boards beneath his feet.

Now. She had to act now or… Billie Rae told herself she could do this. Only a few more feet and if she didn't do something…

The warning signs had been there. She'd noticed even before they'd married that Duane always had to have his way. When she'd tried to assert herself, they'd argued. He had a temper and said hurtful things, but he was always sorry.

She found giving in to him was easier. She hated fighting with him. She overlooked his moodiness and believed if she tried harder to make him happy, everything would be fine. She loved him. And he loved her.

She shuddered as she saw the pattern their lives had taken, her walking around on eggshells, Duane getting furious over nothing at all. Her trying to pacify him. Him needing to be pacified more and more.

And finally Duane taking out all that anger inside him on her.

Billie Rae suddenly thought of the boy her husband had shot soon after they'd moved to Williston. There'd been an investigation, which had put Duane in one of his moods. She'd tried to stay out of his way, but he'd finally come looking for her as if he'd needed to work off some steam by picking a fight with her and slapping her around.

But she remembered what he'd said about the killing. "The boy was asking for it, so it was self-defense."

"I thought he didn't have a weapon?" she'd foolishly pointed out.

He'd given her one of his dirty looks and raised his fists. "See these? They're a weapon. So that makes it self-defense. Even if my weapon that day was a lot bigger and a hell of a lot more lethal."

Fifteen feet, twelve, ten.

Billie Rae thought of that boy as she pulled the gun from her jacket pocket and said, "That's far enough, Duane."

Chapter 13

Duane froze in mid-step as he saw her pull a gun from the pocket of the oversized jacket she wore. He'd wondered where she'd gotten the jacket since she'd left home without one, didn't have her purse so shouldn't have had money to buy one and this one was too large for her. The cowboy. She must have gotten it from him.

"What do you think you're doing, Billie Rae?" His voice sounded amused even to him. Then he remembered the day he'd taught Billie Rae to shoot.

At first she'd been afraid of the gun, which really made him angry. Then she'd finally taken it and seemed to draw on some inner strength because when she'd fired the automatic pistol she hadn't stopped firing until she'd completely obliterated the bull's eye of the target.

He'd been astounded. "Are you sure you haven't fired a gun before?" he'd demanded.

"I told you, I don't like guns."

Duane realized now that she hadn't answered his question about whether or not she'd fired a gun before. Clearly she had.

"Billie Rae, I thought you didn't like guns," he called to her.

"I don't," she called back. "But you've really given me no choice, have you, Duane?"

"You can't shoot your own husband. Come on, put the gun away before you shoot yourself."

In the years he'd been a cop, he'd faced his share of fools with weapons. He'd learned the telltale nervous gestures that could signal if the hand holding the gun was going to pull the trigger.

He stared at his wife now as if looking at a stranger. Her expression was one of calm, cold and calculating. Her eyes were on him, the gun aimed at his chest, her feet spread as she balanced on the moving bridge.

"You can't be serious," he said, even though he knew she was. It went against everything he believed about his wife. Even after that humiliating experience at the gun range, if anyone had asked him if Billie Rae could fire a gun at a human being, he would have guffawed and said the woman didn't have the killer instinct. Now he wasn't so sure.

Could she shoot her own husband?

A few days ago he would have thought the question ridiculous.

Right now, though, he had a bad feeling not only could she, she would.

The only question was whether or not he could draw and shoot her before she got off a shot.

He squinted his eyes against the afternoon sun as he tried to see what kind of gun she held in her hands. "What the hell?" he said when he saw that it was a pistol-shaped taser.

As part of his law enforcement training, he'd been hit with a taser and he'd nailed more than a few suspects with one. He was well aware of what happened when fifty-thousand volts traveling in two small darts struck a body.

His gaze shot to the vertical rope supports every four to five feet along the footbridge and knew that if she pulled the trigger before he reached one, he was in for a long fall—and certain death in the river and rocks below.

Just as Billie Rae had obviously planned it, he realized with a start. The woman had brought him here to kill him.

"You better hope to hell you miss," Duane screamed and lunged forward.

Billie Rae watched in horror as Duane threw himself forward as if he planned to run down the bridge and take the taser from her.

She pulled the trigger. The fifty-thousand volts shot out in two darts that penetrated his shirt to prick his skin.

Her heart in her throat, she saw him instantly lose all muscle control and drop, just like the clerk who'd sold her the taser said would happen.

Duane landed hard on the bridge and would have fallen over the side except for one of the vertical ropes between the footbridge base and the rope handrails.

She only had an instant to stuff the taser into her

pocket again and grab the rope before the bridge swung
crazily with his fallen weight. Beyond him, she saw
Tanner do the same. He was still yards from Duane.

He had stopped and was looking at her as if he
couldn't believe what she'd just done. She couldn't, either. Worse, her plan hadn't worked.

Billie Rae clung to the ropes as a gust of wind rocked
the bridge and she realized what Duane had done. He'd
seen that she had a taser, he'd known what it would do
and he'd managed to get to a spot on the bridge so the
rope uprights kept him from falling off and dropping
to the river below.

A sob rose in her throat as she watched him lying
there. A part of her couldn't believe she'd shot him—
even with only a taser. Worse, that her plan had been
for him to fall from the bridge.

She closed her eyes against the image of him lying
bloody and broken in the rocks below. Even though she
knew it was him or her in the end, she felt sick to her
stomach. How had it come down to this?

With a jolt she realized that she had only a few minutes before he regained control of his body. He would be
even more furious. There was no doubt now that he would
kill her, that she had chosen the spot she would die today.

Her gaze went to Tanner. They would both die here
today. Another sob rose in her throat. She was about to
get them both killed.

"Stay back!" she called to Tanner, but he either didn't
hear or refused to heed her warning as he began moving
toward the spot where Duane had fallen to the bridge
slats. Tanner had something in his hand. Something
that gleamed in the sunlight. A tire iron?

Duane began to move. Billie Rae saw him trying to

get his Glock out of his shoulder holster. He fumbled the gun out, lost his grip. The gun skittered across the planes of the footbridge to drop over the edge. Duane made a guttural sound, then reached for the gun butt sticking out of the waistband of his slacks.

Billie Rae let go of the rope rail with one hand and dug in her pocket for the taser and another cartridge. The wind seemed stronger now. Her eyes burned from it and balancing on the moving bridge was becoming harder, especially as she hurriedly tried to reload the taser.

With shaking fingers she took out the spent cartridge and fumbled to get the new one loaded into the butt-end of the taser, while out of the corner of her eye she watched Duane rise up, the gun in his hand.

A gust of wind swung the bridge. She dropped the cartridge. Like the cell phone, it hit at her feet, bounced and disappeared over the side of the footbridge.

Billie Rae let out a cry of frustration and fear as Duane managed to get to his feet. He pointed the gun at her. They were now no more than eight feet apart. She could see the gleam in his eyes, feel the hatred and anger coming off him in waves.

"This isn't the way I wanted to end it," Duane said from between clenched teeth.

The wind was whistling through the footbridge. That, Billie Rae realized, was why Duane was unaware of Tanner moving stealthily along the bridge behind him. When she'd called, "Stay back," Duane had thought she was warning him.

She fumbled in her pocket for the last cartridge. Duane was watching her almost in amusement. He would never let her load the taser before he shot her and they both knew it.

He took a step forward. She could tell he didn't want to pull the trigger and end it so quickly. He wanted to hurt her. Worse, if he shot her, how would he explain it? But she knew when push came to shove, he would shoot her before he'd let her taser him again—and that could be as much justice as she could get.

"I gave you everything," he said, pain in his voice. "You were my wife. I treated you like a princess."

"A princess you slapped around when you had a bad day," she snapped unable to hold her tongue as she was forced to hang on to the rope with one hand and frantically try to load the taser with the other.

He stopped now only a few feet from her. "I used to watch my old man slap my mother around. I hated him for doing it. But I didn't realize that women push you to hurt them."

"We ask for it, right?"

"Make fun, but Billie Rae, if you had tried harder not to set me off—"

"Stop lying to yourself, Duane. You liked beating up a defenseless woman," she pushed. "It made you feel like you were somebody."

His face twisted in anger. He raised the gun so she was looking down the dark hole of the barrel. "I'm sorry it has to end like this. I really am."

Just pull the trigger. Let's get this over with because I can't live like this anymore. "Yeah, too bad you didn't get to slap me around some more, huh, Duane?"

The face she'd once found handsome twisted into the monster he was. "Goodbye, Billie Rae." He grabbed for her with his free hand, his intent in his eyes. She was going off the bridge. Alone.

* * *

Tanner heard what Duane said as he came up behind him. As he swung the tire iron, the cop must have felt the movement behind him or sensed his presence. He half turned, catching the blow on his shoulder.

The sound of the report from the handgun echoed in the narrow canyon, but all Tanner heard was Billie Rae cry out. Duane fell back against the rope rail and almost toppled over, but caught himself.

He'd managed to still hang on to the gun as he half turned, knocking the tire iron out of Tanner's hand. It fell to the bridge and Tanner lost sight of it.

As Duane turned the gun on him, Tanner grabbed for it and they wrestled on the bridge, making it rock crazily. Tanner's gaze shot past Duane to the spot where he'd last seen Billie Rae.

She was gone.

The cartridge locked in the taser just an instant before Duane grabbed for her. He got a handful of her jacket in his big fist before she could raise the weapon and fire.

She saw his expression and knew that he had sensed Tanner coming up behind him because he only had time to shove her through the ropes of the bridge railing before he was turning to fire again.

Billie Rae saw it all in those few heart-dropping moments. As she fell off the edge of the bridge through one of the spaces between the ropes, she stuffed the taser back into the jacket pocket and closed her eyes.

She could feel the fear contort her face as she fell— not at all sure she would stop before she hit the river fifty feet below. The drop was no more than a few yards, but when the climbing rope attached to her harness caught and she stopped falling, the impact was more jarring that she'd thought it would be. It knocked the air out of her.

She dangled from the bridge cable high above the gorge and fought to breathe. She didn't dare look down. Above her through the bridge slats, she could see Duane and Tanner wrestling for the gun. Still gasping for breath, she reached up and began to ratchet herself back up toward the bridge like the clerk at the climbing store had showed her.

He had made it look so easy on the store climbing wall. It took all her effort to rise the few feet to the level of the bridge, the effort more difficult because of the growing wind. But all she could think about was Tanner. She had desperately needed him the night of the rodeo. Now he desperately needed her.

Just before Duane had thrown her off the bridge, she'd heard the report of his gun. But she hadn't realized he'd shot her until she looked down and saw that the jacket was soaked with blood.

She realized she was losing a lot of blood because suddenly she felt light-headed. She clung to the climbing rope as the bridge above her blurred. Just a little farther. Tanner and Duane were still fighting for the gun. She felt as if she could pass out at any moment.

Pushing herself, she ratcheted herself up the last few inches. As she reached the edge of the footbridge, she pulled out the loaded taser and prayed for a clear shot.

As they fought for the gun, Tanner knew he was fighting for his life. It was almost impossible to keep from losing his balance and falling from the bridge. Duane was strong and wild with an insane need to finish what he'd started. Tanner fought with a craziness of his own, believing that Duane had already killed Billie Rae.

He found himself thrown against the rope railing as they grappled for the gun, the bridge threatening to spill them both into the river far below. Duane kneed him in the groin and Tanner stumbled back, falling to the floor of the footbridge. He would have fallen through the opening had he not managed to grab hold of one of the vertical ropes and get one leg wrapped around the wooden slats on the opposite side.

He was breathing hard from the exertion and the near fall when he looked up to find Duane standing over him. Duane had the gun in one hand and was hanging onto the bridge rope rail with the other. He was breathing hard, sweating, but smiling as he pointed the weapon at Tanner's chest.

Tanner saw the tire iron caught between two of the wooden slats of the footbridge floor. Duane saw it too and slammed down his foot on it before Tanner could grab it.

"You should never have come between me and my wife," Duane said. "Let alone assault a police officer with a weapon," he added as he kicked the tire iron off the bridge. He seemed to watch its descent out of the corner of his eye and Tanner knew exactly what the cop had in mind for him once he shot him.

Like the tire iron, he would be making that fifty-foot fall to the rocks and river below them.

That's when behind Duane, Tanner caught a glimpse of Billie Rae dangling from the bridge. Tanner had never been so happy to see Billie Rae. She was bleeding but he couldn't tell how badly she'd been hit.

With a start, he understood the climbing rope and why she'd attached the end of it to the steel cable. She had been expecting that very thing to happen.

The woman was crazy.

Of course she was. Her husband had driven her to this point where she felt she had nothing to lose.

Tanner thought of her in his arms, her face in the light from the fireworks, the look she'd given him yesterday just before she'd left. She'd known that she couldn't run far enough from the man she'd married. She'd known that one day she would have to end it because if she didn't Duane would kill her.

He couldn't imagine having that kind of monkey on his back.

Duane thrust the gun out in front of him as he took a more careful aim for Tanner's heart. "It was a shame that I had to kill you. But after what you did to Billie Rae. The jealous lover pushing Billie Rae off the bridge when she told you she would never leave her husband."

"Do you really think that will fly?" Tanner said.

"You forget, I'm a cop."

Billie Rae clung to the edge of the swaying bridge, the wind in her face, her vision blurring from the loss of blood. She felt light-headed and feared she might pass out at any moment.

The battle between the two men had driven them both away from her. Duane was a good fifteen feet away from her now—on the edge of the taser range.

But there was nothing she could do about that. She was feeling faint and her arms were trembling from the climb up the rope. She felt as if she was going into shock.

Billie Rae thought about calling down the bridge to Duane to get his attention, but she didn't dare chance it.

She raised the taser and tried to steady it. The last cartridge was loaded. If she missed him—

Duane was clinging to the rope with one hand, the gun in the other aimed at Tanner's chest. She could hear the hum of his voice but she couldn't make out his words. There was no doubt in her mind he intended to kill Tanner, who was lying on his back unable to do more than cling to the moving floor of the footbridge.

Everything began to fade from her vision. She felt herself getting weaker, the taser slumping a little in her hands as the bridge rocked and her eyes dimmed.

She said a silent prayer and pulled the trigger.

Tanner had seen Billie Rae holding the taser. He could see that she was struggling to aim it.

"Any last words?" Duane asked.

"Burn in hell," Tanner said. The darts caught Duane in the low back. He fell against the rope railing and for a moment Tanner thought his weight would snap it—or flip the bridge and both of them off it.

The floor twisted and Tanner was looking down at the water below him. The river was dark now that the sun was lower in the sky, but the rocks just beneath the surface still shone like sun-bleached bones as the water rushed over them.

Duane seemed to teeter on the rope, his body bent over it. Tanner grabbed the weapon Duane dropped and now held it on the man suspended on the rope.

He would later remember it all happening in an instant. Duane suspended there. And then in a blink, gone.

But right now it seemed to happen in slow motion. Duane's heavy body looped over the rope, making the bridge twist to the side, before gravity finally claimed the weight of his limp body. Tanner impulsively grabbed for him as Duane fell over the side of the bridge. But there was no saving him from the river—or from himself.

Then there was only the sound of the wind but he knew that like him, Billie Rae was listening for the moment when Duane landed in the river below them. He saw her hanging like a limp doll from the climbing rope, her gaze blurred with tears.

Tanner listened, but there was nothing to hear over the wind.

He didn't look down either as he made his way toward Billie Rae. She seemed to watch him through her tears. And then he was pulling her up and into his arms and holding her and telling her not to worry.

"Everything is going to be all right."

In the distance he could hear the sound of sirens headed this way as Billie Rae slumped in his arms.

Chapter 14

"I can't believe Emma would do this," Tanner said as he looked around the kitchen table at his brothers. The six of them had gathered at the main house after Marshall had discovered Emma missing.

Dawson shoved the note across the table. "Believe it. It's right there in black and white."

"She took all her things," Marshall said. "Her closet is cleaned out. Everything is gone."

Tanner shook his head. "This is going to break Dad's heart."

"How is Billie Rae?" Dawson asked, changing the subject.

"The bullet wound missed any vital organs," Tanner said. "The doctor is releasing her today."

"The police cleared the two of you?" Dawson asked. He remembered the hours of questioning, the days of worrying about Billie Rae, the awful time spent next to her hospital bed fearing she might not survive. "Mc-Call said it shouldn't be too long before the investigation is concluded and Billie Rae and I are exonerated."

"What is Billie Rae going to do now?" Zane asked.

"Go back to North Dakota for the time being." Tanner had wanted to go with her but she'd insisted she needed to do this alone.

"I can't believe the judge denied bail and Dad has to stay in jail until his trial," Logan said.

"The judge thought he was a flight risk." Colton had been quiet until then. The fact that he was engaged to a sheriff's deputy didn't make him all that popular right now.

"As if Dad would ever leave the ranch," Logan said and looked to the others as if needing to be reassured.

"Dad didn't kill anyone," Dawson snapped, getting to his feet. "Enough sitting around here moping. Emma is gone. We have to finish the fence. I'll go into town for the load of barbed wire. The rest of you get ready to string fence for the next few days. This ranch isn't going to run itself and we have no idea of how long before Dad is cleared and back home."

"Any word on those rustlers that were hitting ranches down by the Wyoming border?" Zane asked.

Dawson shook his head. "I'll ask around while I'm in town. But I can tell you right now, they won't be getting any of our cattle."

"I'm going by the hospital to see Billie Rae and then I'll catch up with you out in the north forty," Tanner said and watched his brothers file out of the house.

He stood for a moment, listening to the silence. It hadn't been this quiet since Emma had come into their lives. He missed her, missed the rich aroma of whatever she had baking in the big kitchen. She'd made the house warmer, made their lives warmer as well.

Tanner still couldn't believe she would turn tail and run at the first sign of trouble. It just didn't seem like her, he thought as he picked up the note off the kitchen table and reread it.

I'm sorry but I can't do this,
Emma

No matter what the others said, Tanner knew his father was going to be heartbroken. Emma had been the love of his life.

Cindy Ross fidgeted in the seat across from the sheriff. "I got your message?" She made it sound like a question. She smelled of soap and her hair was still wet from her early morning shower.

McCall could see the fear in the girl's eyes and wished she had better news. "We haven't found your aunt. As you know we found her rental car." She didn't mention the blood they found on the seat. McCall was still waiting for forensics to tell her whether or not it was Agatha Wells's blood. The lab was testing the blood stain against hair follicles found in a hairbrush in the suitcase.

Cindy's eyes widened in alarm. "You aren't going to stop looking for her, are you?"

The team dragging the river had discontinued their search for Aggie Wells. "Law enforcement will continue to keep an eye out for your aunt."

"That's it? That's all you're going to do?" the girl asked, sounding close to tears.

"Until we get another lead—"

"What about that body you found out there?" Cindy asked.

McCall wasn't surprised the girl had heard about the remains found near her aunt's abandoned car. "That is tied in with another case."

"I know you arrested Hoyt Chisholm for the murder of the woman's remains you found. It was one of his wives that he murdered. He's going to prison, isn't he?"

"The remains were identified as one of his wives, but until his case goes to trial—"

"You know he killed my aunt."

She didn't know that. But like everyone else in town, she suspected he might have. "Have you been in contact with your father?" McCall asked the girl, seeing how upset she was.

"He hasn't heard from her." From the way she ducked her head, McCall guessed the father wasn't happy about his daughter's coming to Whitehorse in search of her aunt, let alone her staying so long.

"You might consider going home," the sheriff said. She knew Cindy had been staying at a local motel, waiting for news of her aunt. "When we have any news of your aunt…" If they ever did, but she didn't say that.

Cindy had slumped in her chair, all the fight gone out of her.

"Do you have money to get home?" McCall asked.

"I have enough to catch the bus back," she said. "I just feel like I should stay here, though, in case—"

"Your aunt will expect you to be in Arizona, right?

That will be the obvious place she would try to contact you."

The girl lifted her head, hope shining in her eyes. "You still think she might be alive?"

"We have no evidence otherwise at this point." McCall didn't want the girl to be so far away from her father when there was news about her aunt. After this much time and what they'd discovered on the seat of Aggie Wells's abandoned rental car, McCall wasn't expecting the news to be good.

Billie Rae was dressed and standing at the window when she heard Tanner come into the hospital room. She knew the sound of his boots on the hospital's tiled floor after all his visits over the days she'd been healing.

She had a lot more healing to do—and not just from the gunshot wound.

As she stared out at the beautiful Montana summer day, she heard him come up behind her. She ached to feel his arms around her, the touch of his lips against her skin, the whisper of his voice next to her ear.

She turned before he reached her, knowing how easily he could destroy her resolve. "I was just thinking about you," she said honestly.

"That's a good start," he said, his Stetson in his suntanned callused hands. He'd been working at the ranch when he wasn't coming to the hospital to see her. He looked stronger, his shoulders seeming broader. There had always been strength and integrity in this man. She'd seen it that first night at the rodeo.

But now there was something different about him. A calm assuredness—and she knew it had something to do with how he felt about her.

He could survive without her, though. She wasn't so sure she could without him.

"I'll come back," she said, her voice breaking as she looked into his handsome face and fought the urge to reach out and feel the smooth line of his freshly shaven jaw beneath her fingers.

"I'm planning on that," he said.

She met his warm brown gaze, saw how hard it was for him to let her go. But he'd helped free her of a man who had tried to hold on to her at all costs. Tanner would let her go—even if it broke his heart—and that was what she loved so much about him.

All the hours he'd spent visiting her while she was in the hospital, he'd talked about everything but the two of them and the future. He'd known she wasn't ready for that.

"I should get going. I'm taking the train back to Williston."

"Do you need a ride to the station?" He sounded so hopeful, she almost weakened. But she couldn't bear another goodbye, especially one in a train station. This was hard enough as it was.

"I have a ride, but thank you."

At a sound behind him, Tanner turned to see his brother Marshall standing in the doorway. When he turned back to Billie Rae, he was smiling. "You couldn't have picked a better person to take you to the train." Then he stepped to her and gently brushed aside a lock of her hair to press a kiss to her forehead before stepping back. "You'd better get going. See you soon. Drive careful, Marshall."

Epilogue

When Tanner saw Billie Rae coming across the field, he thought he must be seeing things.

He'd imagined her coming back to the Chisholm Ranch so many times, this time didn't seem real.

He stood watching her, the sun beating down on him. He'd warned himself that it might be months before she'd come back. There was also the possibility that she wouldn't. She might want to forget everything about what had happened on the bridge that day—and him with it.

Sheriff McCall Crawford had stopped by to tell him that the investigation of Duane Rasmussen's death had been completed. Both he and Billie Rae had been cleared of any wrongdoing. Duane's body had been released, his remains cremated and sent to Billie Rae in Williston.

So many times Tanner had wanted to turn his pickup down Highway 2 toward North Dakota. He'd wake up in the middle of the night knowing that Billie Rae had cried herself to sleep. He couldn't bear thinking of her alone back in Williston and being forced to come to terms with Duane's death and the ashes of her marriage.

But he'd done what she'd asked and he'd waited, counting the days, then the weeks, watching and waiting for her, planning what he would say when he saw her again. He'd hoped she would call, but she hadn't.

In all that time, there had been no word from Emma, either. Tanner still thought it odd. They all missed her and had moved back into the main house to hold down the fort until the day their father was set free.

It had been a waiting game. The only thing that had saved him was work. They had put in miles of new fence posts and were still stringing barbed wire along with all the other chores of running such a large ranch.

Now as Billie Rae walked the rest of the way across the pasture to where he was leading an appaloosa mare back toward the corral, words failed him.

Billie Rae looked so beautiful. Her face seemed to glow in the morning sunlight. Her brown eyes shone with tears as she stopped a few feet from him, looking almost shy. Then she smiled and he realized he didn't need any words.

Tanner let out a whoop, dropped the horse's reins and ran to her. He picked her up by her waist and swung her around in a circle before slowly lowering her down to the ground.

He looked into the depths of her gold-flecked brown eyes and saw love shining out. "Welcome home, Billie Rae."

She smiled through her tears and it could have been

the Fourth of July all over again. Tanner swore he felt fireworks exploding around them as he pulled her into his arms and kissed her.

Billie Rae knew the moment she saw his face that this was where she belonged—in Tanner Chisholm's arms. And then he kissed her and she couldn't believe how far she'd come from that night in July when she'd been running for her life and Tanner had caught her.

Fate? Maybe. Love at first sight? Definitely. She remembered looking up into the cowboy's face and feeling safe for the first time in months.

In the weeks since what had happened on the bridge, she'd struggled with her heart. If it had had its way, she would never have left Whitehorse or Tanner. But her head said she needed time. She had to go back to Williston and take care of the mess she'd made of her life by marrying Duane.

Billie Rae had also wanted time to be sure that what she felt was real. Now as she drew back from the kiss to cradle his face in her hands and look into his eyes, she couldn't imagine anything more real.

"There is something I need to tell you," she said.

He laughed and shook his head. "I love you too, Billie Rae Johnson."

She smiled. "That too." She brushed a lock of his hair back from his forehead and turned serious. Just last week she'd gotten the tests back. "How do you feel about being a father?"

His brown eyes lit up and he let out another whoop as he picked her up again and spun her in a circle.

"Put that woman down!" Marshall called as he came out the back door of the main house.

"Billie Rae and I are havin' a baby!" Tanner called back.

"Isn't that putting the cart before the horse?" Marshall asked, grinning as Tanner led Billie Rae over to him.

"She might be a little gun-shy of marriage," Tanner said, eyeing her. "But I was about to ask her." He got down on one knee. He'd been carrying the ring around in his pocket for weeks like a good luck charm. "Marry me and make me the happiest man in Montana."

Billie Rae let her heart answer.

* * * * *

He knew he had to utilize her somehow, and maybe she could be useful. "All right, you might as well come along. You might come in handy if there's a next of kin to notify." Ronan began walking back to his car. "I'm not much good at that."

"I'm surprised," Sierra commented.

Reaching the car, Ronan turned to look at her. "If you're going to be sarcastic—"

"No, I'm serious," she told him, then went on to explain her rationale. "You're so detached, I just assumed it wouldn't bother you to tell a person that someone they'd expected to come home was never going to do that again. It would bother them, of course," she couldn't help adding, "but not you."

Ronan got into his vehicle, buckled up and pulled out in what seemed like one fluid motion, all the while chewing on what this latest addition to his team had just said. Part of him just wanted to let it go. But he couldn't.

"I'm not heartless," he informed her. "I just don't allow emotions to get in the way and I don't believe in using more words than are absolutely necessary," he added pointedly since he knew that seemed to bother her.

"Well, lucky for you, I do," she told him with what amounted to the beginnings of a smile. "I guess that's what'll make us such good partners."

He looked at her, stunned. He viewed them as being like oil and water—never able to mix. "Is that your take on this?" he asked incredulously.

"Yes," she answered cheerfully.

The fact that she appeared to have what one of his brothers would label a "killer smile" notwithstanding, Ronan just shook his head. "Unbelievable."

"Oh, you'll get to believe it soon enough," she told him. Before he could say anything, Sierra just continued talking to him and got down to the immediate business at hand. "I'm going to need to see your files on the other murders once we're back in the squad room so I can be brought up to date."

He didn't even spare her a look. "Fine."

"Are you always this cheerful?" she asked. "Or is there something in particular that's bothering you?"

Don't miss
CAVANAUGH STANDOFF by Marie Ferrarella,
available June 2017 wherever
Harlequin® Intrigue books and ebooks are sold.

www.Harlequin.com

INTRIGUE

EDGE-OF-YOUR-SEAT INTRIGUE,
FEARLESS ROMANCE.

Save $1.00

on the purchase of ANY
Harlequin® Intrigue book.

Available wherever books are sold, including most bookstores, supermarkets, drugstores and discount stores.

✂

Save $1.00

on the purchase of any Harlequin Intrigue book.

Coupon valid until August 31, 2017.
Redeemable at participating outlets in the U.S. and Canada only.
Not redeemable at Barnes & Noble stores. Limit one coupon per customer.

Canadian Retailers: Harlequin Enterprises Limited will pay the face value of this coupon plus 10.25¢ if submitted by customer for this product only. Any other use constitutes fraud. Coupon is nonassignable. Void if taxed, prohibited or restricted by law. Consumer must pay any government taxes. Void if copied. Inmar Promotional Services ("IPS") customers. submit coupons and proof of sales to Harlequin Enterprises Limited, P.O. Box 3000, Saint John, NB E2L 4L3, Canada. Non-IPS retailer—for reimbursement submit coupons and proof of sales directly to Harlequin Enterprises Limited, Retail Marketing Department, 225 Duncan Mill Rd., Don Mills, ON M3B 3K9, Canada.

U.S. Retailers: Harlequin Enterprises Limited will pay the face value of this coupon plus 8¢ if submitted by customer for this product only. Any other use constitutes fraud. Coupon is nonassignable. Void if taxed, prohibited or restricted by law. Consumer must pay any government taxes. Void if copied. For reimbursement submit coupons and proof of sales directly to Harlequin Enterprises, Ltd 482, NCH Marketing Services, P.O. Box 880001, El Paso, TX 88588-0001, U.S.A. Cash value 1/100 cents.

NYTCOUP0517

**Trouble comes to town for the
Cahill Siblings of Gilt Edge, Montana,
in this captivating new series from
New York Times bestselling author**

B.J. DANIELS

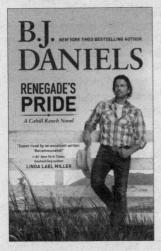

In the nine years since Trask Beaumont left Gilt Edge, Lillian Cahill has convinced herself she is over him. But when the rugged cowboy suddenly walks into her bar, there's a pang in her heart that argues the attraction never faded. And that's dangerous, because Trask has returned on a mission to clear his name—and win Lillie back.

When a body is recovered from a burning house, everyone suspects Trask… especially Lillie's brother Hawk, the town marshal. Will Lillie give Trask a second chance, even if it leaves her torn between her family and the man she never stopped loving?

Pick up your copy today!